To Barbara
with all good
A. K Robert

WARRIORS FOR THE
WORKING DAY

Also by A. K. Robertson:
The Golden Treasure of Athos, The Book Guild

WARRIORS FOR THE WORKING DAY

A. K. Robertson

The Book Guild Ltd
Sussex, England

This book is a work of fiction. The characters and situations in this story are imaginary. No resemblance is intended between these characters and any real persons, either living or dead.

This book is sold subject to the condition that it shall not, by way of trade or otherwise, be lent, re-sold, hired out, photocopied or held in any retrieval system, or otherwise circulated without the publisher's prior consent in any form of binding or cover other than that in which this is published and without a similar condition including this condition being imposed on the subsequent purchaser.

The Book Guild Limited
25 High Street
Lewes, Sussex
First Published 1991
©A. K. Robertson 1991
set in Baskerville
Typesetting by Hawks Phototypesetters Ltd
Copthorne, West Sussex
Printed in Great Britain by
Antony Rowe Ltd
Chippenham, Wiltshire

British Library Cataloguing Publication Data
Robertson, A. K.
  Warriors For The Working Day
  I. Title
  823.914 [F]

ISBN 0 86332 580 7

To Angela, who's memory of the war is still very vivid.

Let me speak proudly: . . .
We are but warriors for the working day;
Our gayness and our gilt are all besmirch'd
With rainy marching in the painful field;
>King Henry V.
>Act IV, Scene III.

CONTENTS

Preface		9
Oakfield Rest Home 1989		11
The War Diaries of Major Colin Marshall		15
Introduction		17
Chapter 1	Blitzkrieg	20
Chapter 2	Battle of Britain	41
Chapter 3	Preparation	52
Chapter 4	Making Plans	73
Chapter 5	Reconnaissance	93
Chapter 6	Commando	101
Chapter 7	Raiders	113
Chapter 8	A Spot of Leave	133
Oakfield Rest Home		152
Chapter 9	Free French	154
Chapter 10	Special Operations	169
Chapter 11	Complications	187
Chapter 12	Back to France	202
Chapter 13	Capture and Escape	216
Chapter 14	The Farm	226
Chapter 15	Countdown to D-Day	245
Chapter 16	In Limbo	273
Chapter 17	Blighted Hopes	289
Aftermath		309
Oakfield Rest Home 1989		318

PREFACE

The advent of the recent fifty-year anniversary of the outbreak of World War II has rekindled memories of those far-off days, but perhaps more than anything it has brought home to those of us who took part that we have now reached old age. And yet we still look back on the war years as an exciting interlude in our lives, and most of us can recall in vivid detail much of what took place during that time, when other, more recent and mundane incidents have long since been forgotten.

Not only was it a short period of history when ordinary men and women performed feats of courage and endurance, but in many cases overshadowing the capabilities of the professional Services. At the same time, they often found an inner strength within themselves which they had never suspected they possessed, only to return to continue their hum-drum lives.

This story is an attempt to bridge the time-gap between those years and the present time by depicting one very small aspect of the hostilities, and a cross-section of the men and women who could have taken part. Although the book has been written as fiction, knowing that all things are possible, it may be that some of the incidents herewith described could have actually occurred. If this is the case, any similarity to a person or persons alive or dead is purely coincidental.

A.K.R. 1990.

OAKFIELD REST HOME

1989

It was close to midnight, and any stranger passing along the road in front of the large old building might be forgiven for thinking that it was unoccupied, since everything was in darkness. But the impression was a false one, because the inmates had long since settled down for the night, each one alone with his or her memories, or seeking solace in the healing qualities of sleep. But at the back of the house a chink of light showed through one of the curtains on the first floor, indicating that someone was still awake.

Inside the room there were three people, two of whom were women. One was young, little more than a girl still in her teens, while the other was middle-aged, plump and motherly. Whereas the youngster's normally smooth and unlined face bore a worried frown, by contrast her companion appeared to be totally relaxed and in command of the situation, mindful perhaps of the former's youth and inexperience.

They were both standing gazing down at a third figure who occupied the bed, but who was oblivious of their presence. He was an old man, his face partly hidden by a neatly trimmed white beard, and although his eyes were open and staring up at the ceiling, they saw nothing. He had the stertorous breathing of someone in a coma, and occasionally flecks of froth from saliva would appear at one corner of his twisted mouth. One arm lay immobile on the counterpane, the fingers deformed by rheumatism, but the hand kept opening and shutting at intervals, almost as if it was a signal to indicate that he was still alive. All these signs, together with the blue-grey tinge of his lips was a sure indication that he had recently suffered a massive stroke.

'Is he going to die tonight, Mrs Mellor?' the girl asked. Her voice was barely above a whisper, and she was unable to conceal the anxiety she felt.

The older woman sighed. 'I'm afraid so, Penny. The doctor saw him earlier in the evening, and didn't hold out any hope. It will be kinder to him if he dies.'

'Oh, Mrs Mellor . . .' she began.

'Does that shock you, dear? Well, I'm afraid he's not the type of man who would accept a long illness.'

'Is there nothing we can do for him?'

'Nothing, I'm afraid, beyond trying to make him comfortable. I know that you haven't been with us very long, dear, but death is something you will get used to here. None of us lives for ever, and this home is the end of the line for many of the inmates. Most of them have already passed their three score years and ten.'

'Why do we always stay when someone is dying, Mrs Mellor?'

'No one should be left to die alone. When we come into the world there is always another person present, and the same ought to apply when we leave it. I know that Mr Marshall was a difficult and unpleasant old man, but at a time like this we must forget that, and think of him only as someone who is needing help. That's what we're here for.'

'Does he know we're with him?'

'I don't think so, but it's difficult to tell exactly how much he understands while he's in this state. I'm going off to bed now, Penny, but if you're worried just ring the bell and I'll come at once.'

As soon as she had been left alone with the patient, the girl felt ill at ease, and wandered aimlessly around the room, unsure as to how she was to pass the time. One wall was almost covered by bookshelves, but the contents were of little or no interest to her, tomes on Political History and Economics, as well as a few classic novels and many paperbacks, but most were written in French.

Apart from the fact that his name was Colin Marshall, and that his age was eighty-one, Penny knew very little about him, since he had rebuffed any attempt she had made to draw him into conversation. She had been bewildered by his aggressive and unfriendly attitude towards both his fellow-inmates, and the staff, who all went out of their way to make his stay as comfortable as possible. Fortunately, for most of the time he had stayed in his room, but at meal-times he had reappeared like a spectre at the feast to go out of his way to needle and torment his companions.

Old Mad Marshall they called him behind his back, but during the eight years he had lived in the home, he had never had a visitor, and as far as Mrs Mellor was aware he had no living relatives. However, on one occasion he had let slip that he had once been married, but he had immediately clammed up on the details. It was generally felt that it was not surprising that he was alone in the world if he had treated his wife in the same off-hand manner. The girl knew that he had been a journalist when he was younger, a foreign correspondent it was rumoured, but no one could be certain.

During the past five years, the old man had spent most of his time confined to his room writing furiously, but so far the fruits of his labours had remained a mystery. One day Penny had asked him outright what he was writing, only to be told in basic terms to mind her own business. Now as she cast her eyes around the room, on the mahogany desk, partly hidden by newspapers, she noticed a large folder, which she pulled out, unable to suppress her curiosity any longer. It was surprisingly heavy and contained many pages written in a neat hand.

After a final glance at the patient, she settled down in the armchair with the manuscript on her knee, and began to read with growing interest and a feeling of mounting excitement.

THE WAR DIARIES

OF

MAJOR COLIN MARSHALL
Royal Marine Commandos

INTRODUCTION

Which ever way you look at it, war is hell for everyone both for those who take an active part in it, or are caught up in it through no fault of their own. It disrupts lives and families, as well as causing hardship and emotional instability to the ones who are mere onlookers. In peace-time the tempo of life is altogether slower and the changes less obvious, whereas during a war the ever moving pattern of events seem to imprint themselves indelibly on the mind so that they are remembered more clearly than other less distant milestones in one's life.

This seems to apply especially to the survivors of World War II, and tales of heroism, personal anecdotes, disasters, amusing incidents and recollections of fear or elation are still exchanged whenever the participants meet together. Somehow the war years were a separate life within a life, something apart which produced a variety of incidents which were an unnatural interlude during which everything we had been brought up to believe in was turned around. For those few individuals who craved excitement it was a heaven-sent opportunity to indulge their fantasies, but for most of us it was a matter of getting through it as best we could, and doing what we were trained to do, even if it was foreign to our nature.

This certainly applied to me, and I hope to demonstrate how my life was influenced by the events of that time. The reader may be forgiven for thinking that after an interval as long as this my memory would be blurred, but the details remain as fresh in my mind as if they had occurred only yesterday.

So, why am I writing this now after such a lapse of time? I had never intended writing my memoirs, until I chanced to overhear a remark by one of the other inmates of the home. I forget who it was now, but it is of no consequence. We were having a discussion about the possibility of war in the Middle East, during the course of which I implied that none of them really knew what war was all about.

'And where were you during the last war?' was the reply. 'Probably skulking about in some so-called reserved occupation, while others fought and died so that you could crawl out unharmed when it was all over.'

I considered that I had developed a thick enough skin over the years to make me impervious to such remarks. But the untrue accusation upset me more than I thought possible, and gave me an irresistible urge to commit my story to paper before I die. Perhaps I am using the opportunity to excuse my anti-social behaviour, or am I merely seeking to justify it? I am in no doubt that the war was wholly responsible for the changes which took place in my personality, and altered my outlook on life — not for the better, I may add. But if anyone should chance to read this, I can only hope they will learn from my mistakes.

Oh, yes, I have made many mistakes, only a fool would think otherwise, but unlike others I have failed to profit from the experiences.

At first I was too complacent, and took what I had for granted so it was only after I had lost it that I came to realise how much it had meant to me. Secondly, I ought to have learned to trust those who had my interests at heart, so my personality changed from a gregarious family man, through a phase of being a womaniser and drunkard, to the thick-skinned, anti-social outcast I have become.

There was no single point at which the changes took place, rather it was a gradual transition brought on as a consequence of the various situations in which I found myself, each one in turn making their mark on me. Although I always did my duty to the best of my ability and was decorated for it, perhaps it was that I was not professional enough to have remained psychologically detached from the aftermath.

However, enough of this self-analysis! The reader can

judge for himself whether or not I am to blame as the story unfolds.

I

Blitzkrieg

When I was in my teens I imagined that my upbringing had been fairly conventional, but it was only in later years when I realised to what an extent these formative years had influenced my subsequent way of life, and the war-time role which I was called upon to perform.

My father was a diplomat attached to the British Embassy in Paris, a post which he held from the end of World War I, until his death in 1937. Although I attended a public school in England from an early age, all my holidays were spent in France, either in the capital, or at our house in the country. I do not remember my mother who died when I was small, and since I was an only child with no one to play with, much of my time and energy was spent in devising ways of escaping the eagle eye of Mamselle. She was always known to me as Mamselle, and I don't think I ever knew what her real name was.

I suppose in a way I must have been a bit of a trial to her, since she was virtually responsible for my welfare. Everyone in the Embassy, from the servants to my father were afraid of her, and she ruled the household with a rod of iron. I certainly did my utmost to undermine her autocratic control over myself, but she continued to carry out her duties with ruthless efficiency, whether it was supervising a formal banquet, or presenting the household accounts which she did regularly once a month. I know my father used to dread these sessions, but Mamselle always insisted that every sou was accounted for.

Her age was indeterminate, but she was probably in her late forties or early fifties. She never attempted to dress in pretty clothes, or use make-up, even on her days off, but draped her thin, bustless figure in black. Her greying straight hair was drawn back severely into a bun, throwing into relief her angular features with thin lips, a longish nose, and false teeth which used to drop occasionally. I was always waiting for this to happen, as it afforded me some amusement. Never once did I remember seeing her smile, and although I dare say she was kind to me in her own way, I suspect that she really did not know how to handle me. I suppose she must have had a family, but I never heard her mention them, and she seldom went away on holiday, certainly never when I was in residence.

Although her presence was a constant threat to my liberty, fortunately she could not keep an eye on me all the time, so I used to escape from the rather sterile atmosphere of the Embassy, out to mingle with the real people of the district who I used to regard as my friends.

There was old Pierre, the street sweeper, who came round every day, and I used to try to intercept him. He was a great talker, and as he worked he kept me amused with a series of anecdotes and unlikely tales, many of which were patently untrue, but I followed him on his round, hanging on his every word. Sometimes, when he had a rare piece of homespun philosophy to impart, he would stop dead in his tracks to emphasise the point.

'You mark my words, young Colin,' he would say. 'One day you'll see that I'm right.'

Then there was Madame Orphier who ran the boulangerie on the corner. She kept a supply of sweets in her apron pocket which she doled out to me while showing me photographs of her grandchildren. There never seemed to be many customers, and she always had time for a chat. After several years, the shop was closed and she went off to join her family in a village close to Orleans.

But Fifi was my favourite. She was a prostitute who solicited in one of the quieter streets adjoining the Embassy. I don't suppose Fifi was her real name, but she stood out in all weathers accompanied by her little poodle who went everywhere with her. Although she was no longer young she possessed a faded beauty which was still evident under the layers of make-up. Her clientele were few and far between, so she had time on her hands to spare for me. Never once did she tell me to go away, although I must have been a nuisance.

I first met her when her little dog slipped his lead one day and ran off after a boy on a bicycle. I was agile enough to give chase and brought him back to her. She was pathetically grateful, and from that day we struck up a friendship which lasted until I was into my teens. Sometimes she took me home with her to her flat nearby, and gave me coffee and cake. Although I was never quite sure what she actually did, I was always fascinated by her apartment, especially the bedroom which was always in semi-darkness except for a dim red light and was pervaded by the smell of cheap perfume. Occasionally I was allowed to peep in, but she never once tried to enlighten me as to what took place in there, and so it remained a focus of mystery to my innocent imagination.

She was always generous to me both with her time and her possessions. Fifi was continually trying to give me presents which I knew I could not accept because Mamselle would want to know where they had come from. One mechanical doll in particular, I used to play with when I visited her; more than anything I coveted that toy, but I resisted the temptation to ask for it, although sometimes the temptation to do so was almost too much for me. She was careful to keep the tools of her trade out of my sight, although on one occasion I found a magazine with pictures of naked men and women in it.

Looking back, I am sure that, like me, she was lonely, and that perhaps I was her only friend apart from her dog. When she had said something which she thought was very funny, she would clasp me to her generous bosom and kiss me on the cheek, then laughingly wipe off the imprint of lipstick she had left there.

But inevitably her easy-going nature and the life she led was her downfall. I was only fourteen when she fell foul to a sexual psychopath, and was the victim of a gruesome murder. It was in all the papers, so I was not spared the horror of all the intimate details. Poor Fifi! She certainly deserved a more dignified end than that.

After leaving school I spent three idyllic years at Cambridge where I did a minimum of work, but added to my already well-developed taste for hedonism. I had always been a keen student of human nature, but this interest took on another meaning during my time at university, and I was able to experience aspects of life I had only heard about previously. However, fortunately I had got it all out of my system by the time I came down with a modest degree.

My father had wanted me to join the diplomatic service, but I was intent on becoming a journalist, and with this in view I served my apprenticeship on one ot the national dailies. Within a short time my talents were recognised and I was assigned to become junior French correspondent. Not only did I speak the language like a native, but I had an understanding of the Gallic mentality, thus I was in a position to produce articles which were both balanced and unbiased. However, my independent views did not always coincide with editorial policy, and my position on the paper became more precarious as time went on.

By now I was married to the daughter of one of France's best known cabinet ministers. I had known her all my life, but we met again after an interval when we had each been completing our education, she at finishing school in Switzerland. We fell in love, and those early years of marriage were some of the happiest of my life. It was she who persuaded me to leave the paper and go freelance, although it was a more precarious way of making a living and I now had two daughters to support. But Claudette, who was rich in her own right, was adamant, because my happiness was her only aim in life. At first I resisted because I was too proud to use her money, but she wore me down and kept the household going until I became established.

To begin with the assignments were slow to materialise, but with the connections I had already made, in time I had all the work I could handle. I must have made a comfortable living, because I managed to support a wife and two children in comfort in a fairly large house in a small village on the edge of the stockbroker belt to the south of London. Although I was away from home for much of the time I was always eager to return to the bosom of my family which I regarded as a haven of peace in a violent and unstable world.

My thirty-first birthday fell on the day after war had been declared, and I was in Paris. It was with considerable difficulty I managed to speak to Claudette that evening.

'Happy birthday, darling', she said. 'Did you have much difficulty in getting through?'

'Yes. I had to book the call hours ago. Yesterday it was impossible. All the lines to London were jammed the whole day, even at night.'

'I didn't really expect to hear from you, but I'm glad you have managed it. Daddy was cut off as he was speaking, which must have upset him. What about the war, Colin? What's to become of us? I worry for the girls most of all.'

I laughed. 'What war? Paris looks as beautiful as ever. Perhaps there are a few anxious faces about, but basically nothing has changed. I wish you were here to celebrate my birthday with me, Claudette.'

I really meant what I said. Claudette was the most exciting companion any man could have wished for, and I never dreamed of looking at another woman.

'I wish I was there too, darling. What are you doing this evening?'

'I'm having dinner with your father and another ex-cabinet minister.'

'It's as well I'm not there then. You'll talk shop all through the meal if I'm any judge. Anyway, have a good time, Colin, and give my love to Daddy.'

I knew her well enough to sense that behind the wifely chatter all was not well, and she was putting a brave face on the situation.

'What's the matter, Claudette?' I asked anxiously. 'Are the girls all right?'

'Yes, darling, we're fine,' she tried to reassure me, but suddenly I knew that she was crying. 'Please, come home, Colin,' she blurted out before I could speak. 'I'm frightened. There is a searchlight unit and an anti-aircraft battery being set up on the common, and sandbags everywhere. I know we're about to be bombed, or something terrible is going to happen. Please, darling, we need you here.'

It was unlike Claudette to panic, but somehow she had managed to work herself into a state of near hysteria.

'You are a goose, you know. Nothing is going to happen. Don't worry! I'll be back in London on Thursday, and home in the evening. Meanwhile . . .'

At that moment we were cut off and there was nothing I could do to restore the connection, nor was I able to telephone home again.

Claudette's sense of foreboding lasted for several weeks, but gradually the fact that we were not subjected to any air-raids, together with my continual assurances that all would be well, managed to allay her fears. Being in a reserved occupation, I was able to be home more frequently than usual, but it was evident that this stalemate would not last indefinitely, and it was in the summer of 1940 that my war began in earnest.

It was May when the German break-through into Belgium, Holland and North-eastern France occurred, and while the Panzer armoured divisions rolled almost unopposed across the hot, dusty landscape, I found myself in the French capital once more. Now, however, it was a very different Paris from the one I had experienced when war was declared. The mood of reckless optimism which had prevailed then, had been replaced by a deep sense of foreboding, which the media and the politicians did their best to reverse. After the Maginot Line had been turned, the mood of the population was one of fatalism, and each person to whom I spoke expected the worst, but was praying for a miracle.

Now there were only two topics of conversation, namely who were the ones to blame for the lack of unpreparedness and the military debacle, or what would happen when the Germans occupied the city. It was no longer a question of "if" they arrived to occupy them, but "when".

People were leaving Paris in droves, all of them determined to escape from the rapidly advancing German armies. As the rumours of atrocities, real or imaginary, grew more rife, so the swelling tide of humanity increased, thus adding to the chaos and congestion already present on the roads. Everything which moved had been pressed into service, cars, buses, taxis, vans and lorries, horse-drawn carts piled high with a variety of personal possessions, together with people on foot carrying only what they could. On the whole there was no panic, only a dogged determination which motivated them with a blind expectation of escape at any price. But escape to where? Many of the refugees had not stopped to think through their situation. Most of them were travelling towards the Channel coast, but the majority would never reach their destination, far less be lucky enough to find a ship to carry them to safety.

So far as I was concerned, when all the sources of communications with England were finally severed, I realised that my presence in France was no longer necessary, and it was only then that I began to organise my own escape.

I decided that my best bet was to go to the embassy to see if any of the staff were still there, because I knew that there were contingency plans laid on for their evacuation. I was very relieved to find that my luck was in. All the personnel had already left with the exception of Graham Barwick, one of the junior assistants to the ambassador, together with two of the female secretaries, a young girl and a middle-aged woman. It was obvious that their departure was imminent, as they were loading luggage into a black Citroen.

'Hello, Colin!' Graham shouted to me, pumping my hand effusively. 'It's good to see you, but I thought you must have left days ago. God, what a shambles! I'm just locking up. The ambassador left yesterday, but we've stayed to destroy code books, and shred documents.'

'How are you getting out?' I asked.

'We have a plane waiting for us at a field near Amiens, that is if we ever get there. Tony Morell was supposed to be with us, but he hasn't shown up, so there's a spare seat if you want it. I'd be glad of your company, Colin.'

'Well, I'm ready to go now,' I told him, unable to hide my relief.

'What about your luggage? We haven't room for more

than one suitcase, I'm afraid.'

'Don't worry, I'll come just as I am.'

The elder of the two women wanted to bring two large holdalls, and became very peevish when Barwick refused. he drove and I sat in the front beside him, while the women settled themselves down in the back. The young girl immediately fell asleep, but her companion sat with her hand over her eyes, saying nothing, and once when I turned to make sure she was all right, I saw a tear trickling slowly down her cheek.

The boulevards of Paris, usually so full of bustling life, were strangely deserted, and the atmosphere seemed to be charged with an air of expectancy, as if something terrible was about to take place. The few individuals who were out and about, hurried along with their heads bowed, looking neither to the left nor the right. The pavement cafes were nearly all closed, and those few which were still open were all empty for the first time in my memory. It was as if the capital had become a ghost town.

We were the only vehicle on the streets, but no one even looked up at us as we passed. It was as if all other traffic had been dispersed so as not to impede our progress. As we made our way through the suburbs and finally sped out into the countryside, we encountered very few refugees, and we began to imagine that our escape would be a mere formality.

What we had not realised was that everyone who intended to leave the capital had already gone, and it was not until we approached an intersection of main roads near Chantilly that the true state of progress was brought home to us. We could see the highway, long and straight in front of us, shimmering in the heat as it disappeared into the distance, but there was no way through. Some buildings at the crossroads had been bombed, partially blocking the route with rubble, and two of the houses were burning fiercely. The way ahead was choked by a static tide of transport of every description, and it was obvious that it would be hours yet before the jam could be cleared. If the bombers should return they would find an even easier target, and be able to commit mass murder. We had no intention of being one of the victims, so an alternative route was imperative.

I made a hurried appraisal of the map to discover that there was a minor road, little more than a cart-track, about a kilometre back.

'It'll be all right if you take this one,' I told Graham. 'It goes through open country, but it leads to another good road further north, and hopefully we can join the main highway again further on. It may be a rough ride, so hang on to your hats, girls!'

We passed through two villages without seeing a living soul, and on the outskirts of a third, we noticed a petrol pump in a courtyard just off the road.

'How are we off for juice?' I asked.

Barwick tapped the gauge on the dashboard. 'I don't think this is very reliable,' he said. 'Perhaps we'd better fill up now, if they have any left.'

After several minutes had passed during which we banged on the door, sounded the horn, and shouted ourselves hoarse, still no one had appeared, and so we proceeded to help ourselves. We argued that it was better we had it rather than leaving it for the Germans.

While we filled up, the two women had gone foraging, returning after a short while with some fruit and a couple of bottles of vin ordinaire. The short break for refreshments helped to lift our spirits, and we set off once more in a more optimistic frame of mind.

For the next forty kilometres we kept strictly to the minor roads, and although we encountered small groups of refugees, they did not hinder our progress to any extent. As we neared Breteuil, however, where there was an intersection of main roads in the centre of the town, we once again found ourselves impeded by an enormous traffic jam which stretched for several hundred metres in all directions. This time there was no way round the obstruction, and so we were forced to sit it out patiently in the hope that whatever was causing the blockage would eventually clear itself.

We certainly made some intermittent progress, moving forward at irregular intervals so that within the space of an hour we had advanced about a hundred and fifty metres. But time was pressing, and it was essential for us to get clear soon in order to meet the deadline when the plane took off.

Immediately in front of the Citroen was a horse-drawn cart piled high with furniture and personal effects. The driver was an old peasant, and there were two passengers perched on top, an elderly woman, and a young girl who was probably their grand-daughter. The poor horse was on its last legs, but the old man kept on beating it whenever they wanted to move a few metres in order to extract every last ounce of energy from the unfortunate beast. Several times Graham sounded his horn in an attempt to make him give us room to pass, but the only response this evoked was a stream of abuse directed towards us at intervals over the old man's shoulder.

Soon the roar of several engines approaching at speed from behind, made us pull over on to the verge before a convoy of lorries belonging to the French Army had caught up with us. They were travelling fast, and miraculously the road in front of them had cleared until now. However, the driver of the cart had established his right to commandeer the centre of the highway, and was determined to stay there at all costs. Without even slackening spped, the leading vehicle caught the cart a glancing blow, knocking it sideways into the deep ditch where it turned over. The contents were scattered over a wide area, and at least one piece of furniture ended up as matchwood, while the poor horse lay on its back not moving except for the quivering of its skinny flank. The occupants were dazed but otherwise unhurt, and it was obvious that any further progress would have to be made on foot.

The old peasant stood at the side of the road, almost hidden by clouds of dust, shaking his fist at the rest of the convoy as it swept past without so much as a sideways glance. The men on board were red-eyed and exhausted, and most were asleep, but the drivers all wore a dazed expression, as if they were not quite sure what was happening to them.

'Bastards! Cowardly bastards! Why don't you go back and fight?' the old man screamed after them, but his words were partly drowned by the roar of engines.

When the last vehicle had passed, Barwick seized his opportunity and accelerated to tag on to the rear of the convoy. Having the road cleared in front enabled us to make good progress for several kilometres, but before reaching Amiens, the column swung off to the left, leaving us to find our own way once more.

When we were close to the airfield, a military policeman insisted that we made a diversion away from our destination. No amount of argument would make him change his mind, and even the production of Embassy and Press passes left him unmoved. No doubt he had had his orders.

For more than an hour, thereafter, we criss-crossed the area trying to find an alternative route on minor roads, some of which were not even on the map, but eventually we arrived at the right location more by good luck than by good judgment. Some workmen, who were in the process of destroying the makeshift airstrip, informed us that we were too late, and that the plane had taken off only half an hour before. Obviously there would be no more aircraft using the field, and so our escape route was cut off.

The news came as a severe blow to all of us, even more so because none of us had even considered the possibility of our being stranded. The elder of the two women wept openly, while the girl looked lost and bewildered. We tried to discuss the situation calmly and rationally, but our passengers were too numb to take part, and so the only suggestions as to what we should do came from Graham and myself.

'I think we ought to continue going north towards the Channel ports in the hope of picking up a boat there,' he proposed.

'On the face of it, that seems the easiest thing to do, but don't forget, most of the refugees as well as the military will also be travelling in the same direction, and remember, the Army will have priority on any sailings,' I argued. 'I think we'd be better off doubling back towards the Normandy or even the Brittany coasts.'

'But we'd be travelling against the stream of traffic,' he countered.

'Yes, but only for a short way. Thereafter the traffic should be less, and I'm sure it will be easier for us to find a boat once we are away from the main body of escapees.'

We discussed the plan for several minutes, but in the end

my argument was carried by a vote of three to one, and without any more delay we began our journey westwards.

Once again, food was becoming a problem. We were all desperately hungry, but every shop we passed was either closed, or empty of goods, and we were forced to ignore our rumbling innards.

Soon we were bowling along at a fair pace on one of the long, straight, tree-lined roads for which France is famous. There was very little traffic, most of it travelling in the opposite direction, and for once we felt that we had made the correct decision. Our conversation had become almost animated, and even the women began singing. We joined in, and for a short time it helped us to forget our hunger. Although it was still light, the evening was beginning to draw in, and the prospect of an overnight stop was an appealing respite. We had been on the road continually since morning, and although Barwick and I had shared the driving, we were almost exhausted.

But our sense of well-being, almost amounting to euphoria was short-lived. Suddenly, and without warning, the people along the road in front of us began to scatter and take refuge in the ditch among the trees lining the highway. It was only after I had switched off the engine that we could hear the unmistakable and terrifying scream of a JU88 dive-bomber making its approach somewhere overhead. The first stick of bombs fell among the trees close to the road, and we watched mesmerised as they exploded at intervals for a couple of hundred metres to our front. Most of them did little damage, but a hand-cart which had been pulled by a young man with his arm in a sling, was overturned by the blast of the bomb nearest to us. The child who was accompanying him, was pinned underneath the cart, while the young man himself had been thrown against the base of a tree and knocked unconscious.

Without a second thought, I dashed out of the car, and ran to assist. As I did so I caught a glimpse of the plane climbing back into the evening sky after its dive. With its wheels down, and silhouetted against the sunset, it looked for all the world like some monstrous bird of prey.

The Citroen was a two-door model, and so the women had to scramble out of the back seat as best they could.

Having got out himself, Graham turned to assist them, but it was his last action. A second dive-bomber was on its way down, and had already released its deadly cargo. The first bomb scored a direct hit on the saloon, and the blast blew me off my feet. It was several minutes before I was able to gather my numbed wits together once more, and as soon as I realised where I was, I looked up to find that where the car had stood there was now a large crater in the road surrounded by several pieces of unidentifiable twisted metal.

It took me some time to absorb the fact that three people together with a vehicle could disappear completely in one blinding flash, and I had to force myself to look again to realise that it was true — they had vanished just as surely as if they had never existed.

Still in a daze, I lifted the overturned cart from the child's body, but I needed no confirmation to know that there was no more life there either. The young man sat sobbing quietly, while all around the eerie silence was broken only by some victim moaning softly further up the road. Both the planes had gone, no doubt congratulating themselves on a job well done.

Now I knew at first hand what it was really like to be a refugee without either protection or transport, and without any definite plan of escape in mind. At least I was unencumbered by personal possessions, thus giving me total freedom of movement. There could be no question now of continuing my journey westwards, and so I decided to go north towards the Channel coast. I considered the possibility that a single person would have a better chance of boarding a boat than four people together.

For three days I walked, mostly during the hours of darkness when the Luftwaffe was not operating. I slept rough during the day in deserted cottages and farmhouses, where I helped myself to food and drink and I managed to purchase a meal in a café at an inflated price, which relieved me of my last few francs. Once I caught sight of my reflection in a shop window, and was horrified by what I saw. I was dirty and unshaven, with unkempt matted hair, and dusty, torn clothes. I looked just like a tramp, and I doubted if even Claudette would have recognised me. I knew that she must be worried about me, not knowing where I was, or what had happened to me, because it was now several days since I had managed to contact her, and she would be well aware of the situation.

I was close to the town of Abbeville, when I came upon a welcome sight. A lorry and a jeep belonging to the Royal Artillery were parked on a piece of wasteland close to the road. Near by, under the cover of a small wood, about a dozen men were sighting a 25-pounder field gun to cover the approach route as it came round a blind corner. A lieutenant and a sergeant were leaning on the bonnet of the jeep studying a map. It was obvious that they had scarcely slept for days because, like the men, they were red-eyed, dusty and unshaven. The soldiers moved like automatons, and there was no sign of the famous humour which the British Tommy is supposed to possess, even in the face of adversity.

'Are you lost, lieutenant?' I asked as I joined them.

Both men eyed me with suspicion when they heard the unexpected English voice.

'Who the hell are you?' the officer snapped, 'and what exactly are you doing here?'

Under the layer of dust, I could see that he was only a youngster, probably still in his teens and certainly too immature to be responsible for the lives of other men. And yet, during the past few days, he had certainly acquired the knowledge and experience of a man twice his age.

I showed him my Press card, and gave him a brief resumé of the events which had brought me there, but he still seemed to be suspicious.

'There have been many incidents of fifth columnists posing as British Army personnel, so you must excuse me if I appear to doubt your bono fides,' he said in a more conciliatory tone of voice.

'You're the first British soldiers I have seen since leaving Paris,' I told him. 'How is it that you're on your own and as far west as this? I thought that the Army was falling back towards the north, especially Calais.'

'We were part of a column which was making its way

towards the Channel coast when we were dive-bombed, and then straffed by fighter-planes. It was the first time most of us had been under fire, and it was chaos. That was two days ago. Then the lorry broke down and we became separated from the main unit, so we decided to go it alone. About forty miles back, someone had moved a sign-post at a cross-roads, with the result that we took the wrong turning, and now we're not sure exactly where we are, or which direction to take from here.'

I pointed out their present location on the map as accurately as I could, and indicated the road which would take them to the Channel ports.

'Are you going to run for it, or make a stand?' I asked.

'Well, the position is this. The lorry has run out of petrol, and the jeep has barely enought to reach the coast. To make matters worse, we've only just heard over the radio that the German armour is advancing fast in this direction and will be here within half an hour. This is a good position to make a stand, and that's what we've decided to do.'

The sergeant was already supervising the placement of the camouflage netting over the gun among the trees. When he had finished, the officer gathered his men around him.

'I won't beat about the bush,' he told them. 'You all know the position. The Germans are at our heels, and if we continue on foot, they will soon catch up with us. If we can stop the leading tank as it appears round that corner, it may delay the others long enough to allow the jeep to get away to safety. I, for one, am going to stay, and I would be glad of volunteers to help me. Sergeant Tovey will take as many as he can in the jeep towards the Channel, and it will be up to you who goes or stays.'

'Sir, we've talked this over amongst ourselves,' the sergeant replied, 'and with your permission, we are all agreed that the married men among us will go. That leaves six men to stay here with you.'

'Thank you, sergeant, that will be an adequate number. You can be assured we'll do our best, and won't let you down. Now, you'll have to move quickly. Leave all your surplus equipment here, but take your small arms with you. You never know if and when you may need them.'

'What about this fellow?' Sergeant Tovey asked, pointing

to me.

'I'll leave the decision to you, sergeant, but remember the jeep will be heavily loaded as it is. I suggest that he'll just have to fend for himself.'

My heart sank when I heard this. I had begun to take it for granted that I would go with them, and now the prospect of being left behind was a bitter disappointment. In spite of that, I knew that the lieutenant was right, and that it was essential to get as many trained soldiers back to England as was possible. However, I was acutely aware of my own vulnerable position. Here I was, dressed in civilian clothes, footloose in the French countryside in the middle of a war, with the Germans breathing down my neck. Finding an Englishman out of uniform would almost certainly mean that I would be regarded as a spy, and I was not yet prepared to face a firing squad.

'Good luck, sir!' Sergeant Tovey said as he shook hands with his officer before saluting him formally. I was glad to see that order and discipline was maintained in spite of the setbacks. 'All the best, lads. Give 'em hell from us,' he said, as he collected some hurriedly written notes to be posted once he had reached Blighty.

'You too, sergeant. We hope you make it back safely.'

As the jeep pulled out, I saw my hopes go with it. Without another word I turned my back on the gun emplacement and began to walk in the same direction. The vehicle had not travelled more than a hundred metres when it stopped, and one of the soldiers called back.

'Come on, sir! I reckon we can find a corner for you after all.'

I could scarcely believe my good fortune, especially having braced myself to accept the worst, and I needed no second invitation as I ran after them and clambered aboard. The heavily-loaded vehicle then set off towards the north. Although I have never been a religious man, on that occasion I admit that I offered up a silent prayer of thanksgiving.

We had driven no more than five kilometers, when from the direction we had come, we heard the faint, but unmistakable crack of the twenty-five pounder, which carried on the slight breeze. This was followed a few seconds later by the noise of alien gun-fire. The artillery exchange must have lasted for a full minute, to be followed by a profound silence. None of us spoke, but the look on the faces of my companions was more expressive than words.

They treated me as one of themselves, even to the extent of sharing what little food they had, while I, for my part was able to assist them with the map reading, and managed to scrounge some wine in a village close to the coast. I vowed to myself that if I managed to get back home safely I would be able to write about the Blitzkrieg from first-hand knowledge, but more important would be to inform the British public of the magnificent effort put up by their fighting men.

Our journey towards the Channel ports was uncomfortable but otherwise uneventful. We were not hampered by refugees, and fortunately the Luftwaffe did not make an appearance. We paid a brief visit to the harbours of some of the smaller coastal towns, but there were no boats leaving for England. On the outskirts of Boulogne, the jeep ran out of petrol, and we were forced to walk the last couple of miles, all the while meeting up with remnants of other Army units as well as some soldiers from the French Army, all of whom were converging on the port.

Soon rumour was rife that there was a destroyer in the harbour ready to embark troops. Normally I have found wartime rumour to be without foundation, but we practically ran the last few hundred metres to the docks. Sure enough, there it was alongside one of the quays, grey and sleek, with her funnels smoking and boilers fired up for departure. But already the decks were covered by a mass of khaki, and no doubt there would be many more below. I felt a moment of panic in case there was no room for us, and this feeling was compounded by the refusal of the Military Police guarding the dock gate, who were reluctant to let me through. I can't say that I blamed them, because I must have looked a sight with my filthy clothes, unshaven face, and bloodshot eyes. Even my press pass together with the assurances of my companions was not enough to persuade them that I had a right to be there. However, their vigil was somewhat lax, and when their attention was diverted elsewhere, I slipped through and made my way up the gangway without further scrutiny.

Once on board, I managed to find a few square feet of unoccupied deck towards the stern, only a few minutes before the vessel cast off and headed out into the Channel. I remember one of the last sights at Boulogne was of a vast parking area containing hundreds of Army vehicles close to the docks, where gangs of men were busy sabotaging them to prevent their use by the enemy.

The normally fast and manoeuvrable destroyer was so laden down by her human cargo that she tended to wallow in the slight swell. In spite of that it did not seem long before the White Cliffs of Dover could clearly be seen on the horizon, and most of us thought that we were safely home. However, the Gods of War had not yet finished with us.

We were no more than six miles from the English coast when a buzz of excited conversation broke out amongst the men on deck, and all eyes were lifted skywards to see a formation of four JU88s which had appeared from behind some clouds overhead. No sooner had they made their presence known when the first one began to dive, and its hellish scream was soon mingled with the chatter of the destroyer's Oerlikons and pom-pom anti-aircraft guns.

I'm sure there was not a single man on deck who did not feel defenceless and frustrated. There was nothing we could do except cover our ears with our hands and huddle closer together, in the vain hope that contact with another human would bring some measure of protection. Someone close at hand prayed out loud. At any moment we expected an R.A.F. fighter to appear, but the Germans had the sky to themselves. In spite of my hatred for them, I felt a sneaking admiration for the pilots who were courageous enough to dive their aircraft straight into the hail of fire.

The first stick of bombs fell wide, but before our ears had recovered from the blast, the next plane was screaming on its way down. The overloaded destroyer was not able to manoeuvre easily, and one of the bombs from the second stick fell close to the hull on the starboard side, which caused the vessel to lose speed, and at the same time she developed a small but definite list.

It was the third plane which delivered the coup de gras.

A direct hit on the bow almost sheared the forecastle in two, and the ship's forward motion was abruptly discontinued. Fortunately there were few passengers at that end of the boat, but within a matter of half a minute or so, the vessel began to go down by the bows, slowly at first, and then at an increasing and alarming rate. There was no panic — there had been no time for it to develop, but every man knew that his survival was in the lap of the gods.

I found myself in the water surrounded by dozens of men. No life-jackets had been issued, and those of us who could swim were ordered by loud-hailer to get clear of the ship. The men who could not swim were either helped by the others, or else they slipped quietly under the surface of the water, never to be seen again. Fortunately the sea was calm with only a slight swell. Together with several others, I managed to swim to what I thought at first was a piece of wreckage, but which turned out to be a life-raft. By the time we had heaved ourselves aboard, we were able to take stock of the situation. The water all around us was covered by debris and men struggling to remain afloat. Of the destroyer, there was no sign, only its scattered remains.

The last plane made its attack unopposed, but instead of releasing its bombs, it sprayed the survivors in the water with machine-gun fire, adding to the number of corpses. The cries of those who had been wounded were drowned by the noise of the aircraft climbing back up to join the others under full boost. It was only then that a lone Spitfire appeared as if from nowhere. It fired a burst at the last JU88, causing it to spiral down trailing a plume of black smoke, but the others had already high-tailed it back towards the French coast.

Some of the men in the water raised a half-hearted cheer, with the exception of one solitary voice which shouted loudly up at the sky, 'Just like the R.A.F.! You're too bloody late!'

Soon we were aware of an armada of small boats coming from the coast towards us, and it was not long before we were transferred on board, cold, wet, and utterly exhausted both mentally and physically. Less than half an hour later, wrapped in warm blankets and with a large tot of rum inside us, we finally put our feet on English soil once more.

I never saw Sergeant Tovey or any of his men again after the destroyer was sunk, but I hope they managed to survive. I will always be grateful to them, because without their help I am certain I would never have managed to make my escape.

The authorities wanted to admit us to hospital for observation, but my one aim was to return to my family as quickly as possible. Although I did not realise it at the time, I was suffering from shock and exposure, but I managed to persuade the overworked medical staff that I was fit enough to be discharged. Since I was a civilian, they could not force me to stay, and I'm sure they were thankful to have one less patient to deal with.

☆ ☆ ☆

When I opened the front gate of my home my younger daughter was playing out in the garden. She took one look at me before running into the house calling, 'Mummy, mummy! There's a strange man at the door, and he's dirty!'

It was not surprising that Claudette failed to recognise me at once, and it was all of ten seconds before she realised who I was. Then she was in my arms, and we were all laughing and crying at the same time.

'We've been so worried,' she told me. 'There have been terrible stories about what has been happening over there, and since we had had no news of you, I began to expect the worst.'

'Don't worry about me, darling,' I assured her. 'You know that I'm a survivor, and will always turn up when I'm least expected.'

'Don't ever say that, Colin, even in fun.'

After I had eaten, bathed, then slept for twenty-four hours, I felt totally restored to health, the events of the past few days being like some continuous nightmare. With my family around me once more, full of love and concern for me, it did much to lift my morale, but after what I had seen I could not help being worried about what the future held for us all. I tried to make light of my experiences, but Claudette knew me too well, and although she managed to extract much of the story from me, I did not tell her everything.

And so I had survived my first encounter with war, but it was ironic that I had gained this experience as a civilian, and not as a member of the armed Services.

2

Battle of Britain

After three days spent doing nothing except enjoying a life of domestic bliss when the war seemed to be far away, the Press Agency, always eager for first-hand accounts of recent events in France and during the evacuation, began to telephone me once more. I was eager to write about what I had seen, and I prepared several factual articles about the Blitzkrieg as I had seen it. However, much of what I wrote was censored and edited to such an extent that the copy was presented as a morale-boosting exercise rather than an eye-witness account. The courage and self-sacrifice of our troops was highlighted, especially the little detachment of the Royal Artillery which was responsible for my escape. I hoped that Sergeant Tovey and his men had managed to read it. But I was obliged to play down the effective use of German dive-bombers, and the absence of air cover provided by the R.A.F.

Once I was invited to air my views on the radio, but again I was not allowed to express opinions which were different from the official line laid down by the Ministry of Information. Rather I was asked to speculate on the future of the French nation, and what I thought would happen over there now that the Germans were in occupation. It was a futile exercise, since I really had no idea what was happening back across the Channel.

It was not long before I was drawn back into the war, but on this occasion I was asked to play a very different role. At the same time as my escape from France, another great escape was taking place, namely the evacuation of the British Expeditionary Force from Dunkirk. Similar scenes were also being enacted to a lesser extent all along the Channel coast, involving many French soldiers who were eventually to form the Free French Army under the controversial, but intensely patriotic command of General de Gaulle. Many of these escapees had to have security clearance before they were allowed to assume the role of a serving soldier once more, and several camps were set up in the South of England to hold them until such time as they could be vetted. Since there was a shortage of Intelligence officers with sufficient knowledge of the country, my expertise in this field was pressed into service. Although I had been used to interviewing people, this was a different technique, and I underwent a brief course of instruction in the art of extracting information from a reluctant suspect, before being given a free hand to weed out fifth columnists.

The centre to which I was sent where this screening was carried out was a large house standing in its own grounds out in the country only a few miles from where I lived. A hastily-built camp of wooden huts had been constructed on the estate where the Frenchmen were incarcerated until they had been cleared. Naturally, many of them resented this treatment, but it was necessary in order to weed out any Nazi infiltrators who may have taken the opportunity to make their way to England during the disorganization of the retreat and subsequent evacuation.

On the whole, it was demanding but boring work, but one which required absolute concentration, making meticulous notes, and looking up numerous cross-references. I was pleased to mark up one definite success in unmasking a traitor, and I also passed on several suspects. My one single triumph happened in this way.

Every morning the interrogators met together to compare notes, so that every suspect was interviewed by at least two of us. I had been working at the centre for about ten days when the colonel in charge handed a file over to me.

'You know something about Brittany don't you, Colin?' he asked.

'Yes, sir. My father used to rent a house at Carnac for the summer when I was a boy, and I've been back for a holiday with my own family just before the war.'

'Good! I thought you had said something about being familiar with that area. Now then, I interviewed a fellow yesterday who's story struck me as being doubtful. He claims that he is in the French Army, but he says that he has lost his uniform during the retreat. The odd thing is that as yet we haven't come across any other men belonging to this so-called unit, and none of our screening groups could give me any confirmation. He also says that he originally comes from Brittany, and he seems to be familiar with the area, but read the file and see what you can make of him, Colin.'

I saw the man that same afternoon when he was brought to my office. He gave his name as Gaston Rouelle, a private soldier in the — Battalion of Pioneers. Although this unit was not on our list, it did not worry me unduly since there were many locally raised small detachments who were part of the French Army of which we had no knowledge.

Rouelle was dressed in an old pullover, and a pair of ill-fitting Army trousers. I would have expected that anyone in his circumstances would have shown a measure of diffidence and uncertainty, but he looked me straight in the eye, and his whole attitude was belligerent and confident.

First of all, he explained in great detail that his battalion had been busy doing maintenance work on the Maginot Line when the German breakthrough had occurred. Due to the confusion, he stated that his small group had received conflicting orders, and thus were separated from the main body. He recited the story as if he had learned it by heart, and even after close questioning he repeated it word for word. Like the colonel I was very suspicious.

When I asked him how he had managed to lose his uniform, for the first time he was hesitant.

'We were passing a small lake close to the road,' he told me, 'and as we were hot and dusty, we decided to stop the lorry and have a swim. When we were in the water, some of us had our clothes stolen, myself included. While we were trying to make up our minds what to do, an enemy plane suddenly appeared and made a low level machine-gun attack. The others were all killed, but somehow miraculously I was unscathed. I took the trousers from one of the dead soldiers nearby, but his tunic was shot through, and quite unfit to wear.'

Rouelle spoke with increasing confidence as his tale continued to unfold. I did not press the matter or show any doubt, but I scribbled a note on his file to the effect that who in their right mind would stop off to have a swim when the enemy was hard on their heels. I immediately switched to another topic for discussion.

'You state that you were born and brought up in Quiberon; at what age did you leave?'

'I was only twelve, monsieur.'

'But you told the colonel that you were fifteen.'

'Er, I made a mistake.'

'Describe the area to me.'

'You must remember it's several years since I left, monsieur.' I sensed a faint reluctance to pursue the subject.

'Never mind! We can all remember the place where we spent our childhood. I know I can. Tell me all you know.'

He proceeded to do so in great detail, with an accuracy which could only have been gleaned from the close study of a large scale map, and guide-books.

I threw in several questions concerning places and buildings in the area which would be known to any resident, but not mentioned in the literature. His hesitant and inaccurate replies following as they did his detailed description led me to believe that his story was untrue, but I decided to give him one more opportunity to redeem himself.

'Now, Monsieur Rouelle, I want you to imagine that you are approaching Quiberon down the causeway from the mainland. When you enter the town, what is the first shop you come to, and which side of the road is it on?'

He looked up at me with a confident smile. 'How can I possibly remember that?' he answered as if it was of no consequence.

One look at my face was enough for him to realise that he had damned himself. As it happened, the shop in question was Simmat's patisserie — a famous establishment in the town which drew clientele from a wide area. It was not possible for anyone to have lived there without knowing about it.

I looked up from writing my notes. 'Thank you, you may go now.'

I could tell from his expression that he was aware he had made the ultimate mistake. He mumbled something about the unfairness of the system, but his shoulders dropped as he shuffled out of the room. It was a further two weeks before I had news of him again.

'Oh, by the way, Colin, do you remember that fellow Rouelle you passed over to Intelligence?' the colonel asked me at lunch one day.

He went on to tell me that the man had eventually cracked under intensive interrogation, and that my suspicions had been well founded.

Apparently, the true story was that he had his roots in the Rhineland, the son of a French father and a German mother. It was the latter who had had most influence on his formative years, and so he became an ardent admirer of Adolf Hitler. Before the war he had been recruited into one of the Nazi cells, of which there were several, since the area was adjacent to Germany. When the Blitzkrieg began the members of these Nazi organizations were now ready to play an active role.

Rouelle had been ordered to make his way towards the Channel ports, and by posing as a soldier in the French Army he thought it would be easy to gain entry to England. Once he was established here, his assignment had been to make contact with another infiltrator who had been here for several years already, and who possessed an illegal radio transmitter. He had not expected to have undergone screening, but he had a story prepared in case he was questioned. Now both he and the mole were under arrest.

'A satisfactory day's work, Colin,' the colonel had commended me.

'Why did he pick Quiberon as his birthplace, sir?'

'Because it was almost as far from his real home as it was possible to be. You were right when you suspected that he had obtained all his information about the place from maps and guide-books. He had never actually been there, and didn't expect to meet anyone else who had.'

'So, what happens to him now, sir?' I asked.

The colonel shrugged. 'We handed him over to the Free

French Forces. I imagine that he will have paid the ultimate penalty. Our Allies don't mess about when it comes to dealing with traitors.'

☆ ☆ ☆

It was about this time when war correspondents were issued with uniforms. These were similar in style to those worn by British Army officers, except that they carried no badges of rank, but had flashes sewn on to the shoulders. With the plethora of foreign uniforms which now abounded in Britain, no one seemed to notice that they were different, and I used to smile to myself when O.Rs. saluted me, but the novelty soon wore off. I was well aware of the soldier's dictum, 'If in doubt — salute!'

Although the evacuation of the British Expeditionary Force from Dunkirk was now long past, and the Germans occupied the whole length of the Channel coast, we were still kept busy. There still remained a backlog of interviews, and every day more Frenchmen were escaping to England before the enemy had had time to re-organize themselves. However, inevitably the supply of people to be processed diminished, and so my services as an interrogator were no longer required. For once I was sorry to return to my previous work as a war correspondent. I had enjoyed my time at the centre, and being able to travel every day to and from my home, was a bonus which I appreciated.

During the months of July and August, there had been an apparent lull in the hostilities during which everyone braced themselves for the invasion of England which we were sure was bound to follow. By the time September came along, much of my work consisted of elaborating official communiques, or writing about deeds of individual heroism and personal experiences. Sometimes, for no apparent reason, much of my copy was suppressed by the censor anyway, so there was little scope for investigative journalism, and I was becoming bored.

As September progressed, the Battle of Britain changed all that. Everywhere one could feel the excitement which was generated during this historic time, when the whole country was once more galvanised into a state of pride in the achievements of our armed services, as they had been at Dunkirk. Now everybody in the South of England, civilian and serviceman alike, felt that they were actually a part of this, the first great battle for mastery of the skies. Whereas the role of the R.A.F. during the retreat through France had been suspect, now they were the heroes of the hour.

Every day, above our house, the skies were criss-crossed by vapour-trails as the dog-fights developed, and it became commonplace to witness planes plummetting out of the sky trailing smoke in their death throes. Naturally some of these landed on civilian property, causing loss of life, but these incidents were few and far between, and during the whole of the battle, our village had remained unscathed.

After a few exciting weeks, the war in the air was won, and the previously invincible Luftwaffe defeated. To us in Britain it seemed nothing short of a miracle, and since then even the historians have spoken about Divine intervention. But whatever the reason, it was obvious that the invasion of England would not now take place. However, the euphoria gave way to concern when the nightly bombing of London began. Since we were living deep in the countryside, we were seemingly immune from this nightmare, and with our friends and neighbours for support, it seemed as if we had built an impregnable fortress around us wherein the worst horrors of the war were kept at bay.

It was then that Claudette announced that she was pregnant once more, and on this occasion she was sure that it was going to be the son she knew I had always wanted. For several days I was walking on air, convinced that the future was assured for all of us. But I was old enough to know that complacency is a dangerous emotion, and I returned to reality one day to find my neat little world ripped apart, a reminder that no one could opt out, even if they wanted to.

☆   ☆   ☆

All my life I have remembered that awful day in November — the seventh to be exact, and the details have remained as fresh in my mind as if it was yesterday.

I had gone off to Southampton the previous day, full of

the joys of living, expecting to be back home that same evening. I really did not need to go at all, but a colleague of mine, who's assignment it was, had taken ill, and he had passed it over to me. Claudette urged me to go because she told me she wanted to do a big wash, and she said it was difficult with me under her feet. Our elder daughter had just begun to attend the village school, and Claudette would collect her in the afternoon. Reluctantly, I agreed to go.

I was to meet and interview some of the survivors from a liner which had been on its way to America full of evacuees, mostly children, but it had been torpedoed and sunk while still in the English Channel. Some of the rescued were in hospital, and I tracked down the remainder in a large hall close to the docks, which had been opened up as a reception centre. The whole exercise took much longer than I had anticipated, and it was late in the evening before I managed to get away.

I was at the railway station when the city was subjected to a severe air-raid, during which many of the lines had been uprooted. A block of flats close by had received a direct hit, and so instead of sitting comfortably in a train on my way home, I found myself part of a rescue squad, digging people out from the rubble. Most of the casualties were already dead, but we managed to pull out some who were still alive, thus giving us the stimulus to carry on. By early morning I was dog tired, dirty and hungry. I tried to telephone home to let them know I was all right, and I wasn't unduly worried when I was unable to get through, because I knew that many of the communications out of the city would have been cut.

Because of the disruption to both the railway and the bus services, it had taken me a long time to get home, and I knew that Claudette would be worried by now. Eventually, after many diversions, I alighted from a relief train at our local station in the middle of the afternoon.

As I walked towards the village I noticed that the atmosphere seemed to be heavily laden with smoke, as if someone had been burning rubbish on a grand scale, but it did not take me long to realise that this was the distinctive smell which follows an air-raid. Along the High Street, everything looked normal, but as I drew closer to home, I noticed that the smoke was denser here. Before I was able to turn the corner into our road, our local air-raid warden, James Mitchell, came to meet me.

'Hello, Jim!' I called out cheerily. 'Have we had an air-raid, then?'

'Well, I suppose you could say that. I guessed that you were away for the night, and I've been keeping an eye open for you, Colin. Come into the house for a minute, will you?'

We were outside his gate, but I said that Claudette and the girls would be worried about me, and that I'd better get off home. My neighbour insisted, however, and led me into his sitting-room.

'Sit down, Colin,' he said, handing me a stiff drink. His normally cheerful countenance had a serious look, and it was not until that moment I realised that something was wrong. I experienced a sudden sinking feeling in my lower abdomen.

'For God's sake tell me what's happened, Jim!' My mouth was so dry all of a sudden that I could barely get the words out.

'Late last night,' he began, picking his words carefully, 'one of the German planes which had been over London passed this way. We think he must have been chased by a night-fighter, because he unloaded a whole stick of bombs on the village. I'm afraid your house was one of the ones which caught the brunt of it.'

I jumped up. 'Claudette and the girls, where are they now, Jim?'

'In the village hall, but . . .'

'I must go to them straight away.'

He put a restraining hand on my arm. 'It's no use, Colin. I'm sorry to have to break the news to you, but they're dead. All of them.'

I felt as if he had hit me a physical blow. It just was not possible, and I scanned his face to make sure that I had heard him correctly.

'The whole house came down on top of them after a direct hit,' James went on. 'Claudette was only just alive when we brought her out, but she died in the ambulance before they could get her to hospital. We dug in the rubble to find you, and it was only then we realised you weren't at home, Colin. If it's any consolation, they were all in bed, probably asleep, so they wouldn't have known anything about it.'

His words of sympathy went unheard. I still could not believe it. It was only yesterday when I had laughingly taken my leave of them all. I still remember the last bantering words we spoke. She had said, 'Don't do anything foolish, now!' To which I had replied, 'What can I possibly do with a boatload of rescued children? Have a good wash!'

What an inane final conversation to have with someone you love. If I hadn't accepted the assignment, and if I had been home in time as I had intended, I too would have been lying dead in the ruins of my house. At that very moment I wished that my corpse had been there beside them in the village hall.

The next few days were a nightmare, which thankfully with the passage of time, is now only a hazy memory. I have no idea who arranged the funeral, and I didn't care. There had been several other fatalities in the area, and they were all buried together in a mass grave, but I could not find the courage to attend, and the platitudes offered by the clergy, instead of giving me comfort, merely irritated me. For several days I wallowed in a sea of self-pity, never quite sober, which must have been an embarrassment to James and his wife Mary, but they took me in, tended to all my physical needs, and did not intrude on my mental anguish. I often wish I had been in a position to repay them.

I had no other relatives, and Claudette's parents were still living in Occupied France, so there was no way of contacting them. Some of our neighbours who had also been close friends had either been killed, were in hospital, or they were too busy trying to rebuild their shattered homes to be concerned with my troubles, and so, apart from the Mitchells, I had to face the ordeal alone.

At last, I emerged from my drunken stupor, but even then I could not bring myself to go to view what was left of my home. It was now a part of my life which was at an end, a closed book, and I was determined to try to erase the memory of those years completely. I even went so far as to tear up the photographs of the family which I carried in my wallet, because I could no longer bear to look at them.

So far as the immediate future was concerned, I decided that there would be no more pussy-footing around with journalism. Now I had only one single thought in my mind, to avenge my loss in the best way I knew how. I was young and fit, and with my knowledge of French and France, I was ready to offer these attributes to help the war effort. And so, after leaving my affairs in the hands of a local solicitor, with only the clothes I stood up in, I left the village where I had been so happy, never to return.

3

Preparation

'Sir George will see you now, Mr Marshall.' The soft, musical voice of the incredibly beautiful WRNS officer broke into my thoughts.

When I left the village I had come straight here to the nerve centre of Combined Operations (Southern Area), which was situated in a large Georgian mansion standing in its own grounds out in the country, but readily accessible to Portsmouth. I had been waiting in this outer ante-room for over an hour, while a stream of high-ranking officers from all the Services came and went. The beautiful WREN was obviously the guardian of the inner sanctum, and seemed to be on familiar terms with many of the men who passed her desk.

Without further ceremony I found myself in the presence of the Co-ordinator himself, Rear-Admiral Sir George Henry Brown, KVO, DSO, RN., who rose to greet me and extended a friendly hand. I had first met the admiral about six months before the war, when he had sat next to me at a dinner, and on that occasion I had found him to be an interesting and entertaining companion. The next time we met was shortly after his appointment to Combined Operations, when we shared a compartment on the train to London. He remembered me, and spent the entire journey pumping me for information about the French coast and the French people. At this stage the Germans were still contained behind the Siegfried Line.

'I could use someone like you in my office,' he had

confided in me before we parted.

I thought he was joking, and I had laughingly informed him that I already had a job. Now here I was face to face with him once more, but this time in different circumstances.

Anyone meeting the admiral for the first time out of uniform, would have been in no doubt that he was a sailor. Although he was now in his late fifties and his thinning sandy hair was tinged with grey, his bright blue eyes, still without glasses, missed nothing as they probed from under bushy eyebrows. In recent years he had begun to show a paunch, and had filled out generally, but in spite of an increase in the flesh around his jowels and neck, his ruddy complexion was as smooth as any woman's. The only blemish on his clean-cut features was a faint scar across one cheek, the result of a wound he had received when he had been a young sub-lieutenant at the Battle of Jutland during World War I.

Sir George waved me into a chair in front of the huge desk, offered me a cigarette, then picked up the telephone beside him.

'Hold all my calls, Rosemary, until I tell you otherwise. If anything fresh comes in from Second Commando, pass it on to Colonel Williams.'

While he was doing this I took the opportunity to have a quick glance round the room. The walls were festooned with large-scale maps, most of which were of the French coast, and were the biggest I had ever seen. At a smaller desk in the corner there sat an RNVR lieutenant taking shorthand notes.

'Well now, Mr Marshall, what can I do for you?'

'Do you remember me, sir? We have met twice before, but I wonder now if we might be of service to each other.'

'Of course, I remember you very well. You have a detailed knowledge of France, if I recall. I know I can always benefit from your assistance, but how can I be of help to you?'

'Have you time to listen to my story, admiral?'

He glanced up at the clock on the wall. 'You have half an hour,' he said.

I told him about my connections with France, glossing over the early days, but in greater detail when I related my escape during the Blitzkrieg, and my experience with the screening unit since then. When it came to describing the events leading to the loss of my family and home, I only just managed to talk my way through it without breaking down. All the time I was speaking, the admiral sat in silence, but I was conscious of his eyes looking into my very soul, or so it seemed. Apart from my voice, there was no other sound in the room, except for the rustle of paper when the RNVR officer turned over a page of his dictation pad.

After I had finished my story, Sir George was silent for a few moments while he drummed the desk with his fingers.

'That was all very interesting, Mr Marshall. You've managed to experience more action already than many professional members of the Services. So, what do you want from me? How can I be of help to you?'

'I want revenge. I don't care what it is, or how it is achieved. My own life means nothing to me now. You once told me that you could use my knowledge and expertise, so here I am. I'm offering myself for you to do with as you see fit.'

'But you're a journalist, Mr Marshall. Surely you can be of great service to the country by doing just that. The pen is mightier than the sword, if you'll excuse the cliché. Public morale is also an essential part of the war effort, don't you think?'

'Maybe that's true, sir, but I'm no longer interested in churning out propaganda. I want to see the tangible results of my personal war effort. I want to kill Germans, or at least be directly instrumental in their death. I don't care what I have to do to achieve this, even if it means sacrificing my own life.'

The admiral sat back in his chair, put the tips of his fingers together, and gazed at me speculatively for what seemed a long time.

'Under the circumstances I can appreciate your reactions, Colin,' he said. 'You don't mind if I call you by your Christian name, do you?'

I shook my head and raised my hand in acquiescence.

'You see, war is a team game, Colin,' he went on, 'and in order to play, one must become a professional member of that team. At this very moment, thousands of young men and women are being transformed from rank amateurs into fighting units which are better and more efficient than the regular Services were before the war. In this context, there is no place for private vendettas, and if you are so emotionally unstable that you allow your personal feelings to over-ride your duty, then you are a weak link in the chain of command. Discipline is the key to all forms of warfare. I hope you understand what I'm trying to say.'

I nodded, and he continued.

'At this moment you obviously feel rage, frustration, and a need to lash out. I can understand your attitude, but frankly, while you are in this frame of mind you are of no use to me. However, provided that you are willing to undergo a period of intensive training through to the end, I do have something in mind for you, but I must warn you, it won't be easy.'

'All right, sir. I'm willing to do anything.'

'Yes, you are at this moment, but don't forget, as time passes, and the memory of your personal loss fades, so your motivation may disappear.'

'I don't think so, admiral. When I take something on, I usually see it through to the end.'

'Good! I have to go up to the War Office tomorrow, and I'm sure I can fix up something for you. You may not be much use to me now, but if you play your part, Colin, you will be, I promise you. Tell me, have you had any military training at all?'

'I did four years in the O.T.C. at my public school, sir, but perhaps that doesn't count.'

'Oh, yes, it does. It has at least instilled you with the basics, so you won't be a complete novice. Now, have you anywhere to stay?'

'No, sir. Since the bombing I've been living with friends in my village.'

'I'm afraid you won't find any hotel accommodation around here, so I suggest you stay at my house for a couple of nights. Rosemary will arrange transport for you.'

'That's very kind of you, sir, but I wouldn't want to be any trouble.'

'No, it's no trouble at all. I'll let my wife know to expect you, but I had better warn you, she isn't very good company at the present time. You see, our only son was a Spitfire pilot, and he was killed during the Battle of Britain only a couple of months ago.'

'I'm sorry to hear that, sir. Are you sure I won't be intruding?'

The admiral shook his head. 'I have my work to keep me occupied, but apart from a few hours of voluntary canteen duty, Connie has had nothing to take her mind off it. I don't get home as often as I would like, so I'm sure she will appreciate having someone else to look after, and you both have much in common. Besides, I want you to be available as soon as I return from London.'

☆   ☆   ☆

Sir George's own staff car deposited me without ceremony at the gate of a small detached house overlooking the Solent, near Gosport. The front door opened in answer to my knock, and I met the admiral's wife for the first time. She was not in the least what I had expected, and I think I may have stared at her rather rudely for a few seconds.

My first impression of Lady Constance Brown was that of a small, rather dumpy woman of indeterminate age, who had let herself go. Her rumpled dress was a faded purplish colour, and did not suit her. It fitted only where it touched, and it had ridden up so that several inches of under-slip was showing below the hem. Underneath she was heavily corseted in such a way that it hoisted her drooping bust and reminded me of a pouter pigeon. Her hair, which had once been bleached, was now showing dark patches at the roots, and by its unkempt condition, it was obvious that she had not visited a hairdresser for a very long time. Although she did manage to smile in greeting, her eyes were sad, and there were lines of worry and grief beginning to appear at the corners. The rest of her face was still smooth, and her complexion like velvet, even without the aid of cosmetics, and I came to the conclusion that she must have been very pretty at one time.

'Please, sit down, Mr Marshall,' she said in a quiet voice, as she ushered me into a pleasantly furnished sitting-room. 'My husband tells me that you will be staying for a few nights. Is that right?'

'Yes, if it isn't any trouble for you, Lady Brown,'

I still had an uneasy feeling that somehow I was intruding, although she was doing her best to make me welcome.

'Not at all, Mr Marshall. I want you to make yourself quite at home here. We have always been used to having young men around the house before . . .' Her voice faltered for a little until she regained control. 'George has told you about our sad loss, I think. I will certainly be glad of some company. I have too much time on my own to think.'

'I'm very sorry. I know exactly how you must feel.'

'Yes, I was forgetting we're both in the same boat. They say that time is a great healer, but I'm beginning to doubt the truth of that statement. It's a couple of months since Andrew was taken from us, but if anything, the emptiness and the pain gets worse.'

She looked away as a tear trickled down her cheek, but she brushed it away with the back of her hand instantly.

'If you are like me, you will feel a sense of unreality at this stage.' she went on, 'But it's when the numbness wears off that you feel it most. My trouble is that I haven't enough to occupy my mind. Try to fill every waking minute to keep your brain active with other matters, but I'm sure you know this already. If you don't want to talk about it, then I won't bring up the subject again.'

I certainly had no wish to talk about it, and so we discussed other matters. After an indifferent meal, I went to bed early, and slept surprisingly well, for the first time since the air-raid. I don't know what time the admiral arrived home, if indeed he came home at all, but by the time I had got up next morning he had already left for London, according to my hostess. After breakfast, Lady Constance went off on her bicycle to spend the day at a canteen run by the local branch of the WVS for sailors, and she did not return until late in the afternoon.

While I was alone in the house, I took the opportunity to look at the many photographs which were scattered around the front room. The admiral's wedding picture showed a tall, slim naval officer, vaguely similar to the portly Sir George, and beside him a small, pretty girl, who gazed up at him with a smile of pure happiness. There were other snaps of them taken separately and together, showing the gradual changes which had taken place as they had got older. On a table in one corner stood two studio portraits in silver frames; one was of a small boy about five years old, and another was that same boy now a good looking young man in R.A.F. uniform.

I spent the day reading from the admiral's well-stocked library, listening to the wireless, and walking in the neglected garden which overlooked the Solent. Two destroyers, a cruiser, and several minesweepers were lying at anchor, and apart from the presence of the warships, the scene looked almost peaceful.

After the evening meal, I made an effort to amuse my hostess by relaying some of the lighter moments which occasionally brighten the life of a journalist, and I felt some satisfaction when one or two of my anecdotes brought a spontaneous smile to her lips. She became even more relaxed after she had raided the admiral's liquor store, and produced a bottle of brandy. By the time we turned in, the bottle was more than half empty.

☆   ☆   ☆

Next day, about mid-morning, a jeep arrived without warning to drive me back to Sir George's office. When I took my leave of Lady Constance I felt that my visit had done her some good, and that she was in a more relaxed frame of mind than when I had arrived, and I politely expressed the hope that we would meet again.

If it was possible, the admiral's office was even more hectic than it had been on my last visit. On this occasion as before, I was kept waiting in the ante-room for over an hour, but at least during that time I was able to feast my eyes on the glamorous Rosemary, which helped to pass the time. Sometimes she caught my eye and smiled at me, as if we were sharing some conspiracy. I was almost sorry when I was summoned into the inner sanctum.

Sir George was sitting at his desk poring over some maps. He looked up as I came in.

'I can only give you a few minutes, Colin,' he said

brusquely. 'I hope Connie has managed to look after you?'

'Yes, perfectly, admiral. I am very grateful.' Secretly I wondered what he would say when he discovered that his brandy store had been raided.

'And I take it you still feel the same about doing something more positive towards the war effort?'

'I haven't changed my mind, if that's what you mean.'

'Right! I have a job in mind for you. I can't tell you yet what it is, but first of all you will have to undergo a period of intensive training. As I have already warned you, it will be hard, and you will have to be utterly dedicated to see it through. Even then, your best may not be good enough, and you may not be able to complete the course. If this should happen, I'm afraid you will be of no further use to me, which would be a pity.'

'May I ask, what is involved, sir?'

'I have made arrangements with Colonel McDonald, who is the commandant of one of the Commando training camps in the North-West of Scotland, for you to go there for six months. The C.O. and the adjutant know all about you, but they are the only persons who do, and I want your past kept a secret. It's not unusual for them to have the occasional odd bod for a period of training there, so your presence ought not to arouse too much speculation. All the time you are there, you will remain a civilian, but you will live and be paid as a private soldier. I cannot stress enough that this is going to take every bit of your courage to see it through to the end. If you feel that you're not going to be able to handle it, then please say so now, before we go any further.'

'No, sir, I'm confident of my own ability.'

'Well, if you find that it becomes too much for you, since theoretically you aren't a member of the Armed Services, then you are free to quit at any time.'

'I won't do that, sir.' I spoke out almost defiantly, because I could feel my resolve beginning to waver. 'Can you tell me what I am being trained for?'

'No. One thing at a time, Colin. The less you know at this stage, the better. Rosemary has your travel warrant and the relevant documents, so you can collect them on your way out.' He held out his hand. 'I need hardly say I hope to see you back here in six months' time.'

The lovely WREN officer gave me a dazzling smile as she handed me an envelope. Inside there was a piece of paper on which was typed out all the times and changes of trains which were necessary to take me to my destination. At the bottom, penned in her own hand, were two words — Good luck! Miraculously, somehow my flagging morale was instantly restored.

☆ ☆ ☆

Four hours later, I found myself in a crowded third class compartment heading north. I was obliged to change trains three times, and each one seemed to be colder than its predecessor, but thirty-six hours after leaving Portsmouth, I was set down on a tiny station platform miles from anywhere, frozen to the marrow, and desperately hungry. Fortunately there was a fifteen-hundredweight truck waiting for me, and as I was the only passenger, I sat beside the driver, a lance-corporal belonging to the R.A.S.C., who kept up a continual line of chatter all during the twelve mile drive to the camp. Thankfully I was not expected to say much, so I was able to look around me at the scenery, and my heart sank. The road surface was not tar macadammed, and full of potholes, the bleak mountains were topped with snow, and partly covered by low cloud, and the trees were bent over by the biting wind. The cold and the damp were all-embracing, and I cursed my luck for having come here during the winter months. I didn't know with any certainty where I was, but I guessed that it was somewhere on the coast of Wester Ross.

At last, after three-quarters of an hour of being buffeted about, the road dropped down to the wooden-hutted camp which was situated close to a few crofters cottages on the edge of a shingly beach with cliffs on either side. This was also the end of the road — it went nowhere else. Through the heavy rain-soaked mist, I could only just make out some scattered islands off-shore. My first reaction was that if this was to be my home for the next six months, then God help me! I must have been mad to agree to come here.

The truck dropped me outside the orderly-room, and I

was immediately admitted.

'This man is to see the C.O., sergeant-major,' Captain O'Brien, the adjutant, told the warrant officer in attendance, after checking my papers, and so I found myself being marched into the colonel's office without further ceremony.

It was quite a shock when I came face to face with Colonel McDonald across the desk. In my own mind I had conjured up the picture of a middle-aged, perhaps Blimp-like figure, but instead I was confronted by a tall, slim, weather-beaten officer wearing khaki dungerees, unadorned except for his badges of rank on the shoulder-straps. He had black, wavy hair, and a smooth boyish face, but his manner was restless, as if he found it difficult to sit still for any length of time. I reckoned that he could not have been more than thirty-five years old.

'Leave us, if you please, sergeant-major.'

The warrant officer's expression remained stoney-faced as he saluted and marched out, but I was willing to bet he was agog with curiosity as to what this thirty-two year old civilian was doing there.

'I know a little about you, Marshall, and why you're here,' the colonel said as soon as we were alone, 'but to begin with I want to assess just how much you are capable of. Tell me what military training you have had in the past.'

I gave him a rough outline of what I had been taught in the Officers' Training Corps at school, but when he questioned me further I had to confess that I had forgotten a great deal.

He made a note on his pad. 'Don't worry,' he said. 'In some ways it's like riding a bicycle. It'll come back to you when you get into the swing of it again. Now, what is your state of physical fitness?'

I had to own up to the fact that I had not taken much exercise in recent years, nor had I played any games since I was married.

He looked at me critically and frowned. 'Hm. Yes, I can see that you're a bit overweight, but we'll soon alter that. Your exercise tolerance will have to be increased, but we'll start you off gradually. Now I understand that you were involved in some of the fighting during the retreat from

France? Tell me about it.'

In as few words as possible, once again I related my adventures. All the time I was speaking he got up and walked about the room, but he listened attentively without interrupting until I was finished.

'Well, at least you've had your baptism of fire, Marshall, which is more than I can say for most of us here. After the ship you were on was sunk, did you have any nightmares about it?'

'Only for a short time, sir. It hasn't worried me now for several months.'

He scribbled another note on his pad. 'Good! It shows that you have no psychological hang-ups, anyway. So far as we are concerned, your time with the Intelligence Service was probably good experience, but it's of no consequence to what you will be doing on this course.'

'Admiral Brown didn't specify what was expected of me here. Perhaps you can fill me in, sir.'

'As you have already discovered, this is a Royal Marine Commando Training Camp. During the next few months we will endeavour to bring you to a peak of both physical and mental fitness, so that you have the confidence in yourself to know that you can achieve the impossible; then we will show you how. This is no rest camp. We will teach you all methods of killing, from unarmed combat to the use of conventional weapons, and a few unconventional ones. You will learn fieldcraft, how to disappear into your surroundings, how to find your bearings by night, and how to creep up on your enemy unseen by day. We will teach you the various techniques of landing on a beach, sometimes under fire, and in between there will be physical training, forced marches, and rock-climbing. Oh, yes, one more little game we have is to take you out on the moors somewhere in a closed truck, then letting you find your own way back with very little equipment. It's all good fun, so they tell me!'

While he was speaking, he displayed considerable enthusiasm, and I could see he was not happy merely just to sit back and watch, but was keen to take part in all aspects of the training.

'Most of the men here come from a hotch-potch of regiments, but they have all volunteered for this course. To pass out as a Royal Marine Commando means something to them. They feel superior to other soldiers, and so they should. The men come from all walks of life, and some of them are pretty rough characters, so be warned. Admiral Brown wanted you to live as one of them and not as an officer, and so you will be treated accordingly, with no special favours. You will be kitted out as a private soldier, but since you remain a civilian, remember you can quit at any time. However, I should advise you not to tell anyone too much about yourself — it could lead to bad feeling. The men and the staff know that you are a civilian, but that's all they need to know. If at any time you wish to speak to Captain O'Brien or myself, one of us is always available, so please feel free to do so. At any rate, I will be sending monthly progress reports about you to the admiral. It must be something pretty important you are being trained for. Any further questions?'

'None that I can think of, sir.'

'Good! Then I'll arrange for you to be billeted, and have a medical examination. Tomorrow you start work in earnest. Good luck, Marshall.'

☆ ☆ ☆

A week later I wondered exactly what it was I had let myself in for, and I was firmly convinced that I would never survive for another week. The training programme meant that we were broken up into squads of twelve men, depending on what stage of instruction they had reached. My party was short of a man, but the others had already been there for four days longer than me, and I was expected to catch up.

Every morning, whatever the weather, we had an hour of intensive physical training out in the open air before breakfast, to be followed by weapon training until lunch. On some days the afternoon was devoted to a cross-country hike over some of the roughest terrain I had ever seen, and each day the distance was progressively increased. Each night I fell into my hard, uncomfortable bunk, aching all over, and scarcely able to hold up my head, so great was my fatigue. But each night I slept right through, and every morning when I awakened, I wondered if I would be able to withstand the day's torture, or if I ought to quit and free myself from this hell. But somehow I managed to struggle through yet one more day.

At least it had the effect of keeping my mind off my personal problems, and gradually the tragic events of a few weeks before began to recede, as if it happened a long time ago. By the end of the second week I found that I was able to cope more easily with the punishing physical routine. In spite of the huge meals with which we satisfied our voracious appetites, I had already lost most of my superfluous weight, and gradually my body was being honed into peak condition. However, although I was managing to survive, my progress was being made all the more difficult because a series of personal vendettas were adding to my tribulations.

All the instructors held the rank of sergeant, and each one was a specialist in his own field. There seemed to be a conspiracy amongst them that there was no way a civilian was to take precedence over fully trained soldiers, consequently I was earmarked for special treatment. If I made the slightest mistake during weapon training, it was highlighted as an example of how not to do it, or if I lagged behind even a yard on the assault course, I was subjected to unbelievable abuse. The sergeant-major, who was no doubt annoyed at having been excluded from my initial interview, took every opportunity to single me out for censure, whether it was on the parade ground, or during our rare moments of leisure. The result was that if there were any extra duties to be undertaken, I was usually the one detailed to do them.

But perhaps it was the unarmed combat instructor who was my greatest threat. Whenever a new hold had to be demonstrated, I was invariably the one singled out as the victim, and naturally I always came off second best. Sometimes, after one of these sessions I would end up with multiple bruises, but next time I was back again for more. I do not believe for one moment that the colonel was a party to this, and although I was tempted, I refrained from making any complaint to those in command. In spite of the fact that the staff seemed determined to break me, as time went on, I became equally determined that they were not going to.

Unfortunately it was not only the staff who were giving me a hard time. The five other men with whom I shared a hut were a mixed bunch, four of them being conscripts and one a regular soldier. There were none of them to whom I could relate intellectually, and I found the conversation to be often inane, especially as it was liberally interspersed with profanity. Even if I tried not to show my displeasure at the endless stream of filthy jokes, I found it impossible to join in, with the result that I withdrew into my shell. In addition, since I remained steadfastly reticent about my past, and my purpose for being there, I was repeatedly referred to as being a "stuck-up bastard", and "His Majesty" often within my hearing.

The only regular soldier among us, a lance-corporal, was in charge of the hut. He was called Jock Ramsay, and was a typical product of the Glasgow Gorbals. It was not surprising that he took an instant dislike to me, so much so that he goaded me in a dialect I could barely understand at every opportunity. On one occasion he provoked me so much that I was forced to defend myself physically. This produced an immediate attack, and he came at me like a bull in a china shop. I fortunately kept my head, and when he found himself on the losing end, in order to save face, he reported me to the sergeant-major for attacking an N.C.O.

Needless to say, I was marched in front of the C.O. who gave me a severe dressing-down, followed by a lecture on the need for mutual co-operation and team spirit. However, I was pleased to note that my adversary was also on the mat, and thereafter he kept out of my way. The fact that I had not divulged the real reason for the fight, went a long way to making the other men more tolerant towards me.

It was an incident during a rock-climbing period during my third month which resulted in a change of attitude towards me by the staff. I had never liked this part of the training programme, as I had no head for heights, and the instructor was well aware of the fact. One bitterly cold day when I was trying to negotiate a short, but very difficult pitch with my heart in my mouth as usual, I felt safe so long as the rope was round my waist to hold me if I should fall. The rock was covered with wet ice, and my fingers were frozen stiff in the chill February wind. My nightmare became a reality when I slipped and fell, but the rope didn't hold. The sergeant who was responsible for belaying me was heard to say, 'This'll make the bugger sweat,' as he let the rope run through for about ten feet. I was on a slight overhang at the time, so I came up with a jerk, and was left dangling in mid-air before I was manhandled back down the face, unable to move.

I spent the next two weeks in sick bay with most of the skin off both knees and four broken ribs. The court of inquiry which followed immediately resulted in the departure of that particular instructor. He was replaced by another, with a different attitude, who instilled me with some confidence on the rock, but it always remained my bête noir. I think that the staff must have been told something about me, because from then on I was treated like all the others, but nothing was said. Even the sergeant-major came to visit me a few times in the sick-bay, and brought me several books he had finished with.

When I returned to duty again, although the attitude of the staff towards me had changed, that of my companions did not. One bone of contention was that as a civilian I was excused guard duty, and even when I pointed out that the arrangements were none of my doing, it did not convince them. My recent popularity with the staff also did not go unnoticed, and caused some resentment.

One day in March, the orderly room received a telephone call to say that a plane belonging to the Free French Air Force had crash-landed in the mountains about fifteen miles inland from the camp. The colonel himself headed the party of volunteers to look for survivors, and as the only French-speaking person there, I was invited to join them.

It was close on twelve hours before we arrived at the map reference, having had to cross over one mountain range, and climb half way up another. The final three hours were carried out in darkness, and a recent blizzard had blotted out many of the landmarks, but we made it. The pilot and the flight engineer had not survived, but we were pleased to discover that two of the crew were still alive. The navigator, who had two broken legs, was barely conscious, but the rear-gunner, having been trapped in his turret, was unhurt although suffering from exposure.

Our party carried out first aid, and I was able to converse with the gunner while he was being freed. I reported the conversation to Colonel McDonald.

'He tells me that there is a fifth member of the crew, sir, the wireless operator. He was injured and has gone off to try to get help.'

'Find out how long it is since he left, and what direction he has taken.'

'He waited until the blizzard had stopped, sir, so it was not more than two hours ago,' I translated, 'but it looks as if he has taken the wrong direction, and gone up the hill instead of across the ridge.'

'He'll never survive in this weather,' the C.O. said in a low voice so that the others could not hear. 'He hasn't any survival gear, and he doesn't know the country. I suppose we ought to go and look for him, but we'll have to wait for daylight. I don't want to put any of our party at risk.'

After a cold and miserable night, the dawn seemed a long time coming, but at least there had been no more snow. After we had breakfasted on iron rations and hot, sweet tea, the colonel took me to one side.

'Look, Marshall, the chances of finding this other man are almost nil. I think we ought to try to get this injured fellow back while he's still alive. Will you tell the gunner why we'll have to abandon the search?'

'Sir, let me go and have a look. At least I can talk to the fellow if I ever find him.'

He considered my request, but was reluctant to allow me to go. At last he nodded in agreement. 'You ought to be able to follow his footprints, but if you haven't found him within half and hour, then make your way back, and that's an order! All right. Marshall? I don't want you taking any unnecessary, risks.'

'Understood, sir!'

'We'll set off back to the camp, but we'll be slow because of the injured man, so you ought to be able to catch us up easily. We'll mark the route for you in case it snows again.'

I set off up the hillside carrying a first aid kit, and a length of rope. As I went higher, so the snow became deeper until it had almost reached my waist, but it made the path taken by the wireless operator easier to follow. Within minutes I was out of sight of the crashed plane, and the only sound in this wilderness of rock and snow was my laboured breathing. After half and hour, the footprints ended abruptly at the edge of a deep corrie.

Standing as close as I dared, I looked over down into the rough terrain far below, but could see nothing. I edged closer, and was able to throw myself backwards as some loose rock under my feet gave way and cascaded out of sight. A few seconds later, I thought I heard a cry, but I could not be sure because of the sound of a waterfall not too far away. I called out, and there was no mistaking the human voice which answered me from somewhere over the rim of the precipice.

Fortunately there was a lone mountain pine close by, a gnarled and twisted tree, bent by the wind, but obviously well established and secure. Looping the rope around it, I lowered myself until I was able to look straight down the face, and there, not twenty feet below me on a wide ledge was the man I had been looking for. He waved his hand and stood up with difficulty, calling out at the same time, but I could not hear what he was saying. It did not take long to abseil down to him, but I had to grit my teeth to force myself to do it, knowing now that I was on my own.

The ledge on which the airman was trapped was free of snow, and sheltered from the worst of the weather, but even then he was frozen so that he could scarcely move. He told me that he had sprained his ankle, and had begun to give up hope of ever being rescued. While I rubbed his frozen limbs, he sipped the hot tea I had brought with me, and I was able to consider our situation. It would be comparatively easy to help him out of here, but getting back to the camp was another matter.

At last we made our move, and with the aid of the rope and me pushing from behind, we were able to scramble back up to the tree. From then on our progress was painfully slow, since every step he took caused him to wince with pain, but after a couple of hours we arrived back at the plane. The other members of the party had long since gone, but they had left some hot drink and a few iron rations.

By now the wind was beginning to rise, and the lacerated fabric covering the wings made a flapping noise. Within the space of an hour the weather had got worse, the wind rising to a scream through the fuselage brought with it intermittent flurries of snow. There was no question of trying to make the camp, and so we settled down to endure another night only half protected from the elements. The airman's lined leather flying jacket and boots had helped to keep him safe from the worst of the cold, otherwise he could never have survived the previous night out in the open.

Fortunately when dawn broke the wind had abated, and it was slightly warmer, and so once we had got our stiffened limbs working again, we set off on the long trail back down the mountain. Unfortunately, the rise in temperature had made the surface of the snow wet and slippery underfoot, instead of firm and crisp, but somehow we slithered our way along to make some progress over the rough terrain. The injured man was forced to lean heavily on me, and before we were half way back I could feel my strength beginning to fail. My companion was scarcely able to walk a step and begged me to leave him, but a streak of obstinacy or bloody-mindedness, call it what you will, was still active and kept me going.

I remember very little after that. I think we may have sat down for a rest and fallen asleep from sheer exhaustion, because the next thing I remember was being shaken roughly. I looked up to see the concerned face of the sergeant-major and for a brief moment I thought I had been caught falling asleep on an exercise.

'Thank God you're all right, Marshall,' he said. 'Here, drink this!'

He put a bottle to my lips, and I coughed as the strong spirit ran down my throat. I tried to get up, but he pushed me down again gently.

'Stay where you are, lad. Let us take you in.'

'The airman, is he all right?'

'Don't you worry! He'll live, thanks to you.'

It was only when I was lifted on to a stretcher that I was aware of the others, including Jock Ramsey, who actually smiled and gave me a thumbs-up sign.

It was pitch dark by the time we reached the camp, and most of the personnel seemed to be waiting to see if I had survived. As soon as I was put to bed in the sick bay, the colonel came to visit me. He told me that the flight engineer had died on the way down the mountain, and they had buried him under a cairn of rocks. The rear gunner had already departed back to his unit.

I made my report about what had happened, adding that we would never have survived if it had not been for the rescue party.

'You don't think we would have left you out there, do you, Marshall?' he said with a twinkle in his eye. 'Anyway, I personally was never in doubt about your ability to survive.'

I don't know if he really believed that, but it did much to boost my morale. The experience had certainly been better than any exercise. I asked how the French airman was.

'The M.O. is with him now, but I think he'll be all right in a few days, thanks to you.'

By the next day I had fully recovered, and was surprised to discover that the ordeal had not affected my health as much as I would have thought. It was proof of my state of fitness, if indeed any proof were needed. Before he left, the airman was vociferous in his thanks to me, so much so that I was embarrassed by his effusive and flowery speech. He kissed me on both cheeks, a gesture to which I was accustomed, but it drew funny looks from the medical orderly.

Thereafter the rest of my stay was quite pleasant, since the attitude of everyone towards me had undergone a complete change. Even Jock Ramsey offered me a swig from the illicit bottle of whisky which he kept hidden in his kit. I suspect it was something of a peace offering, and although I did not want it, it would have been churlish to have refused. My inability to mix with the other members in my hut was now looked on with tolerance, as if they had at least recognised that I did not think as they did.

☆ ☆ ☆

At last, just when spring was beginning to show, the day

arrived when it was time for me to leave. About a third of the men who had started the course had failed to complete it, and had departed long since. Those who had survived were given fourteen days' leave, and travel warrants were issued to wherever they wished to go. I, of course, was the exception. My orders were to report immediately to Admiral Brown, and my travel documents were accordingly made out back to Portsmouth. Before my departure, however, I had one more meeting with Colonel McDonald.

I was somewhat amused to notice that he now addressed me as 'Mister Marshall'.

'I was a bit doubtful about having you up here in the first place,' he told me, 'But Combined Operations were most persuasive. There were times when I had my doubts that you wouldn't make it, but I have since realised that you had been unfairly treated at the beginning. I assure you that was not on my orders, and the fact that you struck it without complaining to me says a lot for your courage and determination. I'm sure that Admiral Brown will be very proud of you. I know that I am, and I'm sure we have given you the preparation necessary to help you cope with whatever lies ahead. You are certainly a different person now from the one who arrived six months ago. Good luck for the future!'

He was right, of course. Having been transformed both mentally and physically, I was now lean and tough, able to look after myself in any situation, and had the ability to withstand hardship and survive. I had also acquired a working knowledge of weapons and explosives, as well as methods of killing an enemy with my bare hands, should the need arise.

But perhaps it was within my mental attitude where the greatest change had taken place. My time here had left me with very little opportunity to dwell on the past. It was only rarely now when I thought about the tragic loss of my family, and the episode seemed somehow unreal, as if it had happened in another life a long time ago. However, I was still capable of feeling guilt when I came to realise that I had not given my dead loved ones a passing thought for several days at a time. Even their likenesses were no longer clear in my mind, and I no longer had any of their photographs to remind me.

My resolve to seek retribution was still there, but it no longer dominated all other considerations, and I had developed a much more professional attitude to whatever job I was given. All during the journey south, I wondered what that job would be.

4

Making Plans

It took me all of five days before I arrived back in Portsmouth, mainly because I took some time off in Birmingham to get blind drunk. Since I had been shut away from civilization with very little alcohol for six months, I had an irresistible urge to kick over the traces, even for a short time. However, I was relatively sober by the time I reached my destination, except that I was suffering from a king-sized hangover.

A telephone call to Combined Operations Headquarters from Portsmouth station brought a truck to pick me up, and once again I found myself in the admiral's outer office where the beautiful Rosemary still presided.

'My, my, Mr Marshall, you're looking well. Scotland must suit you,' she said, as she flashed me one of her dazzling smiles. 'Did you enjoy your course?'

'Enjoy is not the word I would have used, and I don't care if I never see Scotland again,' I replied.

'Well, we're all very proud of you here. We've heard wonderful reports about you. The admiral isn't here, I'm afraid. He's down at Plymouth, but he'll be back tomorrow. We expected you a couple of days ago.'

She looked at me quizzically, but I made no comment as to why I was late.

'Lady Brown sent this note to give you when you arrived,' she continued.

The contents of the letter were short and to the point.

Dear Mr Marshall,

If you have nowhere to stay, I would be pleased to put you up. Come at any time.

         Constance Brown.

When I looked up after having read the note, I had the impression that Rosemary was smirking, but she immediately became serious.

'Be careful!' was all she said, but what it was she was trying to warn me about, I could not imagine.

☆   ☆   ☆

When the taxi dropped me at the admiral's house, I was immediately struck by the fact that although it was springtime, nothing had been done in the garden. When I had been there before it had shown signs of neglect, but now it was a jungle wherein the weeds had been allowed to run riot.

My contemplation was interrupted by the appearance of Lady Constance herself, and I could see that she too had undergone a change. She wore a gaudy housecoat which was none too clean, nor did it fit properly due to the fact that she had lost weight. In contrast to my last visit, she was smiling cheerfully, but when I got close to her I saw that she had been drinking, although it was still early in the afternoon. She greeted me with gushing enthusiasm.

'I'm so glad you could come, Mr Marshall. It's nice to see old friends again. I've been expecting you for the past few days, and I began to think you weren't coming. George is away in Plymouth, but you will have been told that already. He ought to be back tomorrow.'

Once inside the house, I settled down in the sitting-room while she poured us both a stiff gin, taking it for granted that I would have one also.

'Well now, Mr Marshall, tell me about your stay in the wilds of Scotland. May I call you Colin? Mr Marshall sounds so formal, doesn't it?'

I told her something about the rigors of life in the training camp without going into too much detail, and as I was speaking I glanced around me. It was some time before I realised what was different about the room — every photograph which had previously been on display had now disappeared, leaving it looking bare and impersonal.

She fixed me with an intense stare, but I don't know if she was really listening because as soon as I had finished she got up without a word and mixed another drink for us both. When she returned she came and sat closer to me.

'I saw you looking round, Colin, and you must have noticed that there have been some changes here.' She hiccuped, then giggled. 'I suppose you think that I've been drinking? Well, maybe I have, but I have my reasons.'

'I'm sure it's none of my business, Lady Constance.'

'For heaven's sake stop calling me Lady Constance!' she said vehemently. 'My name is Connie. Connie Smith I was before I married George, and I may as well tell you I was a barmaid.' She went on to parody the Cockney accent in a raucous voice. 'Does that shock you, Colin? Well, a lot of water has passed down the Thames since those days, and I've since learned to play at being the lady. Actually, my parents kept a pub in Gravesend, and I used to serve behind the bar on occasions. That's the way to learn about life! It was during the First World War, and George was a lieutenant on a cruiser which used to dock there. He was older than me, but a handsome man then, and a devil with the women. You wouldn't think so seeing him now. In those days I wasn't bad looking either, even if I do say so myself.'

Her voice dwindled to a whisper, and I realised that she had fallen asleep. I rescued the half-filled glass from her hand before lifting her legs up on the couch. Her housecoat fell open to show that she was wearing nothing underneath, and I was treated to a full view of her uncorseted body with its drooping bust, and the folds of slack skin around her midriff. I covered her over with a rug, and left her to sleep off her self-induced stupor.

Poor Connie! To a certain extent I could understand why she had let herself go, and was finding a certain amount of solace from the bottle. She probably didn't see her husband very often, and had no one to whom she could turn to to discuss her problems. Being stuck in this house all alone, several miles from town, with only a bicycle for transport, she must have been desperate for company.

It was a lovely evening, and so I went for a walk. On my return a couple of hours later, I found Connie in the kitchen as bright as a button once more, concocting some dish from powdered eggs. She smiled at me as I came in.

'This isn't like the meals you have been used to in Scotland, but it seems as if it's all we have,' she said cheerfully. 'It won't be long. I knew you would be back before it was dark. Thank you for making me comfortable, Colin. I hope my little lapse didn't embarrass you,' she added coyly.

I thought my presence might put a brake on her alcohol consumption, but after we had eaten an indifferent meal, she was back on the booze again, and now it was neat brandy. I could not stand by and watch without making some comment.

'You don't have to tell me I'm drinking too much, but it's the only way I can make life even half bearable,' she said, glaring at me defiantly.

'Surely it can't be as bad as all that, Connie? No one ever derived real comfort from the bottom of a bottle,' I argued. 'You have a nice home, a husband, and everything necessary to make life comfortable. I know what you went through when you lost your son, but you can't go on destroying yourself because of that. It solves nothing. Even if you are a bit isolated here, surely you have friends who can visit you? What about your parents?'

'They passed away several years ago, and most of our friends are in the services, so they're spread around the country, and travel is difficult. Besides, who would want to come to this dead-and-alive hole? Yes, I lost my only son, but I can't turn off his memory like a tap. I used to go to the canteen to speak to lots of other young men, knowing all the time that I would never see my own boy again. You had your tragedy too, but you've been able to get away for six months and fill your days so that you could forget even for a few hours, but I can't do that. I'm stuck with it.'

'What does Sir George say? Surely you have discussed it with him?'

'He's too taken up with his own problems. As for being a husband, that's a laugh. It's three years now since he retired from the Navy, and we were looking forward to a peaceful future together, after being herded from pillar to post all over the world for the past twenty years or so. This job is killing him. He seldom has any time off, and when he does he can no longer relax and live a normal life. He has become an old man, and I can scarcely recognise him from the well-set-up figure he used to be. That's why I've taken down all the photographs so that it will no longer remind me of the past.'

A tear trickled down her cheek, smudging her mascara. She brushed it away quickly with the back of her hand before continuing.

'Just look at me! I'm only forty-five years old, and I could be taken for a woman of sixty. What man would consider me as a lover, least of all George? I'm convinced he's got someone else, and I'm willing to bet it's that tart Rosemary Stuart in the office. He certainly sees more of her than he does of me. He only comes here to sleep occasionally, and that's all he does — sleep.'

I very much doubted if the lovely WREN officer would harbour any romantic interest in the ageing admiral, since she had so many younger men to chose from. Although I was not in possession of all the facts, it struck me that Connie had developed a paranoia where Rosemary was concerned. She was in full flow now, and there was no stopping her, so I said nothing. Her voice grew more shrill as she continued.

'He seems to have forgotten that I have feelings which need to be satisfied. One night a few months ago, I met a young airman at the canteen. He was obviously lonely, and I was so desperate that I allowed him to take me outside and make love to me. Making love is what they call it, but love didn't enter into it, just a quick bash which was over in a couple of minutes. To him I was just a frustrated old woman wanting a quick screw, and it certainly did nothing to help me. It happened only a month ago, and it's the one and only time I've ever done this. I was so ashamed, and afraid of meeting him again that I have never been back to the canteen.'

She paused and looked at me intently.

'D'you know, Colin, this is the first time I have confided the episode to another living soul. I have never discussed my feelings with anyone, even George. Maybe I ought to have done, but I couldn't bring myself to do it, and my husband has enough on his plate to give him something else to worry about. Now, you'll probably despise me, but I have tried to be honest with you.'

'Of course I don't despise you. I'm flattered that you have confided in me, but I'm afraid I'm not much use when it comes down to this psychological stuff. All I know is that drink is not the answer to your . . .'

'Why don't you shut up?' she interrupted rudely.

'Look, Connie, what exactly do you want from me?' Although I was somewhat taken aback by her outburst, I tried to keep my tone at a normal level.

'Well, if you don't know, who am I to tell you? I thought perhaps you would understand, but maybe you're not a man at all. There's one thing you can be sure of — I didn't ask you here for a sermon or a lecture in psychology.' Her voice rose to a shout before she flounced out of the room.

I swear it was not until that moment when I realised what it was she wanted from me, but I had been too blind to see it. When Claudette had been alive, she had been everything I ever wanted in a woman, consequently I had never looked at anyone else or contemplated being unfaithful. But now she was no longer here, and during my time in Scotland there had been no opportunity to even think about such matters, so it came as something of a surprise to discover that it was more than six months since I had enjoyed female company. Even now I had never considered Connie as a potential partner, so it required some thought.

I sat for some time trying to analyse my thoughts, but my feelings were mixed. I now realised what it was the admiral's secretary was trying to warn me about, although I had no idea how she knew. Whatever happened that night I had an inkling that somehow the news would filter back to the delectable Rosemary, and suddenly for no reason her opinion of me became all important.

My first reaction was that I had no real objection to sleeping with Connie. Surely it could do no harm, and it might even help us both to release some of our pent-up emotions and frustrations. Then a complication implanted itself within my mind. If I could indeed satisfy her lust, what was her reaction going to be? In her unstable condition, Connie would almost certainly wish to make our relationship more permanent, which would lead to embarrassment all round. No, it might be better if I was to keep her at arm's length.

I must have fallen asleep in the chair, because when I awoke all my limbs were stiff, and I felt my head thumping as a result of the spirits I had drunk at Connie's insistence. The house was as quiet as the grave as I tiptoed gently up the stairs and along the corridor to my room. One board creaked loudly as I stepped on it, but when I passed the door of Connie's room everything remained silent, so I assumed that she had fallen asleep. By morning perhaps she would not remember the incident, or so I hoped.

I had just got into bed, but before I switched the light out, the door opened and Connie came into the room. She must have been waiting for me, and she had timed her entrance to perfection. In the dim, diffuse illumination cast by the bedside lamp, she looked almost desirable, and it was evident that she had taken great pains with her appearance. The silk negligee she wore was open all down the front to reveal a nightdress of such flimsiness that it left nothing to the imagination. Her hair had been freshly set and her face carefully made up, not too much, but enough to deduct several years. As she crossed the room a little uncertainly, she exuded a heady aroma of expensive perfume which was not enough to hide the smell of brandy on her breath.

'I'm sorry to barge in on you like this, Colin, but I couldn't sleep until I had apologised to you for that outburst downstairs.' She smiled, and sat down on the bed. 'It wasn't fair to take my feelings out on you.'

'Don't worry about it, Connie.' I tried to sound natural, but I was conscious of the blood pounding in my head.

'That's sweet of you. I'll be happy just so long as we remain friends.'

She leaned over and kissed me on the cheek, her lips surprisingly warm and soft. As she drew away my gaze was riveted on her pendulous breasts which fell forward, almost breaking free from the gaping, flimsy garment. I could feel my resolve weakening and I wanted to put out my hand to touch them. She must have noticed the direction of my gaze because she ran her fingers over the muscles on my shoulder.

'My, you are in good shape, aren't you? You're not going to send me away — are you?' she added in a pleading voice.

I could feel myself throwing caution to the winds, but fate intervened at precisely the right moment, prompted by her next remark.

'Just imagine that I am your wife, Colin.'

In that instant my libido died within me. There was no way I could equate this dumpy, mixed-up, middle-aged alcoholic with the tall, slim, sophisticated beauty who had been my whole life. Connie's moist lips were approaching mine again, but I jerked my head to one side away from her.

'It's no good, Connie! I can't.' My voice was toneless, and I offered her no explanation.

'I see.'

I kept my face turned away from her so that I did not see the hurt I knew to be in her eyes. The door closed quietly behind her, and some time later, I could hear the sound of weeping from the direction of her room.

I suppose I must have slept, but when I awakened, my first thought was to escape from the house as quickly as possible without giving offence. I was unable to suppress a feeling of disgust, not with Connie, but with myself for being unable to fulfil her needs. Although I was up early, she was downstairs before me, her eyes red with weeping. We didn't speak much — there seemed very little left to say. Fortunately the taxi came for me soon.

'I'm sorry, Connie,' was all I could say, as I left her.

'Don't worry, Colin. I'll be all right. Come and see me again, any time.' But we both knew the performance would never be repeated.

As I drove away, I looked back to see a sad and forlorn figure in a dirty housecoat standing like a statue until I was out of sight. I knew that as soon as she returned indoors she would go straight back to the bottle, even at this early hour. I felt guilty because she had always treated me with kindness, and I had failed her when she needed me most. War often makes people act in ways which they would never dream of doing under more stable conditions.

☆   ☆   ☆

The admiral greeted me effusively, but I wondered what his reaction might have been had he known that his wife had tried to seduce me. Perhaps he no longer cared.

Sir George had the appearance of one who had aged considerably during the past six months, and it was obvious that Connie had been quite correct when she said that the job was killing him. He had developed a slight stoop, and his rapidly thinning hair was almost completely white. He also wore half-moon glasses all the time now, and there were bags under his eyes which were from lack of sleep. He had a slight tremor of his nicotine-stained fingers, and the full ashtray was evidence that he was chain-smoking.

We discussed the Commando course at length, before he finally enquired if I still felt the same about my future participation in the war effort.

'Yes, I haven't changed my mind on that score, sir,' I replied. 'Indeed, if anything has changed, it's because I now feel more confident of being able to carry out whatever you think I am capable of.'

'Good! I was hoping for this reaction from you. You knew, of course, that Colonel McDonald has been sending me monthly reports of your progress. I don't mind telling you, Colin, that the first ones weren't very good, and I was beginning to doubt the wisdom of sending you up there. However, you may like to see a copy of his final assessment of your capabilities, which I think is fairly satisfactory, under the circumstances.'

The admiral handed me a piece of paper marked "Private & Confidential". I could feel his eyes watching me closely while I read it:-

> WEAPON TRAINING: Fair. he is able to handle conventional small arms very well, but his marksmanship still requires further practice.
> ROCK-CLIMBING: For someone who was afraid of heights, he has done well to overcome this disability.
> UNARMED COMBAT: Satisfactory, but needs to be more aggressive.

CROSS-COUNTRY & MAP-READING: Excellent. He has a natural aptitude to be able to find his way under adverse conditions.
FIELDCRAFT: Good. Seems to enjoy it.
PHYSICAL FITNESS: Has improved considerably, and possesses a lot of stamina.
TEAM SPIRIT: Has learned to tolerate others but only with difficulty. Still tends to be a loner.
LEADERSHIP: Definitely potential officer material, but must learn to take orders, even if he doesn't agree with them.
IN GENERAL: He has passed out from this course under difficult personal circumstances, having shown a steady improvement during the whole of his stay. He has grit and determination, and a will to succeed, but he is very much an individual. I am sure he has benefited from this course, but he will be more suitable for undercover assignments, rather than having his talents wasted by being committed to regimental duties.

'Well, there it is,' Sir George remarked, when I had passed the paper back to him. 'It's always good to know what other people think about you before you start, then you can make improvements. It's exactly what I want from you. Do you think it's a fair assessment?'

'Yes, sir, I suppose so. The standard they set is very high.'

'It has to be, Colin. They are turning out specialists in the art of killing, and survival.'

He passed another sheet of paper over to me.

'This is a copy of the Official Secrets Act, which you must sign before you can join us. I'm sure I don't have to tell you about it, but basically it means that if you turn traitor we will shoot you officially, and if you don't sign we shoot you just the same. No, I'm only joking, but remember that whatever the circumstances, the safety of the realm must come first at all times, and you must never discuss your business with any person who is not involved in the immediate sphere of the operation.'

'Can you tell me what my assignment will be, sir?'

'All in good time, my boy. You will have to be patient for a little longer. During the next four weeks I want you to make a detailed study of the French countryside between . . .' He went on to give me the map co-ordinates. 'At the end of that period, you must be able to find your way over that piece of country blindfolded. I want you to be familiar with every landmark, every bush, every building. You will have access to all the maps, guide-books, or photographs you need, and you can also be put in touch with Frenchmen who know the area. How much time and effort you put into this research is your own business, but remember, it will be in your own interests to learn as much as possible, because your life, and more important, the lives of others, may depend on it. Have you anything you wish to ask me?'

'What is my status, sir? Am I Army or a civilian?'

'For the present it will be better for you to remain a civilian. As such you may not attract much attention to yourself that way, but as from now you will draw the pay of an Army captain. You will be issued with a railway warrant allowing you unlimited travel, and a special pass to give you access to many secret places, including the archives at the War Office. If you have any problems don't hesitate to come and see Rosemary or myself. There will be an office set aside in this building for you to use exclusively as a base. Remember, Colin, you're on your own. Do not discuss this project with anyone outside this building, and I mean anyone! Is that absolutely clear?'

'Yes, sir, I understand. What about accommodation?'

For one anxious moment I wondered if the admiral was going to suggest my being billeted at his house, and I sincerely hoped not because of the complications such a move would produce. I was told that Rosemary had the matter in hand, much to my relief.

'Now buzz off, there's a good fellow, and allow me to get on with this paperwork. When you report to me again, we will take the assignment a stage further.'

My first look at the map showed me that the area I was to study lay to the west of Dieppe on the coast from Varengeville-sur-Mer to Quiberville, and inland for about six miles to include the town of St Denis d'Aclon. All I knew about this district was that there were some high cliffs along part of the shore-line, with rolling hills and farmland away from the coast. The area covered some twenty square miles, and a detailed study would require considerable effort on my part.

The accommodation which the admiral's secretary found for me was only a bed-sit which was in the same building, but underneath the flat which she shared with another girl. The room was fairly large, but poorly furnished with barely adequate cooking facilities, and I had to share a bathroom, which was not to my liking.

Third Officer Rosemary Stuart, WRNS, was in her middle twenties, having been a personal secretary to one of the big business moguls before the war. Naturally I became quite friendly with her, but the more I saw of her, the less I seemed to understand what made her tick. It was only after several weeks of observation that I came to the conclusion she was three separate people.

First there was Rosemary the secretary, who ran Sir George's office with ruthless efficiency. She knew everyone who visited the office and what their business was, and at the same time she was able to sort out many of the problems herself without troubling her overworked boss. Up to now that was the side of her which I had observed most.

But as time went on I saw an entirely different side of her, namely Rosemary the flirt. Although I did not seem to qualify, she had a string of officers from all the Services in tow, some of whom were quite high-ranking, but young enough to give her a good time. There was scarcely an evening when she was off duty that she wasn't out with some fellow who fancied his chances with her. And yet, in spite of her undoubted sex appeal, I was convinced that she must be frigid, since very few of her suitors seemed to invite her out a second time. This did not agree with Connie's accusation that she was the admiral's mistress, and if Sir George was in fact seeing another woman, which I doubted, it certainly was not his glamorous secretary.

It was Rosemary's third characteristic which surprised me most, since it presented quite a different aspect of her personality. On the rare occasions when she stayed at home, be it either on an evening or at a weekend, I could scarcely recognise her as the same person. Gone was the immaculately dressed, ice-cool, super-efficient secretary, to be replaced by a sloppily dressed, unkempt and untidy young woman, apparently without a care as to how she looked. Whenever she was alone in the apartment, she managed somehow to leave a trail of destruction and mess. God help the poor mug who married her! She would certainly be a decoration around the house, but her undoubted organizing ability did not extend to domestic matters.

The ménage was held together by Rosemary's flat-mate who worked as a nursing sister in a large hospital close to Portsmouth. For the first couple of weeks after going to live there, I only caught glimpses of her since she was on night duty, but it was not long before we were introduced. Her name was Susan Thomas, and I judged her to be older than her flat-mate, probably about thirty. She was tall and thin, with practically no figure to speak of, but she had striking features rather than beauty. Her jet-black hair was coiled up out of the way when she was in uniform, but allowed to cascade in well-groomed pageboy style at other times.

In contrast to her companion, Susan never went out much, either by herself or in company, but busied herself with domestic chores if she wasn't catching up on her sleep. Although Rosemary was always friendly with me, the same could not be said for Susan — in fact she gave the distinct impression that she actively disliked me. Could it be perhaps that she looked upon me as an interloper who might possibly come between her and Rosemary? The idea was ridiculous, as I had no romantic leanings towards the latter, but in spite of that, she continued to harbour an obvious indifference towards me.

On one of the rare evenings when the admiral's secretary was at home alone, she dropped into my room for a chat. We discussed the progress I had made on my assignment, and I was sure she would be passing on the information to Sir George. I managed to work the conversation round so that I brought up the subject of Susan's hostility towards me, and Rosemary told me something about her.

'Don't be too hard on Susan. She's going through a bad patch at the moment. Her husband was a navigator in

Bomber Command, and on one of the first raids over Cologne they were hit by anti-aircraft fire. The pilot managed to bring the plane back to the airfield where they crash-landed. Peter suffered a severe head injury, with the result that he has undergone a complete change of personality and will never fly again. He used to be such fun, but then he had bouts of violence and knocked Susan about. The situation grew so bad that she left him four months ago, and came here to live with me. It's killed any love there used to be between them. It's amazing the changes in people which happen as a result of the war.'

I remembered that I had heard that same phrase used only recently, and thought of Connie and what the war had done to her.

'Where is her husband now?' I asked.

'He's been admitted to a mental hospital somewhere near Southampton. Susan never visits him, and I don't think he knows where she is, if indeed he cares. It's all very sad.'

'I'm afraid she doesn't like me. She seems to go out of her way to avoid me.'

'Don't worry about it, Colin. She feels like that about all men at the moment, so it's not only you. Unfortunately her recent troubles have soured her outlook on life, and so she's not the girl she used to be either. I would give anything for her to return to her old self. Susan and I have always been very close.'

'I — er, I don't know quite how to put this, Rosemary, but are you and she — er, very fond of each other?'

She looked at me blankly for a few seconds before bursting into a fit of laughter. 'Oh, dear!' she spluttered. 'You think that she and I . . . don't you? That's too funny for words. No, Colin, Susan's my sister.'

I felt embarrassed that the thought had even crossed my mind, and I stammered an apology, but justified myself because they seemed to be so different both in looks and in temperament.

Rosemary put her head on one side and looked at me strangely. 'You're not really interested in Susan, are you, Colin?'

When I assured her that I was not, she seemed relieved, but when I said that I had no intention of becoming involved with any woman again, she looked disappointed, and it was some time before the significance of this conversation was brought home to me.

'Anyway,' I concluded, 'I have too much on my plate at the moment to even so much as think about anyone else.'

The subject was left there, but I wondered if Rosemary had told Susan of my gaffe. At any rate, Susan still continued to avoid me.

☆ ☆ ☆

Indeed, it was true that my researches kept me pretty well fully occupied. Gradually I built up a picture of my area in the little back room at headquarters, but there were still gaps in it. I travelled extensively all over the country in order to visit Free French units, and I also managed to interview some of the Intelligence personnel who were responsible for dropping agents into France to organise the Resistance movement, which was in its infancy. I went up to London several times to the Geographical section of the British Museum, where they had some of the largest scale maps that I had ever seen. But one of my luckiest finds was a box of old photographs taken before the war, many of them showing parts of the area.

I saw the admiral only once during that month, when I requested him to arrange a pass for me to visit a top secret establishment. When we had finished our business, he went on to tell me of Connie's misfortune.

'She's been acting very strangely recently,' he said in a flat voice, 'but I have no idea why. Of course I know she drinks, but now it's much more than that. One evening I arrived home to find her sitting stark naked staring into space. I don't know how long she had been there, but she was frozen. Then only last week the police picked her up wandering in the middle of the road with no clothes on in broad daylight. She's been admitted to a private clinic in a very confused state. She is incoherent and rambling, and she seems to have fantasies about you, Colin, and some young airman. They told me it's something to do with the mothering instinct. She's never been the same since our son was killed, I'm afraid. She lived for the boy.'

'Will they be able to do anything for her, sir?' I asked, trying to keep my voice normal.

'No, I don't think so. They have tried to explain to me all about menopausal depression, but I had no idea what they were talking about. What it amounts to is that she will probably never come out again.'

'I'm very sorry to hear it, sir. She has always been very kind to me.'

I walked back to my office with my mind in a turmoil. This had all happened within the few weeks since that disastrous night when I rejected her. It was obvious that I had been responsible for triggering off the delicate mechanism which had changed her world into some sort of living hell. Poor, lonely Connie! She certainly deserved a better fate than this. If only I had realised how desperately she needed me, or perhaps if I had returned to visit her, this tragedy could possibly have been averted, but since I hadn't wished to become involved, she had paid the price.

I sincerely hoped that the admiral harboured no suspicions about my part in the affair. If he had done, it would almost certainly have added to the grief he already felt, but since his attitude towards me remained as friendly as it had always been, I knew that he suspected nothing. This knowledge did nothing for my peace of mind, and I was conscious of a continued feeling of guilt.

☆ ☆ ☆

Eventually my researches were completed, and the moment arrived when I was prepared to be examined on what I had already learned, and to be briefed on the next phase of the operation. After grilling me for over an hour, the admiral declared himself satisfied, and passed a folder over to me. When I opened it, the first thing which faced me was the enlarged photograph of a high-ranking German officer.

'First of all, Colin, I want you to be able to recognise this man even in a poor light. Then study the contents of the file. Everything we know about him is written here. It must never leave this building, and when you are not using it, you will be responsible for its safe keeping.'

He crossed the room to one of the big charts on the wall and stabbed a finger at a point about five miles inland.

'This is the Chateau d'Arlon,' he told me. 'Have you seen it mentioned in your researches?'

'I know where it is, and I've seen reference made to it, sir, but I'm afraid I don't know very much about it.'

'I'm not surprised. It's a very minor chateau, but it's where this man lives. Find out everything you can about the location, and the surrounding area, then I'm making arrangements for you to see it for yourself at first hand.'

'How can I do that, sir?'

'All will be revealed in the fullness of time, my boy,' he chuckled. 'Meanwhile, take this file away and digest it. I'll see you again in a few days.'

The folder contained details of one General Otto Staufen, aged fifty-two. He had had a distinguished career as a pilot during World War I, having been decorated with the Iron Cross on two occasions. At present he commanded a large number of bomber squadrons which were responsible for the London blitz. It went on to list numerous details of a personal nature, together with a timetable of his daily routine which seldom varied. Once a month he visited the various airfields in the Normandy area, otherwise he conducted his business of organising the nightly raids on England from an unpretentious office in the small town of Yevot.

With true Teutonic efficiency, he left the chateau at exactly the same time each morning, returning again in the evening. Although his arrival back at the chateau was not timed so precisely, it did not vary by more than an hour. He always travelled in a staff car with a driver and an armed guard in attendance, and the vehicle was accompanied by two motorcycle combinations, each carrying two men, one preceding and one following the car.

I had no idea how all this information had been collected, but I marvelled at the way such a comprehensive dossier had been compiled.

☆   ☆   ☆

My next scheduled meeting with Sir George a few days

later had to be cancelled due to my contracting a severe bout of 'flu. On the first day I felt terrible, and was barely able to stagger to the bathroom. By evening I was lying on my bed in the darkness, bathed in perspiration with my head bursting, and cocooned in misery. I was unaware that anyone had come into the room until the light was switched on, and I opened an eye to see Susan standing beside the bed with a glass in her hand.

'I don't suppose you have taken any medicine for this?' she demanded in a tone that brooked no argument.

I shook my head, and she helped me to sit up before handing me the glass.

'Drink this!' she ordered. When I made a face, she cast her eyes up towards the ceiling. 'You men are all the same! Now finish it up, and you'll feel better.'

No sooner had I done so than she disappeared, returning a few minutes later carrying a bowl and a towel.

'What's this for?' I croaked.

'A blanket bath, of course,' she snapped. 'We can't leave you to stew in this flea-pit.'

I was forced to admit that I certainly felt better as a result of her ministrations, and for the next couple of days she looked in to see me each morning after coming home from work, and every evening before she left. Whenever she visited me, her manner remained totally professional, and I was given no insight as to what thoughts she harboured behind the facade of benevolent autocracy which she wore like a suit of armour against the possibility of any male intrusions into her emotions.

Rosemary's visits, on the other hand, were few and brief, and I had the impression that her sole purpose was to report to the admiral what my condition was. After a period of three days, the fever left me, and I was able to be up and about again, but I felt as weak as a kitten. During my convalescence, however, Susan continued to come in and see me regularly, and gradually her manner towards me thawed to such an extent that we discussed our past, and I told her something of my life up to the time the bomb fell.

'So, what's your job now, Colin? I know that you're not in journalism any more, but you're tied up with Rosemary's boss somehow, aren't you?'

It was obvious that her sister had told her nothing about my role in Combined Operations, and so I told her that I was undertaking some research work on France for the admiral.

Susan reciprocated my confidences by telling me about her disastrous marriage, and how she discovered on her wedding night that she had made a mistake. Her husband was immature, emotionally unstable, and cared nothing for her feelings. He lived in a world of fantasy, so joining the R.A.F. suited his temperament ideally, and he was able to act out these boyish ideals for real. It also gave him the opportunity to be unfaithful to her. She seemed to be truly sorry that Peter had undergone a change of personality as a result of his wounds.

'I could put up with Peter the way he was before, but now, since he has become violent, there is no way I can live with that on top of everything else. However, there are some new drugs they are using now, which seem to keep him stable, so perhaps there is still hope for him to be able to lead a normal life.'

Although we established a friendly rapport, we neither of us wished to become romantically involved. I think that basically we were both lonely, but Susan gradually became less reserved in my company, and was able to relax and be herself. She seemed to cast aside her veneer of professionalism which discouraged men who wanted to try their chances, and I felt flattered by her attention. But because of the work in which I was engaged, mine was essentially a lonely life, and I wanted to keep it that way.

I tried to draw her out concerning Rosemary, and by dint of careful questioning I managed to find out a good deal about her sister. Whereas Susan had always been the practical one, Rosemary's aptitude had been organisation. It was she who paid all the bills and saw to the correspondence, although she was unable even to boil an egg. It was as well that she was taken out for so many meals, otherwise she would have starved when Susan was not there.

'I'm surprised she has never married,' I suggested tentatively. 'I'm sure there are many men who would have jumped at the chance before now, even if she couldn't cook.'

'In spite of her glamorous appearance and easy manner, Rosemary is a serious person. She has no time for men who imagine that they can lure her into bed at the first opportunity, and there are planty who try. She is intensely loyal, and when she finally does fall in love it will be for keeps.'

'I've heard it suggested that the admiral and she . . .'

'Absolute rubbish! Rosemary looks on him as a father. He has been kind to her, nothing more.'

So now I knew that she was uncommitted romantically, but at this stage I was in no position to become involved.

The admiral was pleased to see me again, and glad to know that I was fully recovered, and he got down to business immediately.

'Now, Colin, the last time we met I told you that you would have an opportunity to view the chateau at first hand, so I have made arrangements for the R.A.F. to fly you over the area so that you can see for yourself how it lies in relation to the surrounding countryside. They will take aerial photographs at the same time, and these can be studied at leisure afterwards. Remember that you will be over the area for only a few seconds, so you will need to have all your wits about you. There is no going back for a second look, and it's a unique opportunity which must not be missed.'

'How soon will it be, admiral?'

'As soon as possible. It's now near the end of June, and we dare not delay much longer. Your illness has set us back ten days, so whenever the weather is suitable, and the plane is available, you will be prepared to go.'

5

Reconnaissance

One evening, a couple of days later, there was a knock at the door of my flat. I opened it to find Rosemary standing there, looking more beautiful than ever. I invited her in, but she shook her head.

'No, Colin. Someone is taking me out, and I'm late as it is. I only came to bring you this, it's your orders for tomorrow.' she laid a hand on my arm briefly. 'Good luck! Let me know as soon as you get back.'

The next moment she was gone, leaving me alone and disappointed that she hadn't stayed longer. At that moment I envied the lucky chap who was her escort for the evening, but I immediately put it out of my mind, knowing that I mustn't become attracted to her.

I opened the envelope, and my orders were that I was to report to ——— airfield at 06.00 hours, the following morning. Transport would call to pick me up at 05.30 hours.

During the early morning drive, I noticed that the sky was clear as far as the eye could see, and the sun was already above the horizon. There was a little hold-up at the main gate because I did not have a pass, but a phone call to the orderly room soon put that right. I was met by the duty officer who introduced me to the pilot. I cannot remember his name, but I do recall thinking that he ought still to be at school, and that he was far too young to be in charge of this sophisticated fighting machine.

The aeroplane was a type that I had never seen before,

and I was informed that it was called a De Havilland Mosquito, of which there were three in our flight. The machine was stubby-nosed with two powerful engines, and I noticed that ours was different from the other two in that it had a plastic bubble in the nose, whereas the others were solid and carried four cannon instead.

I was told that I would occupy the bomb-aimer's position in the nose, and operate the camera when the time came.

'As soon as we cross the French coast, I'll go up to about three-hundred feet,' the young pilot went on. 'Anything lower, and the photographs will be blurred. Besides, you'll get a better look from that height.'

'What do you mean, go up to three hundred feet?' I asked, trying to keep the horror out of my voice. 'What height will we be before then?'

He grinned. 'We'll cross the Channel at what we call zero feet. Don't worry, it's not really as low as that, and we do it all the time,' he hastened to reassure me.

After having been issued with a parachute, I settled myself down in a prone position on the padded couch normally reserved for the bomb-aimer. I was cramped, and hemmed in by an aerial camera which occupied some of the small space, so my lateral movements were limited. I was given some brief instruction on how to operate it; so long as I pressed the button, it would go on taking pictures at one-second intervals, and I was advised to begin filming as sson as we hit the coast.

'All set, then? Here we go!' the skipper's voice came over the intercom, and the twin engines increased their revolutions to a deafening roar.

As the plane began its take-off run, I found myself looking straight down at the ground as it flashed past at an increasing speed. Then my eye caught the trees at the end of the runway, and I watched with apprehension as they began to approach at an alarming rate. Just as I was certain that we must hit them, the nose lifted and the tops flashed past only a few feet below me. As the plane began to gain height smoothly, I was pleased to see the two other Mosquitoes taking station, one on either side of us, and it was only a few minutes before we were crossing the white cliffs, and out over the sea. A small convoy of coastal vessels accompanied by a corvette away to starboard looked peaceful enough, otherwise the Channel seemed to be empty of shipping.

The visibility was perfect, and when we were about half way across, the pilot dropped down to what he had been pleased to call "zero feet". I had to close my eyes, as I was sure that at any moment we would hit one of the waves which seemed to be so close that I could put out my hand to touch them, and I was much happier when we began to gain height in order to clear the cliffs.

'Crossing the French coast now. Start the camera!'

The skipper's voice over the intercom brought me back to reality. I had been so fascinated watching the land coming towards me that I had forgotten all about it.

The countryside speeding by below us looked very similar to that in England, but I was reminded where we were when the pilot's voice said, 'All planes, keep an eye open for enemy aircraft!'

Suddenly the ground directly beneath me seemed to be vaguely familiar, and I realised that I was looking at the area which I had been studying for weeks. There was the chateau with the woods all round and rolling farmland beyond. The road leading down to the main highway and the crossroads with two cottages near by. I tried to see if there were any other buildings close to the chateau, but as we were over the area for only a few seconds I could not take it all in, and I wanted the pilot to take us round again. Hopefully, the photographs would reveal what I had missed. I stopped the camera, expecting the plane to turn for home, but in this I was disappointed.

'We're just going to pay someone a visit,' the skipper's voice broke into my thoughts. 'It seems a shame to have come over here without dropping in.'

We were now flying in single file formation with our aircraft in the middle. A fairly large town flashed by immediately underneath us, and I could see people standing in the streets looking up and pointing at us. In the distance, standing on its own away from other habitation, its tall chimneys belching thick smoke, was our target. The formation gained height until it reached the optimum altitude for bombing, and I saw the first stick fall from the plane in front of us, but we ourselves were over the target before they exploded, so I could not see where they landed. I felt our own aircraft lift as our bombs fell, and as we swung away from the target in a tight semi-circle, I was able to observe that there had been at least two direct hits on the factory itself, as well as one on some nearby storage tanks which were now burning fiercely.

'Good show, chaps! Let's head for home!'

The words were music to my ears, as I considered that I had been cooped up in this flying plastic bubble for long enough, but we hadn't finished yet. A few miles further on we spotted a German Army convoy crawling along one of the straight country roads. It was too good a target to miss.

'Tally-ho, Tally-ho, boys! We can't let this one pass by. Let's give them something to think about,' the skipper radioed to his two companions.

The vehicles came to a halt, and the soldiers scattered like rabbits into the nearby countryside looking for cover. Some of them weren't quick enough and were caught in the fire as the Mosquitoes straffed the convoy from end to end, raking it with machine-gun and cannon-fire. One of the lorries, which had an automatic weapon mounted on the back, fired at the attacking planes, causing one to wobble briefly, but it quickly straightened up and carried on. Three of the wagons caught fire, and one, which must have been carrying ammunition, blew up in a blast of orange flame. In less than a minute, the convoy was a smoking shambles. It gave me great personal satisfaction to witness it, as I still remembered vividly being on the receiving end of an air strike, and I knew how the Germans must be feeling. The most noticeable feature of our sortie had been the absence of the Luftwaffe, for which I for one was truly grateful.

Back at the airfield, we discovered that one of the planes had bullet holes in the wings and fuselage, but there was no real damage, and no casualties. It was at this point that I was informed that not only were the planes a prototype, constructed from plywood and balsa, but also this was the very first occasion when they had been used operationally. If I had been aware of these facts before taking off, I'm sure my courage would have failed me at the last moment.

While we were being debriefed, the film was being

removed from the camera, but as it would still be some hours before the photographs were ready for me to take back, I was invited to spend the night at the station. There was quite a party to celebrate the successful launching of the new plane, and although I was treated courteously as a visitor, I was aware of the general speculation as many of the officers tried to surmise who this civilian was who merited such V.I.P. treatment. The impression was that I was some boffin from the factory which made the aeroplane. For myself, I found it hard to believe that the safety of the realm was held in the hands of these seemingly immature, devil-me-care youths.

☆   ☆   ☆

As soon as I entered the ante-room of the admiral's office I knew that something was amiss. Rosemary's greeting was far from friendly, there was no welcoming smile, and her face was devoid of expression. She spoke to me only in monosyllables, making it obvious that I was in the dog-house, but for what reason I could not imagine.

Sir George was eager to have the full report of my flight at first hand, and when he saw the photographs he was bubbling with enthusiasm, a characteristic which he rarely showed.

'I'll get some of our chaps on to this,' he said. 'They ought to be able to reproduce a detailed, contoured model from these pictures.'

'I'll be glad of that, sir, because I can't quite understand the interpretation of these pictures.'

'Now, Colin, I think the time has come for you to know what all this has been leading up to,' he said while polishing his glasses. 'It's now the beginning of July, so we'll have to move quickly. On the fourteenth of August, we're throwing a major offensive against the French coast at Dieppe. It's not a full-scale invasion, you understand, just a reconnaissance in strength to test out the German defences. We're going to land both troops and armour, and the whole operation is expected to take only a few days. The area which you have been studying is several miles from the main assault, and is not expected to be involved in any of the fighting. We have every reason to believe that General Staufen will not play a part, and we expect him to carry on with his usual routine. While the main assault is taking place, you will be put ashore with a detachment of a dozen men. The details will be left to you, but your objective is to capture General Staufen and bring him back to England.'

He paused for a few seconds while I tried to digest this information.

'In a couple of days from now, you will be transferred to a holding company stationed close to Bognor Regis. There you will set up your own unit, and all the files, maps, photographs which are held here will be sent to you. The model will follow as soon as it's completed. From then on until the actual raid, you will be held incommunicado, but your first job will be to handpick the men to go with you, and in this you have a free hand provided the men are available. As from today you are commissioned as a Captain in the Royal Marine Commandos, but you will draw your uniform from the holding company. The details of the plan, where you land and how you carry it out will be your own, but vetted by me in the final analysis. I need hardly remind you that this raid will be planned in the utmost secrecy.'

'Does Rosemary know, sir?'

He looked at me a little strangely, I thought. 'Yes, she knows, but no one else.'

'Is she all right this morning, admiral? She seems to be somewhat out of sorts.'

'She's probably had a late night,' he grunted. 'She's always out, but she's young and attractive, so I suppose it's understandable. I agree, she certainly doesn't look well, and she was very frosty with me too this morning.'

When I left, Rosemary was not in her office, and so I did not know if she had mellowed towards me. Her attitude was so uncharacteristic that it preyed on my mind all day. I heard her come in about seven o'clock, and knowing that Susan was out, I felt compelled to go up to see Rosemary and have it out with her.

When I knocked at the door of her flat, the door was opened almost at once. Rosemary's greeting was distinctly cool.

'Oh, it's you,' she said in a flat voice.

'Can I come in?'

'I suppose so. I presume you've come to apologise?'

I must have looked at her blankly. 'Apologise? What for? What have I done?'

She looked at me angrily. 'You have no idea, have you? You have no thought for anyone but yourself. I thought that you were different, but you're just like all the rest — silly men playing at being heroes.'

I continued to look at her with a blank expression.

'You still don't know, do you?' she continued in a more moderate tone. 'When I brought you your orders for the flight, didn't I ask you to let me know as soon as you had arrived back safely. All day there was no word, and I was sick with worry. I cancelled a date and stayed in the office until eleven o'clock. It was then that I telephoned the airfield on some pretext, only to be told that you were at a drunken party. It never crossed your mind to give me a ring, knowing that I might possibly be worrying about you. You don't deserve to have friends, Captain Marshall.'

'That's not fair, Rosemary,' I said, putting my hands on her shoulders.

She immediately shook me off. 'Don't you dare touch me! And don't imagine that you can talk your way out of it either.'

'Am I to be given a chance to explain, then? Even a condemned man has a hearing.'

'All right — explain!'

'For a start, I thought that you were merely showing a polite interest when you asked me to let you know of my safe return. I know I ought to have done so, but with the excitement of the flight and everything else, it completely slipped my mind. I had no idea that you were so worried about me. I suppose I have no real excuse, but I hope you'll forgive me all the same.'

'Well, at least you're honest, I suppose.'

'And am I forgiven?'

'No, not yet, but I expect you will be, given time. You've hurt me a lot. I'll have to think about it.'

I had to be content to leave it at that, but it was only then that I began to imagine Rosemary Stuart's solicitous interest in my welfare was more than just a professional inquiry. Thinking about it afterwards made me realise for the first time that I no longer wanted to throw my life away on some grand gesture of revenge, and now I was beginning to feel fear for the future.

6

Commando

I looked around my office, which was nothing more than a partitioned space within a wooden hut, and my heart sank. Office was perhaps too ambitious a word for it, because apart from the bare walls on which photographs and maps were pinned, the only furniture was a desk, two hard wooden chairs, and a filing cabinet. After a couple of days, the model of the area arrived, and stood in one corner. It contained all the details which I had not been able to observe when I was flying over it, and the chateau as well as every building in the vicinity was faithfully reproduced.

Outside, my empire consisted of a small hutted compound within the confines of a larger camp which was heavily guarded as well as being surrounded by a double barbed-wire fence. Entry to the compound was strictly controlled, and although I had a telephone, there was no direct communication with the outside world as all calls were vetted by the central switchboard. When my men arrived, they would be fed by the main cookhouse, while I took my meals in the officers' mess, but apart from that we had very little contact with the other occupants who had no idea what we were doing there. It was little wonder that I felt like a prisoner.

The first person to be assigned to me was a corporal who took charge of the outer office, and dealt with all the paperwork. Strictly speaking, he was not a member of my squad, but merely there to attend to the every-day running of the unit, and so my first, and most urgent task was to recruit my team, all of whom would be volunteers.

For my second-in-command I was offered the choice of two sergeants, one of whom was a regular soldier, and already a member of the Royal Marine Commandos. The other was from one of the Scottish regiments, who had already been in action at Dunkirk. Both were excellent soldiers, but the deciding factor was that the Scot spoke tolerable German, and so Sergeant McKinley became the first volunteer to join me.

During the next couple of weeks I had recruited ten members of my little group, leaving one place still to be filled. They were a mixed bunch of personalities, each with his own particular speciality, so my next task was to mould them into a team and train them for the job in hand. Regarding the last remaining place to be filled, I personally had an idea about that, and set the wheels in motion for a certain person to be located. When I was informed that he was at present residing in Shepton Mallet "glasshouse", it did not really surprise me, but armed with the necessary authority I decided to go and see him anyway.

When I arrived at this notorious military prison, I was escorted to the office of the major in charge, but only after my credentials had been meticulously checked by the Military Police at the camp gate.

'Why is he here?' I asked the major.

'The list is endless. He's been drunk on duty, persistently uncooperative and belligerent. He resents authority, and finally he hit an officer, so naturally he finished up here after his court-martial.'

'Does he still feel that way?'

'I'm afraid so. We haven't had him for long, so we still haven't broken him yet. May I ask why you want him?'

'It's Top Secret, I'm afraid, but just let us say I would prefer that he channelled his aggression against the Germans instead of the British Army. Can I see him alone?'

'Sorry, Captain Marshall, but it's against regulations. One of our chaps must be there at all times, but he'll be very discreet.'

As he had to go and make his rounds, he offered me his office, and as I sat at the desk waiting for my man to be brought in, I began to wonder if this was a good idea after all. A few minutes later, the door was flung open and a figure who I barely recognised was marched in at the double. His hair was cropped close to his head, there was a faint bruise under one eye, and he was thinner than he had been. But his eyes were like those of a caged wild animal, and on his face was the same defiant look I knew so well. He stood rigidly to attention and fixed his gaze on some distant point above my head.

'Private Ramsay, sir,' the accompanying sergeant barked.

'Hello, Jock,' I said quietly.

He dropped his eyes and looked at me for several seconds before he realised who I was. His reaction was typical, and spoken with feeling.

'Jeezuz Christ! I never expected to see you again.'

'Say "sir" when you address an officer, and watch your language, Ramsay,' the sergeant shouted at him.

I waved a hand at the N.C.O. who retreated to stand po-faced in the corner of the office.

'What the hell are you doing here, Jock?'

'Och, I was fed up. After all yon training, I expected to be sent to kill Germans, but I've done bugger all since — just drill and cross-country runs and assault courses. I got fed up with it. I had a few drinks one day, got smashed and hit an officer. I'm not sorry. He deserved all he got, the stuck-up bastard.'

To a certain extent I could sympathise with him, but being Jock he was making his protest in the wrong way.

'Let me tell you why I'm here. I'm getting together a squad for a special job. I'm not at liberty to tell you what it is yet, but I can assure you, you'll get your chance to kill Germans. I warn you, it'll be dangerous, and we'll need a lot of luck to pull it off, but I will want someone like you beside me if we get into a tight corner.'

I could see a flicker of interest in his face.

'I have the authority to get you out of here,' I went on, 'But only if you agree to join us. We'll be preparing for the job for about a month yet, and we're all confined to camp until it's time to go. Since you'll be one of a team, it's essential that you fit in and cooperate with the others. There will be no drinking, and if you behave yourself there is a faint possibility that I may even restore your stripe, but

I must emphasise you'll have to earn it. Any trouble, even of a minor nature, and you'll find yourself back here before you have time even to think about it. Do I make myself clear?'

Jock nodded. He seemed to be struck dumb.

'So, what do you say? Are you willing to join us?'

'Weel, I'm no doin' much good stuck in here, and any place is better than this. Aye, I agree, sir.'

I was pleased to hear the 'sir'. From Jock that was a compliment indeed.

'Good man! I'll make the necessary arrangements, and expect you in a few days' time.'

Two days later, Private John Ramsay reported to the camp, smartly dressed in a brand new uniform, and, so far as I could tell, he hadn't had a drink while in transit, so I thought that this was a good omen. I had not intended to tell any of the others about his recent past, but Jock himself took the matter out of my hands and being basically an honest person, he made no secret of his misdemeanours and where he had come from.

Sergeant McKinley, however, voiced his doubts to me about Jock's ability to fit in.

'He's a bad 'un is that, sir,' he told me. 'I only hope we can rely on him when it becomes necessary.'

I gave the sergeant an account of my past association with Private Ramsay, and he agreed to give him the benefit of the doubt — for the time being at any rate. I hoped that McKinley would not pick on him, but I need not have worried, he was too good an N.C.O. for that.

Now that my team was complete, I considered that the time was ripe for me to divulge something about the forthcoming raid, but I omitted the details and who the target was. I gave them an hour to study the maps, the photographs and the model, before questioning them to find out how much they had learned. The results were not very encouraging, and so I ordered them to repeat the exercise for an hour every day, and discuss the features amongst themselves. After a week most of them had grasped the details, and I began to point out the essential landmarks with which they were to make themselves familiar.

'I take it that our mission has something to do with that castle, sir?' Sergeant McKinley asked one day when we had completed our usual session. 'Are we to attack it?'

'No, it's not the castle that is our prime objective, sergeant, but the man who lives there. Now, I want you all to concentrate on this road junction about half a mile from the chateau. It's heavily wooded on three sides, and you'll notice that there are a couple of cottages adjacent to it. That's where the action will take place.'

I made a point of joining in the P.T. sessions, and the cross-country runs, but while the others were at weapon training or lectures, I spent my time trying to formulate some sort of feasible plan of action. After dinner I would retire to the office to gaze at the model, where already an idea was beginning to germinate.

I was glad to note that my sergeant's predictions regarding Jock had so far not been bourne out. Apparently he fitted in without any grumbles, and generally his conduct gave little cause for complaint, either about his ability as a soldier, or his collaboration with the other members of the team. However, his temper remained on a short fuse, and some of his reactions were uncertain. On the whole, he did not upset the camaraderie which had developed between the squad, and any clashes of personality were soon sorted out.

The admiral came to visit us after our detachment had been in camp for about three weeks. He seemed to be duly impressed by our state of preparedness, and he made a point of meeting every man separately, emphasising how important the mission was. I gave him a run-down of the plan I had considered up to the present, but I was quick to admit that there were still several details to be sorted out. Sir George made a few suggestions, but left me free to make up my own mind whether or not to incorporate them as I thought fit. He pointed out that I knew more about the local situation than he did.

'Tell me, sir, how are we to know up to the last minute if General Staufen is in residence?' I asked.

'The French Resistance are very active in this area, and they have been well briefed in advance of this operation. They are keeping watch on his every movement, and reporting back to us at regular intervals, so you will know exactly where he is at the appropriate time. They are prepared to offer you any assistance, so you won't feel wholly isolated.'

'With so many people knowing about the operation, is there not a danger of it being leaked?'

'I suppose it is a possibility, but we couldn't do it without the French cooperation. Anyway, they don't know the exact details.'

I had to be content with that. I might be glad of help from the Resistance, even if it did increase the possibility of the Germans getting to know that something was afoot.

'Is there anything you need from me, Colin?'

'I have two requests, sir. First of all we need three German Army uniforms. My sergeant and another of the men speak tolerable German, so at one stage I want to impersonate members of the Wermacht.'

The admiral made a note on his pad. 'Yes, that's easily taken care of.'

'The second request is that we be allowed to wear our uniforms at all times, even underneath the German ones. If any of our chaps are captured, I don't want them to be shot as spies.'

'I've been giving the subject some consideration as well, Colin, and I agree with you. As a matter of fact, I want the Germans to know that the raid was carried out by our boys. If they think it was the Resistance, then they will take their revenge on the civilian population after it's over, and I don't want that to happen.'

'That's one big weight off my mind, sir. I take it you'll be letting us know about the method of landing in due course?'

'Yes, naturally. There are just over two and a half weeks to go yet, but I'll be sending you your final orders within the next few days. Meanwhile, if you have any further problems, be sure to let me know.'

As he rose to go, I asked him tentatively how Rosemary was. He didn't reply, but he put a hand in his pocket and took out an envelope which he handed to me.

'I almost forgot,' he said. 'She asked me to give you this. It's not often I'm asked to act as postman.'

He looked at me somewhat strangely, and I wasn't sure if

he altogether approved of any liaison between his secretary and myself. I saluted him formally, and as I watched him drive away I couldn't help wondering how much longer he could keep up the pace at which he was driving himself. It was only after the staff-car was out of sight that I remembered I had omitted to ask after his wife's health. With all the other things on my mind, I felt guilty that I hadn't given Connie a single thought.

Back in the privacy of my office I opened Rosemary's letter. It was written on office paper in her own neat and precise hand.

> My dear Colin,
>
> I hope the admiral remembers to give you this note, because he is becoming very absent-minded about small matters.
>
> I'm really writing to apologise for my outburst when we last met. I'm not in the habit of allowing personal considerations to get on top of me. I know you have enough on your plate to be worried about anything which I might have said.
>
> Susan is well. She often talks about you, and I think she is missing you. I have told her you are up in the North of Scotland.
>
> I hope this finds you well. Be sure to look after yourself.
>
>   Yours affectionately,
>   Rosemary.
> P.S. I am missing you too.

The letter upset me more than I thought possible. I did not need any emotional entanglements now that we were so near to the off. Was Rosemary in love with me? It seemed inconceivable, but I could not ignore what she had said. Perhaps it was only intended as a note of apology, and I was reading more into it than was intended.

On a sudden impulse I picked up the telephone and asked the operator to put me through to Combined Operations. It was several minutes before I was connected.

'Admiral Brown's office,' I asked.

'Third Officer Stuart, Admiral Brown's secretary speaking. Can I help you?' I recognised Rosemary's voice instantly.

'This is the fourteenth detachment, Royal Marine Commandos, Commanding Officer speaking,' I prayed that she would guess that the call was being monitored, and sure enough she was quick enough to realise this.

'Regarding your latest correspondence,' I said, hoping my voice sounded natural. 'The admiral has just left, so I haven't had an opportunity to reply. The contents of the letter have taken a load off my mind, and I hope to be able to discuss the matter further with you in person in due course.'

'Thank you very much, sir. I'll make a note of that.'

The line went dead, leaving me with mixed emotions. Hearing her voice again had started a chain of thought which was unsettling. The last thing I wanted at this moment was to sit down and analyse my feelings. Looking back, I now realise that I had lost sight of the reason why I was there in the first place. Already the memories of my late wife and family were fading into the background.

Three days after the admiral's visit, the German uniforms I had ordered arrived, but our final orders did not come until a week before the raid was due to take place. I waited for twenty-four hours so that I could study them thoroughly, before calling all the members of the team together.

'You'll be pleased to hear that our final orders have come through at last, so now I am at liberty to tell you exactly what you have been training for.'

I went on to tell them about the proposed raid on Dieppe, and that our smaller sortie was scheduled to take place at the same time. When I went on to explain that it was our intention to capture General Staufen, the officer commanding the Luftwaffe in the area, there was a general shuffling of feet for a few seconds, which was followed by instant silence.

'Now I want to get down to details. You can make notes if you want, but these must be memorised and destroyed before we leave. On the evening of the eighteenth of August, that is exactly one week from today, we will embark on a motor torpedo boat at Chichester. This will sail two hours before the main force, and with its superior speed we ought to make landfall about five hours ahead of them, shortly after midnight. The French Resistance will, hopefully, deal with any sentries, then signal to us when it's safe to land. We have chosen this point here, where the aerial photographs show us that apart from a few pill-boxes, there are no fortifications, only a minefield which we will have to cross, so there ought to be little or no opposition. We will row ashore in three inflatable dinghies, hide them, and then make our way inland towards the road junction you have been studying. Yes, Sergeant McKinley, you have a question?'

'Sir, are we to move in a body, or separate?'

'We will move across country in one body. I realise that this could be hazardous, but we are relying to a certain extent on the French to lead us in the dark, and we can't risk losing anyone. We must take up our positions before 05.30 hours, because the main force is expected to land at Dieppe about then. All right so far? No further questions?'

There was a general shaking of heads, and so I went on to discuss the next phase of the plan. I told them how General Staufen came past the crossroads every morning at 07.15 hours precisely, riding in a staff-car sandwiched between motorcycle combinations on either side of him. Sergeant McKinley, Privates Shaw and Ellis, dressed in German Army uniforms on top of their battledress would wait out in the open for the small convoy to approach the junction. The rest of us would take up our stations in the gardens of the cottages which would have been evacuated beforehand, and amongst the shrubbery under the trees beside the stream on the other side of the road.

'Sir, how will we know that the general is coming? With the attack on Dieppe, he may vary his routine,' Private Walkowski asked. He was a Pole who had been an archaeological student before escaping to England, and was known as Wally to the others.

'We don't think that he will be involved in the Dieppe landings, but the Resistance are going to keep watch and signal to us when he is on his way.'

I went on to remind them that apart from the three men at the junction, it was absolutely essential for the rest of them to keep out of sight, as it would be broad daylight at that hour. Sergeant McKinley would stop the convoy and explain that the Resistance had felled a tree which was blocking the road around the next bend. As soon as the staff-car stopped, Ellis and Shaw would approach from either side and take out the driver and the other soldier, while the sergeant got into the back with the general. At the same time, and it must be timed precisely, the party from the cottage gardens were to deal with the first motorcycle combination, while the remainder in the shrubbery would neutralise the one following.

The next thing was to drive the car away to hide it in a wood some distance away. Private Sykes would be responsible for this, and would set a charge with a time-fuse so that it would blow up after we had gone. Meanwhile, the general would come with us on foot back to the beach where we had landed. We would await nightfall in a derelict hut close by, when the M.T.B. would come and pick us up at 00.30 hours. Hopefully, there would be enough activity further up the coast at Dieppe to distract the Germans away from our little sideshow.

I emphasised that although all the German soldiers were to be put out of action, one of them at least was to be only wounded, because it was necessary for the German High Command to know that it was British Commandos who had made the raid. In that event, it was to be hoped that the civilian population would not suffer any reprisals.

At the end of the briefing there were several questions, most of which had already been dealt with, but a few minor points were raised which required clarification. So far as possible, nothing could be left to chance, and I could only hope that I had covered every eventuality. After the men had gone, I stayed behind to look at the plot for the umpteenth time. It all seemed so simple when it was discussed like a training exercise, and the more I studied it, the more I was convinced that it was all too easy.

Needless to say, the next few days were a nightmare of feverish activity. Last-minute instructions kept coming down the line, weather forecasts, the last known disposition of enemy troops in the area, and finally a change in the location where we were to embark on the M.T.B. Amongst all that, there was a memo from Southern Command asking for a list of all weapons and stocks of ammunition held by the unit. This communication was consigned smartly to where it belonged — in the wastepaper basket.

With only forty-eight hours to go, a double set-back caused me to revise some of our plans. Private Ellis, one of our two German speakers, developed an acute appendicitis and had to be rushed to hospital where he was operated on that same evening. It was too late to find a replacement, so I decided to take his place at the road junction myself. This cut down our numbers to only eleven, and it meant that only Sergeant McKinley spoke German.

The second setback was more worrying. Intelligence reported that unfortunately the French Resistance had been infiltrated — with the result that several of their members had been captured in a series of dawn raids the previous day. One of the men to be taken was the one who was supposed to meet us on the beach, and who knew something of our plans. If he was tortured, I could only pray that he could hold out long enough not to divulge his part in the raid. If not, then we could expect the Germans to be waiting for us. At least the Resistance knew little or nothing about the forthcoming raid on Dieppe.

I telephoned Combined Operations and asked to be put through to Admiral Brown's office. It was not Rosemary who answered, and her replacement informed me that neither she nor Sir George were available for the rest of the day. She then transferred the call to the admiral's deputy, Captain James Willoughby-Brook, R.N.

'Marshall? Oh, yes, Marshall! You're running this Commando side-show which someone with a vivid imagination has dreamed up, aren't you? So, what can I do for you? I'm very busy.'

His supercilious drawl irritated me, and I was left in no doubt that he didn't think much of the operation in general, and me in particular. I suppose he was feeling piqued because he had not been consulted at any stage during the planning. Briefly I explained to him what had happened regarding the members of the Resistance who were now in German hands, and asked for guidance.

'What do you want me to do about it, Marshall? I know

nothing about the affair.'

'Then can you tell me where I can contact Admiral Brown, sir?' I asked, trying not to lose my cool.

'I haven't the least idea, old boy. He never tells me where he is going. You'll just have to work it out as best you can, and play it as it comes. If there is any more trouble, then you have my authority to scrub the whole operation.'

He put down the receiver, leaving me fuming with frustration. After all these months of planning and training, I was determined that nothing short of an earthquake would induce me to call it off now. I was only too conscious that I was being given a unique opportunity to avenge myself on the man who had issued the orders to the bomber which had been responsible for killing my wife and family.

But was it fair to risk the lives of others in pursuit of my personal vendetta? I lit a cigarette and found that my hands were trembling, after which I sat for a long time debating what action to take. In the end I decided to carry on. I could only hope that the decision had been arrived at in a professional and dispassionate manner, taking all the facts into consideration.

I saw each member of the squad in my office individually to ensure that everyone knew exactly what role he was to play. Apart from Sergeant McKinley and myself, there was Corporal Smythe (known as Smithy), the radio operator Lance-Corporal Harvey, Privates Shaw, Ramsay, Walkowski (Wally), Coleman, Bridges, Sykes and Bloomfield, making eleven in all.

I tried to contact the admiral next day, but he still had not returned. I knew that he was exclusively involved with the main landing at Dieppe, and that it was useless to pursue the question of his whereabouts. Whatever happened from now on was in the lap of the gods.

7

Raiders

Two lorries transferred us from the camp to the dock where we embarked without a hitch. The motor torpedo boat was even smaller than I had expected, but everyone managed to find some space on board with just enough room to stretch out. I had previously urged my men to try to get some sleep during the crossing, but I for one, was unable to relax. I kept wondering if something had been overlooked, and although I tried to put it at the back of my mind, I was apprehensive as to what was waiting for us on the other side. After making sure everyone was relatively comfortable, we drew away from the quayside, only to drop anchor a hundred yards or so off shore. All around us was an armada of landing craft, some with tanks on board, while out to sea a couple of destroyers kept a watching brief in case of a surprise attack.

The Captain of our mini-warship was a sub-lieutenant in the R.N.V.R., about twenty years of age, and like the pilot of the Mosquito he looked as if he ought still to be at school instead of captaining one of H.M. ships. But in spite of his lack of years I was impressed by the way he handled the craft, and I had every confidence in his ability to deliver us safely at the rendezvous.

After a delay of about half an hour we were off, and no sooner had we cleared the massing armada than we accelerated to full speed. The night was dark with only a small crescent moon showing at irregular intervals between gaps in the clouds, but our creaming white wake was in stark contrast to the black surface of the water as the boat skimmed over the smooth sea. The roar of the twin Rolls-Royce engines was deafening, and the deck shook under our feet while the bows rose up under full throttle, generating a sense of excitement, so that any thought of sleep was quickly dispelled.

I must have eventually dozed off, because as soon as someone touched me on the shoulder I was instantly awake. The engines were only ticking over, and the boat was almost at a standstill.

'The skipper's compliments, sir. Twenty minutes to E.T.A. and would you please join him on the bridge,' the rating said quietly in my ear.

When I squeezed in beside him on what he was pleased to call the bridge, the young officer was scanning the horizon with night glasses.

'Trouble?' I asked.

'No, not really. We've had a buzz over the radio that the E-boats are out in this area, but they're always active round this part, so I think it must be a routine patrol. We haven't seen or heard anything as yet, so we'll carry on at reduced speed. Are all your chaps O.K.?'

I did the rounds and all the members of the team were now wide awake and in good spirits with the exception of Coleman who was suffering from sea-sickness.

'Don't worry about me, sir,' he hastened to assure me. 'I get sick on a rowing boat on the river.'

'We'll go in as close as we can,' the sub-lieutenant said as soon as I had returned to the bridge. 'The dinghies are ready for launching as soon as we see the signal.'

'Are there no mines here?' I asked with some apprehension.

'There's a sandbank just off shore. We've come inside it and the water is too shallow for mines. Fortunately it's high tide, otherwise we couldn't come in.'

It was a further ten minutes before the engines stopped, and we lay wallowing in the rising swell. I could now see the waves breaking against the shore without the aid of glasses.

'This is as far as we dare go without running aground,' the skipper told me. 'We ought to see the light any time now. It will be repeated at two minute intervals.'

It seemed like hours before a pin-point of light from the scrubland behind the shore stabbed the darkness, two long and one short, followed immediately by one long and two short.

'That's it!' I called out. 'Let's go!'

'Good luck, captain,' the skipper said as we shook hands. 'I'll be back here at the same time tomorrow, and again in the early hours of the day after, if you can't make it.'

Transferring from the deck of the M.T.B. into the dinghies proved to be much more difficult than it had been during practice. The sea had risen since we left, and the waves now tossed the small inflatables up and down against the hull at an alarming rate. However, we all managed to make the transfer safely, with the exception of Private Bloomfield, who landed in the water and had to be fished out. I was thankful that it hadn't been the radio operator together with his equipment.

The beach consisted mainly of shingle with a little sand in places, but fortunately the rasping of our boots as we crossed it was drowned by the crashing of the waves behind us. We hid the inflatables in the scrub, while two scouts went forward to meet the guide and assess the situation. They returned after a few minutes in the company of a bulky figure dressed in dark clothing. He introduced himself as Pierre Delame.

'I represent the Resistance,' he said, 'and I have the honour of welcoming you to France.'

I made myself known to him before asking him if he knew where he was to guide us.

'Yes, I know where to take you, mon capitaine, but I do not know why you are here. However, my men will give you all the assistance you may need.'

'I understand that the Germans have captured several members of your organization, including the man who was supposed to be meeting us.'

'Yes, that if unfortunately true, capitaine, but my colleague and friend Raymond Gauthier was the only one who knew the details of your raid. When they took him, he was able to pass a message to his wife giving the radio code, and the time of your arrival.'

'Will your friend talk? If so, we wondered if the Germans would be waiting for us.'

'No monsieur, you can rest assured that Raymond will never talk. They will have to kill him first.'

My immediate concern was whether or not I could trust this fellow. He seemed to be plausible enough, but if Gauthier had already talked, then this man could have been planted by the enemy. In fact, I had no choice but to trust him, but I was alert for the slightest trouble.

'What lies behind these sand-dunes, and where are the sentries?' I asked him.

Delame told me that this section of the coast had not yet been completely fortified. Mines had been laid over some parts, but the sand had blown to uncover a good many, so there was a way through them. He suggested that it might help us to find the path on our return if we marked it as we went along. Apparently they were building pill-boxes on either side of the bay, but these had not yet been completed, and I could only just make out their outline. There were no sentries posted, but an armoured car with a powerful spotlight patrolled the coast road at intervals.

I passed on the information to the others, and we set off in single file with the Frenchman leading, and myself immediately behind him. Sergeant McKinley brought up the rear with one of the men. While the sergeant put in discreet white pegs, which would not be noticeable to the casual observer, his companion raked out our footprints. Hopefully no one would move the markers before we returned.

We came upon the coast road about a couple of hundred yards from the beach, and no sooner had we assembled on the inland side of the highway, than the lights of an approaching vehicle could be seen in the distance. Without any orders being issued, we scattered into the scrub, trying to conceal ourselves as best we could. If it had been daylight, there was no way we could have remained hidden, but fortunately the darkness concealed our presence.

'Do we neutralise this armoured car, sir?' Sergeant McKinley whispered in my ear as we hugged the ground.

'No! If the car doesn't report in they will know that something is amiss. We don't want them to know we're here, so not a move from anyone.'

The vehicle came to a halt directly opposite our hiding-place, and I was prepared for the machine-gun mounted in the turret to open up on us at any moment. However, my fears proved groundless. The searchlight beam swept over the dunes in the direction from which we had just come, and after a few long minutes, much to my relief, the light was extinguished and the vehicle proceeded on its way, apparently oblivious of our presence.

Two hours later, our party arrived intact on the outskirts of the village of Ribeuf, about half a mile from the chateau. We had been guided along little-known paths through thickly wooded country away from the main roads. I had to admit that it would have been very difficult to have found our way without a guide in the darkness, in spite of the fact that I had been studying the area for weeks. By now, I was almost convinced that Delame could be trusted, but I still had one niggling doubt that perhaps the Germans were holding back until they knew exactly what the purpose of our mission was.

A lone dog, shut up in an outhouse barked furiously as we by-passed the village, but no one appeared, and soon it grew quiet. The closer we got to our destination the more carefully we advanced by a series of leap-frogging movements all down the line, with the result that everyone took it in turns to lead along with the Frenchman. The only exception was the radio operator, who stayed close to me at all times.

Just as dawn was breaking, we found ourselves in the vicinity of the road junction, and we washed the blacking from our faces and hands in the little stream which ran alongside the road. As it grew lighter, I was able to distinguish the various landmarks, and I was pleased to note that the cliffs and the heavily wooded slopes on the side of the valley nearest to the junction provided some measure of protection in that we could not be easily overlooked from there. The opposite slope on the other side of the meadow had a sparse covering of trees and undergrowth which would have given insufficient cover for any of the enemy to hide in.

Suddenly the sound of intensive gunfire could be heard some miles away to the east, indicating that the assault on Dieppe had got under way. I made one final visit to all our men to ensure that they were in position, and that each one knew exactly what part he had to play. Sergeant McKinley, Private Shaw and myself then donned our German uniforms over our battledress, so all we had to do now was to await the arrival of our victim who, if all went to schedule, was due to pass here in one hour and twenty minutes.

The vigil passed slowly, and I must have looked at my watch twenty times or more. We didn't talk, but walked up and down close to the junction, and I kept thinking of all the defects in my plan. During this period of waiting, no vehicles passed along the road, only an old peasant on a bicycle who eyed the German uniforms with open hatred, and spat in our direction as a gesture of defiance as he passed. The only sound above the continuous murmuring of the stream was the rumble of distant guns, interspersed at intervals with the occasional rattle of machine-gun and small arms fire, borne towards us on the breeze.

With thirty minutes to go, it was time for our first scheduled radio transmission to base. We gave out the coded message that we were in position, and the acknowledgment was received almost immediately. We had been on the air for not more than thirty seconds, and so there was no chance of the enemy pinpointing the source of the broadcast, in the unlikely event of it having been picked up.

It was also about this time when I discovered that our French guide had disappeared without so much as a word to anyone, but there was nothing I could do about it at that stage.

When zero hour was only seven minutes away, we were all set to deal with the general's car and escort, but to our horror the first vehicle to approach the junction came from another direction entirely. An endless convoy of German Army lorries full of troops, with armoured-car escorts and motorcycle outriders, appeared from the west, obviously on their way to reinforce the garrison at Dieppe. It was too late to slip back into the undergrowth unseen, so the only action we could take was to remain where we were, and brazen it out, hopefully without our disguise being

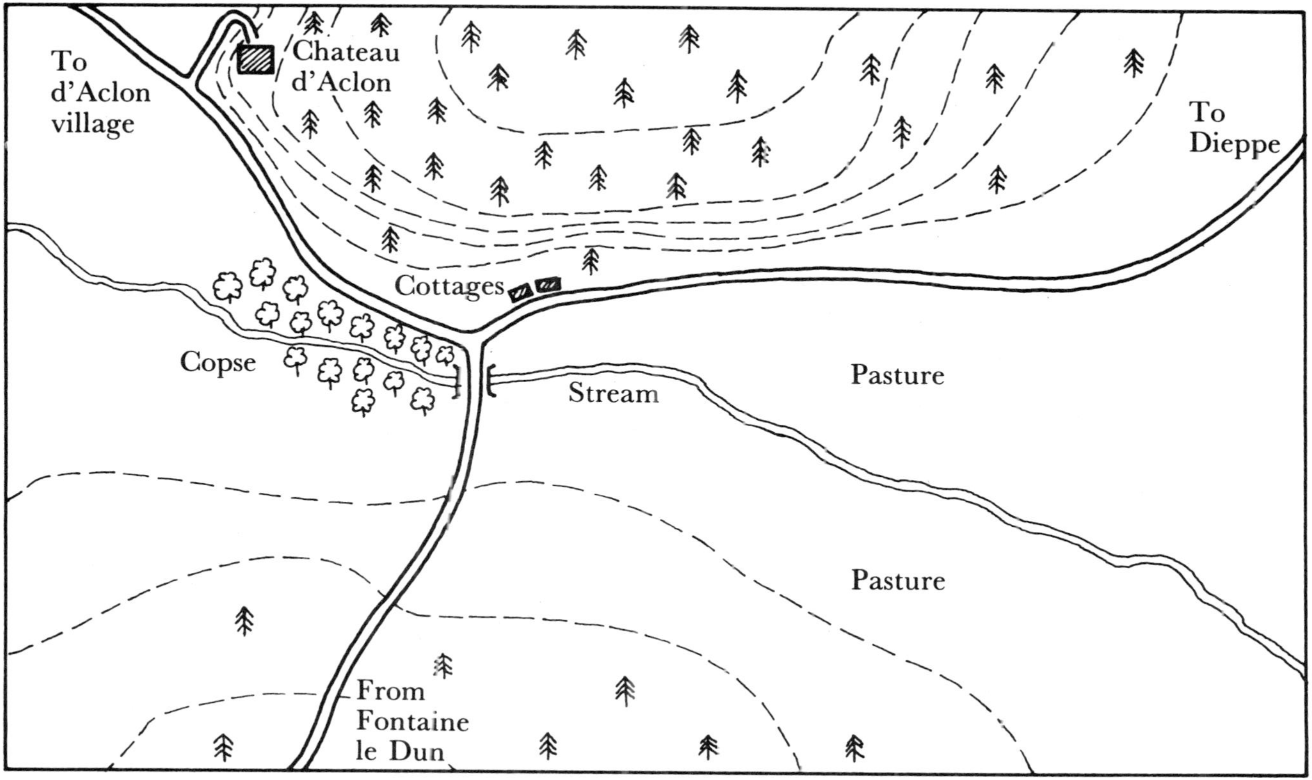
To d'Aclon village
Chateau d'Aclon
To Dieppe
Cottages
Copse
Stream
Pasture
Pasture
From Fontaine le Dun

penetrated.

We waved the convoy through as if we had been positioned there for the sole purpose of directing the traffic. The line of vehicles coming over the brow of the hill seemed to be neverending, and they were still coming when I saw General Staufen's car and escort approaching from the direction of the chateau. With great presence of mind, Sergeant McKinley stepped out into the middle of the road and halted the convoy to allow the general's entourage uninterrupted access into the main highway. We stood to attention and saluted as the vehicle with its shadowy figure inside swept past us, and we continued to watch with mounting frustration as our quarry disappeared round the next bend out of sight.

The sergeant exchanged a few words with the driver of the lorry which had been held up, and a motorcyclist who had come alongside to ascertain what the hold-up was due to. They were doubtless satisfied with what he told them, because the convoy resumed its journey eastward once more.

However, our troubles were still not at an end. A black open Mercedes staff-car, flying a small swastika flag on each of the front wings, was hidden from view behind a large wagon, and we were not aware of its presence until they were almost upon us. The occupants wore the black uniform of the SS, and the car came to a halt close to where we were standing.

One of the officers beckoned me with his finger at the same time as he barked, 'Kommen sie hier!'

In fear and trembling I approached the car, and saw with much relief that Sergeant McKinley was close beside me. He told me afterwards what the conversation was.

'Don't you salute officers of the SS anymore?' The man had complained.

The sergeant duly apologised, and pointed out that the staff-car had not been visible until the last moment.

'That's no excuse! Keep your eyes open in future!' he snapped peering at my uniform. 'What unit does this man belong to?' I had a feeling as if I was under a microscope. 'He doesn't even dress properly. Give me your name, number and unit,' he said to me.

Fortunately, at this moment the other officer reminded him that they were holding up the convoy, and as they pulled away I gave my impression of the Nazi salute with all the fervour I could muster, thankful for our good fortune.

'Damn and blast!' I exploded, as soon as the last lorry had disappeared from view. 'Of all the rotten luck!'

Sergeant McKinley was apparently quite unruffled by what had just happened, and I had been most impressed by his performance under difficult circumstances, whereas it took me some time to regain my composure.

'We'll just have to wait for General Staufen to come back,' I said, 'but then it will not be easy to meet the rendezvous with the M.T.B. in the early hours of tomorrow morning. I believe that these cottages have been evacuated, so get the men inside and we'll rest up until evening. Impress upon them not to make any noise, because we can't risk being overheard by passers-by.'

There was a natural feeling of disappointment amongst the team, but we were all tired and glad of the opportunity to sleep. After a meal of iron rations, I arranged a rota so that there would be someone on watch in each cottage at all times, and we settled down to wait, hopeful that the raid on Dieppe had not caused him to vary his routine. If that was the case then it was possible that we may well have to spend another twenty-four hours in this vulnerable situation, and I knew the longer we stayed there, the more difficult it would be to conceal our presence.

The morning passed without incident, and the majority of us rested and dozed. The cottages were poorly furnished, but it was better than being out in the open, especially when it began to rain. There had been very little traffic on the road during this time. Another convoy had passed, but it was not nearly as big as the last one, and apart from that there had been only the occasional lorry, a couple of ambulances, and several locals on bicycles, but no one looked towards the cottages. On the whole, it was a peaceful scene, except that the continuous rumble of distant gunfire served to remind us that the war was not far away.

The trouble began in the middle of the afternoon, when I was awakened from a deep sleep by a rumpus which emanated from the cottage next door. I hurriedly went to investigate, and the scene which met my eyes made me remember Sergeant McKinley's words regarding Private Ramsay. Jock was being sat on by three of the others, one of whom was holding a hand over his mouth. Somehow he managed to shake himself free.

'Let me get at them!' he shouted. 'I came here to kill the bastards, and by God that's what I'll do! Come on, bring them . . .' At that stage a hand was clamped over his mouth once more.

The reason for the outburst was plain to see. A number of empty bottles of wine lay strewn around the floor. Trust Jock to find them! His affinity for alcohol meant that he was unable to resist the temptation, with the result that he was a danger to us all.

'Stand him up!' I ordered.

He began to shout again as he was hoisted to his feet, but before he could say much I hit him on the point of the jaw, causing him to collapse in a heap, out for the count. The men standing by watching looked relieved, but this consolation was short-lived. Private Bridges appeared at my side looking agitated.

'Sir, a German motorcyclist has stopped outside the cottage next door, and he's looking at it.'

There was instant silence among the men. Two of them stood by ready to gag Jock again if he woke up and began to shout once more.

'Is he alone?' I asked.

'Yes, sir. He seems to be. The road's deserted in every direction.'

'Get Sergeant McKinley,' I ordered, but he was already alert to the danger, and we both slipped into the cottage next door by way of the back garden, hopefully without being seen.

'What do you think, sergeant? I wonder if he's heard the rumpus.'

'His machine seems to have broken down. My God, he's coming up the path.'

Still in his German uniform, McKinley met him at the front door. They conversed for a few minutes before the sergeant invited him in. As the visitor stepped across the threshold, his eyes widened in disbelief when he saw several men in British Army uniforms staring at him from the other side of the room. It was the last thing the poor devil did see. From behind, McKinley dispatched the German with his Commando knife quickly and quietly in the time-honoured manner. The man slid to the floor, a crimson stain spreading over the front of his uniform.

'Get that motorcycle off the road, Sykes,' I ordered. 'Put it round the back out of sight. The rest of you, dump this chap in the shrubbery.'

I asked McKinley what the motorcyclist had said, and if anyone would be likely to come looking for him.

'No, he's been delivering despatches to an airfield near Fecamp, sir, and was on his way back to base. I don't think he heard the rumpus next door. From what he said, he won't be missed for some time.'

'Let's hope not,' I said. 'There's enough gone wrong already with this operation.'

'What are we to do with Jock Ramsay, sir?'

'Let's hope he has sobered up by the time we go into action, but if he becomes obstreperous in the meantime, you have my authority to knock him out again. We can't do anything here, but as soon as we get back to England Private Ramsay is for it.' I added grimly.

At 17.50 hours, Corporal Smythe came to remind me that our next transmission was due in ten minutes' time. I gave him the coded message to the effect that we had failed in our mission on the first occasion, but that we were to try again that evening. This time, the message had to be repeated before acknowledgment was received.

Fortunately, by now Jock Ramsay had sobered up, especially after having been doused with cold water from the pump in the backyard. He knew he was in trouble, and for once he stayed abnormally quiet while keeping out of my way.

At last, the time arrived when General Staufen was due to return to the chateau, but by now much of my confidence had evaporated and I was doubtful if the plan was going to work. Although there had still been no attack on us since Delame had vanished, it was possible that our quarry might vary his routine if he knew that we were waiting for him. Such uncertainties crossed my mind as I stood once more out in the open at the junction, continually checking that there was no traffic coming from the other way. Sergeant McKinley must have read my thoughts, because he grinned in my direction, and gave me a thumbs-up sign.

A few minutes later, the sound of an approaching vehicle could be heard coming from the east, and almost immediately the first motorcycle combination rounded the bend into view, followed by the staff-car and the other escort. Sergeant McKinley stepped out into the middle of the road with his hand raised, bringing the first escort to a halt. By the time he had repeated the story that the Resistance had blocked the road ahead by felling a tree, the staff-car had closed up behind it. Private Shaw and I each approached the vehicle from opposite sides, and as we did so the man sitting beside the driver stuck his head out of the window to ask what the trouble was.

While Sergeant McKinley dealt with the driver, and Private Shaw kept the other soldier under observation, I drew my pistol and opened the back door of the staff-car. There I was surprised to be confronted by not one, but two high-ranking German officers, each with a look of surprise on their faces. I recognised one as General Staufen, but the other man was older and unknown to me. By this time the remainder of our party had emerged from the bushes to surround each of the escorting motorcycle combinations, and so the plan had worked without a shot having been fired.

Alas, once more my confidence took a knock when a cry from the rear warned us that an armoured half-track was approaching. One of the escort, seeing that some of our men had been distracted, opened up with a machine-pistol before he had been disarmed. He had killed two of our number already when he himself was despatched in similar fashion. The incident brought us to our senses, and the remainder of the escort were dealt with in a matter of seconds. I was prudent enough not to take my eyes off the two generals for a second, but a quick glance through the rear window of the limousine showed me that the half-track had stopped about a hundred yards away, and that the heavy machine-gun mounted on the front was now manned.

Sergeant McKinley opened the other rear door and ordered both the officers out of the vehicle. We were about to escort them into the shrubbery close to the road when the armoured car opened up. I watched helplessly while two more of our men went down, one of whom rolled into a stream where he lay face down without moving. I could not even see who it was, since General Staufen and I were pinned down behind the front of the staff-car, and I dared not take my eyes off him.

Suddenly the firing stopped, and an explosion from the direction of the half-track caused me to risk a quick look in that direction. I was delighted to see that the Resistance had launched an attack on the vehicle which was now on fire, and as its crew came out one by one, they were cut down by the Frenchmen. It was Delame who had brought his men to help us, and their arrival was well timed.

I had not yet had an opportunity to disarm General Staufen who, seeing my distraction, drew his Luger, and I turned to find it pointing straight at me. Private Ramsay, who was standing close by, launched himself at the German a split second before he pulled the trigger. Somehow Jock must have interspersed his body between us, because he took the full force of the shot, delivered at almost point-blank range. I had the presence of mind to take the pistol from the general's unresisting grasp before he had recovered from the shock of having failed to put me out of action.

'Are you all right, sir?' Sergeant McKinley called out from behind a nearby wall.

'Yes, I'm O.K.,' I assured him.

I looked down at the Scotsman's body lying at my feet, and for a moment I contemplated the twists of fate. It ought to have been me lying there instead of Jock who had given his life for mine. Whether or not he intended it that way, at least now he would be spared having to face a Court Martial.

The next priority was to clear the road as quickly as possible before any more traffic came along. The motorcycle combinations were wheeled into the undergrowth, but we were unable to drive the Mercedes to the place we had earmarked because of the burning half-track. Eventually, we found that one of the outhouses adjoining the cottages was empty, and so we hid it in there after removing the German uniforms and stowing them in the car as well.

Some minutes later, when we had all assembled under the cover of the trees, I was able to take stock of the situation. Four of our number had been killed — lance-corporal Harvey, Bridges, Bloomfield, and of course, Ramsay. Private Coleman had been hit in both legs, so there was no question of moving him. He was losing blood fast, and in spite of our efforts at first-aid, it was obvious that he would die very soon.

Now that the German officers had been disarmed, their pockets were turned out, but they apparently carried nothing of interest on their person. I had just issued instructions for our dead to be buried, when Delame appeared in company with two of his men.

'You see, we can fight if it's necessary, mon capitaine,' he said with a twinkle in his eye.

I began to thank him for his timely intervention, but he interrupted me. 'You must get away from here at once,' he told me. 'The chateau will have already alerted his headquarters that the general has not arrived, and there will be troops out along the route looking for him.'

'But we must first bury our dead, monsieur, and tidy up here.'

'My men will take care of that for you, never fear. We will also take these two off your hands.' He indicated the two German soldiers who were still alive, but had been kept segregated from the two generals.

I thought it diplomatic not to ask what would happen to them, but now that the members of the Resistance had involved themselves in the affray, it was no longer necessary to cover up for them. I did ask Delame if he knew who the second general was, but he merely shrugged. Soon it would be dark, and the Frenchman was prepared to guide us back to the beach.

We had been travelling on foot for almost an hour when the elder of the two German officers stopped dead in his tracks. Staufen muttered something to him, and they both refused to go any further.

'We must rest,' the Luftwaffe chief told me in excellent French. 'My colleague is no longer young, and he cannot keep up at this pace.'

'Keep moving!' I snarled at him. 'We will stop only when I say so. We have a schedule to maintain.' If it was to be at all possible, I was determined to meet the rendezvous with the M.T.B. before dawn, but I knew that it would be difficult.

General Staufen did not move, even when I pushed him in the back. He turned to face me and protested in tolerable English that he was not being accorded the courtesy due to his rank. His supercilious manner triggered off a loss of self-discipline on my part, and I saw red. Grabbing him roughly by the front of his tunic, I put the muzzle of my pistol under his chin so that it forced his head back.

'Listen to me, you murdering bastard! Your glorious airmen, who are little better than thugs who are capable only of bombing women and children, are responsible for the deaths of my wife and family. Think yourself lucky that you are still in one piece, but if you give me any cause whatsoever, I will personally blow your head off, and enjoy doing it. Do you understand?'

Someone gently, but firmly, pulled me away from behind. The general dusted down his rumpled tunic and looked at me with a certain pity.

'I'm sorry about that, Kapitan,' he said quietly. 'I do understand how you feel. War is hell, and we all suffer. I myself lost my eldest son during the push through Belgium only last year.'

In the half light, there was a certain dignity in his bearing which made me feel almost ashamed of my outburst.

'Very well,' I said gruffly. 'Five minutes. No more.'

He said something to the other German in his own tongue, so I assumed that he did not speak English or French. Sergeant McKinley had already tried to question him, but he did not so much as divulge his name. I was beginning to toy with the idea of disposing of him. After all, it was General Staufen we had come for, and if this other officer held us back, surely we were justified in killing him. However, it would be left to me, as I would never ask any of my men to do it, and I personally did not think I was capable of it, no matter what the circumstances, or how much I hated him.

We set off once more, but our rate of progress was slow, and it was becoming increasingly clear to me that we were not going to meet the rendezvous if we kept up this snail's pace. The darkness had closed around us like a blanket, and if it had not been for Delame there to guide us, I would never have known where we were. The Frenchman must have read my thoughts because he took me to one side.

'We cannot afford to waste any more time, capitaine,' he said in a low voice, so that the others could not overhear. 'There is no suitable place for us to lay up for a whole day near the coast without being detected. We must do everything possible to get to the beach on time.'

'I had considered making a bivouac for the night, here in this wood,' I confided in him. 'It's not a bad place to hide during the day either. Surely no one will find us here?'

'Have you forgotten, mon ami, they will be out in force looking for our two guests. By tomorrow this area will be crawling with troops, and even if they did not find us in here, as soon as we moved out there would be no way through.'

I thought over the situation for a few minutes, and came to the conclusion that he was right.

'Very well! Smithy, I want you to send out a signal now to the effect that our mission has been successful so far, but we are held up. Ask them to pass a message to the M.T.B. to wait for us as long as possible.'

'But, sir, the time for the next transmission isn't due for another hour and twenty-five minutes,' the radio operator reminded me.

'Look, I can't afford to stop again. If we are to reach the boat before it departs then we must keep going. Send the message now, and keep on transmitting until you receive acknowledgment. We'll move on with our captives and mark the route for you. Catch us up as soon as you can. Private Sykes can stay with you for protection.'

I did not want to have to split what was left of our little party, but so far as I could see there was no alternative, even if it meant that there was only four of us left to guard

General Staufen and his unknown companion until Corporal Smythe and Private Sykes caught up with us again. We took it in turns to support the elder of our two captives, one on either side of him whenever the path was wide enough, but at no time did he complain — in fact he never uttered a word. It was the Luftwaffe chief who grumbled continuously until I could have cheerfully strangled him, but I managed to keep my temper under control. Looking back, I'm sure that he did it deliberately merely to irritate me, and to try to push me into a position where I made a mistake.

At last, after what seemed to be hours, we arrived at the coast road tired and hungry, and as we rested among the scrub by the sand-dunes, I was pleased to note that the armoured car patrol was nowhere to be seen.

I decided to go for the beach straight away, and so once again Delame led us through the minefield, quicker this time because of the markers we had put down. Was it only twenty-four hours ago? It seemed like a lifetime. The inflatables were still there where we had left them, but now I was conscious of our exposed position on the open beach. I gave the signal out to sea, but there was no answer. My luninous watch showed me that we were already three-quarters of an hour late for the rendezvous, and the longer we waited, the more uneasy I became.

As we lay on the beach trying to make ourselves inconspicuous, I found myself next to General Staufen. He seemed to be quite resigned to his fate and eager to talk.

'Tell me, Kapitan, why did you not kill me back at the road junction,' he asked me in a friendly manner.

'Because my orders were to capture you, and to bring you back to England. I'm still curious to know the identity of the other officer, he was carrying no means of identification when we searched him.'

'Yes, he managed to fool you there. As soon as the car stopped, he knew something was wrong and pushed his papers down the back of the seat. It has been an interesting exercise watching you trying to find out who he really is. If you ever do manage to get him back to England, I wish I could be there when they discover his true identity.' He actually chuckled as if the idea amused him. He paused for a few seconds, and added quietly, 'I must compliment you on a job well done, Kapitan. What a pity it will all be for nothing, so far as I am concerned.'

'Why is that, general?'

'Because you'll never take me alive, you know.'

I could see him smiling in the darkness, and I wondered what he knew that I didn't. Still there was no answering signal from the sea, and I wondered if perhaps Staufen's words had been prophetic in that an E-boat had been waiting offshore for the M.T.B., in which case we would be stranded. A few more minutes passed before a faint rumble of engines were heard coming towards us. They stopped, and a flash of light stabbed the darkness. It had been the signal we were waiting for.

'There's still no sign of Smithy or Sykes,' Sergeant McKinley said. 'What shall we do, sir?'

'Well, I'm afraid we can't wait for them. They have a few minutes yet.'

At this point Delame came to say goodbye. I thanked him whole-heartedly for his contribution to the mission, adding that we could never have done it without his assistance. He smiled and kissed me on both cheeks, then he turned to go. In a moment he was back again.

'I would be grateful if you would deliver this letter to the address on the envelope,' he said, thrusting it into my hand. Without another word, his bulky figure melted into the darkness, and he disappeared the same way he had come.

After the pre-arranged wait of two minutes, the signal came that it was safe to embark, but just as we were about to launch the inflatables, two figures were visible silhouetted against the night sky up on the coast road. We watched with increasing apprehension as the lights of the coastal patrol armoured car could be seen approaching rapidly at the same time. Before either of the men could cross the road, its powerful searchlight picked them out in the scrub.

Private Sykes did not wait, however. He immediately discarded his equipment, and, holding his rifle above his head, he made a dash towards the beach, but in his eagerness to escape he had omitted to follow the safe path through the dunes. He was almost through the minefield when an explosion rent the night air, thus bringing his life to an abrupt end. We were all too stunned to speak, and the silence which followed was all the more intense.

Smithy, on the other hand, was weighed down by the transmitter on his back, and we watched in frustration while he was captured.

I had taken my eyes off General Staufen during this short interlude, and when I chanced to look back at him he was in the act of putting something into his mouth. I immediately took a step forward and grasped him under the chin in an attempt to prevent him from swallowing whatever it was. However, Sergeant McKinley, seeing what was happening, jumped to the conclusion that my temper had finally snapped, and that I was trying to strangle the German. With difficulty he managed to break my hold, thus allowing the general to stagger free. A few seconds later there was a gurgling sound, and he collapsed on to the shingle.

'You bloody fool!' I shouted at McKinley. 'That was a suicide pill.'

The realisation of what he had done made him hang his head in disgust. 'Oh, my God! I'm sorry, sir. I never realised that he . . .' but he never finished the sentence.

The searchlight on the armoured car was beginning to sweep the beach, thus galvanising us into action to launch the inflatables. Wally and I bundled General Staufen's body into one, while the sergeant and Private Shaw took our other captive in the second dinghy. We had paddled for only a few yards out into the surf when the machine-gun from the road patrol opened up. The first burst was wide, but when they fired again I felt a searing pain in my thigh which I tried to ignore. Wally slumped forward then slid down into the bottom of the boat beside the German's body, so it was essential for me to keep going at all costs.

Before the armoured car could fire again, the twin Oerlikons on the little warship opened up, and I remember watching the tracer bullets passing overhead. The searchlight was immediately extinguished, and simultaneously the firing stopped.

Before I reached the M.T.B. I felt very tired and faint, and I was conscious of a numbness in my thigh. I put my hand down to investigate, and my fingers came away covered in a sticky substance which I knew to be blood. I have no recollection of reaching the warship, or what happened subsequently, and it was a couple of days before I learned how our mission had ended.

8

A Spot of Leave

When I awoke I was immediately conscious of a throbbing pain in my leg, which increased as soon as I tried to move it. My head felt fuzzy, and my mouth was so dry that I could hardly swallow, far less speak. Gradually I began to take stock of my surroundings, the small room with bare, whitewashed walls, the iron bedstead in which I lay, and a bottle of clear fluid hanging from a stand above my head with its tube leading down into my arm. I could hear someone moving about, and a moment later a nurse came into my line of vision.

'I'm pleased to see that you're awake now, Captain Marshall. We began to think that you were going to sleep for ever. No, don't try to sit up! Wait until I help you. Would you like a drink? Steady now, just enough to moisten your mouth. There, that's better isn't it?'

'Where am I?' I managed to croak.

'In a military hospital near Portsmouth. You were wounded in the leg. Do you remember now?'

'Oh, yes. Is it bad?'

'No, it's only a flesh wound, but it was rather a long time before they got you here, and you had lost a lot of blood. You've had a transfusion, and in time you'll be as good as new.'

She helped to prop me up in a sitting position with extra pillows, and I was able to see her for the first time. I remember thinking what a pleasant voice she had, but it was a pity that her appearance didn't match it.

'There, now you can see what's going on,' she said. 'You must be very popular, because you've had a string of visitors. An admiral, no less, and a beautiful WREN officer, Sister Thomas from downstairs, and a Commando sergeant. I'm going to give you an injection now. You'll have a little sleep, then you'll feel much better when you wake up.'

She was right. It was dark outside when I finally came to my senses, and a single lamp on the bedside cabinet cast eerie shadows on the white walls. My head was now much clearer, the ache in my leg was not so acute, and I even felt hungry. I noticed that the drip in my arm had been taken down, then I became aware that someone was holding my hand. I turned my head to find Rosemary sitting beside the bed, and smiling at me.

'It's about time you returned to the land of the living, young man. We were all beginning to be a little bit concerned about you. How do you feel now?'

'Great — I think! What are you doing here, Rosemary?'

'I had nothing better to do, so I just popped in to see how you were. I'll be going now.'

'No, please don't go. How long have I been here?'

'Nearly two days. You certainly look better. I came in a few hours after you returned from theatre, and you looked as if you wouldn't survive for another day.'

'Aw, we're tough, us Marshalls, but . . .'

At that moment the door opened, and Susan came in. She was obviously on duty.

'I heard voices, so I thought you were awake at last. Are you O.K.?' I nodded. 'Hm., Scotland indeed!' she went on. 'You could have knocked me down with the proverbial feather when I saw you lying on the stretcher. I could hardly recognise you.'

'I hope you'll forgive me for the deception, Susan?'

'Oh, I suppose so,' she quipped. 'It's all in a good cause, they tell us. Anyway, I'll come back and see you later.'

Rosemary got up. 'And I must go. We're very busy with the landing at Dieppe, and everything else. Goodnight, Colin.'

She kissed me lightly on the cheek, then she was gone leaving only the lingering fragrance of her perfume.

The next day was filled by a constant stream of visitors,

the first of whom was Sergeant McKinley. He filled me in with many of the details of our trip back across the Channel.

Apparently the motor torpedo-boat had been held up, not because of my request, but because of a marked increase in E-boat activity in the Channel as a direct result of the Dieppe raid. As it was, they had only just managed to beat the tide — another ten minutes and there would have been insufficient water to get close inshore and out again. Even on the return journey we had been forced to make a detour in order to avoid enemy patrols. The result was that it took longer to get back to base, and all the time I continued to bleed in spite of frantic first aid attempts to stem the haemorrhage. In fact, during the final stage of the voyage they began to think that I wasn't going to make it, and had radioed ahead for an ambulance to be standing by. As soon as the boat had docked I was rushed straight here into the operating theatre.

'How many casualties did we have, sergeant?'

'Eight. Seven killed, and one taken prisoner. That's not counting yourself, sir, so only two of us came back without a scratch. Private Shaw has gone off on leave, but he hopes you will have recovered soon.'

'I wouldn't have been here at all if it was not for Jock Ramsay,' I mused.

'Yes. It was a grand final gesture, but why he did it, no one will ever know.'

'What about Walkowski?' I asked.

'He was killed at the same time you were hit. Sir, I'm sorry about that business on the beach with General Staufen.'

'Don't worry about it, Robin. You weren't to know.'

It was the first time I had used his Christian name, but I felt a great comradeship towards him after what we had been through together. He had been a tower of strength right from the beginning, and we couldn't have pulled it off without him.

'I've been writing the preliminary reports, and tying up some of the loose ends, but then when that's done I'm off home for fourteen days as well.'

'Leave the writing of the letters to the relatives of the

men who were killed to me. It'll give me something to do while I'm stuck in here. Thank you for all your help. I hope we will meet again sometime.'

I wasn't merely being polite, I really meant it. I held out my hand, and he gripped it firmly in his huge fist.

'Me too, sir. We made a grand team, didn't we?'

After he had gone, I realised how little I knew about his past or his private life, which was a pity; he was a man whom I could have counted as a friend. If at any time in the future I was called upon to recruit another special squad, his name would certainly be at the top of the list.

My next visitor was the surgeon who had fished the bullet out of my thigh. He explained to me that it had been deeply embedded within the muscles, and had damaged several blood vessels, hence the large amount of uncontrollable haemorrhaging. He went on to reassure me that eventually I would be one-hundred per cent fit again, but that it would take time. Finally, he produced a little box from his pocket, and there, nestling on a bed of cotton wool, was a souvenir of my suffering.

Admiral Brown came to visit during the afternoon, and I was shocked by his appearance. There was no doubt that he had lost weight, because his uniform hung on him, and he had developed even more of a stoop. His eyes were red and sunk into his face from lack of sleep, and altogether he gave the appearance of a man who had been under continuous pressure, and who was now at the end of his tether. There was no doubt that the Dieppe raid had been responsible for yet one more casualty, but it was not one which would appear on any official list.

I thanked him for coming to see me, knowing how busy he must be, and asked him tentatively how the Dieppe raid was proceeding.

He sighed and looked glum. 'It's all over now, bar the shouting, and soon there will be plenty of that. There's nothing left for us except to pick up the pieces.'

'I take it that it was only a limited success, sir?'

He shook his head sadly. 'We lost an awful lot of good men, Colin. The Germans were too strong for us, and we never achieved our objective. However, we've learned a great deal, and we'll put the knowledge to good use next time, so on that basis it wasn't a total waste. After all, it was only supposed to be a trial run, a reconnaissance in strength, if you like. Still, I'm glad your little side-show was such a success.'

'What do you mean, sir — a success? Didn't you read the preliminary report? I lost a lot of good men too, and all for nothing. General Staufen swallowed a suicide pill just before we embarked. We had searched him thoroughly, but obviously not thoroughly enough. I suppose he waited until the very last moment when capture was inevitable before taking it. He had told me before then that we would never take him alive, and I ought to have realised what he was proposing to do. So you see, sir, it was a complete failure.'

Sir George's face lit up for a moment, and he chuckled. 'Ha, ha! Then you haven't heard? Has no one told you just what a prize you did bring back?'

'I don't understand, sir.'

'The other general who was in the car. Intelligence do have their methods, although they may not be as brutal as the Gestapo, and it has taken two days to make him talk. This man is General von Gaetner, who has been personally appointed by Hitler to suppress the French Resistance. Apparently he had only just landed by air, and was going to spend the night at the chateau with Staufen.'

'My God! And I considered him to be a doddering old nuisance. There were several times when I almost eliminated him because he was holding us up. Obviously he didn't have a suicide pill in his possession.'

'Well, according to Intelligence, he is one of the worst of the Nazis. A ruthless butcher who has had a lot of experience in Poland where he was responsible for the massacre of the population of whole villages. The French will be especially glad that he has been captured, and it will strike fear in the hearts of the Germans that we can come in and abduct their top men.'

'I can hardly believe we've had such luck. By the way, sir, Monsieur Delame, the local Resistance leader, gave me a letter to post for him. I haven't looked at the address, but perhaps someone in authority ought to censor it before it is sent.'

After I had fished it out of my bedside locker, the admiral

listened intently to my brief account of the mission.

'I'll be interested to read your official report of the raid, Colin,' he said, when I had finished. 'Fill in as many of the details as you can, but take your time.'

I was tempted to ask him how Connie was, but I thought the subject might be too painful and decided against it.

'Make sure you get well, Colin,' he said when he took his leave. 'When they discharge you from here, there will be a long convalescent leave due.'

I felt strangely elated after he had gone, knowing now that the raid, in spite of its many casualties, had not been in vain after all.

It was late evening when Rosemary visited me again. Although she was still in uniform, she was obviously made up for going out, and I thought she looked more beautiful than ever. I had been dozing, but I woke up as soon as the door opened.

'Hello, Colin,' she said softly, brushing my cheek with the back of her hand. 'Susan tells me that you're improving. I'm sorry I can't stay because I'm off out dancing. My date has some transport, so I persuaded him to bring me here first. I know that you're not supposed to have this, but it might help.'

She handed over half a bottle of whisky which I immediately secreted in my bedside locker. Scotch was as scarce as gold, so I didn't ask where she had obtained it, but I was in no doubt that it had been a present from one of her many boyfriends. Although I felt a twinge of jealousy at the thought of her going out with other men, I was secretly elated that she should take the trouble to visit me on a date.

I did not see the admiral again, but Rosemary kept popping in from time to time, and kept me up to date with the news. On one of these occasions she brought me a letter from Sir George, which thanked me for my report on the raid, and informed me that my prisoner had turned out to be an even bigger prize than they had at first thought. I don't know how they managed it, but they extracted a great deal of top secret material from him before handing him over to the Polish Army. It did not need much imagination to know what his fate would be.

The admiral also confirmed that he had forwarded my recommendation for Sergeant McKinley to receive the Military Medal. What I did not know until later was that he had made his own recommendation for me to be awarded the D.S.O.

By the time I had been in hospital for three weeks, I was beginning to feel restless, and agitated to be discharged, although I was well aware that I was not fit enough to return to active duty. The surgeon in charge of my case took pity on me, and suggested that I have four weeks' convalescent leave, to be followed by another medical examination at the end of that time. What I wanted was some country air, good food and long walks to exercise my leg muscles, but this posed a bit of a problem since I had no idea where to go.

As usual it was Rosemary who came to my rescue. She recommended a small pub which had a few guest rooms in the Cotswold village of Bourton-on-the-Water. She and her family sometimes used to have holidays there when she was at school, and I thought it sounded an ideal solution. I left it to her to fix up, which she did with her usual efficiency, and so in time I found myself being looked after by the motherly Mrs Collins.

I was so unfamiliar with the Cotswold district that I had to look at a map to discover where it was, and the little village of Bourton-on-the-Water came as a revelation to me, since I had never done much travelling in England. The thatched roofs of the cottages, all built in Cotswold stone produced an atmosphere of peace and tranquillity, and with the clear water of the River Windrush running among them, criss-crossed by low bridges, it added a picturesque dimension in addition. There were few people to be seen about during the day, some locals, farmers and their families came to shop from the surrounding district, and several airmen from the nearby R.A.F. station mostly at weekends.

The pub was situated beside the stream which murmured outside my bedroom window, and as I lay in bed on these warm September nights, it was the only sound I could hear. Mrs Collins, the landlady, who ran the pub together with her self-effacing, retired husband, went out of her way to make sure that I had the best of everything. I was fed on anything which the countryside could provide — rabbits, chickens, pork in many guises, eggs and home baking all appeared as if by magic on the table, and when beer and spirits were in short supply, the local cider made an adequate substitute until I began to acquire quite a taste for it.

It did not take long for Mrs Collins to worm out of me what I did, and why I was there. Soon most of the villagers knew me by sight, and were always prepared to stop and have a chat. Even though I wore civilian clothes, the word must have got about because they all addressed me as Captain Marshall. The pub boasted a large library, most of the books having been left by past visitors, so when I wasn't out walking I was either reading, or chatting with the regulars in the friendly bar. Invariably we discussed the war and all its aspects, but it was hard to think about any conflict in this peaceful corner of England.

After I had been there for a couple of weeks, my health showed a big improvement, and I was able to walk for several miles without discomfort. I made a point of exploring some of the neighbouring villages on foot, and found them all to be different, but equally charming. I was growing accustomed to this kind of life, and I would be sorry when my leave came to an end.

One evening after dinner, when there was no one else in the bar, Mrs Collins asked me how well I knew Rosemary Stuart.

I replied that Rosemary was secretary to my boss, and that although I lived in the same building as her, I was away a lot and did not see her all that often.

'You knew it was she who arranged for me to come here,' I told her. 'I understand that her family used to visit you before the war.'

'Aye, that's true, but it's a good few years since she was here with them. She must have been about eighteen the last time I saw her, and a right bonny lass she was too. Is she still as pretty as she used to be?'

'No, I wouldn't describe her as pretty, Mrs Collins — she's beautiful.'

'Oh, aye!' was all she said by way of reply, looking at me quizzically. A few days later she made a request just as I was finishing my breakfast.

'Oh, Captain Marshall, if you're not busy this afternoon, I wonder if you could do me a favour?'

'Yes, of course. Anything I can.'

'I wonder if you could meet the bus from Cirencester. I'm expecting another guest, and I would be grateful if you could help to carry her luggage. Joe isn't up to it, I'm afraid. It's one of his off days. I'll be putting her in the room next to yours.'

Two people, a man and a woman, alighted from the bus when it stopped up on the main street. I stared open-mouthed at the female passenger as she came towards me smiling happily. It was Rosemary, looking ravishing in civilian clothes.

'Surprised to see me, Colin? I hope it's a nice surprise?'

'What are you doing here?' I stammered.

'Well, I sometimes do get leave too, you know, so why shouldn't I come here? It's years since my last visit.'

'Yes, I know. You were eighteen at the time.'

'Oh, so you've been talking about me, have you?' she bantered, but her eyes were shining.

'Only in the nicest possible way,' I replied, having recovered my equilibrium.

Later she brought me up to date with the news. She told me that Susan's husband had made such a good recovery that he had unexpectedly been discharged from hospital. Susan felt it was her duty to look after him, and so they were back together once more, trying to patch up the marriage.

'You'll miss her,' I said. 'Tell me, what was the admiral's reaction when he knew you were coming here?'

'Of course, you don't know! Poor Sir George is no longer in charge. They tried to foist some of the blame on to him regarding the Dieppe fiasco, but now he's got cancer. They operated on him last week, but apparently it's hopeless. He doesn't seem to want to live any more. He is a dear man, and has been like a father to me for the past year. He thought the world of you too, Colin. He told me more than once that you were a very special kind of man.'

'So, who's in charge now?'

'Can't you guess? Our beloved Second-in-Command, James Willoughby-Brook, now promoted to Rear Admiral, no less. I couldn't bear the thought of working for him, so I asked for a posting.'

'Where are they sending you, Rosemary?'

'East Coast Defences. I'll be stationed at Felixstowe.'

I was conscious of a sinking feeling that she was moving away from me, but the disappointment was offset by the thought that I would have Rosemary all to myself for six whole days, and I was determined to make the most of them.

'There are your orders too, Colin. They were to have been posted, but I opted to deliver them by hand.'

She handed over a heavily-sealed buff envelope, which I immediately tossed to one side.

'I don't want to know anything before my leave is up,' I told her emphatically. 'I don't suppose for a moment that our newly-appointed director will want to be encumbered by me, so I hope they have sent me somewhere far away from him.'

'I don't blame you, but how do you know that your new posting will be any better?'

'Of course, I forgot, you know where it is I'm going. Anyway, don't tell me. I don't want to know yet.'

'Fair enough. So what do we do here?'

'Well, I hope you've brought your walking shoes,' I told her. 'There isn't much else to do except walk.'

'Oh, that's a pity. Isn't it possible to borrow bicycles from someone?'

I wondered why I had never thought of that, but for the rest of the afternoon we wandered round the village. Although the weather was warm and sunny, the autumn tints were just beginning to show, giving an added splash of colour. In spite of the fact that she was casually dressed, Rosemary managed to turn a few heads as we strolled, and I felt very proud to be with her.

'Tell me, do you know everybody around here?' she asked. I could see that she was impressed by the beauty of the place, and the friendliness of the local people.

'I think I've spoken to most of them during the past few

weeks,' I replied. 'I've had no one else to talk to.'

Later that evening, when we went downstairs through the bar to the dining-room, the regulars smiled at us, accompanied by a good deal of nudging and winking, but I for one didn't care. Mrs Collins went out of her way to impress Rosemary with her culinary skills, and produced a feast that any five-star hotel would have been proud to serve.

After dinner we talked, and Rosemary encouraged me to tell her about my past life, although she must have already known a bit about me from my records. I was frank about my love for Claudette, and she seemed to understand when I tried to convey the fact that that part of my life seemed to be no longer real. In turn, I tried to draw her out about her own past, but she seemed somewhat reticent to talk about it. I realised that in fact I knew very little about her, but I didn't press the matter.

I was conscious of mixed emotions when I climbed into bed that night knowing that Rosemary was less than a couple of feet away on the other side of the wall. Before falling asleep I wondered how many of her numerous boyfriends had managed to bed her, and if her sexual performance resembled the impression she made on every red-blooded male with whom she came in contact. The question which excited me was, could I possibly be the next? It was more than I dared hope.

After a restless night, I was awakened by the sun streaming through my window. I rose and opened it, to find Rosemary already outside down below watching the trout in the river. She was dressed in slacks and a jumper which accentuated her shapely figure, and I wished that I had had a camera with me. The aroma of frying bacon filled the air, and I realised that I was hungry again. Rosemary seemed to sense that I was watching her. She looked up, smiled and waved when she saw me.

'Come on, lazybones!' she called. 'The day is half over, and Mrs Collins is waiting to feed us.'

Ten minutes later I joined her in the dining-room to be confronted by a plateful of bacon, sausage and eggs.

'Gosh, I'm ravenous,' she said, between mouthfuls. 'If this is a sample of the food, I'm going to be as fat as butter by the end of the week.'

'Lots of exercise will burn it off,' I reminded her, and she curled up her nose at the idea.

We managed to borrow a couple of bicycles, and visited Upper and Lower Slaughter, stopping to lunch on sandwiches and cider at Stow-on-the-Wold. All day Rosemary was full of inconsequential chatter, and I had the impression that she was doing her best to keep the conversation away from any personal or serious matters, but gradually as the day wore on, she became visibly more relaxed in my company. To begin with she had made a point of avoiding any physical contact, but later I noticed that she sometimes put her hand on my arm when she saw something which spontaneously delighted her.

So that first day set the tone for the days which were to follow, and she made a delightful companion. She was enthusiastic about all the places I took her, and for my part it was a delight to share the experience with someone who appreciated it. Each day we went to somewhere new, and by evening we were tired but happy.

On the fourth day our mood changed. The rain was pouring down, and we were both content to settle down to read. At one point Rosemary put her book down, and I considered that the time was now ripe to broach the subject which up to then we had both been avoiding.

'Tell me, Rosemary, why did you come here?' I asked.

She looked out of the window without replying for such a long time that I thought she had resented the question, and had taken umbrage. I waited for the explosion, but then she turned to look at me with a serious expression.

'The alternative was for me to go to London and live it up, or to come here. I decided on this place because I wanted to be with you, Colin.'

I was about to speak, but she held up her hand.

'I know that you don't want any emotional ties, and for a long time I have felt the same way. For these past few days I've been trying desperately to keep our relationship on a platonic level, but I'm finding it increasingly difficult. I know you have wondered why I've been acting funny when we've been together, so now you know.'

'But, Rosemary, why me? You have lots of boyfriends, and some of them are very dishy. I'm sure you would have had no trouble in finding someone to take you somewhere nice. Most men would jump at the opportunity.'

'Up to now, that's been one of my difficulties. I have too many boyfriends. Maybe I give men the wrong impression, because I assure you I'm not a tease, but I like a good time. Most of the ones I've been out with are interested in only one thing, and when they find that I don't come across, they drop me like a red-hot brick. Here I am at twenty-six, not unattractive, but would you believe, Colin, I'm still a virgin? I'm determined not to sell myself cheap — I've seen too much of that in the WRENS. I know that you're not the sort of man to take advantage of a girl, Colin, and I've enjoyed these past few days with you more than I can say.'

I was astounded by the revelation she had just made, but it went a long way to explaining her attitude towards me.

'Oh, hang on, Rosemary! I'm no saint, you know,' I replied. 'I like women as much as the next fellow, but I've never considered you to be a trollope. In fact, up to a few weeks ago, I didn't think you even liked me. I've enjoyed having you here with me too.'

'We still have a couple of days together. That is, if you want me to stay?'

'Please don't run out on me now. I couldn't bear to go on living here without you. You're not really thinking of leaving, are you?'

'No, but let's get one thing straight, Colin. If either one of us feels that the emotional strain is too great, we'll be free to tell the other, and depart if necessary.'

'Agreed!' I said as we shook hands. Her touch was soft, and her hand cool, and not for the first time I felt my heart accelerating. I now doubted my ability to keep my side of the bargain, but I knew that I would have to if we were to remain on friendly terms. I considered the prospect of seducing her, but put the idea firmly to the back of my mind. If there was to be any change in our relationship, I was determined that the advances would come from her.

It seemed like no time at all before our last whole day together dawned. By this time I had fallen hopelessly in love with Rosemary, and I suspected that she felt the same way about me, although neither of us had raised the subject again. We hardly spoke at breakfast, and during the morning our conversation was stilted and unnatural, as if neither of us was sure what to say without upsetting the other. I wanted to tell her how I felt, but that was not part of the bargain.

That afternoon, I took myself off for a final walk round the village. Meanwhile, Rosemary complained of a headache, and went to lie down.

On returning to the inn, I went straight upstairs to ask if she wanted a cup of tea. When I reached the bedroom door, I could hear an unusual sound coming from within. I knocked gently, but, receiving no reply, I walked in to find her lying on the bed face down. Her eyes were red, and the tears running down her cheeks had streaked her make-up.

'Rosemary, whatever is the matter,' I asked gently.

'Nothing! Go away!' she replied vehemently.

'Is it something I've done, or said?' I persisted.

'No!' she snapped. 'Just go away, and leave me alone!'

She was obviously in no mood to discuss the matter rationally, and so I had no alternative but to comply with her request. I went to my room and sat staring out of the window, thinking that I would never understand women for as long as I lived. I don't know how long I sat there, but it was almost dark when someone came into the room. I turned to find Rosemary standing there, looking calm and collected. She had reapplied her make-up, but her eyes were still red. I wanted to take her in my arms and assure her that everything was all right, but before I could rise from my seat she held up a hand.

'I'm sorry about that little display of temperament a short while ago, Colin.' Her voice was trembling a little. 'It wasn't fair of me to inflict my misery on you. All day I've thought of nothing else except that we won't be seeing each other again for a long time, and I'm afraid I let it get on top of me. You see, I know where you are being posted.'

My orders! I had forgotten all about them, but now the time had arrived for me to discover what the future held. I unlocked my suitcase, took out the envelope and weighed it in my hand.

'I wonder what would happen if I threw this away? We could disappear, and we wouldn't have to be parted.'

'It's a nice idea, Colin, but they would soon catch up

with us, and we would be prevented from meeting again until we were both old and grey. You'd better open it.'

The single sheet of paper was dated ten days before, and was terse and to the point.

> Captain C.S. Marshall, Royal Marine Commandos, will present himself to Major J.M. Patterson, R.A.M.C., at Room 162, Mill Hill Hospital, London, for assessment of medical fitness, on 3rd October 1941. (That was two days from now).
>
> Thereafter he will report immediately to Sandford Camp, Wareham, Dorset, where he will place himself under the command of Colonel A. Lautrys, of the Free French Forces stationed there.
>
> A travel warrant, subsistence allowance and letters of introduction are hereby enclosed.
> Signed J. Willoughby-Brook
> Rear Admiral
> Combined Operations
> (Southern Command)

Well, I knew now. I suppose it could have been worse, especially if they had sent me to the North of Scotland, but it was bad enough not knowing what was expected of me, or what I was letting myself in for. The irony was that I now no longer had the same burning desire to avenge the death of my family. Because of Rosemary, I now desperately wanted to live, nor did I wish to end up a chronic invalid, destined to remain in hospital for the rest of my life. Would this be fair to her? Up to then, such an idea had never entered my mind.

She sat on the floor with her legs curled up underneath her, leaning against me with her head in my lap, and I wondered is she had any idea what I was thinking. We stayed there quietly without moving or speaking for a long time, until I suddenly realised it was dark outside.

'Rosemary, it's time to go downstairs,' I said, breaking the silence.

'I couldn't face it,' she replied. 'The food would choke me. You go and leave me, Colin.'

'Well, I suspect that Mrs Collins has spent all the afternoon preparing something special for our last evening. We can't disappoint her.'

'Yes, all right. I'll make an effort. You go and have a drink at the bar, and I'll be down shortly.'

By the time I had bought a round for the regular customers who had come to wish us good luck, Rosemary came to join us. She had changed into a pre-war model dress which still fitted her to perfection, and she stopped all conversation in the room as soon as she appeared. She had made a great effort to repair the ravages of her crying, and my heart gave a great leap when I saw her, especially when she came straight over to me and put her arm through mine.

While Mrs Collins fussed around us, we both made a valiant effort to do justice to the excellent meal, but our hearts were not in it, even after her husband opened a bottle of champagne with the compliments of the house.

'It's been in the cellar for a long time,' he told us. 'We don't get much call for it here, so we would rather it was used for a good cause.'

Later, we sat in the sitting-room making desultory conversation until closing-time, when we slowly climbed the narrow, creaking, wooden stairs. On the landing she turned to face me, and, standing very close, she put her arms around my neck. We kissed passionately for the first time, holding nothing back. Her lips were warm, soft and yielding, and I could feel the contours of her shapely body pressed close against mine.

'Please, don't leave me, Colin,' she whispered. 'I couldn't bear to spend the rest of the night without you.'

'I want you to be absolutely sure about this, Rosemary. Have you considered the consequences?'

'Yes, I've thought about it for days, and have still come to the same answer.'

By the dim light of the small bedside lamp, I watched fascinated as she undressed slowly, her attitude reflecting a mixture of natural modesty on the one hand, and ardour on the other. At last, when she had completely uncovered her perfect figure with its firm breasts and flat, muscular abdomen, I was conscious of my heart pounding and a dryness in my mouth. I felt both privileged and humble, knowing that I was the first man she had given herself to.

As she reached up to pull me down on top of her, she whispered, 'Love me, Colin, but please be gentle with me.'

Rosemary was both apprehensive and tired, and since it was the first time, she did not enjoy it to the full. For the rest of the night we lay locked together on the narrow, single bed, each acutely aware of the other's presence. I woke up at intervals to run my hand over her velvet skin, while she, in turn, would grunt in her sleep and snuggle closer to me. Dawn was breaking when we made love for the second time, but on this occasion she was fully relaxed, and was an eager, responsive and loving partner, who took part with obvious enjoyment.

'So that's what I've been missing for all these years,' she said, as we lit cigarettes. 'Still, I'm glad I waited for you, my love.'

We talked, with myself sitting upright leaning against the bed-head, while Rosemary held on to my arm tightly and rested her head against my shoulder. Eventually, I asked her the one question which had been puzzling me.

'Tell me, darling, why me?' I asked. 'Surely there must have been other fellows who fitted the bill better. Don't forget, I've already been married.'

'I don't think I can answer that, Colin, dear. There's no logic when it comes to a woman's emotions. It was less than a year ago when you came into the office and waited for the admiral to see you. I thought you looked terrible, and it was only later that I learned what you had been through. I don't know what it was, but even then there was something about you which attracted me to you, but of course you didn't know that. Maybe it was because you were like a little boy who was lost, but since coming to know you, Colin, the one thing in your character I like most is that you never pretend to be something you aren't. You've no idea some of the lines men try to impress me with. When you came to live in the flat below us, I tried to keep out of your way because I didn't want to be tied to any one person, but when the opportunity of this leave came up, Susan encouraged me to take it, so here I am. She has always said you were the one for me, and she's right. I'm glad I came, and I'm not sorry for giving myself to you. I only hope my feelings are not one-sided, but somehow I don't think so.'

'You know jolly well that I'm hopelessly head over heels in love with you, Rosemary. There's nothing I'd like better than for us to marry, but the war will almost certainly go on for years yet, and I don't want you to be a war widow, or to end up having you look after me for the rest of my life as a cripple.'

'I don't want that to happen either, but I couldn't bear to be without you now. Even if we're apart, we will keep in touch, won't we?'

'Of course, darling. It'll take nothing short of an earthquake to keep me away from you, but you know as well as I do that I may not be able to tell you where I am, and what I'm doing.'

'Yes, and that will be the hardest part of all, but promise me that you won't try to be a hero, Colin. Don't stick you're neck out unless you have to. I want you to stay in one piece.'

'I'll certainly do my best, but I'm committed to a dangerous job, I'm afraid. I didn't care before, but now I have every reason for staying alive, so I'll promise to keep my head down whenever possible.'

We went down to our last breakfast, both of us dressed in uniform for the first time since we arrived.

'Ee, but you do look a grand pair,' Mrs Collins enthused, looking at us with undisguised admiration. 'It fair makes me want to cry when I see two fine young people like yourselves having to be separated. Now, promise me you'll both come back and see us again, won't you?'

'I have an idea, Mrs Collins,' I told her. 'If it's at all possible, we'll come back a year from now — for an anniversary reunion, so could we ask you to keep our rooms for us then?'

'I'll do better than that, Captain Marshall,' she said in a confidential manner with a twinkle in her eye. 'I'll reserve my best double room for you. I'm sure you will prefer that, won't you? It's not very comfortable for two in a single bed, is it?'

I happened to glance at Rosemary who had turned puce. Mrs Collins put a hand on her arm. 'Don't worry about it, my dear. I was young, too, once upon a time.'

We thanked her for all her kindness to us both, before taking the bus to Cirencester where we caught the train for London. Although it was packed we were lucky enough to find two seats together, but we didn't speak much. Just by holding hands and the occasional look between us, we managed to convey the hurt each of us felt at the prospect of our imminent separation.

I accompanied Rosemary to Liverpool Street Station where she caught the train to Felixstowe, and as I watched it draw out of the platform I was conscious that every turn of the wheel was taking her further away from me. It took all of my self control not to run after it. I also knew that in a couple of days I too would be travelling in the opposite direction, thus doubling the distance between us.

OAKFIELD REST HOME

The proprietress of the home entered the room with a mug of tea which she set down beside the girl, then crossed over to the bed to look at the old man. The clock on the mantelpiece showed that it was a quarter to four.

'Mr Marshall is still alive, I see, but his pulse is much weaker. Are you managing to stay awake, Penny?'

'Oh, yes, Mrs Mellor. I found this manuscript on the desk, and I'm afraid I've been reading it. I hope that it's all right?'

'That's what he's been busy writing for the past five years. You're very lucky. He would never allow anyone to go anywhere near it, so you're the first person to have looked at it. Is it interesting?'

'Yes, very. It's all about the Second World War, and all the things he's supposed to have done. It's awfully exciting, and it reads like a novel, but I can't imagine Old Mad Marshall having done all these things. He certainly hasn't struck me as having been the heroic type.'

'The longer you work here, Penny, the more you'll come to realise that if we're spared, then old age changes us all. When you see the photographs of some of the old women taken when they were young, then you realise that many of them were very beautiful at one time, and you may find it hard to believe that it was the same person.'

'Yes, I've seen some of them already.'

'Many of our residents have a story to tell, but the trouble is that either they don't know how to tell it properly, or they have forgotten. Mr Marshall has always claimed that his memory was excellent, so I suppose there may be some truth in what he's written.'

'Are you going back to bed, Mrs Mellor?'

'Yes, dear. I will have a busy day later, but you'll have the day off, so you can catch up on your sleep then. Call me if there's any change, Penny.'

When the older woman had gone, the girl sipped her tea while looking down at the dying figure in the bed. In spite of what Mrs Mellor had told her, she just could not believe that this unpleasant old man was even remotely similar to the romantic hero who was depicted in the manuscript. Anyway, it made a good story, and in spite of her doubts, she settled down eagerly once more to continue her reading.

9

Free French

After leaving Rosemary at Liverpool Street Station, I had gone on to keep my appointment with Major Patterson at Mill Hill Hospital. There I was subjected to an extensive medical examination which I found to be exhausting as it lasted for more than a couple of hours. Apparently he was satisfied with my progress, but in his opinion I was still not up to the standard required for a member of the Royal Marine Commandos. For the meantime I was advised to remain in an administrative post for a further three months, and I was urged to undertake a series of graduated exercises which he prescribed for me. The prospect of a desk job for several months suited me very well, but when I arrived at my posting I was overcome by a black depression.

Colonel Lautrys turned out to be the exact antithesis of what I had expected. I had imagined him to be fortyish, tall, with an immaculate uniform and beautiful manners, but instead I was confronted by a balding, middle-aged man, small and overweight, who's uniform looked as if it had been made for someone else. He had no manners, and spoke his mind in a blunt, no-nonsense fashion, but he exhibited an apparently insatiable appetite for work, and he expected everyone else who was connected with him to do the same. Perhaps his least endearing quality was that he was prepared to ride rough-shod over everyone and anyone in order to achieve what he wanted, and would take advice from no one in the process. I was later informed that he had been a successful lawyer before joining the Army, in the city of Rouen, where his wife still lived.

We conversed in rapid French while he grilled me on my background, my previous war experience, and whether or not I was prepared to put myself under his command. This last condition had been laid down apparently as a result of the British officer before me who had resented having to take orders from a Frenchman. I assured him that I had no such hang-ups, and he grudgingly accepted me to work with him on a trial basis, but at this stage I had no idea what my duties would be.

Although the camp was surrounded by unspoilt countryside, I reckoned that I would not have much opportunity to appreciate the beauty of the landscape. The best thing about the post was the accommodation which was a small cottage adjacent to a larger house, both of which had obviously formed part of a country estate.

I had imagined that my duties would be something of a sinecure, consisting of some liaison work and acting as interpreter between the Free French Forces and the British. I then received a rude awakening when the true nature of my role was explained to me.

I had been vaguely aware that a traffic had existed whereby the French Resistance was being supplied with arms and ammunition, and anything else they might need, but it was not always possible to drop these by parachute. so there was scope for the use of small naval craft and submarines, both of which were capable of going close inshore, and delivering large quantities of supplies at one time. This was still feasible because the total fortification of the French coast was by no means complete, and there were as yet stretches of coastline with a minimum of protection. It was part of my duty to co-ordinate the delivery of these supplies to the Royal Navy at various ports for onward transfer.

Colonel Lautrys was quite uncomprising in his efforts to make sure the service ran smoothly, and he expected the same dedication from his staff. A single mistake he could forgive, provided that it was not repeated, but negligence he regarded as a personal affront, and at the slightest hint of excessive red tape or bureaucracy, he was instantly transformed into a gesticulating, foul-mouthed moron, who looked as if he would go beserk on the spot. But when he was planning future operations in the quiet of his office, he was decisive and cool-headed, prepared to consider every detail far into the night so that nothing was left to chance. Such was the volatile and almost schizophrenic nature of my new commanding officer, and I was soon left in no doubt that my predecessor could not, or would not, measure up to his high standards.

After a few days, I received my first letter from Rosemary. Apparently the office of the Admiral Commanding East Coast Defences was not a happy place, and she found the work to be both boring and unrewarding. The town of Felixstowe itself did not impress her; it was full of sailors wherever one went, but none of them seemed to stay long, consequently it was not easy to make friends. She was living in a hostel with a dozen other WREN officers, but since they were all on different shifts, it was difficult to get to know them either. Rosemary ended this depressing epistle with her admission that she was missing me more than she had thought possible.

It upset me to think that she was unhappy, and I sat down immediately to reply in a light vein, hoping that it might help to cheer her up. It was difficult to sound elated when I felt anything but, being equally depressed about my own situation.

I was able to see something of the Dorset countryside when my duties took me to other towns occasionally, Poole, Weymouth and Burton Bradstock were all on my rounds, but after a time I began to go further afield to Southampton, and even Plymouth. I looked forward to these occasions when I was on my own without the colonel breathing down my neck.

The other French officers tried their best to be friendly, but I had very little in common with any of them. I even managed to introduce some of them to the institution of the English pub, but they could never acquire a taste for the local beer. As for Colonel Lautrys, he remained both aloof and unapproachable when he was off duty.

Winter was approaching, and we were ordered to plan one more big operation before the weather deteriorated too much. Everything was still in the planning stage, and no details had been thrashed out when the French wanted a couple of M.G.B.s standing by for instant use as soon as everything had been arranged, and the weather was right. It was left up to me to persuade the Navy to comply with the request, but naturally they were reluctant to take two of their boats out of active service, and to remain on stand-by for some unspecified purpose. Much of my time was devoted to obtaining such an agreement, and every day without fail, the colonel asked for a report on the state of the negotiations, so it was necessary to have a good reason for any lack of progress.

An impasse developed, which resulted in a meeting between Colonel Lautrys and a Commodore from the War Office. I was asked to act as interpreter, but when the colonel began to accuse the British of being obstructive and abusive, I was sure that an international incident would ensue. I therefore began to put my own interpretaion on some of the exchanges, thus allowing them both time to simmer down, and eventually a compromise was reached.

Following this incident, Colonel Lautrys sent for me, and proceeded to give me what I reckoned was an undeserved dressing-down for my intervention. It was then that I discovered he knew more English than he had previously admitted. When I pointed out that it was only because of my self-imposed role of mediator that the matter had been resolved, he told me in no uncertain manner that in future when I was asked to act as interpreter for him, I was expected to do so word for word, and no more. When he went on to accuse me of usurping his position, I thought that the time had come for some plain speaking, whether he liked it or not.

'With all due respect, sir,' I said quietly; it was all I could do not to shout at him. 'If it had not been for my intervention, you would have got nowhere. As it is, you may not have got everything you wanted, but something is better than nothing at all. You will have to learn how to approach the British before you are able to put your point across.'

'Don't you dare lecture me, Marshall,' he snapped. 'This is my unit, and it's run my way. I do all the planning, and I take all the responsibility. your job is to assist me by giving me whatever help I require. If you do as you are told and no more, that's all I expect from you, so don't you forget it.'

I wondered how a man who was so brilliant an organiser could be so inept at handling people. I had no intention of allowing myself to be trampled on, and I'm afraid I lost my temper.

'As a British officer, I am expected to think for myself sometimes,' I told him forcefully, while thumping the desk at the same time. 'In our Army, it's called initiative. I am not expected to follow every order blindly like a puppet, more expecially when these orders are impossible to carry out. If you are so dissatisfied with my performance, then I will make a formal request to be transferred just as soon as you can find a replacement — sir.'

For a moment I thought that I had gone too far, and we glared at each other before his eyes dropped, and I was perfunctorily dismissed. Obviously some of what I had said must have gone home, because thereafter our relationship underwent a marked improvement, and although it must have almost choked him, he even went so far as to ask my advice on several occasions. I think he was acutely aware of the fact that I had already seen active service on the other side, whereas he was desk-bound, and it gave him a feeling of having missed out.

Our assignment involving the two M.G.Bs was scheduled to take place towards the end of October, but with only forty-eight hours to go, the true purpose of our mission was released to us. Apparently a number of R.A.F. aeroplane crews who had been shot down over France, together with a number of British soldiers who had been in hiding since the 1940 offensive, had been handed down the line by the Underground. Singly and in pairs they had now been gathered into one group, and it was proposed to use our organisation to lift them from a deserted part of the coast on the Cherbourg Peninsula.

Before Rosemary and I parted, we had devised a crude code, so that I could let her know if I was to be involved in any missions. Although we did not expect our letters to be intercepted or censored, we were taking no chances. Briefly, what it amounted to was that if a raid was imminent in which I was involved, I wrote that Aunt Polly was ill, but we hoped that she would be better soon. This meant that the proposed mission was a short one, and I would let her know when Aunt Polly had recovered.

The low cloud base made the night as black as pitch when we moved away from our moorings in Weymouth harbour, so dark that the long stretch of Portland Bill was invisible on our starboard quarter. As soon as we were out into open water, the throttles were fully opened, and the little warships were soon skimming along at full speed. However, the further we ventured out to sea, the greater was the swell, which was enough to cause the boats to bounce from one wave to the next, forcing me to hang on for dear life. After three hours of this pounding, our apprehension at nearing the French coast was mixed with relief as our little craft was throttled down. I had been very close to being sea-sick, but managed to control it with difficulty. Some of the crew were not so lucky, and I admired their spirit for going out night after night knowing that they would be subjected to this treatment.

Our passage led through some rocks close in-shore through which it was possible to navigate, except at low tide. The boat was barely making steering-way, when a black object appeared above the surface close to our starboard bow.

'Rock ahead, green, forty-five degrees, twenty yards,' the lookout in the bows reported.

I was standing immediately below the little bridge, and could see the object clearly as we drifted past. Its top was smooth and rounded, and I was just beginning to wonder if it was a . . .

Suddenly the skipper's shout confirmed my fears. 'It's not a rock, it's a mine!'

I already knew that this channel was normally free of mines, because it was used extensively by local fishermen, so this one must have broken loose from its mooring and had been washed inshore. How it had managed to get here without hitting anything was a mystery.

A signal was flashed to the other M.G.B. which was following, to warn them of the danger, but before the message was completed, the night was ripped by a massive explosion. The blast nearly knocked me off my feet, and as I looked astern, a ball of fire lit up the darkness to be followed a few seconds later by a hail of debris which rained down on to our deck.

The skipper immediately put the vessel into reverse in order to pick up survivors, but after a search lasting for about twenty minutes, the only person we pulled from the water was so badly burned that he was unrecognisable, and he died a few minutes later.

The captain called to me to join him on the bridge, where I found him grim-faced and despondent.

'We're now running late,' he said, 'and if we're held up inshore the tide will drop making it impossible to navigate the passage out of here. If we're stranded we'll be captured for sure, and I have no intention of allowing that to happen. Since we've already lost half our force, I recommend aborting the mission. Besides, the Germans will soon be along to investigate the cause of the explosion.'

'Don't you think it's just possible that they might think it's one of their mines which has broken loose and been washed on to the rocks?' I argued. 'The people on shore are relying on us. We can't let them down now. How long have we got?'

'Not more than half an hour, and that's cutting it fine.'

'Then let's give them that half-hour. It's the least we can do now that we're so close.'

He agreed, and the vessel proceeded slowly along the passage until a signal was flashed from the shore indicating that we had arrived at the rendezvous. At the same time, not five miles away, we could see the lights of an approaching convoy, and we reckoned that it would be no more than ten minutes before they were here. The skipper caught my eye, and I nodded. There was no way we could take anyone off in time, as we had to make a fast getaway.

While the gunboat navigated its return through the narrow channel, I watched with mounting frustration while the convoy closed on the place where our men were hidden. There was no way we could have warned them of the impending danger, and as we reached open water I looked back to see flashes of gunfire which indicated that they were being rounded up.

I arrived back at the camp exhausted both mentally and physically, but before turning in I wrote an account of the mission while it was still fresh in my mind, and posted a short letter to Rosemary. It was only after I had had a long sleep that the colonel asked me to report to his office.

'I've read this document several times, Marshall, but I just cannot believe what you have written. Tell me it isn't true, and that you have a better explanation than the one you have given here.'

I had expected him to be displeased, but his sarcastic opening comment got under my skin.

'It happened exactly as I have indicated, sir. The failure to reach the rendezvous was due entirely to a rogue mine which blew up the other M.G.B. The skipper of our boat was reluctant to proceed because of the risk of being stranded, and the arrival of the Germans.'

'Yes, yes, I'm aware of all that, but it was only after you had wasted valuable time trying to pick up survivors, of which there were none. If you had gone straight in, you would have been able to complete the job and be away before either the Germans arrived, or the tide went out.'

I was aghast at his attitude, and it must have showed in my face. 'Are you seriously suggesting that we ought not to have stopped to pick up survivors?'

'Look at it this way, Marshall. We lost a valuable boat plus eight men, and all for nothing, in addition to the men on the beach, who by now have undoubtedly been captured. A lot of people risked their lives to get that party assembled, again all for nothing. If you had persuaded the captain of the M.G.B. to go straight in, we might at least have made the pick-up and we would have had something to show for the loss.'

'May I remind you, sir, that I was not in command of the boat. It was the skipper's decision.'

'Yes, but you were in charge of the operation. you could have ordered him not to waste time.'

'No one with an ounce of humanity would have left without looking for survivors, sir.'

His eyes bored into mine across the desk. 'Listen to me, Marshall! We're not in this business for humanitarian purposes. Ours is not a humane profession. It's a bloody awful job, and there's no place in it for anyone with a conscience. Why do you think I don't socialise in the evenings? I'll tell you why! It's because I get drunk. If I didn't I would never sleep. Do you honestly think I like doing what I do? Don't lecture me on the subject of humanity.'

I was still smarting from his remarks, so I was in no mood to continue the argument. It was only later, when I had had time to think about it, that I could see the situation from his point of view.

'Will that be all, sir?' I asked icily.

He appeared to relax. 'Er, no. As a matter of fact, there is something else.' He picked up a piece of paper from his desk and handed it to me. 'This message from Area Command arrived for you yesterday. Your D.S.O. has been confirmed. Congratulations! You must have done something to earn it,' he added, smiling sardonically.

I saluted, and walked to the door.

'By the way, Colin,' he called after me. 'I'm glad that Aunt Polly has now recovered.'

The colonel actually chuckled, and I knew then that my letter must have been censored. I resolved not to post any more to Rosemary within the confines of the camp, since I did not want him reading about my innermost thoughts and emotions. It was not for several minutes, that I realised he had called me by my Christian name.

Shortly after this I was recalled to London for a further medical assessment, and on this occasion I was pronounced fit for active service. I was in two minds about this, as I had become accustomed to office work, and apart from the one mission, I was not asked to put my life on the line. It was necessary for me to spend the night in London, and I had telephoned Rosemary to come and join me, but she was unable to at short notice. It was then that we both arranged to apply for leave over Christmas, and spend it together in London.

Fortunately both of our requests were granted, and it seemed as if the days dragged slowly until then.

My only project during this time was to make a feasibility

study of using submarines to send supplies and agents through the fishing fleets which plied their trade most nights off the coast of Brittany. A simple meeting between a submarine and a trawler was not easy to arrange, however, because the Germans were only too aware of the vulnerability of French boats at sea, especially on dark nights, consequently they made certain provisions to maintain security. I discovered that they always sailed in a fleet, and every trawler was obliged to remain within sight and hailing distance of the others at all times. If any inadvertently strayed away from the fleet, they were promptly rounded up by a couple of E-boats which patrolled around the periphery. In addition, a guard was placed on board one or two trawlers on a random basis, so that the skipper did not know if he was to have a German for company beforehand.

The planners had reckoned that the safest place to make an exchange would be in the middle of the fishing-fleet, or alternatively to draw off one of the E-boats by a false alarm, thus leaving a gap in the defences. Apart from the possibility of getting entangled in the nets, one of the main difficulties was the guard on board the trawlers, who were equipped with flares to alert the patrolling E-boats if there was any trouble. All the fishing-vessels were clearly numbered by white figures on black hulls, which made each boat instantly identifiable.

At one stage, it was suggested that I accompany one of our submarines to the Brittany coast, to see at first hand if the plan would work. I did not relish this prospect, and I was very relieved when the whole idea was scrapped as being unworkable, because there was too much left to chance. I was pleased to discover that for once Colonel Lautrys agreed with my conclusions. It had meant a lot of work on my part, but I was happy doing it, since it helped to take my mind off the approaching Christmas.

The only other event of note happened at the beginning of December, when the Japanese raided Pearl Harbour, thus bringing America into the war.

Ever since the abortive mission on the Cherbourg peninsula, I had been subjected to the occasional nightmares. The scene was always the same. I was on an M.G.B.

which was floating without power through a minefield, until it blew up in a sheet of flame. My blackened body was thrown into the water where I slowly sank, unable to move my charred limbs. I would wake up shouting and bathed in perspiration, but fortunately these dreams were not regular occurrences. I had hoped that sleeping with Rosemary would dispel these unwelcome sub-conscious aberrations.

At last the day arrived when I took the train to London in a fever pitch of excitement. I had not slept properly for several nights, and all during the journey I wanted to shout it out to everybody that I was on my way to meet my love. Any schoolboy on his first date could not have felt more elated at the prospect.

I stood at the barrier at Liverpool Street Station anxiously scanning the various uniforms which came towards me in a mass, all full of eager anticipation at the prospect of spending Christmas away from their units. At last I caught sight of her craning her neck looking for me, and oblivious of the Naval Commander who was dancing attendance on her. As soon as she caught sight of me she broke into a run, not stopping until she was in my arms, leaving the poor chap standing with his mouth open. He probably thought that he had made a hit with this lovely WREN officer, and it must have hurt his pride when he discovered that she was already spoken for.

Once in the taxi, she looked at me closely and stroked my cheek with her hand. 'Oh, Colin, you're so thin. Are you sure you're all right, dear?'

'Perhaps I've been missing Mrs Collins' cooking,' I replied, trying to keep the conversation on a lighthearted level. In truth I had not realised just how much the constant pressure of working under Colonel Lautrys had undermined my vitality. Then there were my nightmares ... I decided not to say anything about these.

Rosemary ran her finger over the D.S.O. ribbon. 'You deserved that,' she said quietly, 'and I'm very proud of you, my darling.'

Ever since we had met, I wondered what was different about her, until it suddenly struck me that she had acquired a new maturity which made her more beautiful than ever, and added to that there was an inner glow which radiated from her as she talked. I felt sure that every man she met must fall in love with her, and it made me feel very proud to know it was only me she cared for. I told her so, and she laughed happily, while every word and gesture indicated that the feeling was mutual.

Once more I was struggling to escape from my watery prison, the only difference being that on this occasion I was actually being physically restrained, and I was vaguely aware of threshing my arms about in a bid to break free.

'Colin! Colin, dear, wake up!'

Gradually I returned to consciousness enough to realise that it was Rosemary trying to restrain me from hitting her. She was holding me with my head cradled against her bosom, rocking me backwards and forwards as if I was a baby. For some unaccountable reason, I began to weep uncontrollably.

'Hush! Hush, darling!' she said softly. 'It's all right now. You're here with me.'

When I had controlled myself, she lit a cigarette and passed it over to me. For several minutes we sat in silence.

'Would you like to tell me about it, Colin?'

In a flat voice I told her about the M.G.B. blowing up, and all the burned bodies in the water. It could have so easily have been us, and ever since the trip I had been plagued with this recurrent nightmare. I went on to tell her that I had hoped being with her would have helped to dispel the dreams, all to no avail.

'Have you spoken to anyone about this, Colin?'

I shook my head. 'I don't want to admit my weaknesses to anyone, not even you, Rosemary. When I began all this, I didn't care if I lived or died, but since coming to know and falling in love with you, I desperately want to live. Now that I'm committed to playing this dangerous game, I'm frightened, love. Scared to death if you must know, and terrified that I'll lose you.'

'I don't understand. Why should you think about losing me?'

'Well, look at me! I'm supposed to be a hero, and instead I'm reduced to a blubbering wreck. How could you go on loving anyone like that?'

'Now you listen to me, Colin Marshall. I'll always be here as long as you want me. I'm so proud of you, and what you've done. Being frightened is only natural, and doesn't make you any less of a man. In fact, doing what you do in spite of the way you feel, shows great strength of character, and is not a weakness. I'm sure that now you have discussed it with someone, and not bottled it up any more will be good for you.'

'Thank you for the psychiatric consultation, ma'am,' I said, trying to make light of it.

'You can come on to my couch any time, young man,' she replied in the same vein.

Whether or not, the logic of Rosemary's words had an impact on my subconscious reasoning, I don't know, but thereafter I settled down to sleep like a baby.

We had four whole days ahead of us, and I wanted so much to make this a Christmas we could both remember. I was also pleased that my display of mental instability did not spoil the pleasures to come. It was difficult for me not to experience a feeling of guilt when I remembered some of the Christmases past with Claudette and the girls, but I reminded myself very firmly that that phase of my life was over, and that Rosemary was part of my life now.

We told each other about the details of our respective duties, filling in all the parts we could not say in our letters. I made her laugh by imitating Colonel Lautrys when he was in a temper, while she admitted that she had come to enjoy her work. Being in charge of the plot in the control room at East Coast Defences was a very responsible job, and it was quite exciting at times when inshore convoys were under attack. However, she still did not like the place, and had made few friends since the personnel were constantly changing.

The next day was Christmas Eve, and we spent the time by going round the shops, not that there was much to buy, especially among the luxury items. I bought her a dress which she admired, but considered was too expensive. I persuaded her to try it on, and when I saw her in it I knew that it was absolutely right for her. That evening she wore it when we went to a nightclub, and drew many admiring glances as we danced the night away. Whatever the reason, that night I had the first dreamless sleep I had experienced for weeks, and cleared my mind of many of the doubts which had previously beset me.

My Christmas present to Rosemary was a brooch in silver and enamel of the crest of the Royal Marine Commandos. She was not allowed to wear it on her tunic, and so she asked me to pin it to her shirt.

'It will be more appropriate to wear it closer to my heart,' she said simply. 'I know that neither of us are religious persons, Colin,' she went on, 'But I want you to carry this with you always. You never know, it may help to protect you in some mysterious way, and I want to leave nothing to chance.'

It was a small leather-bound volume of St John's Gospel which slipped easily into the pocket. Inside, in her neat writing, was a simple inscription: — To Colin from Rosemary, with all my love.

The rest of the people in the hotel were in a party mood, and it appeared to us as if they were forcing themselves to forget the war. Somehow, our feelings did not match the occasion, and after the Christmas lunch, while the air was full of drunken chatter, we slipped away to walk quietly in St James's Park.

Our all too brief time together was soon over, but not before we had savoured every last minute of our meeting. All during the few days we had scarcely been apart, and had made love twice a day.

'What happens if I get pregnant?' Rosemary asked, after one particularly passionate session.

'Then I'll just have to make an honest woman of you. We'll get married and you'll have to come out of the WRENS,' was my simple reply.

She was silent for a moment. 'I couldn't bear the thought of having a husband who is in constant danger. I would never be able to settle down, especially with the additional responsibility of children.'

'There are lots of men who are in more danger than I am. Sailors, for example, and most of their wives seem to be able to cope with the situation. I agree, it's not an ideal basis for marriage, but surely we could survive?'

'No, Colin, just to muddle through is not enough. When I marry there must be total commitment. Besides, it is better for you when you're on a mission, not to have to worry about a family. You've been through all that already.'

'I take it, then, that you won't marry me?'

'Yes, of course I will, darling, but not until this awful war is over, and we can settle down to a normal life.'

'Then we'll just have to trust to luck that you don't become pregnant, won't we?'

The gist of this conversation was to provide me with food for thought during some of my quieter moments in the future, when I came to see the wisdom of her words, but at the time it created a small cloud on my immediate horizon.

10

Special Operations

When I returned to the camp at Wareham I reported my arrival to the orderly room where the adjutant handed me an official-looking letter marked SECRET. Inside there were instructions that I was to report forthwith to a Brigadier Hardcastle at an address in London. I had only a couple of hours in which to pack up all my kit, settle my mess bill, and catch the train straight back to the capital.

I would have liked the opportunity to say goodbye to Colonel Lautrys, but he was away at a conference. In spite of our difficulties, we had established a good working relationship, and had a mutual respect for each other. I wondered if my next assignment would be similar, and so it was with a certain amount of trepidation and speculation that I returned to London.

The building to which I reported was a large terrace house close to Waterloo Station. From the outside there was nothing to indicate that it was a military establishment, and my first reaction was that I had come to the wrong address. Once inside, however, I discovered a different world operating behind the apparently innocuous facade. My credentials were closely scrutinised by armed guards just inside the door, and in a very short time, I found myself face to face with the Brigadier himself.

For the second time that morning I had a surprise, because the man before me did not in any way conform to the image I had built up in my mind. I had always considered that most of the senior officers at the War Office bore a faint resemblance to Colonel Blimp, but this man shattered that illusion. I reckoned his age to be not more than forty, but in appearance he was quite undistinguished, and if it had not been for his uniform I would never have given him a second glance. This apparent commonplace exterior, I was soon to discover, hid a dynamic and forceful personality which compelled one to listen to him.

He extended his hand in a friendly manner, but did not indulge in small talk and got straight down to business. I was surprised to find that he already had a file about me, and that he knew much of my past history and experience, but he continued to interview me in depth, during which I was obliged to lay bare my very soul. He concentrated mainly on my ideas as to how certain aspects of the war ought to be handled, and he tried to acertain what I considered myself to be capable of until I began to worry exactly what I was going to be asked to do.

After an hour of intensive grilling I was feeling exhausted and felt I could not go on any longer, when he suddenly leaned back in his chair and smiled.

'Right! I think you've come out of that rather well,' he said. 'Don't you agree?'

'I'm afraid I'm not in a postion to say one way or the other, sir. I still don't know why I'm here.'

'All in good time, Marshall. Have you heard of an organisation called Special Operations Executive, better known as S.O.E.?'

'I've heard it vaguely mentioned, sir, but I have no idea what they do.'

'That's as it should be. It goes without saying that it's all very hush-hush, and we go to considerable lengths not to advertise our existence. This is S.O.E. headquarters, and I am the officer in charge. There are various units scattered throughout the South of England, and their main purpose is to train and dispatch agents into Occupied France, as well as to collate and disseminate information. We are also in constant touch with the Resistance, who are becoming increasingly active throughout France. Of course every unit consists of personnel from other branches of the Armed Services, Intelligence, Signals, members of the Free French Forces, and a small arm of the R.A.F. for our exclusive use.

I am offering you command of one of these establishments, if you'll be willing to take it on, so how do you feel about it?'

All the way up in the train I had prayed that I would not be sent on another mission, so my worst fears had proved groundless and I was being offered another desk job which would suit me admirably.

'I accept, sir,' I replied with alacrity.

'Good! I'm sure you'll manage admirably, once you are *au fait* with the routine.'

He went on to tell me that the unit was located in Hampshire, several miles from Winchester, and he also informed me that I was to be promoted to the rank of major to take effect forthwith.

'Thank you very much, sir,' was all I could stammer by way of reply.

'Don't thank me yet,' he said grimly. 'You'll earn it. I may as well tell you now that I'm a hard taskmaster, but you'll get used to me in time.'

'Sir, how did you come to know about me? Did Colonel Lautrys ask to have me posted?'

He shook his head. 'No. The good colonel was actually quite flattering in his assessment of you. If you can work with him, you can get along with anyone.'

'Then who could it have been?'

Suddenly he grinned, and the transformation made him look even younger, like a schoolboy about to perpetrate some naughty prank.

'Does the name Pierre Delame mean anything to you?'

'Yes, sir. he was leader of the local Resistance when we captured the two German generals.'

'That's right. He also gave you a letter to post when you arrived back in England. That letter found its way to this office, with glowing reports of what a splendid fellow you were, and how you were admirably suited for this type of work. You must have impressed him more than somewhat, because Delame is not a man to enthuse about anything. The result was that I've been trying to recruit you into this organisation ever since. Then this opening came up, and I insisted on at least giving you the opportunity to take it, if I thought that you were capable of handling it. If not, you would have been sent straight back to Wareham. Anyway, with your background and experience, you know something of the dangers which our agents face. There are very few officers capable of doing this job.'

'How many personnel are there on the establishment, sir, and how will I be involved?'

'At the moment there are forty-two on the staff, plus, of course, the agents in training or in transit, which is a variable number. Although you won't be directly involved in the actual work of these other services, you will be responsible for co-ordinating them so that the unit as a whole functions smoothly. You will be dealing with a mixture of personnel with very differing backgrounds and futures, so it will require tact and patience in order to get the best out of them. Remember, we're all on the same side. The staff who deal with the every-day running of the unit are very good, so you will have no worries there. Your purpose is to concentrate on fielding as many trained agents as possible.'

'What happened to my predecessor, sir?'

Brigadier Hardcastle hesitated before answering. 'Let me give you a word of warning, Colin. Whatever happens, never allow yourself to become emotionally involved. Try to remain detached and professional at all times. This isn't an easy thing to do, and is probably the hardest part of the job. I'm afraid that the officer in charge before you was unable to do this. He took everything personally, and identified himself with every operative who was sent out. If they were captured or killed, he reckoned that it was his fault by failing to train them properly. There was a period recently when we lost several agents in quick succession, all women. Since they had all been denounced to the Germans by a traitor who had infiltrated the organisation, it could scarcely have been his fault, but he couldn't take any more and deliberately drove his jeep at high speed into a wall. He wasn't killed, but he'll be no use to us again.'

'You realise I've never done any of this work before, sir?'

'Don't worry, you'll be fine. I'll keep an eye on you for the first few weeks, but I'm in no doubt you'll be able to cope with the pressure. If ever you require help or advice, don't be afraid to ring this number at any time, day or night. There's always someone here to answer your queries, or know where to get in touch with me. No one will censure you for getting a second opinion, so if you are ever in doubt, make sure instead of making a wrong decision.'

He went on to elaborate on many of the aspects concerning the use of operatives, particularly the women belonging to that peculiar arm of the Services, the First Aid Nursing Yeomanry, better known as Fannies. Each was a volunteer, and much of their work was so secret that their own families had no idea what they were doing.

'I need hardly remind you not to discuss your work with any outsider, Colin. Even your girlfriend, Third Officer Stuart of the WRNS.'

The dossier he had on me must have been very complete.

'Is that necessary, sir. She used to be secretary to Admiral Sir George Brown, who was Chief of Combined Operations, Southern Area, so she's used to keeping secrets. Anyway, she's in Felixstowe now, so I don't see her all that often.'

'Even so, I'm sorry, but I must insist that the rule of secrecy still applies. The fewer people who know of our set-up the better, and any correspondence will be sent through a Box number.' He glanced at his watch. 'You must be famished. Come and have dinner.'

Martin Hardcastle turned out to be a charming and amusing host, and we hit it off straight away. The longer I was in his company the better I liked him, and I'm sure the feeling was mutual. Over the meal we discussed many aspects of the war, and I was impressed by his wide knowledge on a variety of topics. He also told me something about himself and his past life.

I discovered that he was older than I had at first thought, in his middle forties, but still young for the rank he held. For seven years until the outbreak of war in 1939, he had been a lecturer in Modern European History at Cambridge University, where his wife and two sons still lived. Although he had been in the Territorials he was not dedicated to the Army, and had no intention of furthering his career in the Services after the war. He confided in me, that due to the anomalies of the promotion system, although he held the rank of acting brigadier, he was in fact only a substantive captain. His meteoric rise had generated some jealousy and resentment among many of the older regulars in the War Office, especially after he was put in charge of all S.O.E. operations, which included not only France, but Holland and Belgium, and even Germany itself. However, since his appointment had been made by Churchill in person, his position was unassailable.

He encouraged me to tell him of my experiences as a French correspondent, about my escape from Paris in 1940, and to fill in many of the details of the Normandy raid in 1941. He also persuaded me to talk about the loss of my family, something I was usually loth to do. I came to the conclusion that we were very alike, he and I, both loners, freelance personnel who were nevertheless playing an important part in the conduct of the war, but almost detached from the Military machine and the system it produced.

Our dinner lasted far into the night, and after a few hours' sleep at the officers' club, next day found me on a train to join my new unit with a feeling of trepidation.

I alighted at Winchester station where a small pick-up truck was waiting for me outside. A lance-corporal in the R.A.S.C. came towards me and saluted, so evidently my time of arrival had been sent on ahead.

'Major Marshall?'

I nodded, still unused to my new rank.

'If you won't mind riding with me in the front, sir, I'll put your kit in the back.'

I was conscious of a feeling of anticipation when we stopped outside the heavy wrought-iron gates which was the entrance to my new domain some twenty minutes later. There was no indication as to the type of establishment operating within the high walls surrounding the estate, only two notices, one which said PRIVATE — KEEP OUT, while a smaller one inside the gate said W.D. PROPERTY. ALL PASSES MUST BE SHOWN. Two armed sentries scrutinised my papers before telephoning for confirmation that I was expected. While I was waiting, I noted the electrified fence within the stone wall, and I subsequently discovered that roving sentries with dogs also patrolled the grounds twenty-four hours a day, making security a number one priority.

After driving through several acres of parkland, I had my first glimpse of the building through the trees. The unit was housed in one of those isolated Georgian mansions which are fairly commonplace around this part of the country. Before the outbreak of war it had been used as a health farm, which was a recent innovation in those days, where the rich and the famous (or infamous) were pampered and starved at enormous expense, in order to avail themselves of a pseudo-medical regime which was supposed to make them feel better from non-existent ailments.

There were many rooms in the main building, I never did discover how many, all of which had been lavishly furnished at one time, but now the valuable pictures and antiques had been removed to a safe venue, and in their place were W.D. utility fittings. Our footsteps echoed on the carpetless floors, and the once highly-polished parquet was now scratched and unsightly. There were also a collection of outbuildings at the back of the house, all of which had been converted to a variety of uses.

In a letter to Rosemary, I managed to convey the news that I now had a desk job, without actually telling her what it was. She knew enough about the service to guess from the fact that my address was now a Box Number, it was what she referred to as a "Cloak and Dagger" establishment. I also suggested that if she could wangle a posting to the W.R.N.S. Training School at Petersfield, then we might see more of each other. This was enough to let her know the area where I was stationed.

The reply came almost by return of post. She congratulated me on my promotion, and was pleased to know that I had not been banished to the wilds of Scotland. She was also glad to know that I was not actively involved in any missions, at least for the foreseeable future. However, Rosemary was doubtful of her chances of a posting to that area, but she would keep on trying. Her one item of good news was that she wasn't pregnant, although I was beginning to feel that it would be the only way to persuade her to marry me.

She went on to tell me at great length that Susan's husband had started drinking again, and had had to be re-admitted to hospital. Reading between the lines, I was sure

Rosemary informed me of this in order to emphasise that marrying a man who was on active service was a mistake, although she did not actually say so.

It took me several weeks to come to grips with all the various aspects of my command, and, as Brigadier Hardcastle had indicated, the job was no sinecure. Although the routine running of the unit had already been established, there were always complications arising which demanded my personal attention or required an instant decision, consequently I had very little time to call my own. Almost every day there was a crisis of some description due to a variety of reasons — failures of communication, individual carelessness of key personnel due to stress, sudden illness, or agents going missing in circumstances of which we were ignorant often for a long time.

It was a constant source of wonder and admiration to me as to how they managed to recruit the brave men and women who were prepared to go into Occupied France, and yet there seemed to be no shortage. Every one was a volunteer, and if at any stage of the training they wished to opt out, no blame or finger of accusation was ever pointed at them. Of course, they were all thoroughly vetted before they ever came to us, but it was very much to their credit that out of the dozens of agents who passed through our hands, only three failed to complete the course all the time I was there. Each one was briefed as to the difficulties they would have to face on the other side, and they were left in no doubt as to what would happen to them should they fall into enemy hands, but this did not seem to deter them. Each one, particularly the Fannies, had a good reason for going.

I was determined not to make the same mistake as my predecessor, and become personally involved with any of the agents who were either in training or in transit, but it was difficult not to. Many were intelligent and likeable people with whom I would have been proud to be on friendly terms under normal circumstances, but I must have appeared to them as an aloof and unapproachable figure who communicated with them only on a professional level. Even during my rare visits to the mess, I deliberately kept the conversation on general topics.

And yet there was always a background of personal problems to be sorted out among my charges. Most of them had families or loved ones who had no idea what they were doing, and this often threw additional strains on them. The radio operators in particular required delicate handling, as their survival rate in enemy territory was less than any of the others. I may have given the impression that I was bearing the burden of command solely on my own shoulders, but this was by no means the case. There were several social workers as well as a resident psychiatrist to help deal with these problems.

In fact, I had the backing of a marvellously dedicated staff at all levels who knew their jobs, and were able to function adequately without my interference. I left them to get on with it, and it was only when things went wrong that I was involved. Although I led a lonely life on the whole, I did strike up a friendship with several members of the staff, and we formed a tight-knit circle who refused to discuss matters of business when off duty. My especial friend was our resident psychiatrist, Bill Galloway, an amusing and flamboyant character, who had a definite extrovert outlook on life, and I always felt better after an hour or two in his company.

True to his word, Martin Hardcastle came to visit the unit after I had been there for a month. After a detailed inspection he declared himself satisfied that every aspect of the work was carrying on as smoothly as possible, but made a few suggestions of a minor nature. He opted to stay the night which delighted me, and we talked far into the small hours while demolishing a whole bottle of French brandy. He was particularly anxious to know how I was coping on a personal level, and when I informed him of my determination to remain detached, he nodded in approval.

'I think it's the only way to handle the problem, Colin, no matter how much you dislike it. But above all else, you mustn't allow yourself to become too introspective.'

'No, sir. Up to now I've managed to stay more or less normal, but I know it's early days yet. I've made a friend of Captain Galloway, the psychiatrist, you met him at dinner, and I'm hoping he will make sure I stay on an even keel.'

'I told you at the beginning that this would be no soft

option, Colin. Now that the French Resistance is becoming more active and organised, I'm afraid the supply of agents will have to be stepped up.'

'But, sir, we're working to capacity now!' I exploded. 'It's a physical impossibility to process any more.'

'I'm well aware of the difficulties but, nevertheless, the need is still there. I am trying to set up more S.O.E. units such as this one, but the supply of suitable establishments is running out. Most of the big estates have been commandeered already by one or other of the Services.'

'If we try to step up the numbers going through here, we will be turning out operatives who are not properly trained, or psychologically ill-equipped to deal with the dangers on the other side. I wouldn't want to be a party to that, sir.'

'I agree with every word you say, Colin. Nevertheless, I want you to train another ten per cent of your present capacity. There are no difficulties in finding volunteers, I assure you. That number ought not throw a strain on your staff, will it?'

I sighed. 'No, I suppose we will manage.'

The brigadier contemplated his glass. 'This is extraordinarily good brandy. I haven't tasted anything like it since before the war. French cognac, isn't it?'

'Armagnac, actually. One of the agents brought it back as a present. I accepted it gratefully, and didn't ask where it came from.'

Hardcastle's eyes twinkled. 'I don't know if I like the idea of our aircraft smuggling in contraband liquor, so I'll forget what you have just told me.'

Next morning he was gone, leaving me to work out how we were to cope with the extra supply of volunteers. I suppose every S.O.E. unit in the country was having similar problems, but since I had no idea where the others were, there was no way I could contact them to compare notes.

In a roundabout way, I was able to convey to Rosemary what I was doing, but although I was desperate to be with her again, any prospect of leave, even for a forty-eight hour pass, was out of the question.

Another couple of months had passed before Captain Galloway, the psychiatrist, mentioned to me casually in conversation that I seemed to be drinking rather heavily. Up to that moment I had not realised how much I was becoming dependent on the consumption of alcohol to keep up my morale, especially during the lonely evenings when the problems of the day seemed to crowd in on me. I knew it didn't help me to solve anything, but it went a long way to stop me from dwelling on the many problems which always seemed to end up on my desk. I took the hint and consulted Bill Galloway on a professional level.

'I don't want to give you any pills, Colin,' he told me. 'They may afford you temporary relief, but, in the end, the real cure lies within yourself.'

Since I was terrified of becoming an alcoholic, for a time I went to the other extreme and cut out all drink completely. This drastic course of action made me irritable and difficult to approach, but gradually I began to settle down to a more balanced outlook whereby I was able to have a drink occasionally on a social level. Thinking back, I realised that the alcohol was beginning to add to my problems instead of making them go away.

With the coming of spring, I decided that the majority of my staff were in danger of becoming stale and desk-bound, consequently none of us were as fit as we ought to have been, myself included. The result was that I posted an order to the effect that everyone (except those on duty) were to take part in an hour's physical exercise every morning before breakfast, and run a makeshift assault course once a week. I set the ball in motion by being the first to attend the P.T. instructor's parade, a habit which I kept up religiously as an example to the others. Of all the orders I had issued, this one was perhaps the most unpopular, and the M.O. reported a marked increase in the numbers on sick parade. However, he was on my side, and ruthless when it came to weeding out scroungers. After a few weeks, we found that not only did most of the staff feel better for the regime, but a few actually came to enjoy the sessions.

We also made an effort to renovate the tennis courts which up to then had been neglected and overgrown with weeds. Someone managed to acquire some rackets and balls, and soon the sound of games in progress became commonplace on the long summer evenings. We were also able to play the odd football match when things were quiet. The sides were usually picked from officers versus other ranks, because, by the nature of our work, it was impossible for us to play against outside teams, but any sporting activity, even if it was limited, was well attended.

At last I managed to arrange a weekend leave which I intended to spend with Rosemary, but at the last minute, much to my frustration, some of the girls in her department had been struck down by a mysterious infection, and so all leave was cancelled. I went up to London where I wandered about aimlessly, fed up and miserable. Martin Hardcastle, who was aware of my plight, invited me out to a party thrown for one of the staff officers in the War Office.

I took the opportunity to ask him if I could arrange a week's leave in the Cotswolds during a certain week in September. He managed to wheedle out of me as to why it was important, and when I told him he laughed.

'I don't see why not, Colin. You are certainly overdue for some leave, and you've earned it. Put in an application in the usual way.'

After that the world seemed to be a brighter place, especially when I discovered that Rosemary had managed to fix up to have the same week off. I could only pray that nothing now would come along to disrupt our plans.

It is often said that one should never try to recreate the past, and this was certainly true in our case. In spite of our determination to make this the best leave ever, somehow the magic of our former visit was missing. Mrs Collins and her husband were delighted to see us both again, and true to her word she gave us her best double room. Although the inn seemed the same, there was something different which I could not at first identify. Whether it was that the atmosphere of the place was changed, or perhaps we ourselves had changed, but some of the spell had been broken.

The difference was made obvious when we came down to the bar before dinner on that first evening. Instead of a handful of familiar faces from our last visit, the place was packed with American servicemen so that there was barely room to squeeze through, far less find a seat. Loud and unfamiliar accents now filled the normally quiet bar with a babel of noise, and the snatches of conversation which I happened to overhear seemed to me to be gauche and almost childish. I saw nearly all of them sported medal ribbons, in spite of the fact that none of them had been over here for any length of time, and had never been close to any action. Since we were both in civilian clothes, I scarcely merited a second glance, but Rosemary was the recipient of several wolf whistles in addition to some salacious remarks which I'm sure were designed to flatter her in a naive way.

Mrs Collins, seeing our predicament, came over to rescue us. She was very apologetic.

'I'm sorry, my dears. but it's like this every weekend now. They come over from the big American airbase a few miles away. Every pub in the village has the same problem. I don't like it one little bit because it has chased all our regulars away, but my Joe thinks it's good for business. He forgets that we'll still be here, God willing, after they've all gone. Anyway, we're a public house, so by law we have to serve them, so long as they behave themselves. Sometimes we have to send for the Military Police when they get a bit drunk and rowdy, but on the whole they're not bad lads, just different from us. I suppose it's the first time most of them have been away from home, if you ask me.'

There were five visitors in the dining-room as well as ourselves, an elderly couple at one table, and there were U.S. Air Force officers at another. In contrast to their men through in the bar, their conversation was quietly restrained, and they seemed unobrusive by studiously ignoring us. At least I thought so until I noticed one of them winking in Rosemary's direction when he thought I wasn't looking. She herself was not amused by the gesture, and moved her seat to turn her back on the trio.

Immediately after the meal we went upstairs to our room where we listened to the radio and talked quietly. I told her a bit about my life at the S.O.E. unit, emphasising how lonely I was, as well as the distressing aspect of the job, when men and women went missing. I went on to tell Rosemary about what had happened to my predecessor, and how I had begun to drink in order to try to drown my worries.

'I can understand the difficulties, Colin,' she replied, 'but from a selfish point of view, I am relieved that you are in a safe, shore-based job, and are no longer in danger on the other side of the Channel.'

'I don't think this desk job is going to last indefinitely,' I told her as gently as I could. 'There has been an enormous increase in cross-Channel activity recently. I suppose most of it is a build-up to this so-called Second Front we're always hearing about. Nothing has been said officially, but I have a feeling that one day they're going to send me over there again before I'm very much older.'

'Oh, don't, Colin!' she cried, throwing her arms round my neck. 'I don't want to talk about it any more, either now or for the rest of the week. Promise me you won't mention the subject again.'

'That suits me, darling. I came away to forget the war.'

We went to bed early, and Rosemary fell asleep almost immediately, locked im my arms. I lay for some time savouring the moment. This was what I had dreamed about all these months, to have her there beside me, knowing that she was mine, seemed like a glimpse of heaven. It was not long before I too fell into a long, dreamless sleep.

When I awoke the daylight was streaming in through a gap in the curtains, and I was immediately conscious of Rosemary's body in close proximity to my own. Without disturbing her, I moved my hand gently over her thigh, and across her flat abomen to finish up cupping her firm breast. At the same time I felt myself being aroused.

She must have been awake already, and felt the effect she was having on me, because her voice came through loud and clear, 'Well, what are you waiting for, Marshall? I thought you were a man of action, so why don't you stop pussy-footing around and do something about it?'

The next moment she had rolled over on to her back, and was grinning up at me with an expression of open invitation.

'No, I don't think I will,' I said in a mocking tone, 'but I'm open to persuasion.'

I expected her to go along with the charade for a short while, but suddenly the smile left her face.

'All right, if you want me to, will this be enough to persuade you?' she whispered, as she reached up and drew my head down to kiss her warm, inviting lips, which were parted slightly in supplication. That single kiss conveyed all the love she felt for me, thus making it impossible for me to resist any longer. Our union began slowly at first in order to prolong the moment of ecstasy, and eventually reached a frenzied climax. Afterwards, I held her close for a long time as if afraid that she would suddenly be spirited away.

'I do love you, Colin. I don't think you will ever know how much. You won't ever leave me, will you?'

'Not if I can help it!' I replied vehemently, and at that moment I meant it. 'Whatever brought that into your head?'

She shivered as if someone had walked over her grave.

'Even if I don't see you as often as I would like, I can't imagine life without you actually being there, but so much can happen in wartime, that I'm afraid this happiness is too good to last.'

I hope I managed to persuade her that she was being fanciful.

During the next few days the weather was unsettled, but we cycled round our old haunts whenever we could between the showers. The peace of the countryside, however, was disturbed by a number of vehicles belonging to the U.S. Air Force, which seemed to be everywhere. Sometimes the occupants would emit cat-calls and wolf-whistles whenever they passed us. I don't suppose they really meant any harm, but neither of us liked being the object of this childish behaviour.

One evening, just before we went in for our meal, Rosemary complained of feeling chilly, and I volunteered to fetch her cardigan from upstairs, leaving her alone in the bar for a few minutes. Apparently, no sooner had I gone than she was accosted by a group of Americans sitting at a nearby table.

'Hey, honey, come over and join us!'

She shook her head and looked away, not wishing to become involved in any conversation.

'Aw, come on!' another chipped in, 'Good-looking dames

are hard to find around here. Why don't you ditch that civilian, and come and talk to some real man?'

Rosemary flushed. 'You wouldn't recognise a real man if you fell over one,' she snapped. 'That so-called civilian is more of a man than all of you put together.'

Hoots of laughter greeted this remark, until a warrant officer at another table noticing her embarrassment, told them to shut up. At that moment I reappeared and the incident was closed, but Rosemary refused to see the funny side of it, and was spitting fire for the remainder of the evening.

'Don't you ever leave me in there again on my own, Colin. I have never been so humiliated in all my life,' she said when she had finished relating the incident to me later.

'Then we ought to teach them that appearances aren't everything. I know what we'll do. On our last night, we'll have a drink in the bar, with both of us wearing uniform,' I suggested. 'It might help to make them realise that they're not the only ones fighting this war, although to hear them you would think they were.'

Rosemary agreed to the idea, but I had the impression she was not over-enthusiastic.

As we had planned, our appearance in the bar in uniform on our last evening had the desired effect. The buzz of conversation in the room dried up immediately as all eyes followed us, and I was pleased to note that many of the same G.I.s who had ribbed her a few evenings before, were there again. Mrs Collins, smiling broadly, also played along.

'What will you have to drink, major?' she asked.

I ordered a small beer for both of us, while the Yanks sat and stared at us open-mouthed. At last one of them broke the silence which was becoming embarrassing.

'Jeez, major, why didn't you tell us?'

'Tell you what?' I asked innocently.

'That you were one of us. Royal Marine Commandos,' he went on, reading my shoulder-flash. 'I've read about them. That's a shit-hot outfit, isn't it?'

'Watch your language in front of the lady, Gruber,' one of the older men chided his companion.

The next moment I found myself deluged with questions as well as offers of a drink, to which we refused. None of them had seen any action, and they didn't know what to expect.

'Have you seen any of the fighting, major?'

'Yes, some, but not as much as many of our other boys.'

'Whereabouts? In France?'

'Yes. I was in the retreat when the Germans invaded in 1940, and I've been in Occupied France since then.'

'What is it like, being in action? Are the Germans as good as they make out? Is it right that they're trying to fortify the whole of the French Coast?'

I tried to answer their questions as honestly as I could, but some were naive in the extreme. for the most part they were young, but they wanted desperately to be involved in the war now that they were over here, and they also wanted to give the impression that they were equal to the task, They still had not learned that whereas the Americans tend to wear their hearts on their sleeves, the British were usually the opposite.

'If you've been in Occupied France, major, how come you have only one medal ribbon?'

I shifted my gaze to the questioner who was older than most of the others, and displayed three on his tunic.

'May I ask what yours were awarded for, corporal?' I countered.

'I'm a regular soldier, see. This one is for five years' service, this one is for marksmanship, and this one at the end is because I've been posted overseas,' he replied, pointing proudly to each of them in turn.

'I'm afraid the British Army don't give out medals for any of these.'

'Well, what's yours for, then?'

'Let's just say I was lucky, and leave it at that.'

'If you must know, he captured a German general,' Rosemary chipped in, unable to disguise the pride in her voice.

There was an audible gasp all round. 'Singlehanded?'

'Oh, goodness no. I had ten men with me on the raid, but only three of us came back.'

'Jeezus H. Christ!' someone gasped in a loud voice.

By now my embarrassment had reached the point where I wished we had never started this charade. I hated being the centre of attraction, and their undisguised hero-worship made me feel cheap, knowing that they were over here only to service U.S. Air Force planes, and unlikely ever to see any action. Fortunately, at that moment, Mrs Collins came in to tell us that our meal was ready. We didn't return to the bar afterwards, but went out for a long walk in the warm autumn air until it was time to turn in.

Next morning we regretfully parted before returning to our respective units. Leaving Rosemary felt as if part of me was going with her, but she stressed that she was still doing her utmost to try for a posting somewhere near me. For my part, I could only hope that that day wasn't too far distant.

11

Complications

I returned to the unit to discover that they were in the middle of a monumental flap, and that all hell had been let loose. Apparently, two days before I arrived back, S.O.E. headquarters had issued a Top Secret memo to the effect that our coding system had been broken by the Germans several weeks before. This meant that it was possible all transmissions could have been monitored, consequently our whole operation in France was in jeopardy. There had been no time as yet to alter the codes and communicate them to our agents, and it could have meant that they themselves were in danger of discovery. Captain René Delpierre, of the Free French Army, who was my second-in-command, had kept his head, and apart from watching the situation closely he had not been panicked into taking any precipitate action.

There was an urgent message for me to telephone the brigadier on my return, but when I complied, he had very little to say except that he would be coming down in a couple of days' time. In the interval I was not to dispatch any more agents unless the all-clear had been received.

Two days later, Martin Hardcastle's staff car came up the drive at 07.15 hours, which meant that he had left London two hours before. Fortunately, I was already up and dressed when the gate telephoned me to say he had arrived. He was unshaven and bleary-eyed, his face was pale and drawn, and in contrast to his normal friendly approach he was withdrawn and monosyllabic. I immediately offered him the use of my room where he showered and shaved before joining me for breakfast, by which time he seemed to have recovered his equilibrium.

'A bad business this, Colin,' he said, between mouthfuls of bacon and powdered eggs. 'I don't suppose you've had time to grasp all the implications yet?'

'I must confess that apart from reading the memo, and gleaning some information from Captain Delpierre, I'm not yet up to date with all the details. I feel guilty at having been away when it all happened. Perhaps if I'd been here. . . .'

He shook his head. 'It has all taken place on the other side. Even if you had been here, there is nothing you could have done. Anyway, it was essential that you had your leave, so don't give it another thought. Briefly, what has happened was that a couple of days ago, one of the other S.O.E. units received a garbled message. We don't know where it originated, or who sent it, but it must have been someone who knew something about our communications procedures. Up to now nothing has happened. There have been no mass arrests, but the Germans may be content merely to monitor any transmissions for the time being. Of course, we've shut down all but the most essential broadcasts.'

'But they must know we've been alerted, sir?'

'I don't know what to think yet, Colin. All I do know is that we mustn't be panicked into recalling our agents in large numbers.'

'Then the ones who are there will be at risk.'

'Possibly, but the way this has been orchestrated, I have a feeling that the Germans themselves could have made that initial transmission, hoping to throw us into a flap. I must say they have achieved that objective all right.'

'But how could they break into our system, sir? I know nothing is foolproof, but. . . .'

'It's possible one of our agents has been captured and has leaked enough information for them to have made that broadcast. I'm not going to be pushed into doing anything rash, but I'm making contingency plans, so that if arrests do start, we will be prepared to institute a mass withdrawal.'

'I have three operatives ready to go, sir. I take it you

want me to hold them back until further notice?'

'Yes, keep them on stand-by for the time being. Anyway, to change the subject, I'm afraid I have another shock for you. General de Gaulle and some of his senior staff are coming to inspect this unit on Thursday of next week. In view of all this trouble, I've tried to have the visit postponed, but apparently his time is limited and that's the only day he can make it. He's getting very twitchy about this Second Front, and he's pushing it for all it's worth. Be warned, Colin, he's an abrasive character who is used to getting his own way, and he isn't easy to fob off with excuses.'

'Will you be here?'

'I'll certainly do my best. I've met him before, and it wouldn't be fair to let you carry the can, and face him on your own.'

The brigadier spent the rest of the day going round the unit by himself. He stayed for a long time with the Signals personnel and the decoders, as well as having a briefing session with the agents waiting to go out. I stayed in the office trying to catch up with some of the paperwork which had accumulated during my absence. It was half past-four when Martin Hardcastle was ready to leave.

'I'll keep you in touch, Colin,' he said as he climbed into his staff car, 'and, of course, I'll let you know if there are any further developments.'

I remember thinking that it was one of the perks of his position to be driven around the countryside in a comfortable staff-car with a pretty A.T.S. chaffeuse for company.

It was three hours later when the telephone rang in the orderly-room. It was headquarters in London inquiring if the brigadier had left, because he was due to attend a meeting at the War Office, and had not yet arrived. After making further inquiries, we learned that his staff-car had been in collision with a lorry, and had landed upside down in a ditch. The pretty A.T.S. driver had been killed, and Martin Hardcastle himself had been admitted to the military hospital in Aldershot suffering from broken ribs and a dislocated shoulder.

The immediate consequence of this accident was that I

was going to be left to face General de Gaulle and his entourage on my own, which was a daunting prospect.

Fortunately, two days before the French V.I.P. visit, the crisis of communication suddenly resolved itself, and H.Q. informed us that all operations were to be resumed as quickly as possible. It had been discovered that the Germans themselves had been responsible for initiating the rumour with the intention of causing chaos in the S.O.E., and in this respect they had been entirely successful. Two facts emerged to allay everyone's fears. In the first place, it had only just been ascertained that the radio operator who received the original message, had failed to follow the correct procedure, and in his panic he had not checked the authenticity of its source. Secondly, if the original message had been genuine, it would have led to the uncovering of many of our agents' identities, with many arrests, but this had not happened. By the time de Gaulle was due, the unit was operating normally once more, for which I was grateful.

As Brigadier Hardcastle had predicted, the general seemed to be obsessed with the need to open the Second Front, and all his questions and observations were slanted in that direction. He spent a long time talking to the agents in transit, especially two who had just returned from France, while one of his aides showed a particular interest in the communications side of the operation. At no stage did he comment as to whether he was satisfied with our efforts or not, but, by the end of the day, I for one was glad to see them depart. No doubt any criticisms would be passed back to us in due course.

The next day I went to visit the brigadier in hospital. He was now fairly comfortable, although his breathing was still impaired, and his arm was in a sling, but on the whole he was pleased to see me, and eager to talk.

He expressed a regret about the loss of his driver. 'It was my fault entirely, Colin. I kept on at the poor girl to go faster because I had a meeting to attend, and I thought I was going to be late. The conditions were wet and dark, and with hooded headlights she obviously could not see properly. I shall never forgive myself.'

He was clearly upset, but he pulled himself together and returned to other matters.

'Tell me all about de Gaulle's visit,' he ordered.

I furnished him with as many details as I could remember, but I indicated that I had no idea what the Commander of the Free French Forces really thought.

'I wish you had been there, sir,' I concluded. 'He asked me several questions which I couldn't answer. Anyway, I was pleased we were back to normal working. I hate to think what his reaction would have been if he had found us sitting about doing nothing.'

At that moment, the door of the room opened and another visitor was ushered in. Martin Hardcastle's face lit up immediately, and his discomfort seemed to vanish.

'Hello, darling. How are you today?' the newcomer said as she kissed him.

'Letty, this is Colin Marshall,' he introduced me.

'Oh, yes. How do you do, major. Martin has told me a lot about you.'

Her handshake was warm, and her smile friendly, but she was certainly not what I thought the brigadier's wife would be like. Whereas her husband was tall, athletic, and good-looking, Letitia Hardcastle was none of these things. She, too, was tall, but boney and angular, with spreading hips but little or no bust. By no stretch of the imagination could she be regarded as beautiful or even striking in appearance. Nor did she make any effort to improve her looks — her hair was cut short without any attempt to have it styled, and her rather sallow complexion was devoid of make-up, except for a little lipstick, which gave the indication of having been slapped on anyhow at the last minute. The overall result was that she seemed to be older than her husband, although they were probably the same age. She had a pedantic and precise way of speaking in a beautifully modulated voice, giving the impression that at heart she was more of a blue-stocking than a housewife.

When I came to know her better, I learned that she had indeed been a brilliant student when she was at Girton College, Cambridge, but she had abandoned all ambition of an academic career when she met the young Martin Hardcastle who was at that time a struggling lecturer. From then on she had been happy to bury her own personality in order to devote the rest of her life to her husband's welfare, and the needs of her two sons, and she had never regretted it. The boys were seventeen and fourteen years of age respectively, both of them away at school in the country, and until the war had intervened they had been a close and happy family. I know that the brigadier appreciated the sacrifice his wife had made on his behalf because he always treated her as if she was the most beautiful woman in the world, and deferred to her opinion when domestic matters had to be decided. It gave me a funny feeling to realise that they had the same sort of rapport that Claudette and I used to enjoy.

I stayed for about twenty minutes making small talk, but I could see that they wanted to be on their own, and so I made an excuse that I had another appointment, and left.

Two weeks later I received a letter through the post. It was written in a neat and precise hand on pale mauve notepaper:

> Dear Major Marshall,
> If you have nothing to do over Christmas, Martin and I would be happy if you could come and spend it here with us in Cambridge. Your friend, Miss Stuart, will also be most welcome. We have nothing exciting planned, just a quiet family get-together over the festive period. Please don't feel that you are obliged to come, if you have made alternative plans we will both understand.
> Yours sincerely,
> Letitia Hardcastle.

I telephoned Rosemary that same evening to pass on the invitation, but she was immediately apologetic.

'Oh, darling, I'm so sorry. I was going to write to you tonight to tell you that I can't get away. The roster for December was posted yesterday, and I am on duty both Christmas and Boxing Day. I went to see the Chief Officer who reminded me that I had last Christmas off, so I suppose it's fair enough. It would have been lovely, Colin. Please thank them for me.'

'Is there any point in my coming up to Felixstowe?'

'None, I'm afraid. You couldn't stay here, and apart from

not being able to leave the station, I could be called out at any time. No, you go to the Hardcastles. There's no need for us both to be miserable.'

'I'll be miserable without you anyway,' I told her.

'Please, try to telephone me on Christmas Day, darling.'

'Yes, of course I will.'

We went on talking about other matters until the operator cut us off with apologies.

The taxi drew up in front of a large Victorian terrace house in a tree-lined avenue on the outskirts of Cambridge. The area had an air of quiet respectability, and out of the corner of my eye I could see one of the curtains twitch in a window on the opposite side of the street. The Hardcastles' house was on three floors plus a basement, with a postage-stamp garden separating it from the pavement.

I scarcely recognised the brigadier when he came to the door in answer to my knock. Hitherto, I had always seen him dressed in his immaculate uniform, but now he wore an open-necked shirt, a pair of old slacks, and a sportsjacket with leather edging at the cuffs and patches on the elbows. He looked lean and fit, and told me he was returning to full duty just as soon as the holiday was over.

Inside the house there was chaos, with books and newspapers strewn about, but the atmosphere was homely, and Martin's wife went out of her way to make me welcome.

'As you can see, we don't stand on ceremony here, so just make yourself at home. We eat when we're hungry, and if you want anything, sing out. I'm afraid I'm not very organised, but we seem to be well stocked with food and drink.'

'Thank you very much, Mrs Hardcastle,' I murmured.

'Before we go any further, let's get this straight,' the brigadier chipped in. 'I'm Martin and this is Letty, for the holiday anyway. Let's try to forget the war for a few days.'

I produced a bottle of perfume for my hostess, and a bottle of Champagne for Martin. He looked at them both and grinned.

'Do you know, Letty, this fellow here has an amazing way of producing bottles, especially French bottles, out of thin air. I wish I knew how he does it?'

I smiled back, and, entering into the spirit of the conversation, I tapped the side of my nose with one finger. 'I never ask how they appear. I just accept everything gratefully.'

'I must look into this when I return,' he said, still smiling, but I wondered if he was joking.

It was only when I met the two boys, John and Peter, aged seventeen and fourteen, that I detected an aura of unease which made them all a bit edgy. The elder boy made himself scarce and did not reappear until the evening meal was on the table, but even then he ate very little, and any attempt on my part to draw him into the conversation was met with monosyllabic responses. After dinner, when we three adults had settled down, and the boys had gone to their room that I learned what the trouble was.

Apparently John Hardcastle had been caught in a compromising situation behind the bicycle sheds with the caretaker's sixteen-year-old daughter a few days before the end of term. Needless to say, he had been sent home in disgrace, and his parents were naturally embarrassed about the whole affair. He was a well set-up, good-looking young fellow, and I could imagine him breaking many hearts in the years to come.

'We thought we'd better tell you what was going on. John is normally very outgoing, and chatters to everyone. I hope it doesn't put too much of a damper on the Christmas festivities. I think we're just beginning to realise that he's growing up, and is likely to get into scrapes. He himself feels that he has let us down, but you know what boys of his age are like. I'm not too bothered, but Letty has taken the incident to heart.'

'Well, I should think so,' she said. 'The affair will be all over town next week.'

'Rubbish!' Martin laughed. 'Apparently the girl is well known for hanging about the older boys, and it's just bad luck that John got caught. By tomorrow I expect he'll be back to normal, especially if we stop making a great thing out of it. What would you do, if you were in my shoes, Colin?'

'Well, you know as well as I do, that all boys of that age

have dirty minds, but most never have an opportunity to put the theory into practice. I was no better. I remember in my last year at boarding school one of my classmates used to invite one of us home for the weekend, occasionally. His mother was still quite young and married to an older man who was away a lot. It was rumoured that she used to come to the friend's bedroom at night, but I don't know if this was true, or just wishful thinking. Even though I couldn't stand the fellow, I tried for six months to get an invitation, but nothing came of it.'

'You men are awful,' Letty said forcefully. She was obviously not amused by our cavalier attitude towards the problem.

'I wouldn't worry about it too much, if I were you,' I tried to reassure her. 'It shows he has a healthy interest in the opposite sex, and it'll all be forgotten in a week or two.'

'I suppose you're right,' Martin replied, 'but what bothers me is that we'll have to find another school for him. He still has a year to do before the Army takes him.'

I was pleased to find that on Christmas morning the atmosphere inside the Hardcastle household was much more relaxed, and their elder son was evidently back in favour. he was a likeable lad who was old for his years. He reminded me of myself when I was about twenty.

After breakfast, I asked Martin if I could use the telephone to ring Rosemary.

'Oh, I think we can do better than that,' he replied with a twinkle in his eye. 'We aren't eating our main meal until late afternoon, and John has a motorcycle which he won't be using today. I'm sure he'll let you borrow it, but it's up to you, Colin. The roads will be quiet so it will take just over an hour to reach Felixstowe, and you can be back in time easily. It would be an ideal opportunity, if you can get in to see her.'

John readily gave his permission, and I had a feeling that the proposal had already been discussed between them. Within twenty minutes I was mounted on an old Norton, which, although noisy, bowled along at a reasonable speed. The morning was cold but dry, so I made good time. However, it took me an extra half-hour to find Rosemary's outfit because of the lack of signposts, and there was no one about whom I could ask, but eventually I arrived at the right place.

It was lucky that I was wearing uniform, because the sentry at the gate took me at face value. He didn't ask me for a pass or any other credentials, but directed me to the officers' mess without question. I expect he was fed up having to do guard duty on Christmas Day, but no saboteur could have had an easier entry. I found the mess without difficulty, but no sooner had I opened the door than an orderly asked me my business. When I requested to see Third Officer Stuart, he ushered me into a large messroom without a word.

Inside, Rosemary was seated on a couch drinking coffee, while an RNVR lieutenant-commander opposite was leaning towards her as he talked animatedly in a low voice. Whatever his line of chat, it was obviously having little or no effect because she looked bored and miserable. I gave a little cough and they both looked up. Rosemary's expression was immediately transformed to one of surprise and delight as she ran across the room straight into my arms.

'Colin! I was waiting for you to telephone, and here you are in person,' she cried, after kissing me several times. 'My fairy godmother must be working overtime. It's the best Christmas surprise I could possibly have had. How ever did you manage to get here?'

She turned to introduce me to the other officer, only to find that he had gone.

'Who's your friend?' I asked casually, trying not to appear jealous.

'That's only the officer of the day. He fancies himself as a ladies' man, but his wife has him well and truly under her thumb. Let me organise some fresh coffee for you, darling. You're frozen.'

I told her how I came to be there, and we carried on talking for about an hour, holding hands all the time. I could see two WRENS watching us through the serving hatch and nudging each other, but I didn't care.

'How long can you stay, Colin? Will you be able to stop for lunch? It won't be much, I'm afraid, because most of the staff have gone off duty for the day.'

I explained that I had to leave early in the afternoon, but we continued talking until a WREN messenger appeared.

'I'm sorry, ma'am. Orderly officer's compliments, could you please join him in the plot-room. I'm afraid there's a bit of a flap on.'

'Damn!' Rosemary exploded. 'You'd think they could leave us alone today of all days. Look, my love, if I'm not back in an hour, there's no point in your staying. Look after yourself, darling. I'm still trying my best to wangle a posting somewhere close to you.'

She kissed me and was gone, leaving the room empty and dismal. For about an hour and a half I casually flicked through a pile of magazines, but when she didn't reappear, I had to admit the fact that the duty officer would certainly see more of her than I would that day.

The journey back to Cambridge was very different from the morning's ride, however. Shortly after leaving Felixstowe it began to rain which was soon mixed with sleet. It was bitterly cold and the wind blew straight into my face, making the conditions very unpleasant, but worse was to follow. The engine began to mis-fire, and when I was only half way, it stopped altogether. There was no one around to ask for help or advice, so I did the only thing I could think of, namely, cleaning the plug, which was heavily sooted up. Fortunately the engine started once more, but I had two further unscheduled stops before I arrived back in Cambridge after dark, cold and hungry.

'We thought you had decided to stay,' Martin said with a twinkle in his eye.

I explained what had happened, and the elder boy looked somewhat sheepish.

'John hasn't yet learned the value of vehicle maintainance,' the brigadier told me. 'He imagines that all you have to do is to pour petrol into the tank when his ration is available, and it will keep going for ever. Let this be a lesson to you, young man.'

On Boxing Day evening the Hardcastles threw a party, a bring-your-own-bottle affair which was attended mainly by university staff, their wives and families. Most of the conversation tended to be on the academic side, and much of it over my head, but I hope I didn't look too bored. As one of the few unattached males present, my company was much in demand, especially when they learned that I was in the Commandos. One such female who was slightly drunk and blatantly predatory, told me that her husband was away in North Africa, and asked me outright to take her upstairs. I had quite a lot of trouble getting rid of her, as I didn't really fancy her in the first place. I was not sorry when the last guest had gone, and I was able to escape to the privacy of my room.

The Hardcastles had been perfect hosts, and the leave was by no means a disaster, but I had missed Rosemary not being there, and I felt a twinge of relief when I was back in my unit once more. Fortunately, this time there had been no alarms during my absence, and life very soon settled down into the old routine once more.

Three months slipped by, and although I did not want to admit the fact, I was becoming bored. Captain Delpierre had been posted elsewhere, and his replacement was the exact opposite. He was a young Frenchman, almost a dandy who fancied himself as a ladies' man. He also wanted to change much of our established routine, and it was necessary for me to keep a close eye on him. However, he was also as keen as mustard, so I had to be careful not to dampen his enthusiasm too much.

At last I had a letter from Rosemary with the news I had been waiting for. Not only had she obtained a posting to Petersfield, but she had also been promoted to Second Officer. I was over the moon, and my boredom vanished overnight until I received a message that the brigadier was coming to visit me during the next forty-eight hours.

'You're looking very pleased with yourself, Colin,' he remarked after he had sat down in my office.

'I didn't think it showed, sir,' I grinned. 'Yes, I have something to celebrate. At long last, Rosemary has been posted to Petersfield, and she's had promotion as well. I'll be able to see her fairly often from now on.'

He didn't reply immediately, but sat staring in front of him with an expressionless face for what seemed like an age. It was then I realised he had brought bad news, and I began to experience a sinking sensation in the pit of my stomach.

'I'm sorry, Colin,' he said in a flat voice. 'I thought I had better come down and tell you myself. A piece of paper is so impersonal somehow.'

'I'm not being posted, am I?'

He nodded. 'I'm afraid so. General de Gaulle himself has asked for you personally. Apparently you impressed him very much when he was here a few months ago. There's nothing I can do to prevent it. The order came from much higher up.'

'Damnation!' I exploded, thumping the desk with my fist. I then turned to look out of the window so that he would not see the tears in my eyes. 'What does it involve, sir, do you know?'

'I'm not absolutely sure, but from what I've gleaned I think it will mean going back to France. I know it's rough luck, old lad, but I have no doubt that you'll be able to take it in your stride.'

'So, when do I leave here?'

'Not for a few weeks yet. We still have to find a suitable replacement, and then give him a few days to take over. It's a pity Delpierre is no longer here. This present fellow is quite unsuitable. So, when does Rosemary arrive in Petersfield?'

'The day after tomorrow. How the hell am I going to tell her?' All my euphoria had by now evaporated, and I was almost dreading having to face her.

'Well, at least the delay will give you a little time together.'

After he had gone I studied the order for my posting, but the bald statement told me nothing. I was to report to the Free French headquarters in London on the twenty-sixth of April 1943 at 14.30 hours for an interview, following which I was to be prepared to move immediately to another location. Just who was to do the interviewing, and for what purpose, time alone would tell.

'Colin, darling, what's the matter? Something's wrong, I know it. Ever since I have been down in this part of the country, you have been withdrawn and pre-occupied. And this evening in particular, you've hardly said a word. Have you gone off me, or have you got another girl-friend, or what?'

'You know that's not true, Rosemary.'

'Then tell me! I'm a big girl now.'

We had spent the evening in a quiet pub out in the country where we had sat scarcely speaking, and were now parked in my little pick-up truck outside her dormitory block at Petersfield, savouring the last moments before she was due to go in. It was true what she had said about my attitude towards her ever since her posting here. Each time we had been together I had made up my mind to break the news to her, but when it came to the point my courage had always failed me. Now, tonight, there was no way I could postpone the awful moment any longer.

As gently as I could I told her everything, but I was not able to look at her as I did so.

'I just couldn't bring myself to admit the truth to you before, Rosemary. You were so happy to have been posted near me, I didn't want to break the spell. There was no use in us both being miserable.'

Suddenly, she burst into tears. 'How long is it before you go?' she asked, gulping between sobs.

'The day after tomorrow,' I answered in a flat voice. Her obvious distress was tearing me apart.

'Will I see you again before you go?'

'I don't think so, my love. It will take me all day to hand over to my successor, and I couldn't face another parting. That's why I've told you tonight. If I'm not able to let you know of my whereabouts, contact Martin Hardcastle and he may be able to give you a rough idea as to my location. Here is his address and telephone number. He knows all about you, and will be willing to keep you informed, so don't be afraid to get in touch with him.'

Our last kiss was brief because Rosemary pulled herself away from me, and a few minutes later I watched her disappear along the path until she was lost in the darkness. She walked slowly with her shoulders slumped, and her head down. I wanted to run after her and take her in my arms, but I knew that it was too late. I was also conscious of the fact that it had been brutal of me to have broken the news to her at the very last moment, but even if she had known beforehand, it would have added to her misery too, knowing what was coming. I remember wondering at the time if I would ever see her again.

12

Back to France

No one could have been more surprised than I was when I found myself being ushered into the presence of General Charles de Gaulle in person. There was one other officer present, but it was the Free French leader himself who conducted the entire interview, and whose personality dominated the proceedings absolutely. I sat in a chair while he walked around the room, stopping every now and then to look down at me from his great height with piercing eyes which appeared to note my every reaction. For my part, I was fascinated by his aquiline nose which seemed to swivel like a direction-finder, and I had to stop myself from laughing at this irreverent thought. Throughout the meeting he remained aloof, detached almost, as if he was trying to give the impression of being a god-like figure without warmth or humanity. In spite of this, the longer I remained in his presence, the more I came to have a sneaking admiration for him.

After he had questioned me in great detail as to my background and previous war experience, he began to probe into my political affiliations, as well as my attitude towards his fellow countrymen. I considered this to be a very strange line of inquiry, and he was astute enough to pick up my thoughts.

'You may imagine that politics has nothing to do with the conduct of the war, Major Marshall, but it is necessary for me to know exactly where you stand before I decide whether or not you are the right man for the delicate mission I have in mind. So far I have received nothing but obstruction and non-cooperation from Churchill and the British War Cabinet, so I must have someone who will give me absolute loyalty. Do I make myself clear?'

'Not exactly, general. I might be able to give you a more accurate answer if I knew what was expected of me.'

What he told me had merely confirmed what was already common knowledge, namely that the War Cabinet and this autocratic and nationalistic leader of the French nation in exile did not see eye to eye on a number of issues.

'All in good time, major. As I have already indicated, the mission is a very delicate one, but it will be vital to the success of the Second Front, if and when this ever takes place. Eisenhower wants time to build up his forces before attempting a landing, but every month we delay means that the German European fortress grows stronger, and the enemy become better organised. If they were to push us back into the sea, it would set the war back ten years. In the meantime my countrymen are suffering at the hands of an army of occupation which is probably far more oppressive than any other throughout history. I cannot stand by and watch this go on day after day, while the British remain obdurate, and the Americans don't care.'

All the time he had been delivering this homely he was staring out of the window so that I could not see his face, but now he swung round to watch my reaction. I could see his point, and I told him so, but reminded him that in my position any change was out of my hands.

He crossed the room to his desk, sat down and regarded me intently for a time before answering.

'That's not altogether true, Major Marshall. You have it in your power to ensure that any landings on the French Coast met with success. You could help me — er, us to achieve this.'

'I'm flattered, general, but surely this is a job for a Frenchman, whatever it is?'

'That's true, but the British and Americans will only agree to this scheme if it is carried out by a British officer, and so far you name has been the only one which has been considered. Having met you already, Major Marshall, with a few reservations, I am prepared to place the fate of my country in your hands.'

I considered this last statement to be a bit over the top, but I let it pass. Whatever the operation, it was obviously an important one, and apparently had been agreed at the highest level. De Gaulle continued to watch me closely.

'As you are aware, sir, I have had a long connection with your country, and have the greatest admiration for your people, but if there is any resentment at my appointment, then surely it will cause friction with those whom I am supposed to be helping?'

He gave an exaggerated shrug. 'That may be so, but I'm sure it is a small price to pay. They will realise the value of your contribution in time.'

'Would it be possible for me to discuss the matter with Brigadier Hardcastle, general?'

I was desperately trying to find a way out. Whatever my feelings had been when I had embarked on this type of work, my heart was now no longer in it.

'Hardcastle already knows all about it,' the general said coldly. 'He is also aware that this mission is of the utmost importance, so his views are irrelevant.'

If this was the case, then there was no way out short of a blunt refusal, but if I did turn it down, then what would my future be?

'Very well, sir, I accept.' The words had slipped out before I could stop them.

He nodded as if that was what he had expected me to say, then he crossed the room to where a large scale map of Normandy hung on the wall and beckoned me to join him.

'The landings for the Second Front will almost certainly take place in this area,' he told me. 'The exact details and timing have still to be finalised, but in order to increase our chances of success it will be necessary for the Resistance to play its part by attacking German lines of communication and isolated units simultaneously with acts of sabotage at key points. At all costs they must be prevented from reinforcing their troops on the coast. You understand me so far, major?'

I nodded.

'At the moment, the Maquis are disorganised, with their various groups operating independently of each other. It will be necessary to formulate a plan whereby they become one effective unit with a single purpose. It will be your job to organise this, so that when the time comes, they will each have a separate role to play, hopefully without confusion. This will not be easy. You will appreciate that the men and women of the Resistance are naturally very suspicious of any control from an unseen distant source, and are resentful of strangers coming into their midst. They prefer to fight their own war in their own way.'

'Then how am I to manage it, general? If what you say is true, how can I make them listen to me?'

'I personally will broadcast to the Resistance throughout the whole of France. In this way it will avoid pin-pointing any one area in particular. I will inform them that you are coming as my emissary, but in general terms so that they will be prepared for you. They will listen to me. As soon as you have made contact with one group, it will be a matter of passing on to the next, and the word will get round.'

'Why cannot these orders be passed by radio, sir?'

'We dare not take the risk. Should the Germans monitor our broadcasts without us knowing, it could blow the whole thing wide open. No, it will have to be done on a personal level.'

'How will I be landed, sir, and where?'

'You will be dropped by parachute, but up to now the exact location has not yet been decided. There is still a great deal to do before we reach that stage. In the meantime, you will be taken to a secret location where you will be fully briefed and undergo parachute training. It could be as long as two to three months before you actually make the drop. No doubt I will meet you again before that time. Thank you, for your co-operation, major.'

With a casual wave of his hand, I was dismissed. The other officer, a colonel, ushered me out, still without uttering a word.

Once more I found myself installed in one of those large country estates which had been commandeered for the duration of the war. It was not dissimilar to the one I had just left, this time it was situated in Hertfordshire, about twenty miles from London, and close to a small aerodrome.

I was anxious to begin my mission and get it finished as quickly as possible, but this was not the case, and I very soon realised why it could not be achieved in a short time. Each day I was fed with more and more data to commit to memory — the names of Resistance leaders and where they were to be found, the specific tasks which every group was to undertake when the signal was given, and the changes in codes to be implemented prior to D-Day.

It was a Herculean task, and I quickly discovered the reason why the second man had been present during my interview. His name was Colonel Lamotte, and not only was he my briefing officer, but I subsequently learned that he had been responsible for collating and planning the mission, which was destined to cause the maximum disruption behind the enemy lines immediately before and after the landings. Each day we discussed a fresh aspect of the assignment until my head was reeling with a jumble of facts. There was no way that I would be able to carry written instructions, therefore every single detail had to be committed to memory. The task was harder than I had imagined it to be, but Colonel Lamotte approached it with patience and understanding, so that gradually the proposed pattern of events began to be filed somewhere within my grey matter.

Facilities at the detachment were adequate, if not luxurious. We had a swimming pool, tennis courts, and there were a few organised games such as net-ball and five-a-side football. The mess-rooms were comfortable, there was a comprehensive library, and twice a week we were treated to a film show. Perhaps the greatest imposition was the fact that we were not allowed to communicate with the outside world by any means, and I found that this restriction on my personal freedom particularly hard to bear. Not being able to send or receive any letters was soul-destroying, and there were many times when I longed to telephone Rosemary. Even the sound of her voice would have helped to sustain my morale, but all calls were strictly taboo.

There were ten of us altogether at the centre, three men and seven women, but I never discovered what part they were playing since none of us discussed our reason for being there at any time. For two months, my routine never varied. There was P.T. before breakfast, then the remainder of the morning was devoted to refresher courses in weaponry or unarmed combat. We were also given a working knowledge of radio procedure in case we were ever faced with using a transmitter in an emergency. After lunch we went our separate ways, and for three days a week I had a couple of hours with Colonel Lamotte, but most of my free time was devoted to memorising the details of my mission.

After a couple of months I began parachute training which I found to be a harrowing experience. I had never had a good head for heights, and even the gradual progression from jumping on to rubber mats on the gymnasium floor, through the harness and captive wire stage, to the final drop from a balloon, I found daunting in the extreme, and I was forced to grit my teeth in order to go through with it. It was on my final jump when the accident occurred. Just as I was about to hit the ground, a sudden gust of wind twisted me sideways, with the result that I landed awkwardly, tearing a ligament in my ankle which put me out of action for a whole month.

Perhaps it was a blessing in disguise because it enabled me to catch up with my briefing which continued unabated.

One day, when I was sitting outside in the sunshine trying to memorise a particularly difficult passage containing several map references, a shadow fell across the paper I was reading. I looked up to find Martin Hardcastle standing smiling down at me. When I tried to stand up he pushed me gently back into my seat and drew up a chair.

'So this is what you get up to when I'm not there to keep an eye on you?' He grinned as we shook hands. 'How are you feeling, Colin?'

'Fed up, immobile, and wishing that I was somewhere else,' I replied without enthusiasm.

'I heard about your accident, so I managed to pull some strings and come and visit you. I understand it will delay your departure for several weeks.' He looked around. 'Still, it's not a bad place to be laid-up, even if it does feel like an open prison. I wouldn't mind having a couple of weeks here, doing nothing.'

'I'm glad to see you, sir. I've been wanting to discuss the whole project with you, but de Gaulle said you knew all about it.'

'That's not strictly true, but what's on your mind, Colin?'

'What are the chances of my opting out? I know this is a big assignment, but my heart isn't in it. Up to now, everyone has assumed that I can do it, but I'm beginning to doubt my ability to see it through, even if I make it to France.'

He shook his head. 'There's not a hope of you backing out now, old lad. I know how you feel, but this project has the blessing of Churchill himself. Besides, if you did refuse to go through with it at this stage, you know that they would lock you up until it was all over, which may be several months yet. They dare not let you go free with all the knowledge you have acquired. I'm sorry, Colin, but there is nothing I can do for you.'

At that time I did not know that Churchill had agreed to this mission only to keep de Gaulle from pestering him about the Second Front which was still a long way off as yet. Certainly he never mentioned it in his War Memoires, so whether or not my mission was strictly necessary I will never be sure. If I had been aware of this at the time of the brigadier's visit, I wonder if I might not have taken the risk of going to prison instead of putting my life on the line in order to placate the French leader.

'I never thought of that,' I answered in my ignorance. 'It seems an even worse prospect than going ahead with it, so I may as well accept the inevitable. I'm sorry, you've caught me at a bad time, sir. As you can see, I'm feeling a bit sorry for myself.'

'Well, I suspected that you might need cheering up, so perhaps this may help.'

From his pocket, he drew out an envelope and handed it to me. Although there was nothing written on the outside, I knew as soon as I touched it that it was from Rosemary.

'You've seen her, of course?' I asked eagerly.

He nodded. 'At the end of last week. A beautiful and charming girl, Colin. I can understand now why you don't want to be separated from her. You're a lucky man. Go ahead and read it if you want to.'

He tactfully went off for a walk while I tore open the envelope with trembling fingers. The letter was dated five days before.

> My darling Colin,
> I have just received a visit from Brigadier Hardcastle who is waiting for me to finish this note to you. It was kind of him to take the trouble. Please thank him for me.
> How are you, my love? A silly question. Of course, you can't answer, but I often think about you and wonder what you are doing. The fact that he can deliver this letter to you must mean that you are still in this country, and I'm glad about that.
> Wherever you go, Colin, please look after yourself, if only for my sake. Don't worry about me. I'll be all right, so long as I know you are safe. I'll start to live again when you have returned safely.
> God bless and watch over you, my love. I'll be counting the days till you are here with me again.
> Your own,
> Rosemary.

For several minutes I sat without moving. Of course it was wonderful to hear from her, and the letter ought to have cheered me up, but in fact it had the opposite effect. It merely emphasised how much I was missing her, and it was frustrating to know that it would be a long time before I saw her again.

By the time Martin Hardcastle returned I had managed to pull myself together, and we sat down to talk.

'I was looking through your file the other day, Colin, and I noticed that your official next-of-kin is a solicitor in Surrey. Would it be in order if I asked him to notify Rosemary if anything should happen to you, otherwise she may not know for some time. I don't want to be an alarmist, but as things are, I'm sure it's important for both of you.'

'Yes, of course, sir. It's something I was going to do myself some time ago, but I never got round to it.'

'One more thing, Colin. I want you to remember that

you are still an officer in the Royal Marine Commandos, and are only on temporary secondment. When this party is over you'll be returning to us. I wouldn't want you to think we have abandoned you.'

I was glad he had cleared up that point, because it did much for my morale. We continued talking for about an hour while he brought me up to date with all the news, but when it was time for him to leave, I watched as he strode purposefully down the path out of sight, and it seemed to me that my last link with home and safety went with him, leaving me alone with my thoughts.

Towards the end of September I was declared fit once more. I had also completed my parachute training, and Colonel Lamotte was satisfied that I had absorbed all the facts relating to my mission. During his final session with me, I put a question to him which had been worrying me for several weeks.

'What will happen if I am captured and fall into the hands of the Gestapo, sir? I'm not sure if I would be able to stop myself from talking under torture, in which case they will discover what we are planning.'

'Hopefully, it won't come to that, major. Unlike the Germans, we don't issue suicide pills to our operatives. However, you will scarcely come under the category of a spy, because you will be able to wear your uniform under civilian clothes. If you are unlucky enough to be caught, you may have the opportunity to get rid of your disguise and declare yourself to be a member of the Armed Services, in which case you are subject to the protection of the Geneva Convention and escape interrogation.'

'The Germans may not view my clandestine presence in their midst with such leniency, sir.'

'Well, if the worst happens, you can be sure that someone has made contingency plans. Try if possible to throw the enemy off the scent by admitting that your mission is a blind, and that the real invasion will take place close to Calais. I am sure that is what they want to hear.'

And so it came to pass that in the early hours of the morning on the 28th of September 1943, I was parachuted from a light aircraft into a field surrounded by dense woods somewhere between Caen and Falaise in Normandy. I remember nothing about the actual drop. At the time I was so terrified that I must have erased it from my memory. My sole recollection is that I landed safely without damaging my injured ankle.

No sooner had I gathered in my parachute, when a pinpoint of light flashed the recognition signal from the edge of the trees adjoining the field. With some trepidation, I made my way towards it, keeping my hand on my pistol all the time. I was prepared to throw myself to the ground as half-a-dozen shadowy figures emerged from hiding, but I was greeted effusively, while the silk canopy was taken from me to be buried somewhere deep within the wood.

'We're pleased to see you, major. We have had warning of your arrival, but right now we must hurry to a place of safety. Whenever a light aircraft comes over, the Germans know it is here either to drop agents or supplies, and they are always quick to send out patrols, so we must clear the area immediately.'

Half running and half walking, I was guided through dense woods and scrubland, along paths which must have been known only to poachers and members of the Resistance. Several times we stopped to listen, but no sound of pursuit was evident, and in a short time our little party arrived at a large, isolated farmhouse where we went straight to the barn. We climbed a ladder into what appeared from below to be a hayloft, but when I reached it, I saw that an area had been cleared behind the facade of straw bales. There were no windows, but one of the men lit a paraffin lamp which cast eerie flickering shadows on the roof. The leader pointed to some bread and cheese together with a carafe of red wine which had been set out.

'You must be hungry, major. Tomorrow we will talk, but now we will leave you to sleep here. There is some loose straw in the corner. No doubt you are used to something more comfortable, but I'm afraid this is the best we can do for the time being.'

With that they all melted away into the night leaving me alone with my thoughts. The bread was freshly baked and the local cheese excellent. I was hungrier than I thought so was able to do justice to both, but the rough red wine was not to my taste, so I scarcely drank any. I turned out the lamp and lay listening to the scurrying of the mice or rats who were doubtless upset by my invasion of their domain, and the snuffling of the two big horses in the stalls below. I must have slept soundly, however, because the next thing I remember was that the barn doors were wide open, allowing the morning sunshine to flood in.

I was aware of someone moving about underneath me, and I peeped cautiously over the edge of the loft to see a young lad in his teens harnessing the horses. If he knew of my presence he gave no sign, and led the animals outside without so much as a glance in my direction.

A few minutes after he had gone I heard a different lot of footsteps entering the barn.

'Psst! Monsieur!' A voice called up to me.

An old man stood at the foot of the ladder and beckoned me to follow him into the house. In a large stone-flagged kitchen an old woman and a young girl of about twelve busied themselves with their domestic chores. Breakfast consisting of ham, bread and milk was already set out for me, and while I ate alone not a word was spoken. It did not require a great deal of intuition to know that my presence was not welcome. I washed and shaved at the pump outside in the yard, but before I had finished my ablutions I was startled by a man's voice behind me.

'Good morning, major. I hope you slept well.'

I must have jumped visibly because the man laughed at my discomfort. I was relieved to find it was the same person who had led my reception party in the earlier hours of the morning, because I had not heard him approach.

'It's as well that I was not a German, monsieur. In this work one must have eyes in the back of one's head.'

We went into a room in the farmhouse which looked as if it was seldom used. because a thick dust covered much of the old-fashioned furniture. My companion produced some clothing which he handed to me — a blue denim jacket and trousers such as the peasants wore, a scarf and a beret. They were suitably oversized so that I was able to wear them over my uniform, the result being a passable imitation of a local Frenchman. He then handed me an identity card made out in the name of Emile Barouche together with a small knapsack.

'Carry your papers at all times,' he told me, 'but your pistol produces too much of a bulge under your clothing, and I advise you to carry it in the bag, major. The Germans hereabouts usually do not bother to search us in the street. The fact is they are becoming careless and war-weary. Most of them just want to go home.'

I asked him what his name was, but he shook his head.

'We have no names, monsieur, just as I do not know yours. It is safer that way. After you leave here, you have never seen me before, and you will not recognise me even if we pass each other in the street.'

We discussed the role which his group was expected to play in the event of the impending invasion, and I passed on the codeword which would be broadcast when they were to go into action, but he was apparently unimpressed.

'When will this come about, major? We are ready now, and have been all summer, but with winter approaching I cannot visualise any landing before next spring.'

There was little I could say except to reassure him that the Second Front would open just as soon as the Allies were ready. He tried to press me for a date, but of course I was unable to give him one.

Two days later, a guide took me on to the next Resistance group, avoiding any contact with the Occupying Forces.

For the next couple of months I travelled over a wide area covering almost half of Normandy, staying in a variety of locations. Mostly my billets were in isolated farmhouses, but I also lived in a chateau, a basement flat in a large town, and several private houses both large and small. But no matter who I contacted I was treated as an outsider, someone who was not quite to be trusted, although they usually came to accept the necessity of my mission after I had spoken to them. Always I was asked the same questions.

'When will the invasion come? Where will it take place?' All I could do was to advise patience.

Occasionally I managed to make contact with members of the S.O.E., and so was able to notify London by way of their radio transmissions as to the progress I was making. I sometimes wondered if any of this information would filter back to Brigadier Hardcastle, who, in turn, could notify Rosemary that I was all right, but somehow I doubted it.

On the few occasions when I was stopped and asked for my papers by the Germans, they were given scant inspection, especially now that I had acquired all the characteristics and mannerisms of a French peasant. I had slipped into the role so easily that at any given time I could have passed myself off amongst the local population as one of themselves. In fact I had had so little difficulty in travelling around the area that inevitably I grew careless.

One morning in mid-December, I was on my way to visit yet another Resistance group in a village which was in the centre of a scattered rural community. My mode of transport was a horse-drawn cart driven by a young girl who was unaware of my true identity. Because of the heavy sleet which the wind blew straight into our faces, we were huddled together under a tarpaulin giving us only a limited view of the road ahead, and impairing our hearing so that we were oblivious to any vehicles approaching from the rear. We were therefore unaware of the fact that a German scout car was trying to pass us on the narrow road.

Eventually, by dint of much hooting, we pulled off on to the verge, thus allowing the vehicle to pass, but as it did so, the passenger, a German officer, peered at us closely before continuing on his way.

If I had had my wits about me I perhaps would have noted his abnormal interest in us, and made a diversion, but I thought no more about the incident. When we entered the next village some fifteen minutes later, I noticed the same scout car was parked outside the gendarmerie on the main street. Still the penny didn't drop until a soldier stepped out from a doorway into the road and signalled us to stop. We were ushered into the building where we were shown into a sparsely-furnished room in which the same officer was sitting at a table. He examined our papers meticulously without a word being spoken, then sat back in the chair looking us up and down, smiling sardonically. I was conscious of the soldier who stood by the door immediately behind us.

'Forgive me for interrupting your journey,' he said in

excellent French, 'but I am curious as to why it is necessary for you to be travelling in an open cart in weather like this. Your journey must be very urgent.'

'This young lady's mother is ill, and we are going to visit her,' I said, trying to sound as convincing as possible. This explanation was ready in my mind in case of such an eventuality.

'I see,' he said softly. 'And what is the address of this ill mother?'

I gave him the name of a fictitious farmhouse, hoping that he would not bother to follow it up, but if he did it may give me a little more time to consider my next move.

'Take them both away, and lock them up in separate cells,' he ordered the soldier.

As I turned to leave the room he called me back, and pointing to the satchel I was carrying, he ordered me to open it. For a moment I was taken aback at the unexpected request, and stood motionless with the bag in my hand so that he was obliged to repeat the order in a voice which was raised several decibels. I glanced over my shoulder to see if the sentry was still there, but he was, and with his rifle pointed at my back.

The officer jumped to his feet, knocking over the chair, but he did not appear to notice.

'Open it!' he shouted, thumping the desk with his fist.

There was no escape now. I drew out the pistol, and holding it by the barrel I handed it over to the German. It was now his turn to be surprised, but he recovered quickly.

'Well, well,' he said softly, 'and what have we here?'

13

Capture and Escape

I felt strangely calm and detached, with my mind crystal clear, but I was conscious of my heart hammering rapidly. My companion stood in a corner of the room weeping softly, and my first priority was to try to obtain her release.

'This girl knows nothing about me,' I said to the officer. 'She was genuinely going to visit her sick mother, like I told you, and I persuaded her to give me a lift. Let her go, please. She is quite innocent.'

'And do you honestly expect me to on your say so? You terrorists are all the same. You make use of everyone, even little children, and hope that we will overlook the fact. No, the girl will stay until I have finished with her.'

He turned his attention to the revolver, which was a Smith & Wesson .38, standard British Army issue.

'So, how did you come to have this in your possession?' he asked, after he had examined it.

I saw by the flashes on his tunic that he was a member of the Abwehr, the German Military Intelligence, and so I knew I would have to be careful. This man was a trained interrogator, and my answers would be subjected to scrutiny, but in spite of that I decided to bluff it out a little longer.

'I watched some men come out of a hut in the woods,' I told him. 'After they had gone I went in and found the satchel lying there.'

He looked at me with contempt. 'You must consider me to be a fool if you think I will swallow a story like that.

Here you are with a loaded British revolver which can be used for killing Germans, and you try to fob me off with childish lies. Is there any reason why I shouldn't have you taken out and shot, right now?'

Events were beginning to take a serious turn, and I decided that the time had come to reveal my true identity, but before I could do so, my adversary had held out his hand for the satchel which I passed over to him without a word.

He then proceeded to empty the contents on to the desk, fresh underclothing, a little food, and right at the bottom the little leather-bound volume of the Gospel of St John. He opened it and read the inscription out loud. 'To Colin from Rosemary — with all my love.' In his mouth it sounded dirty. 'An interesting item this. And who, pray, is Colin?'

Without another word I peeled off my civilian outer garments and stood in my battledress which had major's crowns on the epaulettes, but no unit flashes or other embellishments. For several seconds he looked me up and down, but there was nothing in his expression to give an indication of what he was thinking.

'My name is Colin Marshall, my rank is major, my Army number is 604272, and I claim Prisoner of War status under the Geneva Convention.'

I stood rigidly to attention and looked him straight in the eye as I spoke, but my mouth was dry and I tried to control the trembling in my limbs. This was my last card, and I knew it. From now on it was up to him as to how I was to be treated.

He picked up the overturned chair and sat down again, resting his elbows on the desk with his finger-tips together and his thumbs under his chin. His unblinking grey eyes were fixed on my face, but he could not hide his interest in me. He remained in that position without moving for what seemed to be a long time.

'What would you say if I suggested to you that you had found this uniform also?' he asked, speaking slowly as if measuring every word. 'Here you are in German occupied territory dressed in civilian clothes, under which you are wearing a British Army uniform. For all I know it may have been stolen like you say the revolver was, and you speak French like a native. It all points to you being a member of the Resistance, so what makes you think that you are entitled to P.o.W. status?'

'Do you speak English?' I asked him, switching to my native tongue.

'Yes, I do, as a matter of fact. During the early 1930s I was a student at Oxford University.'

'Then you know what I say is true,' I persisted. 'You won't have me shot.'

'And why not, may I ask? One word is all that is necessary to have it carried out here and now.'

'Because I interest you,' I said, still speaking in English with a confidence which I did not feel.

He threw back his head and laughed, but there was no mirth in the gesture.

'Well now, that may or may not be true. It all depends on how much information you are prepared to give me.'

'Not a lot, beyond my name, rank and number.'

He frowned with annoyance, and picked up the little Gospel. 'Who is Rosemary? Wife, girl-friend?'

'My fiancée,' I replied. 'She hoped that it would help to keep me safe from harm.'

He shook his head. 'What a strange notion that is. How can a little book like this save you from the might of the German Army? Still, it's an interesting concept.'

He put it down and picked up the revolver, turning it over in his hand. There was no sound in the room, even the girl's sobs had abated now.

'You must be aware, of course, that we have the means to make you tell us everything. It would be a pity to have to inflict such an ordeal on a fellow-officer,' he said, leaning forward in a confidential manner. 'Why don't you make it easy for yourself.'

'Ah, so you admit that I am a fellow-officer. In which case my name is Colin Marshall, my number is 604272, and I claim P.o.W. status under the Geneva. . . .'

This obstinacy caused an immediate change in the German's attitude. He jumped to his feet once more, his face red and his eyes blazing with anger, while his previous tone of measured reason was replaced by uncontrollable shouting, which produced flecks of saliva on his lips.

'You may think you are being clever,' he screamed, 'but don't imagine for a moment that I am so easily fooled. I have a colleague in Paris who will be very anxious to meet a so-called British major who poses as a French peasant.'

In our lectures we had been warned about this method of interrogation whereby the simulated frenzy was supposed to instil fear and uncertainty into the prisoner. When he saw that his outburst did not have the desired effect, he sat down again and smiled sardonically.

'It's interesting to speculate that this little book has in fact kept you safe. For one thing, it has convinced me as to your identity, otherwise I might have treated you differently. Since you won't be needing it anymore, I think I will hang on to it. Who knows, maybe it will bring me luck also, although I don't believe in luck. However, I'm afraid I must send you on to Paris. There is a directive that all British Service personnel caught helping the Resistance will be interrogated there. A pity — I'm sure we could have found much to talk about, but the matter is out of my hands.'

With a jerk of his head, the girl was led away. What her eventual fate was I do not know, because I never saw her again. The officer pushed a button on the desk, and a few seconds later an elderly gendarme appeared.

'Take this fellow away and lock him up overnight,' he ordered. 'I will arrange for him to be transferred to Paris in the morning.'

In the bare, unheated cell, I was given only a dirty blanket for warmth. Was I to be handed over to the Gestapo? If so, there would be no point in my insisting to be dealt with as a P.o.W. Besides, who knew that I had been captured, and either my present whereabouts, or where I would finish up? At least the search of my clothing and personal belongings revealed nothing except for the pistol.

I had never really contemplated being tortured before now, and the lectures on the subject gave us only an inkling of what to expect, and how to cope with it. While sitting comfortably in a classroom, one had always imagined that it would happen to someone else, but here I was in that very situation for real. My mind was now in such a turmoil that I could no longer recall the advice I had been given.

It was still dark outside when the elderly gendarme brought me a bowl of thin soup and a piece of dark bread, which he passed through the grill in the door. I expected him to go away immediately, but instead he waited until I had collected the food from the narrow ledge.

'Do not worry, monsieur,' he said in a voice so low that I could scarcely hear him. 'You have not been forgotten, and help is at hand. In one hour, the Germans will come to take you away. You must be prepared.'

I could scarcely believe my ears. Prepared for what? Had I heard him right, or had I misinterpreted what he had said? Perhaps it was a ruse so that I would not make any trouble in expectation of being freed. At any rate, it would appear that the Resistance did know of my whereabouts, and would be able to relay the news back to London. It was then that another thought entered my mind. Supposing a sniper had been positioned outside on the buildings opposite to finish me off so that I would not talk. It wouldn't be the first occasion such a drastic solution had been put into operation.

They had taken my watch, so I did not know what time it was, but through the filthy window I could see the first streaks of daylight filtering through the rain-laden sky when I heard the escort approaching. There were two German soldiers with a sergeant in charge, who bound my hands tightly behind my back before I was marched out. The N.C.O. barked unintelligible orders in my ear as he continually kept pushing me forwards from behind. I suspect he did this merely in order to stamp his authority on the proceedings, and to make me feel inferior.

Out on the street, a lorry with a canvas cover was parked, together with a motorcycle combination which had a machine-gun mounted on the sidecar; a small armoured car completed the convoy. I stood blinking in the doorway, and for a brief moment I saw two familiar faces amongst the few people who had gathered to watch. I wondered if this would be the time when an assassin's bullet would put an end to my life, but I was hustled towards the back of the lorry, and made to climb in without incident. The two armed guards sat opposite me, and as we moved off I knew that the Germans had discovered how important a capture they had made, so it was essential to ensure my safe arrival in Paris.

By the time we had reached the next village, the rain had turned to sleet, and I was shivering with cold since I had no overcoat. As time passed, and we drove further away from the area, I was conscious that every turn of the wheels was taking me closer to the capital where my fate would be decided. Ten, fifteen, twenty kilometres had passed without incident, until I had given up hope that the gendarme's comforting words held any meaning. By now, my two guards had relaxed visibly to the extent that they were smoking and carrying on an animated conversation, ignoring me completely. Through a chink in the canvas, I saw that the countryside was heavily wooded, but, apart from that, I had no idea where we were.

I thought of leaping out over the tail-board, even with my hands tied, but when I looked out, the menacing presence of the armoured car was still following close behind.

When I had given up all hope of rescue, there was a sudden explosion, followed by several bursts of small arms fire. The lorry bucked violently, and before the startled guards could rise to their feet, the vehicle overturned and rolled over three times down a steep bank beside the road. I was thrown about violently and uncontrollably like a pea in a drum, until the vehicle came to rest upside down a few seconds later. I found myself mixed up with the bodies of the two German soldiers, the three of us all in a heap, fortunately with myself on top.

When I gathered together my scattered wits, I saw that one of the men did not move, and I had the feeling that he was dead. The other soldier began to stir, but my body was lying face-down across his legs, thus preventing the German reaching for his rifle which was at the front of the truck, a couple of metres away. I could do very little with my hands tied behind by back, but with an effort I managed to struggle to my feet and kicked him full in the face with all my strength, just as his finger-tips touched the weapon. He suddenly went limp, but I did not wait to see what happened to him. My one instinctive reaction was to put as much distance between myself and my captors as was possible, and as quickly as I could.

With a desperation bordering on panic, I somehow extricated myself from the lorry which was lying in a small stream at the foot of a steep bank covered with thick undergrowth, and surrounded by trees. Up on the road, the shooting and the sound of men's voices, with the occasional grenade exploding, could still be heard. The heavy machine-gun mounted on the armoured car was firing intermittently, which meant that the Resistance had not yet managed to overpower my escort. I certainly had no intention of hanging around to await the outcome. If the Germans were the victors, they would waste no time in coming after me, and so I set off into the forest in the opposite direction.

Progress was difficult because the lower branches of the trees constantly scratched my face, while underfoot the ground was wet and marshy. An additional complication was the fact that my hands were still tied behind my back, and my second priority was to find means of freeing myself. I ploughed on for perhaps ten minutes more, stopping every now and then to listen for any sounds of pursuit, but I could hear nothing beyond the noise of sporadic firing far away in the distance. Eventually this stopped, but of course I had no idea who had won, and so I knew I had to get away from the area.

Get away — but where to? I didn't even know my location, but a small voice inside urged me to keep on running. I veered off to the left and continued for quite a distance until the trees suddenly thinned out so that I found myself standing on the edge of the forest overlooking an uncultivated field which sloped away from me down into a lush valley full of small orchards, with fruit trees now bare of leaves. Nestling amongst them was a farm with a few cultivated fields on the far side. The house itself was small, dwarfed by the out-buildings which were adjacent to it on three sides to form a sizeable yard in the centre. Close by, a cow and a couple of tethered goats grazed peacefully, but even from that distance I could see that the whole establishment had a run-down, delapidated appearance. An unmade, rough road, little more than a track ran up to the yard, but I was unable to see where it came from because of a wooded spur of land around which it disappeared from view.

Although there was no one to be seen outside, I knew that the house was almost certainly occupied, because a thin wisp of smoke rose from one of its two chimneys.

Until that moment, all my actions had been as the result of blind panic, but now, for the first time since my escape, I stopped to think about what my next move ought to be. I was sensible enough to know that if I walked straight down to the farm and asked for help, I could be in trouble once more, since not all the French were patriotic, and for a number of reasons there were those who either through fear, or for promises of favours to come, would turn against their countrymen or their allies, if they considered it was in their own interests to do so.

As if to reinforce this line of reasoning, even while I watched, a solitary German on a motorcycle came down the track and rode straight into the yard. Having dismounted he entered the house without knocking, which pointed to the fact that he was on familiar terms with the occupants. A few moments after he had entered, a female emerged and went into one of the out-houses, but whether she was young or old I had no means of telling from that distance.

By now, I was firmly convinced that the German was part of an organised search for me, but at that moment it seemed unimportant. I felt a combination of extreme physical exhaustion and depression wash over me, and my euphoria at having escaped was replaced by the realisation that alone and on foot, with nothing in my pockets, it would be almost impossible for me to get away completely without the assistance of others. I remember thinking that I would rather have died of exposure out here, than take the risk of being captured again.

There must have been some factor which drew me to the farm because I continued to keep a watch on it. I was looking through a fence immediately in front of me, without actually seeing it, until my eyes changed focus so that I was looking at the strands instead of through them, and I realised then that it was made of barbed wire. It took longer than I imagined to fray through the ropes binding my wrists, and not only had I to dig deeply into my reserves of strength, but during the process I was forced to stop for a rest on several occasions. By the time I was free I could scarcely stand, and my limbs were shaking uncontrollably, partly due to exhaustion and also due to the intense cold.

Without thinking, I ran my hand over my face which felt wet from the rain, and sticky because of what I thought was excessive sweating. The roughness of my chin reminded me that I hadn't shaved for a couple of days, but when my fingers touched the upper part of my cheek and around the eye, I felt a stab of pain. I stared at my hand which was now covered with fresh blood, and on looking down at my clothing I saw that the front of my tunic was stained dark red in large patches. I realised then that when the lorry turned over I must have split open my cheek, but it had been made worse by the branches which had continuously scratched the wound during my escape through the forest.

I reckoned that the German must have been in the farmhouse for about an hour before he emerged and mounted his motorcycle once more, roaring away at high speed with the noise of his engine still audible long after he himself had disappeared from sight. What had he been doing all this time? Since he was alone, it was more than likely that his purpose in visiting was private — official visits invariably involved a number of men. In that case, I surmised that whoever lived there must have been of a friendly disposition towards the Germans, which boded ill if I wanted their help.

The rain grew heavier, driven by a gale-force wind which blew straight into my face. I retreated back into the wood for shelter, and found a dry place underfoot where the trees above were thickest. I lay down on a carpet of pine needles, too tired to take any more interest in my surroundings. A rabbit scuttled past so close that I could have almost put out my hand and touched it, while all around there were rustlings in the undergrowth to let me know that there were other wild creatures who perhaps regarded me as one of themselves.

I must have fallen into a deep sleep, because when I

awoke for the first time, it was already dark. In spite of my rest, I still felt exhausted, and I had to force myself to get to my feet. I managed it with an effort, and when I looked down at the place where I had been resting, there was just enough light for me to notice that a fairly large pool of congealed blood had collected under my head. Now I knew that my feeling of excessive tiredness was not due to fatigue, but the result of haemorrhage, and I was sensible enough to realise that if I stayed there I would almost certainly bleed to death. I decided to take a chance by going down to the farm and asking them for help.

I hoped that in the darkness I would be able to make a reconnaissance without being detected. This would give me a chance to discover who the occupants might be, and to be sure that there were no Germans about. The house was further down the hill than I had at first thought, and towards the bottom each step became a conscious effort, since my legs felt that at any minute they were going to give way under me. Fortunately it had stopped raining, but the ground was still wet and heavy, making it doubly difficult to plough over the uneven terrain.

Even before I had entered the yard, a dog in one of the out-houses began to bark, and I drew back into the shadows until I was sure that no one was coming out to investigate. Whoever was inside the house either didn't hear the dog's warning, or else they had better things to do. I staggered across the yard towards a window where a chink of light was showing, and by dint of propping myself on the sill, I was able to peep through a gap in the curtains. My view was somewhat restricted, but I saw two women sitting at a table eating a meal, but it wasn't what I saw which interested me, it was what I could hear. At first I thought there was also a man in the room whom I could not see, until I realised that the words I was listening to were being spoken by a newsreader from the French Service of the B.B.C.

No sooner had I knocked on the door than my legs finally gave way under me. I vaguely remember two anxious female faces peering down at me, but at the same moment I lost consciousness.

14

The Farm

How long I had remained unconscious I did not know, but when I came to I found that I was lying on a mattress and covered by blankets which had been used as a makeshift bed. At first I had no idea where I was or how I had come to be there, but gradually the events which had led to my present situation came back to me, and I was able to take note of my surroundings. Some daylight filtered into the room through the cheap curtains, enough to enable me to see that the room was bare of furniture and without any carpeting. A carafe of water and an enamel mug had been set down beside me, and when I sat up to pour myself a drink, I discovered that I was wearing a man's nightshirt which was made of some rough material and far too big for me. I had been washed, and the wound in my face dressed, but there was no sign of either my boots or my uniform.

    I tried to stand up, but found that I was too weak, and so I lay down again to contemplate my future. I remembered the German on the motorcycle, and wondered if I was going to be handed over to the enemy, but something told me they would not have gone to all this trouble if that was to be my fate. In my present state I was in no position to resist, especially without any clothes.

    It was sometime later when I heard the creaking of footsteps ascending the wooden stairs, and the door opened enough to allow a woman's head to peep in at me. As soon as she saw that I was now awake she crossed the room and drew back the curtains, letting in some hazy sunshine. The sudden daylight hurt my eyes for a few moments, and by the time they had become accustomed, the woman was standing smiling down at me in a friendly manner.

My first impression was that her age was somewhere about forty, but it was difficult to assess. She was very tall, with an Amazonian figure which the loose smock she wore only partly concealed. The lines on her face, which was devoid of make-up, were the result of hardship rather than the passage of years, and I would have said that she was handsome rather than pretty, although I suspected that she must have been a beauty when she was younger. She had long black hair which was taken back severely from her face and coiled up in a rough bun at the back of her head. Her sloppy dress and lack of grooming all indicated that she took little pride in her appearance.

By contrast, when she smiled I noticed that her teeth were beautifully white and even, and her dark brown eyes were alive with interest in me. She bent down to adjust the strips of cloth used as bandages for my face, and I saw that her hands were rough and red, the finger-nails dirty and broken, and I could feel the calloused skin on her palms. Although she emitted a faint body odour undisguised by perfume, it was not overpowering or unpleasant. On the whole, I felt I could trust her.

'You are Breetish, yes?' she asked in halting English.

'Yes, I am an officer in the British Army,' I told her, and she was visibly relieved at my use of French. 'Where is my uniform?'

'My daughter is cleaning it now, monsieur. It was very dirty and blood-stained.'

'How long have I been here?'

'You arrived on our doorstep yesterday evening, and now it is the middle of the afternoon. You have lost a lot of blood, and it will be some time before you are fit again. By the way, I am Yvonne Bernard. There is no one else here except my daughter, Marie, so you have no worries about being discovered, monsieur.'

'My name is Colin Marshall,' I told her. At this stage I did not consider it necessary to mention my rank or why I was there. Nor did I ask about the German visitor.

'What about my face?' I asked. 'Could I have a mirror,

please?'

The woman hesitated for a moment before replying. 'You have received a very severe cut, monsieur. I have pulled the edges of the wound together as best I could, but it is better that the dressing should stay undisturbed for several days.'

'You are a nurse, then?'

'Unfortunately, no, but out here in the country we have to look after many of our own injuries without any medical assistance.'

'I think it's only fair to warn you, madame, that I have escaped from the Germans who were taking me to Paris for questioning. It happened some distance away from here, but they will certainly be looking for me. I should hate to put you in any danger by being here.'

She shrugged her magnificent shoulders. 'We'll discuss that when you are well again, Monsieur Marshall. In the meantime, try to get some more sleep, and we will bring you something to eat later.'

With that she slipped from the room, and I heard her footsteps descending the stairs until she was out of earshot.

I must have dropped off to sleep again immediately, because the next thing I remember was being aware that there was someone else in the room. It was dark outside, but a small paraffin lamp gave a poor illumination of my immediate surroundings. I could not see the girl very well, but she was built in the same massive proportions as her mother. When she bent down to give me the plate she leaned forward provocatively, but the sight of her deep cleavage had no effect on me at all.

'Does monsieur want anything else?' she asked in a soft voice. 'Anything at all. It's no trouble.'

'No thanks, Marie, not at the moment. This food is all I need.'

By way of answer, she flounced out of the room and stamped down the stairs. I knew then that I was going to have to be careful of this girl in the future.

I had not eaten for over twenty-four hours, so I was ravenous, and tucked into the food without giving it a second thought, but before I had finished I discovered that I was eating German sausage and black bread. So how was it that an isolated farmhouse came to have these luxuries, when most of the French population was going hungry? Then I remembered the motor-cyclist, and was determined to find out the answer as soon as possible.

For several days I was confined to what I subsequently discovered was the attic of the farmhouse, while Madame Bernard and her daughter attended to all my needs. Whereas the mother remained detached and polite, Marie was inclined to be over-friendly. When I saw her properly in daylight, her looks somewhat resembled those of Yvonne, but she still had a child's face with rosy cheeks, and displayed none of the suffering which was apparent in the older woman. Even when she flirted with me shamefully, there was something naive and gauche in her manner. I put her age at about fifteen or sixteen, and in spite of the fact that she was as tall as her mother, much of her apparent voluptuousness was due to puppy fat which would no doubt disappear during the next few years.

My uniform had been returned to me clean and freshly pressed, and each day showed an improvement in my physical condition, but I began to hate the four walls which seemed to close in on me like a prison. I longed to be out in the open air, even although it was the middle of winter, but when I broached the subject with Madame Bernard she was not very enthusiastic, and advised patience.

'I know we are isolated here,' she told me, 'but occasionally people do drop in unexpectedly, and it would be very foolish to risk being seen.'

'What kind of people?' I asked.

'Oh, you know, neighbours, the occasional passers-by who are lost, and — er, others.'

'Such as German soldiers?'

She flushed and looked away. 'How did you find out? Has Marie been telling you things about which she knows nothing?'

I assured her that her daughter had not brought up the subject, but I went on to describe exactly what I had seen from the edge of the wood on the day I arrived. To my surprise she began to cry silently.

'I had better tell you everything,' she said, after she had composed herself. 'If you are to be here for some time, it's probably better to clear the air now, so you will know exactly how things stand. I feel as if I can talk frankly to you, Colin. You don't mind if I call you by your first name, do you?'

Although she pronounced it Coleen, I indicated that I had no objection in the least.

'I'll begin at the beginning,' she said, and proceeded to unburden herself as if she was in a confessional.

She told me how she had come here from Paris as a new bride in 1927, but had immediately regretted it. She had married Jean Bernard mainly to escape from the life she had been leading in the capital, but when she had arrived at the farm it did not take her long to discover that the life she had left was no worse than the one she had adopted, which was dominated by hard work and poverty. Yvonne confessed that she had never really loved her husband, but he had been a kind man who had worshipped her. Marie was their only child, born a year after the marriage. Then in 1939, her husband, who had been in the Army Reserve, was called up, and after war had been declared, she never saw him again.

The German occupation did not affect them much, apart from the chronic shortage of food and other commodities, but she felt it was her duty to keep the farm going in case Jean should return. She had fully expected him to do so after the fighting had ended, but as time went on she knew that he was gone, although she had never been officially notified that he was dead. Anyway, she was sure that they would be better off here than trying to survive in the capital where work was scarce, and she knew no one. The Germans did not bother her apart from the odd foraging party, who helped themselves to whatever food they thought she could spare, leaving her sometimes with barely enough to live on.

One day, about four months ago, when she had been shopping in the village which was a couple of kilometres away, she fell in the street and sprained her ankle, making it impossible for her to return to the farm without assistance. A German sergeant who had witnessed the accident, offered her a lift on his motorcycle. At first she refused, but he was insistent and kindly with it, so finally she accepted his offer. He seemed a decent sort of man who told her that he originated from farming stock in Westphalia, the result being that he sometimes came to the farm to help her with some of the heavier manual work.

After he had visited her once or twice, he informed her that he was married, but he was missing his wife and home comforts so much that he would like to form a liaison with Yvonne on a regular basis in return for his help and presents of food or other luxury items which were unobtainable. His visits became a routine, and it was on the day of one of these assignations when I had seen him.

'Don't blame me too much, Colin. I'm not proud of what I'm doing. There's no love involved on either side, only a release of animal passion. After he has gone, I try to wipe away the memory of his touch by washing myself all over. I make no excuses. It helps Marie and I to get a little extra, and I believe that we all have to look out for ourselves in this life. My daughter is a growing girl, and I don't want her to go hungry, even if I have to do a bit of whoring to prevent it.'

'Poor Yvonne!' I muttered. There was little else I could think of to say.

'I'm afraid, there's more. Before Hans, that's the German, started visiting, one of my neighbours, Jacques Blazzard by name, who is a widower, began to come round here a lot. I could see what his intentions were, but he's a horrible old man, and I would rather have the German than him. Eventually we had a showdown during which I gave him his marching orders, and told him not to come back. Then when Hans started coming, Blazzard got wind of it. He has some standing in the village, and he has successfully managed to turn everyone against me, so now Marie has to do all the shopping. I haven't been away from the farm for the past three months. Perhaps this may make it difficult for you to leave, Colin.'

'Why is that?' I asked, immediately interested.

'Because no one will trust me, consequently I know nothing either about escape routes, who the members of the Resistance are, or how to make contact with them. If I tried to find out, they would certainly imagine I was going to betray them to the Germans.'

'But surely if you were to tell this Blazzard that you were hiding a British officer who wanted to escape back to

England, he would do something about it?'

Yvonne shook her head. 'What has happened elsewhere is that the Germans have planted stooges into some of the escape routes, with the result that the persons involved all down the line have been arrested. I'm afraid it wouldn't work, Colin, we'll have to think of something else.'

We talked for a little while longer in the course of which she asked me if I was married. I told her all about my late family, and the abrupt fate which they met, but for some reason which I shall never understand, I failed to mention my association with Rosemary. Nor did I divulge anything concerning my Army career, or what the purpose of my visit to France had been, and Yvonne herself had sufficient sense not to inquire about these matters.

As soon as she had gone back downstairs, my thoughts switched again to Rosemary, and it came as a surprise when I discovered that I had been suppressing my memories of her during the past few days. Would she know that I was still alive, or would I have been posted as — Missing, Believed Killed in Action? There was no use my fretting about it, since there was nothing I could do at the present time. Later, perhaps, when I was stronger, I might try to get away without involving anyone else.

A couple of days passed, and while both the women were out in the barn milking the animals, I took the opportunity to remove the dressing over my wound in front of the kitchen mirror. When I saw my face for the first time I received quite a shock. A long Y-shaped gash, deep enough to expose the bone in places, ran from just in front of my ear across my cheek. One branch finished close to my eye, while the other went towards the corner of my mouth forming a triangular flap of skin which Yvonne had tried to repair by pulling the edges together with adhesive plaster. This makeshift attempt at restoration had been only partly successful, and the scar which was now forming was red and angry-looking, with serum oozing out where it had become infected.

The whole of that side of my face looked grotesque, and required expert suturing. When the women returned to the house I asked Yvonne why medical help could not be sought. The simple reason was that the village doctor was apparently on friendly terms with the local German commandant, and therefore could not be trusted to keep his mouth shut.

The next day I was reminded that Hans, the German sergeant, was due to visit Yvonne that same afternoon.

'I would rather you didn't stay in the house while he is here, Colin,' she told me. 'He never goes up to the attic, but it would be a precaution in case you inadvertently happened to make a noise. Marie always goes out to the barn as soon as he arrives, and perhaps you could join her.'

I did not tell Madame Bernard that I had no intention of being left alone with her daughter in these circumstances. I was sure that given such an opportunity she would try to seduce me, young as she was. It was not that she felt any affection for me, but just because I was an available man, and she was unable to resist anyone in trousers. I knew that all she expected from the exercise was a bit of fun, and so it would be up to me to restrain her enthusiasm.

It was dry, but cold when I took myself off up the hill to the spot where I had first seen the farm. As I watched the peaceful scene, Hans arrived on cue and went into the house just before Marie came out and crossed the yard into the barn. I passed the time by trying to analyse the situation in which I now found myself, but could not come up with any immediate solution. I stayed there until the German reappeared, and as soon as the noise of his machine had vanished in the distance, I walked back down the hill to the farm.

When I entered the kitchen, Yvonne was standing with her back towards me washing herself at the sink. She was completely naked with her long black hair hanging down her back as far as her waist, but I was able to note her broad shoulders and strong arms, as powerful as a man's, while her long legs were topped by muscular thighs without an ounce of spare flesh. She turned round when she heard me come in, but made no attempt to cover herself, and I was treated to a full frontal view of her magnificent bust, which in spite of its size was still firm enough not to sag unduly. There were fresh love-bites on her neck and shoulders, a reminder of Hans' attention.

I stared at her spellbound for perhaps ten seconds while she glared back at me belligerently.

'Well? Have you seen enough? Does it meet with your approval?' she demanded sarcastically. 'You men are all the same! The sight of a woman's naked body seems to bring out the beast in you.'

I stammered an apology and immediately went up to my room. She was right, of course — the sight of that magnificent torso had aroused basic instincts within me, which I had kept suppressed since I was last with Rosemary.

That same evening, Yvonne, now calm and collected once more, tried to explain the reason for her outburst.

'I'm sorry for venting my feelings on you this afternoon, Colin,' she said quietly, 'but I usually feel bloody-minded after Hans has been, so it's better that you don't come near me for a couple of hours. There is a good reason for my resentment. When I told you about myself yesterday, I deliberately didn't tell you about my work in Paris before I was married.'

'You don't have to tell me if you don't want to, Yvonne,' I interrupted.

'Yes, I do want to, then perhaps it will help you to understand. I was a dancer in one of these sleazy revue bars in the back streets behind Pigalle. When I said I was a dancer, what I meant was all that was required of me was to do topless gyrations, and being well endowed I drew in the crowds. All I wanted was to be recognised as a person, and not as a sex object for men to sit and drool over. On occasions, one of the V.I.P. customers, of which there were plenty, would request the management for one of the girls to spend the night with them. We dared not refuse or we would have been out of work, and jobs were not easy to find, even jobs like mine. I know it was only one degree better than prostitution, but after that there was only one way to go, and that was downwards.'

'How did you manage to get away?'

'One night, one of the customers came back stage looking for me. He explained that he was on holiday in Paris, and that he had been to see the show for the past three nights. He invited me out for supper, which clients often did.

However, I quickly found that he was different from the usual punter who nine times out of ten was elderly, fat and balding, but they were the ones with the money, who continually pawed you, and thought they had bought you body and soul. Jean was a big, strong lad, but desperately shy, and so was lacking the usual line of chat to which I was accustomed. When I was with him, he somehow brought out emotions I hadn't felt before — I suppose they were more maternal than anything else. By the end of a week I agreed to marry him.'

'Was that such a bad thing?'

'I had thought that living on a farm would be healthy after what I was used to, but after a week I was quickly disillusioned. Jean's father, who was a widower, was here then to help with the work, but I was not prepared for the degree of poverty under which we lived. Then when the old man died, I realised that I had merely exchanged one life of drudgery for another. I considered returning to Paris, where at least I was warm and well fed, but one of my few virtues is loyalty and so I stuck it out until Jean went off to the war.'

'Surely, there's nothing to stop you from going back now?'

She continued as if I had not spoken. 'For a time I expected him to come striding down the road like he always did, but gradually I came to realise that he had gone for ever. If I went back to the city, what was there for me? The chances were that I would possibly have finished up in a German brothel, and I couldn't have stood that. Here, at least, I have some sort of future and a small measure of independence. I know it isn't much, but there's also Marie, who needs me now as much as she ever did. She is nearly sixteen, and sex mad more so than I was at the same age. What she needs is a husband when she is old enough, and there's more chance of that here than in Paris.'

'I may as well tell you, Marie is causing me a bit of a problem too, Yvonne. I don't want to be too brutal and send her packing when she makes approaches to me, so what am I to do?'

'I know that you are a man of some sensitivity, Colin, and I'm thankful for that. All I can do is to trust you not to take advantage of her foolishness. I'm sure you will find a way to divert her emotions into other directions.'

That was easily said, but keeping Marie Bernard at arm's length was not easy, and I considered my best line of approach was to try to be a father figure to her.

Christmas passed by almost unnoticed except that we drank a bottle of vintage champagne, no doubt supplied by Hans. I remember being somewhat withdrawn as I recalled other happier festivities in times past. Yvonne seemed to know what I was thinking, and left me with my thoughts. She, too, was quieter than usual; no doubt she had memories of her own. At least Hans had gone back to his home in Germany for two weeks leave, and so we were spared the uncertainty of an unexpected visit from him.

Around noon during the first week in January 1944, with the first snows of the year covering the ground, the yard was suddenly filled by German soldiers who poured out of the back of two lorries. I immediately thought that the worst had happened, and that someone had denounced me, but who? So far as I was aware only Yvonne and Marie knew of my existence. I was not unduly worried for myself, but for Yvonne, who would undoubtedly face a firing squad if I was found, and such fears went through my mind as I watched the troops line up through a chink in the curtains of the attic bedroom.

Yvonne went outside and spoke to the N.C.O. in charge for a moment before returning to the house. The troops then moved off up the hill towards the head of the valley, leaving one of their men behind with the transport. Several minutes later I heard footsteps coming up the stairs, and I hid behind the door until Marie came into the room.

'It's all right, Colin,' she reassured me. 'They know nothing about you. Apparently an American bomber was shot down and crashed near here early this morning. The Germans are going out to try to find the crew.'

I ought to have realised that they would not have sent out twenty or so soldiers to capture one unarmed man, so I was worrying about nothing.

Having passed on the message, I thought Marie would return downstairs, but she continued to regard me with a thoughtful expression. A sensual smile began to play around her mouth while her eyes looked me up and down in contemplation.

'You'll have to stay up here until they depart, Colin. They've left a man outside in the yard, so you'll have to be especially quiet, won't you? I can help you pass the time,' she added sensuously.

She put out her hand and began to caress my shoulder and upper arm, at the same time wriggling her body from side to side in a manner which left me in no doubt as to what she wanted from me, but there was also something ingenuous about the crude gesture.

'Why don't you let yourself go for once? I'm not a virgin, you know, and you must be in need of a woman,' she said, licking her lips in anticipation.

Marie clamped her arms around me and began to rub her body against mine, pressing her enormous breasts against my chest so that I could scarcely breathe. Before I could protest, she fixed her lips firmly on to mine like a leech, and with her tongue darting in and out of my mouth, only a saint or a eunuch could fail to be stimulated. The fact that I had been starved of sex for so long made the temptation almost irresistible, but I was conscious of my promise to Yvonne concerning her daughter only a few days before. With an effort I managed to shake my head free as if I was coming up for air, causing Marie to draw away a little, but she continued to stare at me with a puzzled frown.

'What's the matter with you?' she hissed with obvious annoyance. 'You're not queer, are you? Don't you find me attractive at all?'

'That's just the trouble, Marie. I am a normal man, and I am attracted to you. Too much, if you must know.'

'Then why don't you make love to me?'

'Because whatever you feel, you are still a child, and as such you must be protected, even from yourself.'

She moved away with a look of defiance.

'I'll show you whether or not I'm a child,' she said, breathing hard between clenched teeth. Slowly she undid her dress and let it fall to the floor, showing that she had nothing on underneath. 'Just look at me, Mr High-and-

Mighty Englishman! Do I look like a child?'

Marie stood in front of me in an exaggerated pose to show off her womanhood. She was as tall as her mother, but the folds of puppy-fat made her look like the advertisements of the Michelin Man. The nipples of her balloon-like breasts were still small and pink, compared to her mother's which were as big as loganberries with dark brown surrounds three inches across. Any transient feeling of desire which I may have felt was now evaporating rapidly, and I tried to reason with her in a convincing manner.

'Can't you see that I'm old enough to be your father, Marie? I'm sure you will be more at home with some of the younger men from the village.'

'Huh! They're only boys. All they want to do is to fondle me, but they're afraid to go any further. You're a grown man, and have had experience, so you know how to make love properly. Sometimes the German soldiers whistle at me, but I never have anything to do with them.'

'One day you will meet a man who will want you for yourself, Marie, and not just for sex. Then you will find out that making love is a wonderful experience when there is affection as well. If you look on it as a means of satisfying a biological urge and nothing more, then you are missing a great deal.'

'Don't lecture me about sex without love! Look at my mother with that horrible Hans. One afternoon when they were in bed together, I crept back into the house and watched through the door which was partly open. He was banging into her, while she just lay there biting her lip with tears in her eyes. Even if she doesn't enjoy it, I bet I can.'

'Your mother's situation is entirely different, and she has her reasons. For the most part she does it for love of you, and I hope that one day you will come to realise the fact. As yet you're not mature enough to understand the implications. Growing up can be a painful business in a number of ways, but we all have to learn to control our emotions, and that's not always easy. Personal discipline enables us to live together in a civilised society, although I agree that there are many uncivilised things taking place in Europe today, but that is only for a short period in history which will soon pass. I hope you understand what I've been saying, Marie.'

'Stop lecturing me as if I was a naughty schoolgirl! If you don't make love to me right now, I'll start screaming, and that soldier down below will come up here and find you.'

Although she looked at me defiantly, I'm sure she knew in her heart that it was no use.

'No, you won't do that, Marie,' I said softly. 'If they find me here, it would mean that both you and your mother will face a firing squad. If you stop to think about it, you know that what I say is true. Now put your clothes back on again, there's a good girl.'

She hung her head, and her shoulders drooped, then slowly she began to dress, crying silently all the while. I hoped that for all our sakes she had come to terms with what I had told her. I was reminded of the old adage that a woman spurned is dangerous, and so I hoped that she did not go to the authorities in a blind rage, before she had had time to think about it.

After she had gone I felt exhausted and emotionally drained. I must have slept for a time because I was awakened by the soldiers retiring to the farmyard. I peeped out carefully to see two bodies being carried on stretchers, and two U.S. airmen in bomber jackets surrounded by the troops. One of the Yanks was wounded and was being helped along by the other, but without delay they were loaded into the back of one of the vehicles, and a minute later the yard was empty once more.

In the days which followed my encounter with Marie, her attitude towards me was one of outright antagonism, and she did her best to avoid being alone with me. She seldom spoke to me, although I continued to treat her as if nothing had happened. Whatever had been the effect of my little lecture, it had certainly dampened her ardour. Yvonne must have noticed the change, so I was obliged to tell her what had taken place, but if she had discussed it further with her daughter, she never mentioned the fact to me.

Towards the end of January the weather continued to be cold and wet, interspersed with occasional showers of sleet or snow. Apart from looking after the animals, no other work was possible on the farm, and we lived in a vacuum whereby each day was the same as the one before. Food was scarce, and we relied on the fruit and vegetables which had been carefully stored after the previous year's harvest. Our diet consisted mainly of those, together with eggs and the occasional chicken. The cow and the goats provided milk and cream, which were used to make butter and a rancid kind of cheese. Looking back, I suppose we were better off than the majority of the French population.

At night we sometimes listened to the Free French Service of the B.B.C. The women always expressed disappointment when there was no mention of an Allied landing, but I knew that any such hostilities would have to wait until the better weather. This meant that, barring a miracle, I was destined to remain here for several months yet, and the farm was beginning to feel like a prison to me. I also wondered how Yvonne and her daughter could possibly manage to keep me hidden here for that length of time.

In addition to my dangerous situation, I now had two more things to worry about. My uniform was becoming threadbare, and was no longer fit to wear day in and day out, so it was put away until such time as my escape could be arranged. Instead, I wore a shirt and a set of blue dungarees which had belonged to Yvonne's husband. They were much too large for me, but with some alteration they were made to fit.

The other complication involved the scar on my cheek. As the weeks passed, so the wound had undergone contraction, which drew down the lower eyelid, and at the same time lifted the corner of my mouth, thus giving my face a lopsided appearance. The scar itself had finally healed, but it was now a bluish-red colour which caused it to stand out in contrast to the pallor of my skin. The result was that I would be instantly recognisable wherever I went, and if, at some future date, I risked walking to the village, then I would be unable to blend into the background. It was bound to arouse a certain amount of suspicion as to where I had come from, and as I no longer resembled the photograph on my identity card, it seemed that any attempt to move away from here would be even more dangerous than staying put.

One evening, when the wind was howling outside, there

was a loud knocking on the door. Suspecting the worst, in fear and trembling I only just had time to hide in the larder before Yvonne opened it. Monsieur Blazzard stood on the doorstep soaking wet, so there was no alternative but to invite him in. He took off his coat and sat down, while Yvonne poured him a large glass of cognac. It was a superior blend, one which Hans had brought, and which simple peasants never taste in a lifetime. Monsieur Blazzard smacked his lips appreciatively as he looked first at her and then at the bottle. Yvonne herself did not have any, and if she had indeed noticed the inference, she gave no sign of the fact. The visitor must have been conscious of the hostile atmosphere towards him, but he continued with small talk as if he was a welcome guest.

I watched and listened through a crack in the pantry door which was slightly ajar. It was only after another glass of cognac when he began to discuss the real reason for his visit.

'I don't know if Marie has said anything to you, dear Madame Bernard,' he said in a smooth, ingratiating voice, 'I understand that she and Pierre, my son, have been seeing each other quite frequently in recent weeks.'

'So that's why she's been so keen to go for walks by herself?' She looked at Marie, who blushed scarlet. 'No, Monsieur Blazzard, she has told me nothing.'

'Well now, it isn't often that I have the honour to be the bearer of good tidings, but I think this liaison could be good for both of us.'

Yvonne was about to speak, but he held up his hand and continued. 'Oh, I know we haven't seen eye to eye about some matters in the past, but I'm willing to let bygones be bygones if you will, Yvonne. I may call you that, may I? And you can call me Jacques. Like I said, a union between our two families would be a great blessing for us both. The possibilities are infinite if we joined the two farms together. Who knows, maybe sometime in the future, you and I might ... I have been a very lonely man since my wife died.'

He leaned forward confidentially, and put out a hand to cover hers, but she drew it away immediately.

'I'm afraid that is out of the question so far as I am

concerned, Monsieur Blazzard,' she replied coldly. 'I'm certainly not leaving here under any circumstances.'

'Well, that's as maybe, but think about it. I know that you have, er — another friend, whom you entertain from time to time.' He leered, then became serious. 'However, a word of warning, dear lady. Don't become too involved with the enemy. The war won't last for ever, and it could lead to trouble. Still, you know your own mind best.'

'Whoever comes here is my business, but on the whole, I'm happy with my own company, Monsieur Blazzard, and I will never leave this farm except in a coffin.'

As he was putting on his coat, he looked at Yvonne again with undisguised admiration.

'You're a fine figure of a woman; I've always thought so, and you can't blame a man for trying. Still, I hope the young ones make a go of it, whatever our differences may be. Marie is a big lass like yourself, and will bear many children. She can come over and visit us whenever she wants.'

With that he went out into the night. Yvonne watched him through the window until he was out of sight, before letting me know it was all clear.

'God, the cheek of the man!' she exploded angrily. 'It's obvious that he knows about Hans coming here, but who is he to make judgments? The goods he is supposed to have bought on the black market have all come from the German commandant for services rendered.' She rounded on Marie. 'I'm surprised at you consorting with one of the Blazzards.'

'Oh, it's not as bad as all that, Mama. Pierre is not really like his father. He may not be very bright, but he's hard-working, and the old man uses him like a slave for very little wages.'

'Well, I had better warn you, Marie, that if ever you go there visiting, you will probably spend all your time cleaning. I once went over there before the war, but with no woman to look after them, the house was like a pigsty. I suspect the old man is just looking for a housekeeper, and you will end up being a slave like Pierre.'

Marie merely shrugged, but said nothing.

Much to my surprise, the thought of Yvonne and the odious Blazzard together aroused a feeling of mild jealousy within me. There had not been any physical contact between her and myself since the beginning when she was looking after me, but the longer I lived here the more I came to realise how much I enjoyed just having her around, and there was no doubt we got on very well. The fact that she had kept me hidden for all these weeks at great danger to herself, and was apparently prepared to go on doing so indefinitely, made me wonder is she had a soft spot for me also. Now that Marie had found someone of her own age, I could only hope that her attitude towards me had undergone a change.

One problem which was always at the back of our minds was Hans. Since he had gone on leave at Christmas we had had no news of him, so we began to speculate as to what had happened to him. He may have been taken ill, deserted, or been posted elsewhere, but we lived in constant fear that one day the sound of his motorcycle in the yard would announce his reappearance, and I for one was particularly careful to be on the look-out for him.

Since I had a lot of time on my hands to think, I began to compare my feelings towards Yvonne with my love for Rosemary. The two women were completely different in every way, and yet it came as a shock to discover that the memory of the latter was becoming blurred. I felt guilty about this, but I excused my lack of loyalty by the fact that I had no tangible reminders of her. For all I knew, by now Rosemary may have been notified of my death, or perhaps that I was missing, but even if she still held out any hopes that I was still alive and waited for me, how was she going to react to my appearance?

Rosemary was so beautiful that in my twisted logic I wondered how she would contemplate a future with someone as ugly as I now was. Oh, she would certainly stay with me out of loyalty, but it would be like beauty and the beast. My twisted features would be a talking point behind my back wherever I went, and people would be bound to compare her physical perfection with my disfigurement. In an orgy of self-pity I decided that the time would come when she wouldn't want me hanging around in the background, afraid to lead a normal social life. I came to the conclusion that even if I did get out of here, I would put all thoughts of returning to her to the back of my mind, but I also knew that such a drastic step would not be easy and I deluded myself that I was doing this for Rosemary's sake.

Having made the decision, it was inevitable that Yvonne and I should be drawn even closer together.

15

Countdown to D-day

The last week in January and the first week in February were particularly unpleasant, with blizzard conditions which was followed by a hard frost. After a good deal of discussion and persuasion on Marie's part, Yvonne finally allowed Marie to visit the Blazzard farm. She left early one morning, and was expected to return that same night, weather permitting. Now that Yvonne and I were left alone in the house the atmosphere was somewhat constrained as if neither of us knew what to talk about. The sun had come out, and although it was cold, the snow was crisp underfoot and the conditions ideal for a walk. This was something which I did frequently when the conditions were suitable, in order to get some fresh air and to try to throw off the feeling of being imprisoned. I told Yvonne to expect me back in a couple of hours.

I set off up the valley, now familiar to me, keeping to the path which ran beside the tiny stream which I could hear gurgling under its mantle of frozen snow. Although the cold was nipping my ears, I was happy to be out of doors and away from the claustrophobic atmosphere of the farmhouse. I walked slowly, but before I reached the head of the valley where the deep forest began, I had a feeling that I was being watched. I had noticed a flash of sunlight reflected on glass at the edge of the wood away to my right about a hundred metres distance, and my senses were immediately alerted. My first instinct was to hurry away, but I resisted it.

I stopped, ostensibly to retie my bootlace, which gave me the opportunity to try to discover who he might be. His face was covered by the binoculars, but I noticed that there was also a rifle lying beside him. Knowing that it was only the Germans and members of the Resistance who carried guns, I hoped it was the latter, but I was not prepared to take any chances. It would have been folly to have returned to the farm leaving a trail of footprints for him to follow, and so I continued on in the same direction. The path took me past his vantage point about seventy-five metres away — hopefully not near enough for him to identify me, but nevertheless too close for comfort. I kept my head down until I drew level with his position when I risked looking up, only to discover that he was no longer there.

I didn't know what to do. Had the man disappeared from view so that he would be able to follow me? Were there others about, or was he a lone hunter on a foraging expedition? I veered off to the left, and using dead ground I climbed up to a small copse where I hid in the undergrowth hoping to be able to catch sight of him again, but he had vanished completely. After half an hour I was stiff with cold, and was about to make a move when a single shot from the depth of the forest reverberated over the valley. I came to the conclusion that the man was a lone hunter who did not wish to be seen any more than I did myself. There were deer in the woods, and I knew that the Germans were also short of food.

Immediately after the shot, there was a shout from the same direction, and I was startled when two more German soldiers emerged from cover away to my right. They hurried up the valley towards the sound, so hopefully if their friend had made a kill it would keep them occupied.

I dared not cross their path because my tracks in the fresh snow could easily arouse their suspicions. I therefore drew back into the forest and began to walk away from the farm with the intention of doubling back later, but when the trees thinned out, I found myself to be in unfamiliar country, with no idea as to my whereabouts. The sun had disappeared, and with it my sense of direction. To make matters worse, the wind was beginning to rise, bringing with it heavy clouds which threatened a further fall of snow.

Soon it was dark, and I was still uncertain as to which course to set for home. By now it was snowing heavily, enough to obliterate my footsteps, and I was both cold and hungry, having reached the stage of near physical exhaustion. At one point I fell through the crust of frozen snow into a bog, and spent considerable time and energy trying to extricate myself. I stumbled around in ever widening circles hoping to pick up a familiar landmark, but it was some time before I was successful. I was close to collapse when I recognised the path leading down the valley back towards the farm, and on two occasions I fell from sheer fatigue when I was not more than a hundred metres from the yard.

When I tried to open the door of the house it was locked, and I was forced to hammer on it with my fist, until Yvonne called out uncertainly from within.

I tried to answer, but my mouth was too dry, and I continued thumping on the door until I collapsed into the snowdrift which was piling up around my feet. It seemed a long time before the door was opened a crack, then the light flooded out and Yvonne was there.

'Colin! What has happened? I heard a shot hours ago, and I thought . . . Come, let me help you.'

I felt her strong arms lift me, and with my last reserves of strength I managed to stagger into the house. The next moment she was in my arms crying softly on my shoulder, but after a few moments she pushed me away.

'Where on earth have you been?' She demanded angrily. 'Don't you know I've been half mad with worry. I was sure you'd been captured, and that the knock on the door was the Germans coming for me. What has happened? Don't you dare do this again!'

She handed me a generous measure of cognac which I managed to sip with difficulty while telling her in a few words about my adventures that afternoon. I felt that she was going to be angry again, but she just shook her head and became instantly practical, divesting me of all my sodden clothing and rubbing me down with dry towels. I was shivering so much that I was physically incapable of doing anything for myself. Even trying to drink the fiery liquid was not easy because my hands were shaking so much.

I noticed that the table had been set for two, but cooking was the thing furthest from our thoughts. All I wanted to do was to lie down and sleep.

'I don't expect Marie to come home tonight in this heavy snow,' she told me. 'Blazzard's farm gets cut off very quickly.'

I tried thawing out in front of the fire, but it was not having much effect. After a few minutes, Yvonne led me upstairs, but guided me into her own bedroom where she pushed me into the big double bed with its soft down mattress. In a moment she was naked beside me, wrapping her long arms and legs around me, until I could feel her warmth pervading my chilled bones.

'There, you'll be all right now with me,' I thought she said, but I may have imagined it, because I was immediately overcome by a deep sleep.

When I awoke it was still dark, and I felt quite fit apart from some residual muscular stiffness. I stirred and was conscious of Yvonne's wonderful body pressed close to mine. I put out a hand and touched her gently, stroking her all over until I finally reached her Amazonian breasts. She murmured something and I thought she was about to succumb to my overtures, but suddenly she leapt out of bed and donned an old dressing-gown. I looked up at her in surprise.

'What's the matter, Yvonne? Don't you want me?' I was all too aware of my state of arousal, and I could feel the blood pounding through my veins.

'No, Colin, not like that!' she said sharply. 'I won't be taken like an animal — I've had too much of that in the past. I want to be courted like any normal woman. If the word "lover" has any meaning, then I will accept you only on these terms. I'm not prepared to be merely an object for your self-gratification. I hope you can understand how I feel, Colin, and be prepared to go along with it.'

I nodded in agreement, but I was nonplussed until I realised that sex for its own sake was not enough for her, and that she wanted an intimate relationship with all the emotional involvements which such a liaison implied. She must have been well aware that up to now my feelings towards her had been nothing more than pure lust, but she preferred more than that. She was a big, strong woman, and there was no way I could have taken her against her will. If seduction was necessary then I was willing to use it, but I was sensible enought to know that if I put a foot wrong, then I would get nowhere.

'Listen, Yvonne, you can hardly blame me for wanting to go to bed with you. Here I am living in close proximity to you for months now, seeing you every day makes it difficult not to feel that way. Any normal man would think the same. Apart from the frustrations of being close to you, and not being able to touch you, I suddenly find myself in a situation where all my fantasies seem about to be fulfilled. Can you wonder I take it for granted.'

She smiled and shook her head. 'No, I know only too well, Colin, but up to now something has always made me hang back.'

'Then why did you take me to bed last night, Yvonne?'

'That was for purely practical reasons. As you see, I had no intention of allowing you to take advantage of the situation. I want love, not just a brief moment of passion to relieve our feelings. If you can't give me that, Colin, then I'd rather you said so now, and we'll end this charade.'

'It's no charade, ma chere. I wish I knew how to convince you that my motives are sincere. Why can't you relax and let nature take its course?'

'It's difficult for me to do that, I'm afraid. Every time I look at you, I am reminded of the differences between us.'

At that moment we were interrupted by a loud knocking at the door. Yvonne looked out and announced that Monsieur Blazzard was below with Marie. Drawing the gown closely about her, she went downstairs and the next moment I could hear her drawing back the bolts on the door.

'I've brought Marie back, Yvonne,' I heard Blazzard's voice from downstairs. 'She couldn't get through last night because of the snow, but I'm sure you weren't worried. I'm afraid she doesn't feel very well. It's just a little fever, you understand, but she wanted to come home. I expect she thought that you might be a little lonely, but I see that you have had company anyway.'

Later I asked her how he knew there was anyone else here.

'Damn him!' she exploded. 'I know he thinks Hans is here. I didn't clear the table last night, and he saw it was laid for two. Anyway, let him think what he wants. It might help to keep him away.'

'How is Marie? is she really all right?'

'Yes, I think so. I'm keeping her in bed for the day. She does have a little fever, but she's not really ill. There's something else bothering her, but she hasn't said what it is as yet.'

Later in the day we resumed our interrupted discussion, when I asked her why she thought we were so different. 'I know why we're different,' I joked. 'You're a woman, and I'm a man.'

'Be serious, Colin! That's not what I meant. You have been brought up as a gentleman; you're intelligent and have a sensitive nature. You're different from all the other men I have ever come into contact with. I can't imagine you wanting anyone with my background and history.'

'But in spite of your doubts about yourself, you are a beautiful and desirable woman, and you have qualities which any man would admire, whatever his background. You know, I think that you're just flirting with me, and you have no intention of allowing me near you.'

Yvonne smiled enigmatically. 'Time alone will tell,' she replied.

Marie had remained in bed all day, and when it came to evening Yvonne was busy preparing the meal which had been abandoned the night before. At one point she said to me, 'Why don't you go and look in the water-butt outside the door? I'm just going to change.'

I could not imagine what the water-butt had to do with the meal, but I dutifully did as I was told and broke the ice on the surface. When I put my arm down into the freezing water my fingers came into contact with the neck of a bottle, and I pulled out a magnum of vintage champagne which had obviously been put there when I was out walking the previous day, for dinner the evening before.

Yvonne appeared a few minutes later, having changed into a skirt and a blouse which I had never seen before.

The latter had a plunging neckline, and the buttons threatened to give way under the strain since her ample bosom more than filled the space available. She had piled her long hair into an elaborate coiffeur on top of her head, which made her appear taller than ever, and she had even applied lipstick for the first time since I had been there. A heady odour of expensive perfume seemed to pervade the room.

She saw where my eyes were drawn, and giggled self-consciously. 'I'm afraid it's too small. I haven't worn it for several years.'

I cannot remember what the meal consisted of, beyond the fact that it didn't amount to much, but the champagne made it feel like a banquet, and by the time it came to an end, we had finished the bottle. It was the first time I had seen Yvonne take anything which Hans had brought, but it helped to relax her mood. I had great difficulty in keeping my eyes away from her plunging neckline, and at first she seemed embarrassed about it because she kept pulling the edges of the blouse together, but gradually as the alcohol took its effect, so she appeared no longer to care.

After dinner Yvonne became quite coquettish, laughing more than I had ever seen her, and flirting with me openly. She pulled the pins from her coiffeur, allowing her jet-black hair to tumble in disarray over her sholders. This altered her appearance completely, giving her an abandoned and almost untamed look which was quite at variance with her normally severe image.

During a lull in the conversation, I took the opportunity to ask a question which had been bothering me the whole evening.

'Tell me, Yvonne, why all this provocative dressing-up, and the champagne. It's very nice, but there must be a reason.'

For a few seconds she looked at me with an enigmatic smile. 'Well, I decided that being courted is a two-way process. It wasn't fair that you should have to make all the running.'

'You're not playing games with me, are you? Leading me on and then . . .'

She became instantly serious, and by way of an answer

she leaned over and took my face in both of her hands before kissing me gently on the lips. She then drew away, and shook her head.

'No, I wouldn't do that to you, Colin. You see, the way I feel about you, I couldn't put into words.'

Ten minutes later I was back in the big double bed, to be joined once more by Yvonne after she had made sure that Marie was still sleeping. On this occasion our mood was very different from that of the previous night. We lay close together, kissing frequently and exploring each other with gentle hands. At first I remembered that this was where Hans and she ... but that image was soon dispelled. Yvonne matched my every move until we were united physically and mentally towards one purpose which manifested itself in an explosive climax such as I had never experienced before either with Claudette or Rosemary.

Afterwards we slept locked together, both oblivious of the outside world and all its troubles. We awoke late, but felt the need to talk rather than make love again.

'You may not believe me, Colin, but that is the very first occasion when I have known complete fulfilment,' Yvonne told me. 'It's only now that I know what love is really like?'

Eventually I got around to the subject of what the future held for both of us. 'How long can you go on putting up with my being here? I worry every minute in case someone detects my presence. We've been lucky so far, but it may not last. God knows I have no wish to leave you, but all the time I am afraid that someone will turn up unexpectedly and see me, or that Marie will inadvertently say something when she's in the village. I must get away if only for your sake, Yvonne. Besides, I was trained to do a job of work, and it doesn't help the war if I am stuck here doing nothing. Please, help me!'

She cocked her head to one side and smiled. 'So, you're determined to go and leave me already, are you? That's not very flattering, is it?'

I knew she was only joking, but there was a grain of truth in what she said, and I could not let it go at that.

'I'm not in the habit of flattering anyone, my dear, but I have never met a woman like you before, and even if I do manage to escape, you can be sure that I will come back one day.'

'Don't you believe it! Once you get back to your lady love you'll forget all about me.'

I took hold of her by the shoulders and looked straight into her eyes. 'By now, the chances are she has been notified that I am dead, but even if I do meet her again, how do you think she will react when she sees me looking like this? Do you suppose that any woman as beautiful as Rosemary would want someone as disfigured as I am hanging around her for the rest of her life?'

Before answering, Yvonne kissed me gently on the scar, then ran the tips of her fingers along its length.

'Why shouldn't she, Colin? I for one, would feel proud to have someone like you, as you say, hanging around. Your looks are only superficial. You're the same person underneath, except that in your case you are beginning to be obsessed by the wound. I'm sure the doctors will be able to do something once the war is over.'

'You may be right, but now there is another matter which has begun to worry me. I don't know if or when Hans will ever come back, but if he does I won't be able to stand by and do nothing, the very idea of him touching you, fills me with an irresistible urge to kill him.'

For an instant I thought that she was going to cry, but she managed to compose herself.

'It was hard enough before to have him near me, but now it will be ten times worse. But whatever you may feel, Colin, please, promise me that you won't try to come to grips with him. He is easily provoked, and has a nasty temper, especially if he is crossed. The second time he came to see me, I refused to do what he wanted and he immediately thumped me, I had a black eye for a couple of weeks afterwards. I know he tries to buy my favours, but at heart he's an animal, and a very big, powerful one at that.'

'I'll try to keep out of his way, but it won't be easy. We mustn't forget that I'm still a soldier and he is the enemy. Still, let's hope that he's gone for good.'

'Since I have let you make love to me, I feel quite different, as if my life is starting all over again, and all the other men have never existed. Even my poor Jean was quite ignorant as to a woman's needs.'

At this point we could hear Marie moving about, and Yvonne went through to make sure she was all right. I went out to milk the animals while Yvonne prepared breakfast, and Marie joined us. She had obviously recovered, but looked depressed. Her mother had been right when she thought that something else was troubling the girl.

'Did you enjoy your stay with Pierre?' I asked.

She shook her head vigorously. 'No. I thought it would be nice to be with someone of my own age,' and she looked at me purposefully, 'but Pierre is a drip. He is completely under his father's thumb, and does everything the old man tells him without question. The house is a tip, and all they want is a woman to see to their needs — all their needs. Even old man Blazzard suggested that .'. .' and she shivered at the recollection. 'I couldn't get away fast enough.'

Yvonne was furious, but I think she was also relieved that she was not likely to be related to Jacques Blazzard by marriage.

Somehow Marie had matured overnight, probably because she had been free from her mother's over-protectiveness even for a short time. She seemed to accept without comment the fact that Yvonne and I were sleeping together, as if it was a normal development in our relationship, and she made no more advances towards me, for which I was truly grateful.

At that stage, I did not consider myself to be in love with Yvonne, but as time passed I grew to rely on her more and more. Not only did she look after all my needs, but she was also a source of encouragement and inspiration when I was feeling depressed. She was an excellent manager who fed all three of us on a minimum of resources, as well as being a loving bedmate. In short, my life was being made easy until I reached the stage when I no longer wished to get away, which was probably what she wanted.

Yvonne repeatedly reminded me that she was in love for the first time in her life, and indeed her appearance confirmed this. She was more cheerful, she looked younger, and she now took more trouble with her appearance. An easy rapport had developed between us, which occasionally boiled over into an intense passion as we were together in the big brass bed. Our relationship was like a volcano which lay dormant most of the time, but bubbled under the surface and would then explode into a frenzied release of tension. Was this love or mere lust? At the time I never stopped to think, but accepted the situation as a matter of course.

But the even tenor of our life could not continue for ever. One evening when we were sitting round the fire, the sound of a motorcycle entering the yard brought us back to reality. Yvonne's face was a study of misery, and I only had time to secrete myself behind the pantry door before the massive figure of Hans stood in the kitchen. He was smiling benevolently, and his flushed face and glazed expression showed that he was drunk. It was then that I realised what a big fellow he really was. Although I topped six feet, he was a good six inches taller, and he must have weighed half as much again as myself.

I had had a vague notion of using unarmed combat on him, but his size and undoubted strength would make it difficult, and, because of my enforced idleness, I was not as fit as I had been when I arrived in France. I reckoned that the time he was most vulnerable was when he was naked in bed, but his pistol was always to hand, and I did not want to involve Yvonne. The risk would be terrible, and if I failed, I shudder to think what the consequences might be for all of us. Besides, there was the difficulty in disposing of the body.

All this went through my mind as I listened and watched from my hiding-place. In terrible French, he explained that he had been away on a motor maintenance course, but now that he had returned he hoped to resume where he had left off. Apparently he had just arrived back from Germany that day, and had come to let her know and to expect him at any time. Unfortunately he was unable to stay that evening as he had another engagement, but all the time he was talking he looked at Yvonne and licked his lips in anticipation. And so, ten minutes after his arrival, the sound of his machine could be heard disappearing back down the track leading to the main highway.

As soon as he had gone, Yvonne slumped into a chair and sobbed as if her heart would break. Marie and I both tried to comfort her as best we could, but it was no use, and for the next few days she withdrew into herself, scarcely speaking to either of us. It put a strain on our relationship knowing that Hans would turn up out of the blue unexpectedly, and the atmosphere within the house changed overnight.

It was one day when I was out chopping firewood when he arrived without warning. Fortunately, I had heard the sound of his motorcycle in the distance, so I had ample time to hide before he appeared. I wondered what was happening to Yvonne when he came out of the farm, obviously very drunk an hour and a half later. He stopped outside the back door swaying unsteadily, then calling to Yvonne to join him. They spoke together for several minutes before he staggered over to his machine, mounted it with difficulty, and weaved his way down the track.

Instead of going back indoors, Yvonne came across the yard to the barn where I was standing. Before she spoke I could tell that she was agitated about something.

'Colin, he saw the freshly-cut firewood stacked outside, and wondered who had been cutting it for us.'

It was something that I had never thought of, and I was surprised that Hans had even noticed it in his inebriated condition.

'So what did you tell him?' I asked.

'I couldn't think of anything to say for the moment, and so I told him that it was Marie, and that she was big and strong enough to do it. That was the worst thing I could have said.'

'Why, for God's sake?'

'Apparently where he comes from, it is always the men who do this type of work, but that's not all. Hans said that he had had his eye on her for some time. He told me that I am getting too old, and my performance isn't what it used to be. The next time he comes, he wants Marie. She's only a child, Colin, and I can't let her be subjected to his type of vicious lechery, can I?'

'We'll just have to think of something before then.'

She went out and I resumed chopping the wood, but a few minutes later a shadow fell across the doorway. Thinking that Yvonne had come back, I looked round to see the huge, menacing figure of the German sergeant standing watching me. He was obliged to prop himself against the doorpost, and he obviously had difficulty in focusing his eyes, but I knew that he could still be dangerous.

'So, here is the man who cuts the wood,' he said in his gutteral French, made even more unintelligible by the slurring of his words. 'Come into the light where I can see you better, then you can tell me who you are.'

I felt strangely calm, although I knew that this was the showdown which I had been expecting. Instinct told me that I must not get too close to him, because even in his inebriated state he was still much stronger than me. On the other hand, I was conscious of the Luger in its leather holster, whereas I had no weapon apart from the small axe I had been using. I stopped about two yards away from him, and he peered at me through bloodshot eyes.

'Well! Who are you?' he demanded.

'Madame Bernard has employed me to work on the farm.'

'So! And how long have you been here?' His body tilted sideways as if he had difficulty in remaining upright.

'Three weeks,' I stammered, hoping that I sounded convincing.

'You lie,' he growled. 'I was here a few days ago in the evening, and you weren't here then.'

'No, I was down at the café in the village. There is nothing to do here in the evening.'

'Where do you come from?'

'From Rouen. I was injured in the bombing there, as you can see, and I am fit only for labouring work.'

'Then why did Madame Bernard tell me it was Marie who had chopped the wood. Why did she not tell me that you were here?'

I shrugged as if I did not know what he was talking about.

'Your papers!'

'I — er, they aren't here. They must be in the house.'

There may have been something about my appearance, what I had said, or the way that I had said it, which alerted him to the fact that I was lying. He went to draw his pistol, but before it cleared its holster, I hit him a glancing blow on the arm with the axe. He cried out in pain and dropped the weapon, then staggered towards me with his arm outstretched. I tried to hit him again, but this time his huge hand caught hold of my wrist and twisted it backwards until I was forced to drop the chopper where it lay close to the Luger.

Unfortunately, I had now got too close to him, he caught me in a bear hug with my arms trapped by my sides, and because of his enormous strength, I could feel the breath being squeezed from my lungs.

I tried to knee him in the groin, but he was too tall, and I was too close to him. I then attempted to head-butt him, and although I managed to make his nose bleed he did not release his hold. However, I could feel that he was slightly off balance, and so I pushed forward making him stagger back against the wall, the impact of my body against his making him grunt. The surprise was enough for him to relax his grip just enough to allow me to tear myself away, and now we were both unarmed and I was fighting for my life. I was under no illusion that he was going to kill me given the opportunity. He may have been drunk, but his speed and strength were still a threat, even if his co-ordination was not all it should be.

With my right hand I aimed a karate chop to the side of his neck, but the blow was delivered in panic so it did not land properly, and with the thickness of his muscles it had virtually no effect. A split second later I kicked him in his private parts with all the strength I could muster. This time it landed fair and square on the target, causing him to double up and slide to the ground in agony. If for a moment I thought he was done for, I was soon disillusioned. His left hand landed straight on the Luger, and I was staring down the barrel while Hans' features changed from being screwed up in agony to a twisted grin of triumph.

'Back off!' he ordered.

I had no option but to comply, and only when the distance between us was several yards did he attempt to rise to his feet, keeping the pistol pointed straight at me all the while and never taking his eyes off me for a second.

'For a simple labourer, you seem to know a great deal

about unarmed combat,' he said, still breathing heavily. 'No one does that to me and gets away with it. Now you will pay the price, whoever you are.'

At that moment Yvonne came into the barn, her eyes wide with fear when she saw what was going on. Hans heard the noise behind him and wheeled round to see who it was. It was my one and only chance. With a single movement I stepped forward, picked up the axe and swung it at his head before he had time to turn and face me again. He was wearing a helmet, but the chopper hit him on the side, denting the metal. He dropped the gun and went sprawling face down, where he stayed without moving. Thinking that he was concussed I lifted up his head to look into his eyes which were glazed with widely dilated pupils. His neck was unduly mobile, and at that moment I knew that it was broken, and that Hans was dead.

When I told Yvonne, she began sobbing hysterically, and stood kicking the body in blind fury. It took all my strength to drag her away out into the yard where I tried to calm her down, but there was no reasoning with her. First of all I grasped her by the shoulders and shook her, but this had no effect, and I was obliged to slap her hard across the cheek. She collapsed sobbing in my arms, and it was some time before she had collected her wits enough to discuss the situation more or less rationally.

'We must get rid of the body quickly,' I told her. 'He is bound to be missed before long, and they'll come looking for him. Besides, I don't want Marie to know about this, so we must do it before she comes back from the village.'

'Can we bury him somewhere?' she suggested.

'I don't think that's a good idea. It will take time, and if they come here looking for him, any freshly-dug patch of earth will be suspect. I might be able to drag him into the forest and hide him in the undergrowth.'

'He's much too heavy for you to do that, Colin. What about the pond?'

'What pond?' I asked.

'Half way along the lane, before you come to the main road, there is a pond surrounded by trees. You must have noticed it when you have been out walking.'

On the last occasion when I was walking past there, the

water had been frozen over and covered with snow, so I had barely noticed it.

'How deep is it?'

'Deep enough, I think, Jean used to go swimming there in the summer sometimes.'

'It sounds a good place' I said. 'If we can mount the body back on the motorcycle, I can push it there and run it into the water. I only hope it's deep enough to cover both him and his machine. If not, there is no way I can drag him out again. It must be made to look like an accident. There are no marks on the body, and the dent in his helmet could have happened if he was thrown. The Germans must know about his drinking. Let's get on with it before Marie comes. When I'm away, you look round the barn and make sure nothing belonging to him has been left behind. There must be no trace of his ever having been here.'

'What about his pistol? You ought to keep it, Colin, You never know when you might need it.'

I was sorely tempted to take the Luger, but if Hans' body was found minus the weapon, the authorities would rightly suspect that it had not been an accident. Reluctantly, I replaced it in its holster.

It took all of our combined strength to drag the dead weight out into the yard and manoeuvre the body across the saddle so that I could wheel the machine with him on it. It was made even more difficult by the fact that Yvonne could not bear to look at the German's face, but somehow we managed it, although it took longer than we intended.

The pond was certainly bigger than I had imagined it to be, and it was an easy matter to run the machine with the body on it off the road and into the water. The motorcycle immediately sank out of sight, but the body remained floating on the surface. I got hold of a rotten branch and prodded the corpse so that it moved further out into the pond, and after a couple of minutes it too sank out of sight, leaving the surface of the water smooth and unruffled. Before departing from the scene, I did my best to eradicate my footprints, leaving only the tyremarks which led straight into the water.

I was just about to leave when I heard the sound of footsteps coming down the lane, and Marie came into view weighed down by baskets of shopping. She expressed surprise at seeing me there. I assured her that I had come to meet her in order to help carry the supplies, at which she gratefully handed them over. I took one final look at the pond, but the ripples on the surface had disappeared and all looked normal once more.

As soon as I got Yvonne on her own, I told her what had happened, and managed to assure her that Marie had seen nothing.

That same evening we went to bed early, partly because we were exhausted by the day's events, but mostly because we wanted to discuss the situation and anticipate any repercussions which may have resulted. It was necessary for Yvonne to get her story absolutely straight, since it was she who would bear the brunt of any interrogation. She was to say that she had expected Hans to come that same afternoon, but he had never arrived. All that was required of Marie was to admit that the German came to visit her mother from time to time, but she was ignorant of what had occured while she was in the village, and so could not say anything to the contrary.

Although my presence on the farm had been a complication and posed a threat to Yvonne before, it was doubly so now. At any time we expected the Germans to come round asking questions, and so, apart from meals, I stayed out of the way, dividing my time between the outhouses when it was raining, and up on the hill in dry weather. It was even too risky to sleep with her in case they came in the middle of the night, as they were wont to do. I think I missed that more than anything, because sleeping in straw after the delights of Yvonne's bed did not please me overmuch. If she was aware of the cause of my short temper, she made no comment, but she must have known the reason, which was essential for her safety.

But as the days passed by, nothing happened, and Marie had heard nothing up in the village about Hans' disappearance. It was possible that he had not confided in anyone about his off-duty visits to the farm, not wishing to share Yvonne's favours with any of his comrades. I put this to her one day, and she was in agreement.

'That's more than likely. He was always a loner, and never seemed to mix with the other men. I suppose it was difficult because of the work he did.'

'What do you mean, because of the work he did?'

'Hans was always cagey about what his duties were, but one day when he had had too much to drink, he let slip that he was an interrogator in Military Intelligence. That's partly the reason why I hated him to touch me. The very idea that those same hands were used for — ugh!' She shivered at the thought. 'He knew immediately the effect this knowledge had on me, but he said that if I didn't co-operate with him, both Marie and I would be taken into custody, and that was too awful to contemplate.'

'My poor Yvonne. Why did you not tell me this before?'

'Because I knew how strongly you felt about this kind of work, and the men who carried it out, and I had a feeling you would do something which you might regret. You never asked about Hans' work, and so I let it pass.'

'But the night he came back, he told you he had been on a motor maintenance course?'

'That's what they always say when they are asked about what they do — motor maintenance.'

'If I had know before, I would certainly not have stood by and let him . . .'

She put a hand on my arm. 'Dear Colin! I was afraid you would have allowed your heart to rule your head, and tried to kill him before this, possibly with disastrous consequences.'

'Because of his training, he must have know instinctively that I was lying about the wood,' I told her. 'Even though he was drunk, he was sharp enough to come back and investigate. You're right, he would have killed me if you had not appeared on the scene at the right moment. That's the second time you have saved my life, Yvonne. I will never be able to repay you.'

'But you have repaid me already, Colin, just by being here. Before you came, I was in the depth of despair, and if it hadn't been for my daughter, I would have done away with myself a long time ago. Not only have you given me hope for the future, but you have also given me love which I have never known before.'

This speech was quite uncharacteristic of Yvonne, who

normally said very little regarding her true feelings. I felt like a hypocrite as I listened, knowing that one day, after we had been liberated by the Allies, I would walk out of here, and out of her life. In our more intimate moments we had often exchanged declarations of love, and it wasn't until that time I realised how much she had meant it, whereas I ...? I knew that there could never be any future for Yvonne and me, but I wondered if she had ever thought that far ahead. She would not fit into my world, and I certainly had no intention of spending the rest of my days here. Sometime soon the problem would come to a head, but for the present I was prepared to allow matters to go along as usual.

One day, shortly after this discussion, Yvonne announced that there was no more money left over from the sale of the previous year's produce, and that in consequence we would be forced to tighten our belts and live only on what the farm could produce. Besides, most of the shops were now empty, and the only food to be had was available on the black market. There was nothing more coming in from Hans, and so when we had run out of sugar and ersatz coffee, I considered the time was ripe for me to do my bit.

I gave Marie a fistful of money to go to the village to buy whatever we needed, even if it came through the black market, but her mother was instantly suspicious.

'Where did that money come from, Colin?'

'I had it with me when I came here,' I lied.

'That's not true, and you know it!' Her eyes flashed angrily. 'You forget that I washed all your clothes when you arrived here, and there was none then. It could only have come from Hans' body, didn't it?'

I had to confess that this was the case, but I had left some on him so that anyone who discovered the body would know that he had not been robbed. I pointed out that he had no further use for it, and that it was a shame not to profit by it. She was reluctant, but eventually I managed to make her see the logic of the argument.

It was another couple of weeks before Marie inquired what had happened to Hans, since he had not been visiting. Yvonne told her that he had been posted elsewhere, and she accepted the explanation at face value.

After three weeks of sleeping rough, since no one had come asking questions after the German's disappearance I moved back into the house. If the authorities had suspected anything they would certainly have been round long before now. It was marvellous to be reunited with Yvonne in her bed once more, and we celebrated in royal style.

The spring of 1944 began with a long hot spell with very little rain, reducing the streams to a trickle and drying out the ground. One day, Marie came back from the village with the news that the level of the pond had dropped sufficiently to reveal the handlebars of a motorcycle sticking out above the surface. There was nothing more I could do about it, so I immediately moved out of the house once more. It was as well that I did so.

At dawn next morning, I watched in fear from my hiding-place at the edge of the wood, while an officer and four men drove into the yard and hammered loudly on the door. Yvonne told me later what had transpired.

Naturally Hans' body had been discovered, and the investigations were under way, so while his men made a thorough search of the house and outbuildings, the officer had remained in the kitchen to interrogate the two women.

Yvonne realised that she had two options open to her. One was to deny all knowledge of having known the German sergeant, or that he had ever been to the farm. The alternative was to tell the truth and admit that he came to visit from time to time. Since it was possible that old man Blazzard might have alerted the authorities about this, and that the Germans already knew about the sergeant's involvement with her, she decided on the latter option.

The officer began his interrogation by showing Yvonne a photograph of Hans together with a large, plump, bovine-looking woman, presumably his wife.

'Do you know this man, madame?' he asked.

'Yes, monsieur. he has been here several times since last June.'

'And what was the purpose of these visits?'

'Hans told me that he was a farmer, and he came here from time to time to help out, since there is no man about the place to do the heavy work.'

'And your daughter confirms this?'

Marie nodded.

'I see. When did you see him last?'

'Oh, not for some time, now. Perhaps it was as long as three months ago.'

'And you have no idea where he has been since then?'

'No, monsieur. I assumed that he had been posted elsewhere.'

'But three months ago the weather was unfit for any farming, was it not? Could he have come here for some other purpose?'

'Well, yes, I suppose that's true. He was a lonely man, and homesick, and . . .'

'. . . and you offered him some solace, madame, since you have no man of your own.' He looked her up and down, and licked his lips lasciviously. 'I can see for myself what the attraction was. It was very patriotic of you to — er, entertain a lonely German soldier.'

'May I ask, monsieur, has something happened to him?'

The officer gazed at Yvonne with expressionless eyes from behind steel-rimmed glasses. He didn't reply immediately, but instead he threw out another question.

'Tell me, Madame, had you noticed anything different about Sergeant Gruber when you saw him last?'

'Yes, monsieur. Even before he went away at Christmas he was nearly always drunk when he came here.'

'Have you actually seen him drinking?'

'Yes, indeed. He usually brought a bottle with him. He drank schnapps, cognac, anything.'

'Did he visit you regularly on a certain day, or did you know in advance that he was coming?'

'No, monsieur. He turned up at any time, day or night.'

At this point one of the soldiers entered the room, the search having been completed.

'All clear, Herr Oberleutnant. We have found nothing.'

The officer followed him out, but when he got to the door he turned round. 'Thank you for your honesty, madame. I am sorry to inform you that Sergeant Gruber met with a fatal accident. It happened some time ago, but we have only just discovered the body. We think he was on his way here at the time. As you yourself remarked, his drinking was beginning to be a problem, not only for himself, but for everyone else. There is no doubt it was the cause of his death.'

He paused and licked his lips while looking at Yvonne in a manner which left no doubt as to what he was thinking.

'Now that your lover is no longer able to visit you, Madam Bernard, perhaps you will consider accommodating another. I myself would be honoured to fill the gap. I'm not a bad man once you get to know me, and I can appreciate a beautiful woman. Even if I am unable to help out with the farm work, you will find that I can be very generous in other ways.'

He clicked his heels and saluted her formally. 'We will meet again, madame, you can be sure of that.'

'Oh, no!' I exclaimed when Yvonne repeated the conversation. 'Now that we've managed to get rid of one German, another one comes along to take his place, and this fellow could be infinitely more dangerous than Hans.'

But the officer never did return, much to our relief, although the idea that he might made us very uneasy for several weeks. Perhaps his non-appearance was due to the fact that the Occupying Forces were now under extreme pressure. Everywhere, a vast redeployment of German troops was taking place, and on the rare occasions when I ventured out to overlook the main road, I was able to see for myself the convoys of lorries, troops and armour which passed by in a never-ending stream. We knew from the broadcasts that the invasion of France was imminent, but where or when the landings would occur, was still a matter for conjecture.

During the first few days of June, the tension was almost unbearable. I remained glued to the radio for long periods, and in doing so heard several of the codewords used which I had been asked to pass on, so I knew that Normandy was almost certainly the area. Marie ventured into the village some days for no other reason than to pick up the latest gossip, but returned with stories of an improbable nature, rumours and counter-rumours. One such was that British Paratroopers had landed nearby and were coming to liberate us at any moment. Then someone with an even more vivid imagination swore that they had actually seen American tanks only a few kilometres away. Both Yvonne and Marie naively believed these tales, but I could not bring myself to tell them that it was all rubbish, thus dispelling their illusions.

At last it was announced that on the morning of the 6th of June, the Allies had landed on the Normandy coast, and so I had some satisfaction that perhaps my mission all these months before, had not entirely been a waste of time.

That same evening, Yvonne produced another bottle of champagne which she had been saving for the occasion, but as we drank a toast "To Liberty", she looked at me with an expression of infinite sadness, and there were tears in her eyes. I knew she was conscious of the fact that as soon as the Allies got here I would leave her, and that now I had become part of her life.

She said as much to me later that night after we had made love with a desperation on her part as if my departure was to take place immediately. I tried to reassure her that whatever happened I would never abandon her, but my stumbling words must have sounded hollow and insincere, the result being that she cried herself to sleep in my arms.

Next morning she was quiet and introspective at first, but as the day wore on so her mood became more outgoing and she even began to make optimistic plans, but I feel now that this was a deception so that I would not feel concerned for her. It has since made me realise that she was the most unselfish person I have ever known.

If we had expected the Allied Armies to come sweeping through France, it certainly did not materialise. I knew that the beach-heads would have to be consolidated before any advance could be made inland, and although the German propaganda machine announced that the initial attack had been pushed back into the sea, after a few days it became obvious that several permanent footholds on the Normandy coast had been established. At that time, the size of the operation was beyond my comprehension.

I had expected the French Resistance to step up their activities, but we were situated more than eighty kilometres from the actual fighting, and in our immediate area everything remained calm. Apart from the troop movements passing through on the main road, and a slight increase of air traffic, there was little evidence of change.

One morning we were awakened by the sound of distant explosions which Yvonne was sure was gunfire, but the noise lasted for only a few minutes, and we heard later that the R.A.F. had bombed a German convoy about three kilometres away. This brought back memories of my journey through France in 1940, only now the enemy was on the receiving end.

Because there was no active part that I could play, on the farm all we could do now was to sit tight and await events. I had hoped to make myself known to the Resistance at this stage with a view to joining them, but if there were any in the district, they certainly kept a low profile, and I had no idea whom to contact.

Food had always been scarce during the Occupation, but now because of the difficulties of distribution, the average Frenchman was reduced to starvation levels. At least we had some home-grown produce put by, and with some more of the crops ready for gathering, we were in a fortunate position. At dawn one morning, I looked out of the window to see a couple of men raiding our vegetable garden. I was about to go out to chase them off, but Yvonne stopped me.

'Their need is greater than ours,' she said, 'and we have more than we can use.'

It was about this time when I began to notice a physical change in Yvonne. We had never really been short of food, but she was beginning to put on weight without any apparent reason, and at the same time her face developed a pale, pinched appearance. She herself did not seem to notice, and never made reference to the change, but when I tried to bring up the subject, she merely shook her head and tried to reassure me that there was nothing wrong. I tried my hardest to persuade her to see a doctor, but she remained adamant that her health was never better.

For about six weeks after the landings, the Allied Forces were still being held in a large bridge-head in the area between Caen and Falaise, where heavy and bitter fighting continued. The German propaganda put out over the radio made the most of this, until we began to almost believe their claim that one more big counter-attack by them would be enough to push the Allied Armies back into the sea. However, we heard on the B.B.C. that the Americans had broken out of the beach-head and had swept west to cut off the Cherbourg Peninsula, which offered us fresh hope. Eventually, at the beginning of August the German High Command admitted that it had made a strategic withdrawal, which meant that their resistance had crumbled, thus allowing the Allies to pour through the breach on the road towards Paris.

One day, soon after this news, we really did hear the sound of distant gunfire, which came closer by the hour. I made a sortie to see what the position was on the main road, and found to my joy that the Germans were now in chaotic retreat. The regular and orderly convoys which had headed towards the coast some weeks before, were now in jumbled disarray travelling in the opposite direction. Armour, lorries and men on foot jostled for space on the road, while overhead the R.A.F. harried them unopposed. The German troops, tired, dusty and unshaven, with their morale at rock bottom, looked exactly like the British Forces when they were retreating to Dunkirk in front of the Blitzkrieg, and I gleaned a great deal of personal satisfaction from the spectacle. My one fear was that the Germans would turn and make a stand in our area, thus putting the farm in the middle of a battlefied, but I did not voice this anxiety to Yvonne.

The livestock were brought into the confines of the outbuildings for safety, and it got to the stage when none of us ventured out. I shaved off the growth of beard which I had allowed to cover my scars. The redness of the weals was not so obvious, but the contraction of the wound had twisted my face to an even greater extent, so I could scarcely recognise myself in the mirror. My uniform, after having been cleaned and pressed, had been kept hidden up in the rafters wrapped in cloth, but now I wore it continuously.

During these past few days I had been aware of the mixed emotions which all three of us felt, although we never voiced them openly. Marie lived in a state of suppressed excitement. Although it was four years since the Germans had come, she could scarcely remember a time when they had not been occupied. Yvonne seemed to retreat into a world of her own, and refused to discuss my departure, which made conversation between us stilted and unnatural, in contrast to our free and easy dialogue hitherto. As for myself, part of me was reluctant to leave, but the thought of returning to England was uppermost in my mind. It was hard to believe that I had survived here in enemy territory for over seven months, and that my days at the farm were now numbered.

The jeep which swept into the farmyard was manned by four soldiers, and had a heavy machine-gun mounted on the back. At first glance I thought that they were Americans because of the large white star which was stencilled on top of the bonnet, but when I saw the stripes of the N.C.O. in charge, I realised that they were British. I walked out to meet them, conscious of the fact that Yvonne and Marie were watching me through the kitchen window.

'Glad to see you, corporal. I thought you'd never get here,' I said. It was the first time I had spoken English for almost a year.

He looked me up and down in amazement before answering in a broad Scots accent. 'Ye'll be British, then? Jist whoo might you be, and whit are ye doin' here?'

'I'm Major Colin Marshall, Royal Marine Commandos, attached to the S.O.E. and the Free French Forces. I have been over here for almost a year. I was captured by the Germans, but managed to escape, and I've been holed up in this farm ever since then, that was nearly eight months ago.'

The corporal's attitude underwent an immediate change. 'Ah'll hiv to ask ye for some proof of identity, sorr.'

The other three men stared at me with expressionless faces. One of them chewed gum noisily.

'I'm afraid I have no papers of any kind,' I replied. 'I was being taken to Paris for questioning when I managed to escape, but I assure you I am who I say.'

The corporal rubbed his chin and looked doubtful. I could see he was not sure what to do with me.

'Murphy, git through to H.Q.' he told the radio operator. 'Tell them aboot the major here, and ask whit we're to dae wi' him.' He turned back to me. 'Will there be ony Germans hereabouts, sorr?'

'No, none. The war seems to have passed us by until now.'

'Aye, it's certainly a rare backwater this. Ye'd niver realise it was here.'

'What brought you along this way, corporal?'

'Looking' for Germans, sorr. The advance units 've gone through already, but some are holed up in odd places and are takin' pot-shots at some of our lads. Others hide away ... a bit like yerself, maybe. No disrespect intended, sorr.'

While we were talking, the radio had been crackling in the background. At last Murphy passed on H.Q.'s message.

'They say we're to take him to this map reference, corporal.' He passed over a piece of paper to the N.C.O.

I asked if I could go back inside the house to take my leave of the occupants.

'May I ask who's in there, sorr? We're supposed to see all the men, Frogs an' anyone else.'

'There's no men here, corporal. Only a girl and her mother — and me, of course.'

The corporal nodded. 'Tak five meenutes smoke, lads.'

Inside the kitchen the only noise was the slow ticking of the ancient clock on the wall. There was little left to say, we had said it all already, many times. When I kissed Marie, her eyes were sparkling with excitement in anticipation of what the future might hold, but with Yvonne it was a different picture. We held each other close and in silence for perhaps a full minute. I could feel her body heaving with suppressed sobs, but when I kissed her, the salty tears ran into my mouth.

'I'll be back, Yvonne, I promise you. If I can return tonight, then I will, but if not, don't worry. It may not be for some time, and if I can't come in person, I'll certainly be in touch. Do you understand?'

She did not reply, but merely nodded dumbly. Not wishing to prolong the agony, I turned on my heel and left the house.

It was a bit of a squeeze in the back of the jeep because of the mounted machine-gun, but as we drove down the lane, I kept looking back until the farm was out of sight, and when we passed the pond where I had dumped Hans' body, I noticed it was all peaceful once more, so no one would know of the grim secret it had held for all these weeks.

Out on the main road there was a considerable volume of traffic, but this time it belonged to the Allies, all bearing the stencilled white star, and travelling in the direction of Paris, while despatch riders weaved in and out between them. After waiting at the junction for a convoy of tanks to pass, we took our place behind them. A few kilometres further on they turned off into a field, leaving us to continue with the road to ourselves.

We had reached a point three kilometres further on where there was a major crossroads, but this intersection had been receiving intermittent attention from enemy artillery. A house close by was totally demolished, and the ground all around was pitted with shellholes. The surface of the road had not escaped and we were forced to slow down to a crawl to avoid the numerous potholes, some of them quite large. Suddenly the German gunners opened up, and a shell whined overhead scoring a direct hit on a truck somewhere to our rear, but before the next one arrived, the corporal had ordered us out of the jeep.

He was too late. I never heard the next shell coming, but it burst almost right under our bonnet lifting the vehicle into the air. Being at the back I had already got out, so the blast was cushioned by the bodies of the men in front of me. At that moment, my war ended, but it was not until some time later that the memory of these events came back to me.

16

In Limbo

I have a vague recollection of lying in an uncomfortable position with my legs twisted up underneath me, but how long I remained there I do not know because I kept drifting in and out of semi-consciousness. In my few lucid moments I was aware that more than one body was lying on top of me, and when I attempted to wriggle free, I was physically incapable of doing so. I had no recollection of how I came to be there, or indeed where I was, but somewhere at the back of my mind was the thought that something terrible had happened, and then the red mist would close in on me once more.

It was during one brief period of clarity that I heard people talking above and around me, and shortly after the weight was lifted from me, but I was still unable to move.

An anonymous voice said, 'Who's this fellow here? He's not one of ours, is he?'

'Then how come he's with this lot,' someone else replied. 'He's certainly wearing British Army battledress.'

'He could have picked that up anywhere. There are major's crowns on the shoulder-straps, but just look at his face. That's a hell of a wound which has been neglected. If he was one of us, that wouldn't have been allowed. Besides, he has no equipment either.'

'So what'll we do with him?'

'We'd better play safe and take him back with us to the Field Hospital. They can sort it out there.'

I tried to speak, but almost immediately I lost consciousness once more, and this time it was complete oblivion.

My next memory was that I was lying on a stretcher in the company of other wounded. Looking up I could see the outline of the red cross on the canvas roof of the big tent, and all around there were sounds of feverish activity. There was another stretcher next to mine, but when I turned my head to speak to the occupant, I saw that he was dead. A few minutes later he was carried out at the same time as an R.A.M.C. officer, a Nursing Sister, and two orderlies came to look at me.

'Who are you? Tell me your name,' someone asked.

It was at that moment I discovered that I could no longer remember who I was, or where I came from. In my panic I answered in rapid French, but I don't think it made any sense, and I could do nothing to stop it.

'Does anyone understand the French lingo? I don't know what he's trying to tell us.'

'No? Oh, well, it doesn't matter. He must be French, but where did he pick up this uniform?'

'There are plenty of bodies lying about, sir.'

'Then who brought him here?'

'We don't know, sir. He was just dumped on us. He has no papers or other means of identification.'

'Well, we may as well have a look at him.'

I felt expert hands examining my limbs, chest and abdomen, then a light was shone in my eyes which I resisted by turning my head away.

'He's certainly badly concussed. There's some neck rigidity, and his pupils are very sluggish, but there seems to be nothing else. How this scar came to be on his face I can't imagine, but it's going to need plastic surgery sometime in the future.'

'What are we going to do with him, colonel?' The sister's voice sounded as if it was coming from far away.

'We'll have to hand him over to the nearest civilian hospital, I suppose. Let them deal with him. We've enough of our own chaps to see to. Give him a sedative before he goes.'

Once more I could feel myself slipping into unconsciousness before I could protest. I was quite oblivious to the fact that I had been transferred to another hospital, but when I finally came to my senses I was in a very different environment.

The dormitory was large and airy, containing perhaps some twenty beds, most of which were occupied. Nuns in blue and white habits glided silently about, quietly ministering to those in need. I was seated in a chair by the window, dressed in a nightshirt tucked into a pair of old trousers which were held up by a piece of bandage. On my feet were a pair of slippers with one toe peeping through, and in my hands I held a religious book, whose title I cannot remember. It was open on my knee, but I don't think I was reading it.

I had a strange feeling that I was having a dream, and yet when I looked down the ward it all seemed very familiar, as if I had been a part of this scene for some time. One of the nuns who was doing the rounds, talking to each patient in turn, eventually came to where I was sitting.

'Is there something wrong, Monsieur Mardi? You look puzzled about something.'

I frowned. 'Why do you call me Monsieur Mardi?'

'Because you were brought to us on a Tuesday, and we have no other name for you.' She spoke quietly without a hint of impatience.

I shook my head as if to clear it. 'But that's not my name,' I protested.

'Then who are you, monsieur?'

It was on the tip of my tongue, but somehow I just could not cross that final barrier. I put out a hand and gripped her arm. It must have hurt, but she did not flinch. I was so close to . . . suddenly the mists parted, as if they had been blown away, and I jumped to my feet, dropping the book to the floor.

'I'm Major Colin Marshall of the Royal Marine Commandos, attached to the S.O.E., and . . .'

The nun did not wait to hear any more. She quickly crossed herself and whispered, 'Praise be to God!' before running off down the ward calling, 'Sister Angelique! Sister Angelique!' at the top of her voice.

Sister Angelique was evidently the one in charge, but it was some minutes before she could be found, during which the events of my time up to leaving the farm came flooding back to me. In a few sentences I managed to convince her of my true identity, and how I came to be in this position, but when I asked to be released at once to the nearest British Military Hospital, she looked at me rather strangley before answering.

'There are no British near here, major. They have all departed a long time ago.'

A horrible thought began to dawn on me. 'Tell me, sister, how long have I been here?'

'You came to us in August of last year. It is now March 1945.'

'But ... but that's impossible! It was only a few days since I left the farm.'

'Look out of the window, monsieur.'

A dusting of snow covered the ground, and there were icicles hanging from the eaves of the building. It had been a hot, summer's day when I had lost my memory.

'Where am I, Sister, and how did I come to be here?'

Patiently she explained to me that I had been unconscious as the result of a head injury when I was transferred from the Field Hospital. The fact that the British had rejected me as one of their own men, and when I spoke it was in French, had left them in no doubt that I had been a civilian who had been caught up in the war. After a few days I had regained consciousness, but I was unable to furnish them with any details as to who I was and where I had come from. Since then I had apparently spent the time in a state of cataleptic amnesia, sitting staring in front of me between eating and sleeping.

When the doctor came to see me, I asked him to explain what had happened to me.

'That's very difficult to answer, major. Our knowledge in that field is still very limited. The brain is a delicate organ which requires only a slight trauma to throw its basic functions out of synchronisation. A severe shock will upset that mechanism enough to produce a block, thus preventing recall of anything which it does not wish to remember, but you must realise that much of this is conjecture.'

'Surely it is unusual for the function to return after all this time?'

'Yes, it is unusual, but similar cases have been reported

from time to time whereby people have regained their memory after years of amnesia, since some parts of the brain have the ability to lie dormant, but can always recover. Why this is so, is still a mystery.'

'Will I be normal in the future, doctor?'

'Oh, I think so. You will require a complete neurological examination, of course, and depending on how much permanent damage has been sustained, you may or may not have total recall. After a short rest, the chances are that you will not have any ill-effects.'

I was cheered by this news, and thanked him for all the trouble he and his staff had taken on my behalf.

'It is satisfying to have such a satisfactory conclusion to a case, major. Many patients are not so lucky.'

The hospital for mental illnesses was situated in a convent close to Verneuil, half way between Caen and Paris. Although France had been free for some time, there was still a Military Mission in the capital manned by representatives of the Allied Forces. Sister Angelique promised to get in touch with them immediately, but I could not be discharged until the necessary papers were made out.

It was several days before an officer from the War Office turned up to see me, and in the intervening period I had an opportunity to catch up on the news of the war. It was obvious that the Allies were now poised for a final push into Germany, the hostilities were almost at an end. In one way I was sorry that I had missed the party, but that was the least of my troubles.

I pictured Yvonne waiting for news of me back at the farm, and she must have thought by now that I had deserted her. I still had every intention of returning as soon as it could be arranged, as I had promised, but now it was as if my life there was only a hazy memory, a time-warp which had taken place long ago.

Then there was Rosemary who must imagine that I truly was dead, and I did not think it right that I should give her a sudden shock by reappearing from the grave, so to speak. At the same time, my twisted reasoning felt that I could not bear for her to be lumbered with anyone looking like I did out of sympathy.

Colonel Mallory who arrived from the War Office to

make inquiries into my case, was cautious in his approach, and tried his best to remain non-committal until he had heard my side of the story. He went through it in great detail step by step while making copious notes, right up to the moment when I left the farm. Everything after that still remained a blank, except that I now had a vague recollection of the Jeep being lifted into the air. At last, after several hours of gruelling and intimate questioning, he declared that he would have to return to London immediately to verify some of the facts.

'There is one more matter which requires correction,' he said in his pedantic manner, after we had finished. I was willing to bet that he had been a lawyer in civilian life. 'I took the liberty of looking at your records before I left, and I find that your next-of-kin,' he flicked over some of the pages of his notebook, 'is Marcus Hobart, a solicitor. He has already been notified that you have been believed killed in action, so I take it you will want me to rectify this.'

'If you don't mind, sir, I would rather tell him myself. I have personal reasons for this request.'

He shrugged. 'It's your decision, of course, but if I may make a suggestion, major, it is my opinion that you would be well advised to reconsider. Perhaps there are other people involved, who would also want to know.'

He looked at me in such a way that I wondered if he knew about my involvement with Rosemary, and by dint of careful questioning, I found myself telling him about the lawyer's arrangement to notify her. I also confided in him the fact that I did not wish her to see me until I had undergone plastic surgery. His reaction was that of mild surprise, and once more he urged me to change my mind.

'I appreciate your concern, sir, but I have thought about the problem for some time. Rosemary is a very beautiful woman, so how will she react to seeing me the way I am?'

'Perhaps you have had time to study yourself for so long that in your own mind the problem has been magnified. I, for one, do not consider your appearance to be unduly offensive.'

'Thank you, colonel. I'll think about what you have said.'

'I have one more piece of news for you. Some time ago you were awarded the Croix de Guerre by the Free French

Forces — posthumously, of course. It will go well with your D.S.O.'

I was quite unmoved by this information. At this stage medals meant nothing to me since I had other, more pressing matters on my mind.

'Would it be possible for me to visit Madame Bernard at the farm, sir. I promised to let her know where I was, but it has been so long that she must think I have forgotten her. I owe her my life.'

'I'm afraid that won't be possible. Why don't you write to her? The postal service has more or less returned to normal.'

'Yes, I'll do that. So, what happens to me now, sir?' I asked anxiously.

'After I have returned to London and verified your story, I will make arrangements for you to be picked up from here and brought back to England. It will mean going straight into a Military Hospital, but at least you will have regained your identity by then. What happens after that is for the doctors to decide.'

I thanked him for the efforts he was making on my behalf, and he departed, leaving me alone with my thoughts once more. My first task was to write to Yvonne telling her everything that had happened to me, and about my imminent return to England. The nuns promised to post the letter for me, and at that stage I had no reason to doubt their word.

The reader may consider it strange that I was willing to notify Yvonne about my survival, when the most important person in my life was being kept in ignorance. Possibly Colonel Mallory had put his finger on the answer when he indicated that I had developed an abnormal fixation concerning my appearance, and what I thought Rosemary's reaction would be. However, I remained adamant that I could not take the risk of seeing her shrink away from me, or to renew our love affair merely out of sympathy. I remembered Susan's husband, and the effect his wounds had on their marriage which may have had something to do with it. At the time, I thought that I was being noble and self-sacrificing, but now I can see that my motives were prompted by vanity, and that I hadn't enough faith in the very person I professed to love.

It was six days since Colonel Mallory's visit before anything happened. I passed the time by helping out with some of the chores on the ward, and reading avidly about the course of the war through a pile of old newspapers which I found in a cupboard. It was at the back of my mind to walk out of there and somehow find my way to the farm, but I had no money and no clothes, so the idea was a non-starter. All the same, I was anxious for something to happen, and I snapped irritably at those who were looking after me.

After what seemed an age, one day a staff-car belonging to the French Army drew up at the hospital to transfer me to the nearest airbase. They provided me with a battledress and a pair of shoes, but although none of the items of clothing fitted properly, I was thankful to be rid of the hospital hand-me-downs. A couple of hours later I found myself on an R.A.F. transport plane taking off from an aerodrome somewhere north-west of Paris, and close to the capital. How dearly I would have liked to have had the opportunity to see the city in its liberated state, with the lights blazing, but a low cloud base prevented me from even catching a glimpse of it from the air.

With surprisingly little red tape, my transfer to a hospital somewhere in Cambridgeshire was carried out smoothly. I was given a room to myself, which was in contrast to the often noisy ward where I had spent my past few months. By the time I had settled in, I felt utterly exhausted, which was the first indication that I was not as fit as I had thought, and for this reason the doctors waited a few days before subjecting me to a series of tests.

They took several X-Rays of my skull, then I had various electrical brain tests, which were followed by a needle being inserted into my back, an uncomfortable and painful procedure. After that came a full psychiatric assessment, which I am sorry to say I treated with a good deal of levity to the annoyance of the young and earnest medical officer who carried it out. The result of all these examinations showed that whatever the original cause of my amnesia, there was no residual brain damage so far as they could tell.

They assured me that, given time, my health would return to normal, although it was doubtful if I would ever achieve the degree of physical fitness which would be required to keep me in the Commandos, but this did not worry me since I had no intention of putting myself in the lion's mouth again.

The plastic surgeons were not so optimistic, however. The first one I saw was uncertain as to the prognosis. He called in a senior colleague who agreed that the original wound would not have been difficult to treat if I had received immediate surgery, but the infection of the scar followed by months of neglect had produced a deep-seated contraction, which would be difficult to correct. They were honest, and told me that I would require several operations, but even then there was no guarantee of success. I was determined that I was not going through the rest of my life with a twisted face, and so I agreed to undergo the surgery.

I had telephoned Marcus Hobart shortly after my arrival. Naturally, he had been very surprised to hear from me, but came straight to the hospital the very next day. I told him that I did not want Second Officer Stuart to be informed of my survival as yet, and that had been the reason why I had waited to notify him in person. He, in turn, gave me the news that since reporting the circumstances of my presumed death to her, he had had no further contact with her, and so he had no idea as to her present whereabouts.

He went on to tell me that my estate was still intact. As was usual in such cases, he had delayed asking for probate until the war was over, so that my demise could be confirmed with absolute certainty.

My second visitor was Colonel Mallory who had come ostensibly to make sure that I had settled in, but I learned later that the real reason was to discuss with the doctors what my physical capabilities would be, so that the Army would know what to do with me. He had brought with him a fresh set of identity papers and other documents for me to complete in order to re-establish my existence after having been officially presumed dead. I was glad he did not reopen the subject of notifying Rosemary, because as yet I was not prepared to come to terms with that situation yet.

My next visitor was a Captain from the Army Pay Corps,

who went over all the details of my previous service and activities before going to France. I considered that this was a bit unnecessary because he could have obtained the information from my records, but I suppose he came to satisfy himself that I really was alive, and I was who I claimed to be. He went off after promising that I would be eligible for a large sum in back pay which had accumulated during my absence.

The day before my first operation, a general from the French Army, accompanied by a colonel from the S.O.E., arrived unexpectedly to present me with my Croix de Guerre in a private ceremony, which was a makeshift affair, and which I found to be both farcical and embarrassing. The general started off by trying to read the citation in English, but he had difficulty with the translation, and half way through he reverted to his native tongue. When he had pinned the medal on to my hospital gown, it was noticeable that he kissed me on only one cheek, instead of both as was the custom.

I had thought about Rosemary so much that I decided to find out if she was still at the same unit, and so one day while I was recovering from my first operation, following an impulse I rang Petersfield. The telephonist was singularly unhelpful, but eventually I persuaded her to put me through to the duty officer, having first ascertained that Rosemary was no longer there.

The WREN officer who took my call was brusque to the point of rudeness. I explained that I was a friend of Second Officer Rosemary Stuart, and as I had just arrived back from overseas, I was trying to contact her.

'We have no officer of that name here,' she snapped. 'Did the switchboard operator not tell you that?'

'Yes, she did,' I replied patiently, 'but I wondered if you would be able to tell me where she had gone?'

'I'm sorry I can't help you. It would take too long to look up the records. I've been here for three months, and I have never even heard her name mentioned. Try the Admiralty!'

With that, she hung up, leaving me feeling like a small boy who had been a nuisance to his elders.

I took her advice and rang the Admiralty, but I met with

no success there either. After being handed from one department to another, I was finally told that no information regarding the whereabouts of their personnel could be divulged over the telephone.

I began to wish that I had allowed Colonel Mallory to have contacted her on my behalf, but it was too late now to rectify the omission.

I wondered why Brigadier Martin Hardcastle had not come to see me, because he must have known about my return. Fortunately, I still remembered his office number, but when I tried to make contact I was told the S.O.E. was no longer operational, and that the unit had been wound up several weeks before. The brigadier had gone off to Canada with his wife on a lecture tour, and would be away for some months.

Rosemary's apparent disappearance began to worry me, and the problem of contacting her occupied most of my waking thoughts. There had to be some way whereby I could obtain news of her, but so long as I was confined to a hospital bed it was difficult. I considered putting an advertisement in the newspapers, but there were already many such notices, and I knew that she never read the papers anyway.

I continued to send letters to Yvonne with an address where I could be contacted, so it was a further cause for concern when I received no reply from her.

Just before V.E. Day, and two weeks after my second operation, I was discharged to take up a desk job at the War Office. The results of the surgery so far had been very satisfactory, and although the scar was still visible, it was now very faint, and the lopsided contraction of my face was barely noticeable. It would still need further attention after an interval of about six months, but my confidence had returned to allow me to go out and meet people without embarrassment, and I was no longer conscious of the deformity.

I managed to find a tiny flat in Central London for which I paid an exorbitant rent, and, having been kitted out with a new uniform, I took up my post with a minimum of delay. The job itself was a sinecure, which involved translations of memoranda from the French Government regarding the time when their troops had been stationed over here, and involved mainly claims for compensation.

On V.E. Night, along with some fellow officers, I went out on the town to join in the celebrations. The crowds were such that I became separated from them, and ended up half drunk in a pub somewhere in Chelsea. There I was picked up by a very liberated young woman who made no secret of the fact that her husband was already on his way home from Northern Italy, and so she was determined to make whoopee in the short period of freedom which remained to her. She returned with me to my flat, and it was not until almost noon on the following day when she left again.

This encounter was typical of the many temptations which lay in wait for officers with time on their hands in the capital. London was full of spare women who were there for the asking. They came in all ages and sizes, some beautiful and many of them nondescript, but it would have taken the self-discipline of a saint to have resisted the temptations which were on offer. There were those who blatantly made a living from pedalling sex, and others who latched on to lonely servicemen for what they could get out of them. I kept clear of both of these groups, but there were plenty of enthusiastic amateurs who wanted nothing more than a good time, or a quick thrill without strings. Such was the climate of lax morals in the city during the immediate post-war period, and I found myself in the middle of it.

Since I had been more or less isolated from all forms of social contact for so long, I certainly made up for lost time, especially when I found that my presence at parties was much sought after, but on the whole I was lonely, and although I formed several liaisons, none of them gave me any satisfaction and were more or less restricted to one night stands since I had little in common with any of them. One such casual affair was typical, but fortunately it brought me to my senses, and turned out to be my last.

I was sitting at the bar of a pub close to the Houses of Parliament one evening when I became aware that I was being watched. The woman in question was of indeterminate age, but what drew my attention to her particularly was the fact that the clothes she wore were very expensive, although they did not appear to fit very well. Around her shoulders was a mink cape which kept slipping down to reveal her figure, displayed for all to see by the low scooped-out neckline of her model dress which fell away so much that it threatened to expose totally her firm, but unsupported breasts every time she leaned forwards to pick up the fur. She caught my eye in the mirror above the bar several times, and smiled tentatively as if she was unsure of herself, but eventually she came over and sat beside me.

'You don't mind if I join you, do you? It's quiet in here this evening. You're not waiting for anyone special, are you? There's no point in us both staring at each other without speaking, is there?'

I made some polite remark and ordered her a drink, but I remember being puzzled by the fact that her voice sounded unnatural, as if she was making an effort to disguise some sort of accent, and it did not quite match up to the expensive image which she represented. After some small talk, she told me that she was the wife of a well-known knighted Member of Parliament, and that her name was Patricia. She also let slip that her husband was away visiting his constituency that weekend, the result being that after several more drinks she invited me back to her flat for a nightcap.

'I'm not in the habit of picking up young men,' she giggled, 'but with my husband away I was feeling in need of company. You look a nice sort, and I'm sure you don't mind spending a few hours with a lonely old woman, do you?' She looked at me archly as she spoke.

I hesitated for a moment, but already the alcohol had removed the last of my inhibitions, and I was curious enough to play along to see what transpired.

The flat in Belgravia was certainly sumptuous, and had not been touched by the bombing. There were rare pieces of antique furniture everywhere, original oil-paintings on the walls, and deep-pile carpets into which one's feet literally sank. With a Joe Loss record playing softly in one corner of the room, and the concealed lighting suitably dimmed, I sank into a brocade couch while my hostess produced two balloon glasses containing a very fine vintage brandy such as I had not seen since before the war.

Patricia sat at the other end of the settee with her legs drawn up underneath her. The dress did not seem to fit her very well, because one side kept slipping down off her shoulder repeatedly. At first she pulled it up every time, but finally she gave up, thus allowing even more of her anatomy to be revealed. She must have noticed my difficulty in keeping my eyes away from the exposed expanse of bare flesh, but she made no reference to it, and when we had finished our drinks she rose to her feet. I tried to do likewise, but it was then that the evening's consumption of booze caught up with me, and the room seemed to spin round so that I fell back on the couch, unable to stand.

'I think it's time I went home. Could you please ring for a taxi?' My words were slurred and I found it difficult to articulate.

Patricia laughed. 'I don't think you're in any fit state to go, are you? Don't worry about it. I'll look after you.'

I suppose she must have undressed me and put me to bed, because I remember nothing until I awoke in broad daylight feeling like death. I had a pounding headache, and my mouth was so dry I could hardly speak, but the king-sized bed with its silken sheets in which I found myself was so comfortable that I was prepared to stay there all day. I became conscious of Patricia's naked body beside me, with her legs wound round my own. She was already awake, and was watching me with an enigmatic smile.

'Feeling better, are we? You weren't much use to a lady last night, were you? Still, I'm sure you can do better now. Ah, yes, I can feel that little Colin has become big Colin at last, and I have a friend waiting specially for him.'

Normally I didn't get turned on by this line of chat, but there was an earthy appeal about her, and what she lacked in finesse, she more than made up for in enthusiasm. She certainly displayed an inventive turn of mind, and she made no excuses for the fact that she enjoyed having a romp with a lusty male. I don't think I experienced any other emotion except that she was so eager to please, in a way I felt sorry for her.

It was only afterwards when the absence of make-up, and

the slackness of her uncovered body was apparent, that I arrived at the conclusion she was quite a lot older than I had originally thought, probably into her fifties.

We must have slept again, because I was awakened by her shaking me vigorously, and her manner was very agitated.

'Quick, get up! 'Er laidyship's come back. 'Ere, taik yer clothes and get dressed in there!'

As she bundled me into the dressing-room, I noticed that her Cockney accent was now very pronounced.

'Be sure you stay there till I come back for you,' she whispered as she handed me the rest of my uniform.

While I dressed hurriedly, I could hear the sound of raised voices in another room, but they were too far away for me to distinguish what was said. After what seemed an age, during which I began to worry that I would never escape, the two women came into the bedroom.

'I shall have to tell Sir Gerald about this, Patricia. It isn't the first time you've done this sort of thing. Sleeping in our bed is bad enough, but I do object to you wearing my clothes. I only hope you haven't been entertaining any of your gentlemen friends. You know that we don't like strangers being allowed into the flat.'

'I'm very sorry, my lady. I assure you it won't happen again.' Patricia's voice was suitably contrite. I wondered what her ladyship would say if she knew I wasn't more than a couple of yards away from her.

'I hate having anyone in my employment whom I cannot trust. You've been a satisfactory housekeeper up till now, Patricia, so don't go spoiling it. You can tidy up in here while I have my bath.'

A few minutes later, the door of the dressing-room was opened, and I was hustled out towards the front door.

'Good-bye, Colin,' she said as she kissed me. 'You've been a gentleman, and a real sport. I hope we'll meet again, sometime soon. I'll keep a look-out for you.'

I made sure that I kept well away from that district in the future.

Some years after this episode I was introduced to her ladyship, who was as I had imagined her to be, tall and angular, with an aquiline nose and a haughty manner. I wondered what her reaction would have been had she known that I had once slept in her bed. I was tempted to ask her if Patricia was still in her employment, but I refrained.

This incident preyed on my mind for a time, until I began to see the funny side of it, but it served to remind me that I was getting too old for such adventures, and I made a vow that from then on I would stop indulging my appetite in any more casual affairs, or one night stands.

Yvonne had still not replied to any of my letters, and I was beginning to think that she wanted nothing more to do with me, having decided that our brief affair was merely as a result of circumstances.

I therefore redoubled my efforts to find Rosemary, and at last, more by good luck than anything else, I received news of her quite by chance, and so was convinced that my future happiness was now assured.

17

Blighted Hopes

Although I had made several amicable associations with colleagues in the War Office, there were very few whom I could regard as being real friends. Most of the personnel had been in their posts for a long time, some had even worked there throughout the entire war, and had commuted from their homes on the outskirts of London just like any businessman. Since I was basically not cut out to be an office wallah, I had very little in common with them, and so they regarded me as something of an interloper.

Now that the war was over both in Europe and in the Far East, the social round became quite hectic, and open invitations to all kinds of functions, both private and public, came flooding in. I turned down many of them, but I did make an attempt to attend a selected few in order to avoid being branded as anti-social altogether. Looking back, I suppose I was quite lonely, because it is possible for one to feel very isolated in a big city like London.

It was at a party in the American Embassy when I had my first news of Rosemary. The social gathering was euphemistically described as a cocktail party, but it turned out to be the same old drinks and snacks affair, where one either imbibes too much, or stands twirling an empty glass. By the same token, there was just enough food circulating to take the edge off one's appetite, but not sufficient to be regarded as a meal. There was the usual throng of bodies consisting mostly of men from the U.S. Services, but there were also a few women in uniform, and a sprinkling of civilians. In order to avoid the worst of the crush, I manoeuvred myself into a corner from where I was able to observe my fellow-guests openly without being considered rude.

After a few minutes I was joined by a high-ranking U.S. Army Officer — I can never sort out their insignia, even now. When we had exhausted our quota of small talk, he asked me what my opinion was about the future of the Commandos, and their strategic use. He seemed to have a wide-ranging and detailed knowledge of the subject, and when I sounded him out, he replied that he had been on the General Staff of Combined Operations since long before D-Day. He went on to tell me that his office was staffed by personnel from all nationalities, and that his personal assistant had been English.

'Best secretary I have ever had, and I've had a few,' he said with enthusiasm. 'She was an officer in your Womens' Navy, you call them WRENS over here. Very efficient she was, and a real cracker as well. Most of the chaps in H.Q. were in love with her, but she wouldn't have anything to do with any of them. Oh, she was quite friendly, you understand, but that's as far as it went. Given the opportunity, I would have made a pass at her myself, but it was strictly hands off so far as she was concerned.'

My heart gave a great leap when I heard this, and I knew at once that he was talking about Rosemary.

'Where was I? Oh, yes,' my companion continued. 'The reason I mention it is because she was engaged to be married to one of your chaps, but a few months before the Allied landings she received a message to say that he was missing, believed killed. She confided in me that he had been over in Occupied France for some time on some hush-hush mission. I take my hat off to those fellows, and women too, I believe. A dangerous game that was, but they did invaluable work behind the enemy lines.'

'Can you remember her name, sir?' I asked, trying to sound as casual as possible.

'Yea, it was Rosemary — same name as my wife's sister, I remember. Rosemary — er . . . something short.'

'Stuart?'

'Yea, that's it! When she got news about her fiance, it

broke her up completely, poor girl. After that she really wasn't up to the job, but we held on to her for a while, because we felt sorry for her. Eventually, though, it got on top of her, and she was posted to an easier billet. Say, you must know her, don't you?'

I nodded. 'Could you possibly tell me where she went after she left you, sir?'

He rubbed his chin and looked doubtful. 'I dunno. It was a long time ago. There's a lot happened since then.'

While he was speaking he kept looking at my medal ribbons. 'Tell me, major, what ribbon it that? I recognise the D.S.O., but this other one has got me beat.'

When I told him it was the Croix de Guerre, he frowned and repeated, 'Croix de Guerre,' to himself thoughtfully, then he suddenly looked me straight in the eye.

'Holy Cow! Wait a minute! It was you, wasn't it? You're the fellow I've been talking about. I'm glad you made it, son. Rosemary must be over the moon.'

When I told him that I hadn't seen her since my return, he looked shocked at first then stared at me in disbelief.

'Jeezus, buddy, if I had a girl like that waiting for me, I'd have moved heaven and earth to get back to her. Where the hell have you been hiding yourself?'

I gave him a brief resumé of my trip to Normandy without going into too many details, and explained what had happened to me since. I went on to tell him that I had been looking for Rosemary, but she seemed to have disappeared, and that this was the first news I had had of her.

'Jeez, that's terrible! I'll tell you what I'll do, major. When I get back to the office, I'll try to find out where she went when she left us. It won't be easy because we're packing up and our records are all over the place, but I'll see what I can come up with. Give me your address in case we strike it lucky.'

I didn't really expect anything to transpire as a result of this encounter, but a letter arrived for me three days later. True to his word, the general had found out to which posting Second Officer Stuart had gone, and wished me good luck in finding her. Since it had been more than twelve months since it had happened it was a long shot, but

I decided to follow it up.

The advanced training camp to which I had been directed was now disbanded, but there was a holding office with all their records still intact, so they were able to tell me where she had gone from there. The trail took me to a large transit camp run by the Americans somewhere in Berkshire, about forty miles from London, but the officer I spoke to was less than helpful.

'Listen, buddy! I have a staff of three hundred here, and there are another two and a half thousand men and women waiting to be sent back to the States. They come and go all the time. We're in chaos, and I haven't the manpower to go hunting for the records of some broad who may or may not be here.'

I must have looked very crestfallen, because when I turned to go, he relented and called me back before I reached the door.

'Look, we're having a big farewell dance here tomorrow night. We always do before a large draft is shipped home. Nearly everybody will be there. You're welcome to come along. That's the best I can do for you, I'm afraid. If you have any trouble getting past the guard at the gate, tell them to clear it with Captain Cohen — that's me.'

I went back to London in a feverpitch of excitement. I could neither eat nor sleep, and somehow, deep down inside, I was sure that this was the end of my quest. If I didn't find her now, then I never would, but I kept reminding myself of the stories I had heard of couples who had been separated by the circumstances of war, and had managed to come together again after an interval sometimes lasting for years.

The following afternoon, I put on my dress uniform and Sam Browne belt which I hardly ever wore, and took an early train which arrived in the nearby town several hours before the dance was due to begin. I passed the time by going to the local cinema, but it was not enough to take my mind off the forthcoming event, and I must have looked at the clock as much as I did at the screen. At last, at the appointed time, my taxi drew up at the camp gate where I was admitted without question and directed to a large building in the centre of the hutted compound.

The hall, which doubled as a gymnasium and recreation centre, was already half full, with a ten-piece band trying to emulate the sounds of the late Glenn Miller. Eagerly I scanned the dancers, but I could not see her anywhere. I had to tell myself that the night was yet young, and after an interval while I prowled about, I was joined by Captain Cohen. He turned out to be a pleasant young fellow, who apologised for his brusqueness the previous day.

'I was having one of those days, major, you know how it is, and I guess you caught me at a bad moment. Anyway, feel free to go anywhere you want, and I hope you manage to find whoever you are looking for.'

He offered me a glass of punch from one of several large bowls set out on a table at one end of the hall. I don't know what it was laced with, but after one sip I decided that a single glass was sufficient if I was to remain clear-headed throughout the evening. An air of euphoria was evident among the assembled company, but there were also those who did not appear to be enjoying the revelry. When I mentioned this to Captain Cohen, he told me that the majority were due to be sent back to the States the next day, but there were a few, including himself, who were earmarked for further duty in Occupied Germany.

Another hour dragged past, during which I stayed close to the punch table, but kept my resolve not to have any more. Then through a gap in the crush of people on the dance-floor, I caught a glimpse of her standing inside the entrance at the far end of the room She was in the company of three officers, all middle-aged, and for a time they stood and watched as if they were uncertain whether or not they would join in. I was conscious of my heart pounding, my mouth was dry, and I had a sinking feeling in my gut. Now that my quest was at an end I was doubtful how to approach her, because I did not want to cause her embarrassment, or to make our reunion a public spectacle, so it took a great deal of self-control not to rush over and put my arms around her.

I thought how lovely Rosemary looked, perhaps a little thinner than before, but it also seemed as if much of her former sparkle had faded. She chatted amiably with her three companions who hung on her every word, and at one stage she put her hand on the arm of one of them. I was surprised to see that she was not wearing uniform, because I had assumed that she was on the staff of this establishment, but this was a minor consideration, and I was happy just to feast my eyes on her again.

The decision of how to approach her was taken out of my hands when the quartet came over to the table where the punch was constantly being replenished. When she was not more than a couple of metres away, Rosemary looked in my direction and caught my eye briefly. She frowned for a few seconds, then she stood as if fixed to the spot and stared at me in wide-eyed disbelief before falling to the floor in a dead faint.

A considerable commotion followed, during which one of the officers she was with, who I discovered later to be a doctor, took charge, and she was spirited away to a small office off the main hall. Some time passed before he emerged grim-faced and came straight over to me.

'She didn't want to see you at first,' he said, 'but I persuaded her to. It's only fair that you should have a chance to talk with her. Take your time, but remember, she's had a nasty shock, so be gentle with her.'

Rosemary was seated on a chair in the almost bare office with a glass of water in her hand. Her face was deathly pale and her hair had come adrift, but she seemed quite composed and in full control of her emotions. She looked up at me impassively when I entered the room.

'Hello, Rosemary, It's been a long time, but I'm glad that I've managed to find you at last.'

This trite phrase was not what I had meant to say, but somehow the words just slipped out. I had been prepared for a big reunion whereby she would throw herself into my arms, but instead she remained completely detached. For the first time I experienced a twinge of fear that winning her back was not going to be so easy, but I was confident that once she had heard my side of the story, all would be forgiven.

There was a pause during which the only sound was the distant beat of the dance band.

'I always said you were a survivor, but I must say I was quite unprepared for anything as dramatic as this. I assume that you have some explanation.' Rosemary's voice was ominously flat, and she avoided catching my eye.

I told her of my work with the French Resistance, how I came to be captured and my subsequent escape, during which I had sustained the wound to my face. I glossed over much of my life at the farm, and considered it tactful not to mention my relationship with Yvonne. Perhaps at a later date, I would confess to her, and hopefully she would understand. The period during which I was shut off because of my amnesia, and my subsequent hospitalisation back in England seemed to have taken place a long time ago, and when I tried to explain why I had made no effort to contact her earlier, the excuse sounded feeble and unconvincing. I went on to tell her about the many difficulties I had encountered in tracing her, otherwise she would have known that I was still alive before this.

'Now that I have managed to find you again, Rosemary,' I concluded, 'you can't imagine what a load it is off my mind, and I can only hope that, given time, we can resume where we left off.'

If I had expected a reaction or some sign that I was getting through to her, I was disappointed. She never once looked at me, but kept her eyes focused on a distant point in the corner of the room. It was some time before she replied.

'I don't think you appreciate the shock I experienced when I received the news of your disappearance, Colin. I was utterly devastated, even more so after your boss told me the awful news that you had been captured. I imagined every kind of horror which might be happening to you. Fortunately, Martin Hardcastle kept in touch and informed me about the rescue bid by the Resistance, but when they found you weren't in the truck, they thought the Germans had fooled them, so no one knew where you were. After Paris had been liberated there was still no news of you, and then I had a message from your solicitor to the effect that you were officially presumed dead.'

She paused to look at me directly for the first time, and although her face was devoid of expression, I saw that there were tears in her eyes.

'I can understand why you were unable to contact

anyone while you were in hiding,' she went on, 'and, of course, when you were suffering from amnesia, but it is beyond my comprehension why you deliberately made no effort to have me traced as soon as you had returned to England.'

'Perhaps I wasn't thinking straight, but at the time it seemed to be the right thing to do. Before I had plastic surgery my face was a mess — a twisted caricature of my former self. You are so beautiful, Rosemary, I couldn't bear the thought of you marrying me out of pity. I remembered the trouble Susan had with her husband, and I didn't want us to end up the same way, hating each other.'

For a second she looked at me in disbelief.

'You profess to love me, Colin, and yet you believe me to be so shallow as to worry about your appearance. If so, then you don't know me very well. It was probably the most foolish decision you have ever made. I was always proud to be seen with you, and I would have felt the same way even if you had no face at all. If it was as bad as you say, then the surgeons have certainly done a good job, although you may have to undergo another operation. But why could I not have been there to share the trouble with you?'

'Because they couldn't guarantee that it would be successful, and I wouldn't have wanted you to have to go through the uncertainty as well. I always hoped that it would turn out all right, but there was a chance that I would have nothing to show for it in the end.'

'I still think you ought to have given me the opportunity to have made up my own mind, but I'm rapidly coming to the conclusion that I don't really know you either.'

'So, because I made one stupid decision, you're going to force me to eat dirt, and plead for you to come back to me? I though better of you, Rosemary, but I will if I have to.'

She shook her head slowly. 'I'm sorry, Colin, but I'm afraid it's too late for that.'

'What do you mean, it's too late?'

She looked straight into my eyes with the tears coursing silently down her cheeks. For the first time I had a terrible foreboding that my life was about to fall apart, and that all my dreams and expectations for the future were about to come to nothing.

'The American colonel who was with me when I was brought in here, is a doctor, His name is Walter Zelinsky, and I met him eight months ago.' Rosemary took a deep breath. 'Probably one reason why you couldn't find me is because my name is no longer Stuart. I married Walter three weeks ago, and we are due to sail to the United States tomorrow.'

She uncovered her left hand which up until then she had been keeping hidden from view, so I could now see the massive solitaire diamond together with the heavy gold wedding ring. I felt numbed, as if I had received a physical blow, and a thousand questions came into my mind.

'But surely you can't love him, Rosemary?'

She didn't answer for a few seconds, but when she did, her voice was flat and toneless.

'He happened to be there at a time when I was in need of support and friendship. I am aware that he's a lot older than me, and that he's been divorced, but he's kind and considerate, and that's what matters most to me now. So long as he's around I will never need to worry about anything ever again. I hope you can understand how important this is to me now, after the worries of this awful war, especially during the past year.'

'Does he know about me?'

'Yes, of course. We have no secrets from each other.'

'So he knows that I am here?'

'Yes. It was his idea that I should see you on my own. He's a very understanding person. Whatever my feelings for you have been in the past, that's all over now. Goodbye, Colin! I don't suppose we will meet again, but I hope you manage to find happiness.'

For a moment I was forced to hang on to the edge of the table to stop myself from keeling over as the room began to spin round. I shook my head to clear it, and without another word I stumbled from the room.

Outside the door, Colonel Zelinsky was waiting patiently until our meeting was over. As I came out, he tried to speak to me.

'I'm sorry about this, Major. I didn't know . . .'

I strode past him as if he didn't exist, and my mind was a

blank as I marched on through the throng of revellers, looking neither to the right nor the left, oblivious of the curious stares which no doubt followed me. Once outside, the cool air seemed to bring me to my senses, and I stood leaning against the wall of the building for a very long time. The temptation to go back inside was very strong, but I was sensible enough to realise that it would merely complicate matters, and make no difference to the outcome.

I have no recollection of how I got back to the station, but I think I must have walked all the way and caught an early morning train. I knew that I only had myself to blame for what had happened. If only I had made an effort to locate her when I was in hospital, or if only I had made an even bigger effort to get in touch with her after my discharge instead of playing fast and loose with all and sundry while celebrating my new-found freedom, we may have been together at this very moment. If only . . . if only we could see what the future held for us we might live our lives differently, but now I had to bear the consequences of my actions, and I had lost her for ever.

Shortly after, I was demobbed and left the Services, although they tried to persuade me to stay in the Army as a Regular, but I was certain that the military life was not for me, and I was anxious to resume my career in journalism. Before doing this, however, I indulged myself in bouts of heavy drinking and womanising once more, in a vain effort to eradicate the feeling that destiny had kicked me in the teeth. Fortunately I soon managed to pull myself together before I turned into a complete rake, and after I had dried out, I was duly appointed as Paris correspondent to one of the large daily newspapers.

Before my demob I had been sent for to have the final operation to my face, but I decided against it. There seemed to be no point now, and I had become accustomed to it as it was. After leaving the Army I grew a beard which adequately camouflaged any remaining imperfection.

My house, which had remained derelict ever since it was bombed, was now sold at a good price for building land which was in short supply. I still could not bring myself to go back and look at it, even after all this time, but my solicitor coped with the sale which brought me sufficient capital to purchase a small flat in the centre of London close to Fleet Street. At the same time, I changed my will whereby Rosemary no longer figured as a beneficiary. I knew now that I had to put her right out of my mind, but it was not easy, and there were many times when I had to force myself to think of other matters.

Although I had written several times, I still had had no reply from Yvonne, so I concluded that she did not wish to resume our liaison. I could understand how she felt, because our worlds were so far apart that she would have found it difficult to adapt to my way of life, as I would to hers. But even if we were quite incompatible by upbringing and background, I would have liked to meet her again, if only to thank her for all she did for me, and the risks she took on my behalf.

Three years later, I happened to be in Normandy to interview a former cabinet minister at his chateau. I was driving back to Paris when I discovered that I was close to the village where I had been taken prisoner, and as it was only a short detour, my curiosity got the better of me. The last time I had travelled up the main street I had been perched on a horse-drawn cart in the pouring rain. Now it seemed to be a nondescript place which looked different from how I had rememberd it, and yet my last visit here had heralded a milestone in my life. I went into the gendarmerie where I had been questioned briefly and held overnight. The policeman in charge regarded me curiously until I explained the reason for my visit, but there was no sign of the elderly jailer who had given me words of encouragement.

From there I took the same road the Germans had brought me, until I came to the spot where the Resistance had ambushed the little convoy, thus giving me the opportunity to make my escape. A look at the map showed me that the farm was a considerable distance away, and I was amazed that I could have covered such mileage across country in my condition. Somehow I seemed to be drawn by invisible threads towards the area where the farm was situated, and it was with a feeling of suppressed excitement that I drove towards it.

My first stop was at the village, where I went in to the local bistro for a glass of wine. There were several men in the bar chatting among themselves, but when I casually asked the proprietor if Madame Bernard was still living in the district, the atmosphere immediately changed. Everyone stopped talking, and although no one answered, they all looked at me, and I could detect a certain amount of hostility. I decided that I was not likely to glean any further information there, and so I finished my drink and left in silence.

The track leading down to the farm was in an even worse state of disrepair than it had been before. There were potholes and ruts everywhere, and the branches of some of the adjacent shrubs and trees hung down over the road. The pond where I had dumped Hans' body was still there, but the foliage had grown in, making it smaller than I remembered it. As I entered the farmyard, a man whom I had never seen before came towards me. He was wheeling a bicycle as if he was about to leave.

'This road goes nowhere,' he told me in an aggressive tone. 'If you're looking for a short cut, there isn't one. I'm fed up with you motorists coming into the yard. You'll have to go back to the main highway.'

He was still young, probably less than thirty, but years of hard toil made him look older. His hair was long and unkempt, and he had several days of unshaven stubble on his chin, which did not enhance his appearance. Although he was big and powerfully built, he was already running to fat, and wheezed as he spoke. He was obviously anxious to get away, which meant that perhaps he would be disinclined to stop and tell me what I wanted to know.

'Does Madame Bernard still live here?' I asked.

'Marie!' he shouted towards the house. 'There's someone here to see you. I'm off!'

With that, he mounted his cycle and pedalled off down the lane, leaving me standing all alone.

I scarcely recognised her as she emerged from the door of the house, wiping her hands on her apron. I knew it was Marie all right, but the intervening years had not been kind to her. She had piled on weight until she had now reached enormous proportions. Her shapeless figure bulged out of a dress which no longer fitted her, and her general appearance was that of a woman who did not bother about how she looked, although she could not have been much more than twenty years old. A child of about two hung on her skirts, while a boy of perhaps four followed behind at a distance.

She peered in my direction, shading her eyes from the glare of the sun which was directly behind me, but I could see that she didn't recognise who I was. Probably the beard gave me a certain degree of anonymity. Her greeting was as unfriendly as the man's had been.

'What do you want from me now?' she demanded. 'If you have been sent by that crooked lawyer, you can go straight back to where you came from. I said all I'm going to say to the other man who was here a couple of days ago.'

'Don't your know me, Marie?'

She came closer and scrutinised my face. It was several seconds before a look of recognition finally crossed her face, but the reaction was not what I had expected.

'What are you doing here?' she asked in a flat voice. 'I thought we'd seen the last of you.'

'Where is Yvonne? Is she still living here?'

Marie hesitated before answering. 'You'd better come inside,' she said.

The kitchen looked much the same, except that whereas Yvonne had always kept it clean and tidy, it was now in a state of chaos. The sink was piled high with dirty dishes, a half-eaten meal was still on the table, there were bits of stale food scattered over the floor, and I don't think the furniture had been dusted in years. Everywhere there was a distinct odour of soiling, and I had to pick my way past a screen on which clothes were steaming as they dried.

Both the children stared at me with wide-eyed hostility, but neither uttered a word. The younger child never let go of Marie's skirts, but the boy remained quietly aloof. I didn't know who he was, but he was a good-looking youngster, and there was something vaguely familiar about him.

'Why have you come?' Marie asked, after having sent the boy outside to play.

'Is there any reason why I shouldn't come back to see

you? I would have thought it only natural, since I spent several months in this house. I can see that you're not overjoyed to see me, but I came to visit Yvonne. Is she not here?'

'No, she isn't. You promised you would come back, so why has it taken you so long?'

'I wrote several times. Didn't she receive any of my letters?'

Marie shook her head, but a shifty look came into her eyes, and she turned away so that I could not see her face.

'I want you to tell me exactly why you didn't return as you had promised,' she persisted. 'You made use of my mother when you were here, but you had no intention of coming back, had you?'

'That's not true, Marie. If you had received my letters you would have known why I was unable to keep my promise.'

I went on to relate the events which had taken place since I had left the farm. She listened intently with a strange expression on her face, which was a mixture of disbelief and horror. Suddenly she burst into tears, covering her face with her hands.

'Now tell me the truth, Marie. I want to know what's going on, and where your mother is. I think I have a right to know, don't you?'

I found a seat which was reasonably clean and waited until she had recovered sufficiently to relate what had happened. It took her some time, but eventually she spoke without looking at me directly.

'After you left us, life went on as usual, except for the fact that Yvonne expected to hear from you at any time. The expectation grew worse until it became an obsession, and she could talk about nothing else. Allied troops were stationed close by the village for a time, and it wasn't until they had left that the trouble started.'

'Trouble? What trouble?'

'It was all started up by old man Blazzard. You remember my mother would have nothing to do with him, so he was determined to get his revenge. He knew about Hans' visits and he spread the rumour that she had entertained German soldiers here at the farm. At this time there was a witch-hunt going on throughout France, and anyone who had given any assistance and consorted with the enemy were the victims of so-called justice which was carried out summarily by the rest of the population, who acted both as judge, jury and executioners.'

'But surely, old man Blazzard was as guilty as anyone? How did he manage to get away with it?'

'The crafty old devil let it be known that he had been acting as a spy for the Resistance. I'm quite sure there was no truth in that, but no one disagreed with him.'

'So, what happened?'

'Early one morning a crowd gathered out in the yard, and demanded that my mother came out, or they would set fire to the barn. Blazzard wasn't even there — he hadn't the guts to face her. Anyway, eventually Yvonne went out to confront the mob alone.'

'Didn't she tell them about hiding me here?'

'She tried to, but no one would even listen. You knew that she was pregnant, didn't you?'

'No, I never suspected. I knew she wasn't well when I left, but I never realised . . .'

'They made out it was the German's bastard she was carrying, but that wasn't true. Hans was already dead when she conceived.'

'Do you mean to tell me that boy outside is . . .?'

'Yes, that's your son. Yvonne wanted to call him Colin, after you.'

In the next few seconds I was conscious of a variety of emotions. There was elation that I was the father of a son, anger that he was born in such circumstances, and remorse that I had failed to realise what the situation was here, and to do something about it. Yvonne in her unselfish way must have known before I went away, but she had deliberately withheld the news from me so that I would not feel a sense of obligation towards her.

'What did they do to her?' I asked. I didn't really want to hear all the details, but somehow I felt I owed it to her.

'They stripped her naked, and made her stand against the barn door while they threw muck at her and hurled insults. It was awful, but there was nothing I could do to help her. They then cut off all her hair and shaved her head. At no time did she raise her voice in protest, but just stood there like a statue, as if she had been carved out of stone. If the mob had expected her to plead for mercy, they must have been disappointed. Finally, they drifted away, leaving us both in a state of shock, but it wasn't really until later that the true effects of the incident made themselves felt.'

'What about the police? Did they not try to protect you? They must have known what was going on.'

'Somehow they were never in evidence at times like these. After that, life in the village became very difficult for a time. Even the shops refused to serve us, and they did their best to drive us out. But this is our farm, and we own the land, and so we refused to budge. However, as time passed, things slowly returned to normal. I think some of the villagers were secretly ashamed of what they had done, because by now they discovered that the Blazzards were not as pure as they had been led to believe.'

She paused for a moment, but I did not interrupt.

'My mother never really recovered, and she continued to be abnormally depressed. Eventually, she gave birth to a son, but the confinement was not an easy one, which made her health suffer even more. She became very withdrawn, just sat hour after hour staring into space. She hardly ate anything, and wore herself down to a shadow.'

'But she managed to look after the baby?'

Marie shook her head. 'No, she showed no interest in him, and so it was left to me to bring him up. Although she never actually said so, I knew she always expected you to come back even after all that time.'

'I have already explained why I couldn't come.'

'Yes, but we didn't know that at the time. I was certain that you had never really cared for Yvonne, and had no intention of returning. After all, what was there here for you to come back to? A broken down farm, and two women who doted on you. You didn't know then that you had a son.'

'But what about my letters? Didn't she receive any of them? I sent one from the French hospital as soon as I knew where I was, and there were three more at intervals later.'

'The first one we didn't receive, and I destroyed the

others.'

'You! But why, Marie?'

She looked at me defiantly. 'I knew they were from you, because of the English stamp, but I never even opened them. By then my mother was incurably insane, and I firmly believed that hearing from you at that stage would have made matters worse. God help me, I may have been wrong, but I did what I thought was best at the time.'

'Was that the only reason?'

'No. I was all mixed up, and still angry with you because you had treated me like a child, Colin. All the time you were with us, I fancied you something rotten. The frustration was almost unbearable at nights when I lay listening to you both through the wall making love. In spite of my resentment, I continued to look after her, and your son, to the best of my ability. I never thought it would end the way it did.'

A feeling of foreboding gripped me. 'How did it end, Marie? What happened?'

'It was on the first Christmas Day after the war was over. As usual she had sat all morning staring into the fire and never speaking. I was upstairs so I didn't see her go out. It must have been a couple of hours later when my husband went into the barn to look for her, and found that she had hanged herself from one of the beams.'

For a few minutes there was a deathly silence while I tried to comprehend the awful news. First of all, I thought of Yvonne with all her lovely long hair cut off, standing naked while her neighbours reviled her as they stared at her swollen Junoesque figure. Then I contemplated the picture of that same figure, now emaciated and lifeless, dangling from the end of a rope. I was conscious of two emotions — grief and profound remorse. I was convinced that I was to blame for everything which had happened, but it was too late to make amends. It was almost as if history had repeated itself, because this situation was similar to the circumstances which had led to my losing Rosemary, once again through my procrastination, and the same two words kept buzzing round inside my brain — if only!

'And what about you, Marie? You're married now, and have a child of your own.'

'Yes,' she sighed, as if the cares of the world were on her shoulders. 'Even before my mother died, we couldn't possibly manage to keep the farm going, and I seriously considered selling up. Then, out of the blue, we heard from a distant cousin of my father's. His son was out of work, and so he came to live here and help out. After a few months I found that I was having a child, and so I married him. He has no head for business, and leaves all that to me, but he works hard, and we have managed to survive.'

'And are you happy now, Marie?'

She shrugged. 'We get along, I suppose. He's not much of a husband, and he drinks too much, but he's quite prepared to bring up little Colin as his own.'

'So, what about the boy? Does he know that you aren't his mother?'

'No, I don't think he would understand as yet, but some day he'll be told.'

'So that means that you are prepared to go on looking after him, Marie? If he came to me I am in a position to give him lots of things, including a good education.'

'You aren't married, are you, Colin?'

'No, but what has that to do with it?'

'And you are away from home a good deal?'

'Yes, but I can afford to have people look after him for me. He can have everything money can buy.'

'Everything except love, Colin. I know that this is a pigsty, and that it may not be the ideal place in which to bring up children, but at least we can give him a stable family background. It would be criminal to take him away from the only home he has ever known to live with strangers. Even his own father is a stranger to him. When he's older I will tell him the truth, and he can make up his own mind about what to do.'

'I'll send you an allowance every month. It will help out not only for him, but for all of you.'

'We don't need your charity,' Marie said, flushed with anger. 'We have managed up to now, and no doubt we'll continue to do so. You can't repair the damage you've done with money.'

'Well, that's up to you,' I countered, 'but I'm going to open a bank account in his name, anyway. If you want to make use of it, then do so. If not, it will be a nest-egg for him when he is older. Don't deny him that, Marie.'

'Very well, if it will salve your conscience,' she agreed reluctantly.

'When I arrived, you thought I was someone else, and you mentioned lawyers. What's going on?'

'The authorities want to build a proper road through here, but I won't agree. This is Bernard land and my home, and it is mine by right of succession. They are trying to make out that since my mother didn't make a will, the deeds are not mine legally, but I know that's not true. The business has been going on for nearly a year now, and they are trying to harass us to get us out.'

'But surely they have offered to buy it? They can't just throw you out.'

'Oh, yes, we know that. The sum on offer has already been increased, and they think I'm just holding out for more, but I'm determined to fight them, only I don't know how much longer we can keep it up.'

'Have you not consulted a lawyer who can look after your interests?'

'Lawyers cost money, and you can see how we are placed. The authorities know this, and harass us continually.'

'I know a good one who would take up your case, Marie. Shall I ask him to get in touch with you? I guarantee it won't cost you a sou. Please, don't look on it as charity. It's the least I can do to help you, as you once helped me.'

She agreed, again with a certain reluctance, and, knowing that our discussion was at an end, she called the boy back into the house. I was able now to have a good look at him, and there could be doubt as to his parentage, because I remembered a photograph I used to have of myself at the same age, and it was as if I was looking at a replica of it. More than ever I wished that Yvonne had been here to see me meet my son for the first time, but I felt guilty that this state of affairs was now impossible.

Young Colin remained just inside the door eyeing me with a certain amount of suspicion, but when he saw that Marie was smiling, he relaxed visibly and came across the room towards us.

'This is Monsieur Marshall,' Marie told him, omitting my

Christian name. 'He was here during the war. Say "How do you do," to him.'

The boy dutifully held out his hand, and I experienced a strange sensation when I took it in mine. Had I felt the same way about either of my daughters? I could no longer remember, but much as I had loved them, this was somehow different. I decided then not to interfere with his upbringing, because I realised that whatever the shortcomings, this was where his roots were, and that he would be happiest here. All I could do in the future was to make sure that the family wanted for nothing until he was old enough to decide his own destiny.

AFTERMATH

The events which I have related in detail are not quite the end of the story. My impulsive visit to the farm had upset me more than I realised, the immediate result being that I stepped back metaphorically to look at myself, and the way I was conducting my life. I could not dismiss from my mind the fact that most of Yvonne's suffering had been due to me, and although I had not been in a position to help her at first, if I had made an effort to do so as soon as I was able, maybe she would have been alive today. Instead, I had been living it up in a vain attempt to forget my own frustrations.

The outcome of this self-analysis was that my attitude underwent a change. No longer was I the gregarious person I had been up to then, no longer did I leave things to chance hoping that they would turn out all right in the long run, and whereas I had used alcohol to try to blot out unpleasant memories, I now threw myself into my work with a fervour which amazed my colleagues. At the same time I became more painstaking, more business-like, and more conscientious.

The effect was that my reporting became more accurate and always arrived on time, but to the critical reader it also began to display a degree of cynicism which had not been in evidence previously. I became increasingly intolerant to all forms of human failings, even my own, and red-tape, bureaucracy, inefficiency and negligence were an anathema to me, to such an extent that I must have been impossible to work with.

This attitude also affected my private life, although I managed to convince myself that such a state of affairs did not worry me, consequently I developed a technique for keeping people at arm's length, the result being that I led a lonely existence. Former friends drifted away, but I didn't mind as I was determined to avoid any familiarity at all costs. It is said that we tend to grow more tolerant with age, but in my case the opposite was true, and I became unapproachable, bitter, and even downright hostile towards those with whom I came into daily contact, including the few friends who stuck by me, and who had only my interests at heart.

So far as women were concerned, after the shock of Yvonne's suicide, I made up my mind that never again would I allow myself to indulge in any emotional entanglements. It was not a decision which I took lightly, but after a good deal of heart-searching, I reached the conclusion that when it came to affairs of the heart, I was too much of a Jonah to become mixed up in any meaningful relationships. With Claudette and Yvonne both dead, and Rosemary out of reach, I began to view the opposite sex with cynicism and indifference to the extent that I avoided meeting women if it was at all possible, so the temptation of starting another affair was never put to the test.

One evening, I went with friends to the Paris Opera House for a presentation of Madame Butterfly, which up to then had been one of my favourites. It was not until the middle of the performance when I suddenly realised that the plot of the opera bore a marked similarity to my own situation, whereby I could easily have been cast in the role of Pinkerton, with Yvonne taking the part of Madame Butterfly in real life. The feeling was so strong I was compelled to leave my seat at the end of the second act, and not return. Naturally my friends were anxious about me, but I made the excuse that I was feeling unwell.

Never again have I been able to attend a performance of this work. Even listening to the music brought back memories of the farm, thus renewing the burden of guilt which was never far away. I do not wish the reader to imagine that I had given up on life altogether. I continued to enjoy travelling to new locations, and was still able to regard any fresh interview as a challenge to be met, so much remained to keep my interests alive.

However, in spite of my philosophy, the Fates decreed that I was to be permitted one solitary glimpse of what the future might have held for me.

Fifteen years must have passed since that terrible night when Rosemary broke the news to me that she was married, and it was quite by chance I saw her again. I was in Harrods before Christmas purchasing a new suitcase when I happened to hear an American accent close by. For no apparent reason I turned to look at the speaker, and there she was standing not more than ten metres away from me. At first I thought that I was mistaken, but there could be no doubt that it was her. Since she was giving her whole attention to the purchase she was making, using a pile of luggage as a screen I edged closer without her seeing me, and managed to keep her under observation while trying to make up my mind whether or not to approach her.

The first thing that struck me was the change in her appearance. I suppose her beauty was still there if one looked for it, but now in her mid-forties, she demonstrated all the characteristics of the typical American matron who was desperately trying to keep the ravages of time at bay.

Her hair was dyed an unnatural brassy colour with pink highlights, but the most obvious feature was the extra flesh which she had piled on over the years. Her obesity was partly hidden under a full-length ranch mink coat which was open enough to show her heavily-corseted figure cocooned in an expensive dress. She wore lizard skin shoes to match her handbag, and under her double chins there hung a string of real pearls, but my eyes were drawn to the podgy fingers which were festooned with expensive rings, including the large solitaire I had seen that night at the transit camp.

It was obvious that she wanted for nothing, and I knew only too well that all these precious stones were more than I could have ever given her. But in spite of that they could not compensate for the change which had taken place both in her physical appearance and her personality.

She half turned in my direction, thus enabling me to see

her face properly. It was heavily made up, but the dense application of lipstick could not disguise the fact that the mouth which I used to find so kissable was now drawn into a thin line, and turned down at the corners as if she rarely smiled. I remembered how her eyes use to come alive and sparkle when she saw me, but now they were hidden behind tinted glasses. The whole image was that of a pampered but dissatisfied woman who was indulged in all material things, but whose life lacked purpose and excitement.

Suddenly Rosemary called out, 'Stanley, come here!'

For one anxious moment I thought she must have seen me, and I was about to reveal myself. Stanley is my second name, and she knew that I hated it, so if at any time she wanted to tease me, she used to call me that. Before I could move, however, she was joined by a boy of about thirteen years of age. I thought it ironic that she should have christened him by that name.

'Where have you been?' she asked in a shrill voice with a marked American accent. 'Don't run off again when Momma's busy. It's easy for you to get lost in here.'

The youth, who was sucking a lollipop, was overweight and spotty, with thick pebble glasses making him singularly unprepossessing in appearance.

'I'm bored, Momma. I wanna go and see the toys.'

'You just wait right there until Momma's finished, then we'll go and see what we can find.'

A few minutes later she moved away out of my life for ever. The change in her had been something I was unprepared for, and the encounter had left me with mixed emotions.

Although Rosemary had obviously got what she wanted, namely wealth, stability and a position in society, she still appeared to be unhappy. I could not help wondering if she would have looked the same way at this moment in time if she had been married to me. Did the fact that she called her son a name she knew I had hated, have any significance? Did she still harbour a lingering affection for me deep down, and did she ever wish that it was my arms around her when Walter and she made love, if indeed they ever did now.

Suddenly I had an uncontrollable urge to find the answer

to these questions, and I hurried off after them, but I was too late. They had been swallowed up in the crowds, and even in the toy department they were nowhere to be seen. Perhaps it was just as well, because meeting Rosemary again face to face could have reopened old wounds which had been partially healed with the passage of time.

Through an intermediary I was able to keep in touch with what was happening at the farm. After my visit, I had briefed a well-known Paris lawyer to represent Marie's interests regarding the compulsory purchase of the land. He managed to obtain a court hearing in the course of which he put forward a cast-iron case that it was prime farming land with rich soil, and that to acquire it for the sole purpose of building a road would be tantamount to an act of vandalism. The adjudicator awarded such a large sum by way of compensation that it caused the authorities to reconsider, and the result was that an alternative route was found.

I had laid down certain conditions in return for this help, one being that the farm was to pass to my son when he came of age. Marie had readily agreed to this, because it was obvious that her husband was quite incapable of taking charge should anything happen to her.

In the meantime, I continued to deposit a moderate sum regularly into a trust account for Marie to use if it was necessary. For several years the account accumulated without any withdrawals until a substantial amount lay in credit. However, her husband got to hear of it, and demanded that it should be used to tide them over a particularly hard winter. His continual and increasing drinking had been largely responsible for their declining fortunes, and for much of the time he was incapable of doing even the minimum work necessary to keep the place going, so a downward spiral began to develop. It was with extreme reluctance, therefore, that Marie was forced to resort to the fund, although the bank official who was in charge of the trust was astute enough to allow her to withdraw only the accrued interest without touching any of the capital.

The situation resolved itself one evening when Marie's

husband was on his way home from the village, staggering all over the road. He was hit from behind by a vehicle which did not stop, and received injuries which were so severe that he died on his way to the hospital.

Marie accepted the situation with some relief. Their life had not been easy over the past few years, but now she felt that she was free to be able to make her own decisions regarding their present finances, and planning for the future. Young Colin at sixteen years of age, was barely old enough to fill his foster-father's shoes, but he was young and strong, and quick to learn, so gradually they began to enjoy a better life-style.

Shortly after his eighteenth birthday, Marie developed cancer, and in a very short time she was transformed from a grossly overweight woman into a living skeleton. Before she died, however, she told young Colin that she was not his mother, but his half-sister, and went on to disclose who his father was, as well as the circumstances leading to his birth. So here he was, less than twenty years of age, in sole charge of a farm, and with the backing of a fairly substantial trust fund at his disposal.

Some youngsters might have gone off the rails in a similar situation, finding themselves heir to such wealth, but my son turned out to be both level-headed and industrious. With the assistance of two hired hands, by the age of twenty-two, the farm had reached a level of prosperity hitherto unknown to its last owners.

The same could not be said for young Pierre Blazzard, who took over the running of his father's estate some time after. The property was run down and now so heavily in debt that my son was able to offer him a knock-down price which was duly accepted. Thus old man Blazzard's dream of uniting the two properties came true at last, but not in the way he had envisaged. The result was that young Colin was now one of the biggest landowners in the district. At the age of twenty-eight he married a local bank manager's daughter, and now I have five fine grandchildren.

About six years after his marriage I made my second visit to the farm merely out of curiousity. I was met by a pleasant looking young woman in an advanced state of pregnancy whom I surmised was my daughter-in-law. I spun her a tale that I had lost my way, and that I was looking for another address, but the excuse sounded thin and unconvincing. We continued chatting for a time during which she observed me closely, then suddenly changed the subject.

'You're Colin's father, are you not?' she asked.

I admitted it, and inquired how she knew.

'Apart from the beard you are very like him. I suppose you have come to introduce yourself to him?'

'Well, not exactly. I came mainly to see for myself the changes that had taken place here, but is there any reason why I should not meet him?'

'For one thing, he's not at home. He has gone to buy some farm machinery, and will not be back until tomorrow.' She hesitated before continuing. 'Naturally he has told me everything concerning the circumstances of his birth, which I have always considered to be very romantic, but he himself does not think so. For some reason which I do not understand, Colin is ashamed of being labelled a bastard, and some people who are jealous of him, do call him that behind his back. They refer to him as "That German bastard," but we know different, don't we?'

She didn't wait for an answer, but continued. 'He is also aware of the financial assistance you have given him over the years, and it's not that he doesn't appreciate it, but he's a very proud man, and does not wish to acknowledge the fact because he likes to think that he has got where he is today solely by his own efforts. So long as he doesn't meet you face to face, and be put in a position where he has to show his gratitude, then he will be content.'

'Are you trying to tell me that he doesn't want to see me now or at any time in the future?'

'Colin has never actually said so, but I know my husband very well, Monsieur Marshall, and I'm sure he will prefer to go it alone from now on without any further help. Perhaps I have expressed myself badly and have misrepresented the situation. He vaguely remembers your last visit here when he was a small boy, and although he did not know why at the time, he has since told me that he was conscious of a feeling of embarrassment even then. I have an idea that somehow he blames you for the fact that he was born out of wedlock, and so long as you remain a shadowy figure from the past, he is prepared to leave it at that, but if you were to materialise now, I'm convinced that he would not view that meeting with any pleasure.'

'Very well. I suppose I must accept that,' I replied with reluctance, 'but I would like to keep in touch.'

'Don't worry, Monsieur Marshall. I will keep you informed from time to time when there is anything to tell you, but please do not reply. Colin would know if any correspondence came for me, and I would be obliged to tell him what I had been doing behind his back, so he would never trust me again. Give me an address where I can reach you.'

We went inside the house so that she could write it down, and I was able to appreciate the transformation which had taken place. The kitchen was well furnished and fitted with modern units, reflecting the prosperity which the farm now enjoyed. Everything was so clean and well-maintained that I could scarcely recognise it as the same place. On the sideboard was a photograph of my son which had been taken recently and the likeness between him and myself was uncanny. There could be no doubt as to who his father was.

I went up to the attic bedroom where I had spent so much of my time, and found it tranformed into a nursery where my eldest grandson lay asleep in the heat of the day. From the window I looked out up the valley where some of the forest had been cleared, thus extending the fields where a herd of pedigree Charolais were grazing peacefully. The sound of a tractor echoed in the distance, and I could see one of the lower pastures being fertilised by a farm hand. The whole scene bore no resemblance to the overgrown and neglected estate which was in my mind.

I was glad that my son had found happiness and contentment, even if I could not share it. It was obvious that his wife adored him, so I could not ask for more. True to her word, at intervals over the years which followed, she sent me news of their continuing prosperity, and my son's standing within the community. Sometimes she enclosed photographs of the family, especially when there had been a new addition.

For my part, I too kept my side of the bargain, although

it was hard sometimes not to go and see with my own eyes how they were getting on, and to meet my grandchildren. However, I did break my promise on one occasion. Several years before I came here to Oakfield, I had an illness which at the time I thought was terminal, and I wrote to inform them of the fact. Even after all that time my son must have felt the same, because from that moment on, all correspondence ceased.

Just over twenty years ago I received a letter from Rosemary, which was addressed to the newspaper where I worked. It was to inform me that her husband had died, and that her only son had disappeared some years before, so she was now quite alone. The letter ended with a suggestion that we perhaps ought to meet again.

She was obviously ignorant of the fact that I had seen her several years before, and perhaps it was for this reason that I made no effort either to reply or to get in touch. By this time I had come to terms with living by myself, and had no desire to try to rekindle a past which was dead and buried long ago.

I have no idea if she is still alive.

Was I wrong to act as I did? Perhaps, but we can't put back the clock however much we may want to, and hindsight is a wonderful reminder of one's shortcomings. Now I am only too aware that I have become an embittered and lonely old man, and yet, when I read over what I have written, it has brought home to me what a full life I led in my younger days. It has also made me realise the opportunities I have missed, due mainly to my own folly. If only . . .

I don't feel very well, but I have finished my story now, so I can only hope that someone will read it and understand.

OAKFIELD REST HOME

1989

'Mrs Mellor! Mr Marshall has just died. At least, I think he has, because he has gone suddenly quiet.'

'Thank you, Penny. Did he say anything?'

'A couple of hours ago he made a noise which sounded like "Romay". I think I know what he was trying to say, but he has never regained consciousness.'

'Penny, you're crying! You mustn't allow this to upset you. While you are here you will see many people dying. It happens to all of us eventually. Anyway, I was under the impression that you didn't like Mr Marshall?'

'I'm all right really, but you see, I've only just finished reading this manuscript, and I have a totally different impression of him now. If what he says is true then perhaps he had an excuse for being unpleasant to everyone, but I find difficulty in believing that what he has written actually happened. How could anyone have done all these things, and had so much excitement in real life?'

'Ah, yes, the Marshall manuscript! He took ill just as he had completed it. I'm glad someone has read it. It would have been a pity if all that effort was thrown on one side, and all to no purpose.'

'He must have been a smashing fellow when he was young, during the war. I wish I had been around to meet him then.'

'You'll learn that many of our elderly inmates were quite different both in looks and in behaviour when they were in their prime. Old age can be very cruel, Penny, but we all have to go through it, if we are spared.'

'What happens now, Mrs Mellor?'

'I'll let the doctor know, and notify the undertaker. After breakfast I'll go through his effects since I am one of his executors, and am responsible for the disposal of his possessions. His lawyer is the other one. So far as I know he has no close friends or relatives. You go off to bed, Penny. You must be tired.'

'If you don't mind, Mrs Mellor, I'd like to stay and see it through to the end. I feel as if I have come to know him quite well, and I would also like to discover how much of what he wrote was the truth.'

'Well, if you're sure you're all right, dear, I don't mind.'

Some time later, after the body had been removed, the contents of Colin Marshall's room was divided into two separate heaps. On the bed lay his clothing and other personal items, but it was the second, smaller pile on the desk which interested Mrs Mellor and her companion. Apart from the bulky manuscript there was a large envelope containing papers, together with an old, battered, cardboard shoebox.

'If this is all that there is to show after eighty-one years of life, it isn't much, is it? Anyway, let's look at these items here first.'

Mrs Mellor then opened out the contents of the large envelope, and put them on one side.

'This is his will, and these are share certificates. This is a building society pass book, and these are the latest bank statements. There doesn't seem to be much in his account. I'll hand these over to his lawyer to deal with. Now, let us see what is in the box.'

As the lid was removed, the girl leaned over eagerly in order to obtain a better look. On top was a photograph of an officer in the W.R.N.S. on the back of which was a faded inscription:- To Colin, with all my love — Rosemary.

Mrs Mellor gasped in admiration. 'Goodness! Isn't she beautiful? She's just like a film star.'

Penny gazed at it for some time. 'He must have been very upset when he found that he had lost her.'

'What did you say, dear?'

'Nothing, Mrs Mellor. What's this other photo?'

'Here she is again, this time together with him in uniform. He was a good-looking chap, wasn't he? Don't they make a handsome couple? I don't know why he grew a beard, he was much better without it.'

'It was to hide the scars on his face,' Penny replied. 'He got those escaping from the Germans during the war.'

'Do you know, Mr Marshall has been with us for eight years, and you have been here for only ten days, Penny, and yet you appear to know more about him than I do.'

'It's all written down in here, Mrs Mellor. You really ought to read it.'

'I was never much of a reader. Milnes and Boone has been my level if I wanted a book. It certainly seems to have made an impression on you, so maybe I will give it a go. Now, what have we here?'

She pulled out a packet of perhaps half a dozen letters held together by an elastic band. On top of the bundle were some photographs of children.

'Oh, dear, these are written in French. Do you understand it, Penny? I'm afraid I never learned.'

'The letters are from his daughter-in-law, and the photographs are his grandchildren. His son is a big landowner in Normandy.'

'I must say, I never realised that he had a son. He told me once that he had had two daughters, but they were killed together with his wife during the war. I suppose he must have married again. I don't know if he's been in touch with his son recently, but he has never come to visit him here. If there's an address there, then they must be notified at once.'

'He — Mr Marshall, that is, was not married to the mother, and his son has never recognised him as his father, but his daughter-in-law does, and has written to him from time to time in the past.'

'All the same, Penny, I think I ought to write to this address and notify them. People sometimes look on their relatives differently after they have passed away. This is especially true of families who have not got on for several years. Now, then, here are his medals!'

She brought out several with multi-coloured ribbons attached which were lying loose at the bottom of the box.

They were the usual service medals distributed to all Service personnel depending on the theatre of operations in which they served. There were two more in velvet-lined cases together with official-looking documents.

'What are these, Mrs Mellor?' the girl asked, pointing to the pieces of paper.

'They're called citations, Penny, and they tell how he won the medals. This one is for the Distinguished Service Order, but the other is written in French.'

'It's the Croix de Guerre. He was in France for a long time before the invasion.'

'Well, there's no doubt that they belong to him. His name is on them both — Major Colin S. Marshall. I knew that he had been in the Army, but I never imagined that there was anything like this.'

'So everything he wrote is true,' Penny told her. 'I can hardly believe it even now. Is that the lot Mrs Mellor?'

'No. There's a letter here right at the bottom. It has an American stamp on it.' The older woman read it through quickly before handing it over to the girl. 'Does that mean anything to you, Penny?'

The letter was dated 1968, and bore an address in Philadelphia. It was dog-eared and tattered, as if it had been folded and unfolded many times, but the writing, although faded, was still legible.

> My Dear Colin,
> I expect you will be surprised to hear from me after all this time, but I just felt that I had to get in touch with you again. I am sending this letter to the newspaper in the hope that somehow it will reach you.
> First of all, I wanted to tell you that Walter passed away six months ago, and I am now on my own. I have never really settled here in America, even after all these years, and consequently I have made very few friends. To make matters worse, my late husband's relatives have never liked me, and there has been a great deal of unpleasantness over his will, which has left me more isolated than ever.

I do have a son, but he has turned his back on society and left home a couple of years ago to become a hippy. I don't know where he is, or even if he is still alive, because he was heavily into drugs before he ran away.

Secondly, and more important, Colin, I must confess to you that I have known right from the start I made a big mistake in marrying Walter. He was kind to me at a time when I needed support, but we were never really compatible. The sight of your stunned face that awful night when I discovered that you were still alive, and broke the news to you, has haunted me for the rest of my life. I ought to have had more faith and waited a bit longer to make absolutely sure you really were not coming back, even though the War Office said you were officially dead. I have since heard of similar cases whereby men have turned up out of nowhere, even years after the war had ended.

Still, it's no use crying over what might have been, although I have done my fair share of that over the years. I am now what is laughingly referred to as a rich widow, but I am also a very lonely one, Colin, and I long with all my heart to see you again. In the interval you may have remarried, in which case tear this up, and I will make no attempt to contact you in the future. In the meantime, I do hope that you can find it in your heart to forgive me for the hurt I caused you, and arrange for us to meet again, if it isn't too late.

Yours always,
Rosemary.

P.S. I am enclosing these photographs taken in happier times. They were forwarded to me after you were reported missing. I have always kept them, and I know you will not have any to remind you of our time together.

There was silence in the room for a few minutes. Penny sat with the letter clutched in her hand, and the tears running down her cheeks.

It was Mrs Mellor who broke the silence. 'So, he never replied! I wonder why. Anyway, he'll be at peace now, and I hope he finds happiness on the other side.'